A STUDY IN SABLE

The
ELEMENTAL
MASTERS

Available now from Mercedes Lackey and Titan Books

THE ELEMENTAL MASTERS
The Serpent's Shadow
The Gates of Sleep
Phoenix and Ashes
The Wizard of London
Reserved for the Cat
Unnatural Issue
Home from the Sea
Steadfast
Blood Red
From a High Tower

THE COLLEGIUM CHRONICLES
Foundation
Intrigues
Changes
Redoubt
Bastion

THE HERALD SPY
Closer to Home
Closer to the Heart
Closer to the Chest (October 2016)

VALDEMAR OMNIBUSES
The Heralds of Valdemar
The Mage Winds
The Mage Storms
The Mage Wars (September 2016)
The Last Herald Mage (March 2017)
Vows & Honor (September 2017)
Exiles of Valdemar (March 2018)

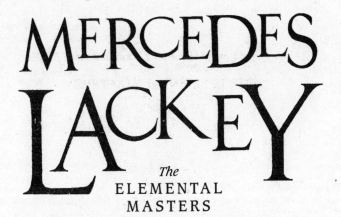

MERCEDES LACKEY

The
ELEMENTAL
MASTERS

A STUDY IN SABLE

TITAN BOOKS

The Elemental Masters: A Study in Sable
Print edition ISBN: 9781785653506
E-book edition ISBN: 9781785653513

Published by Titan Books
A division of Titan Publishing Group Ltd
144 Southwark Street, London SE1 0UP

First edition: June 2016
1 3 5 7 9 10 8 6 4 2

This is a work of fiction. Names, characters, places, and incidents either are the product of the author's imagination or are used fictitiously, and any resemblance to actual persons, living or dead, business establishments, events, or locales is entirely coincidental. The publisher does not have any control over and does not assume any responsibility for author or third-party websites or their content.

A CIP catalogue record for this title is available from the British Library.

Printed and bound by CPI Group (UK) Ltd, Croydon, CR0 4YY

Did you enjoy this book? We love to hear from our readers.
Please email us at: readerfeedback@titanemail.com

To receive advance information, news, competitions, and exclusive offers online, please sign up for the Titan newsletter on our website:
TITANBOOKS.COM

To the memory of Alan Rickman. Always.

PROLOGUE

A feller did not survive as a London street Arab for long, let alone prosper, if he couldn't keep his wits about him under any and all circumstances. And he didn't rise to the heady heights of the front ranks of the Irregulars and the good graces of the guv'nor without having nerves of steel wire and a mind like a rattrap, ready to snap on any bit of information that came his way. Wiggins himself trusted Tommy as his right-hand man, and the guv'nor trusted no Irregular more than Wiggins.

With that sort of regard resting on his shoulders, a feller had to be smart, quick, and steady as Windsor Castle. A feller couldn't let himself get the wind up about anything, no matter how spooky it was. There was more than enough peril in the alleys and shadows without letting your imagination make more.

But Tommy Grimes had to admit to himself that the toff he was following through fog-wreathed streets was giving him a lot of goose bumps. That was strange, because there wasn't much that put the hair up on Tommy's head, and he'd poked into more nasty places than most. And it was strange, because so far, the gent had only acted a bit peculiar, and Tommy followed fellers who had acted quite mad before without getting collywobbles about it. So, he was getting the cauld grue, and it was for no obvious reason that *he* could see.

It wasn't how the blighter looked; he was well dressed, in a long, double-breasted dark coat and matching trousers; without an overcoat, which wasn't unusual tonight, but without a hat, which was. His graying black hair was cut longer than most, wavy, and a bit disheveled, but in a manner a lady would likely say was "artistic." As gents went, he'd probably be reckoned handsome, by ladies anyway. Except for his hair, everything about him was fastidiously tidy. No one was giving him a second glance as he passed by. But then, this was a nice neighborhood; good thing it was dark and no one could see the tattered state of Tommy's clothes. Not that people like this paid any attention to a lad like him anyway, so long as he didn't get within an arm's length of 'em, on account of if he got close, they'd likely think he was about to stick his hand in their pockets. This toff, though, he fit right in and only occasioned a slight smile from a lady, or a nod from a gent as they passed each other on the street. Simple politeness among the gentry.

Not that there were many of the gentry out at this time of night. Folks what lived around here were all asleep, trusting to their locks, their servants, and the police to keep 'em safe. Mostly they were asleep in their own beds, though sometimes they were in beds where they didn't rightly belong, but that was none of Tommy's business, 'cept when the guv'nor made it his business.

But this toff had caught Tommy's attention on account of Tommy could tell he wasn't just strolling, but paying right close attention to whether or not there was anyone about. Once the street was clear, he stopped dead still, inclined his head as if he was listening to someone—nodded, and then whispered a word or two back—and then continued on his way with the determined step of someone who knew exactly where he was going. Tommy'd thought maybe the old gent was a bit barmy, until he did it a couple more times, and each time he did, it was pretty obvious he was getting directions. But directions from what?

The second time he'd listened to something that weren't there, Tommy knew his instincts hadn't been playing tricks on him, and there was something even the guv'nor might not be able to explain going on. He thought about breaking off at that point and letting the gent go on his way, but you never knew what scrap of odd knowledge might be worth something to the boss. *Maybe not the boss, though. Maybe the Major. Talkin' to things as ain't there's more his line.* That was all right. The Major paid just as well as the boss did.

And, as they got closer and closer to the Thames, and the respectable types gave way to loungers and drunks and whores, no one but Tommy saw him make tiny little gestures and whisper a few more words, and then go on as completely unmolested as if he was invisible. *That* made Tommy go cold all over and think again about continuing to follow the man. Surely he had enough, even for the Major.

But it didn't seem that the man knew he was being followed, so Tommy gathered his tattered courage about him and put everything the boss had taught him about tailing a gent into immediate use. Because the Major would pay more, a lot more, if he knew what the man had been getting directions *to*.

But when it became very clear that the gent was heading for the waterfront and the docks themselves, Tommy grew very unhappy indeed, and for a whole different set of reasons than just unchancy behavior. This wasn't his lay; another set of gangs ruled the waterfront, and they didn't much like the Baker Street boys cutting in. Sure, some of them answered to the boss, but plenty more didn't, and no telling who was in which until there was a knife looking for your liver and you found your luck had run out.

But whatever was making the fancy toff invisible to the gangs seemed to be working for Tommy, too. No one harassed them; the waterfront was uncannily quiet. The man's path took him away from the taverns and alehouses, down silent, darkened byways Tommy would have got lost in on his own, avoiding anything other than the occasional night watchman. On they went, first to and then under the docks. And oh, even to Tommy's nose, inured as he was to smells, this place *stank*. Sewage warred with dead fish, which in turn warred with the smell of rotting things best not guessed at. The tide was going out; it was the hour of the mudlarks, as the Thames left its odorous leavings on the mudbanks, and anything could be found, from a silver coin from the time of the eighth Henry to a deader, though most of what washed up was rags and bits of wood and rotten stuff. Needless to say, the deaders outnumbered the silver coins by quite a lot. There was the suicides, of course; there was always one or two of those a night.

But there was also them as hadn't gone into the water of their own free will. And accidents, though it was hard to tell them from the ones that was pushed.

Tommy didn't dare follow the gent out into the mud (though somehow he wasn't sinking ankle-deep in the stuff like any proper human would), but he skulked in the shadows on the rocks under the docks and watched with all his eyes as the gent went straight to—something—lying asprawl in shallow water in the silvery moonlight.

The gent turned the thing over with a curious air of reverence, and a particularly strong beam of moonlight revealed a white, white face and long golden hair, and a fan of pale dress splayed out on the mud like so much seaweed.

"*Perdóname, querida,*" said the gent, and the blade of a very sharp knife flashed for a moment in the moonlight.

Tommy felt horror grip him. It was one thing to cut up a man who meant to cut you up. It was quite another to cut up the dead. The dead should be left alone.

Then clouds covered the moon, and as Tommy found himself caught in a paralysis of terror, the man . . . did something to the corpse. Tommy heard a roaring like the sea in his ears, and everything went dark for a moment, and when he came to himself again, clutching at the wet, barnacle-covered support he'd hidden behind, the gent . . . was gone.

Quite gone, as if he had vanished right into thin air, like a conjurer. Except that Tommy knew quite a lot of conjurer's tricks, thanks to the boss, and no man that *he* knew of had ever been able to vanish from off a mudflat on the banks of the Thames without leaving a trace of his passing.

So, when Tommy managed to gird up his courage and make his way out to where the body lay, he found that, to his relief, the cove had made a decent set of footprints going back besides the set he'd made going out. So at least he hadn't been following some mad spirit or . . . demon. . . .

Even if those prints *were* far shallower than they had any right to be, as if the man had weighed no more than a child.

But then he discovered what the man had been after, and the discovery sent him floundering back to the banks, to the wharves, and racing for his life for the familiar and understandable evils of drunken savages and opium fiends and twelve-year-old prostitutes and murderous thieves.

For what manner of decent, upright man could possibly have wanted the arm bone of a poor drowned girl and her long, muddy, golden hair?

And most of all, in the name of all things sane . . . *why?*

1

It was just after luncheon, in a neighborhood that mostly catered to working-class people. The buildings were all three and four stories tall here, several had little shops on the ground floors, or the offices of those professional men who could not afford more prestigious neighborhoods. A very few were still the dwellings of single families who could afford several servants. For the most part, however, the place was chock-ablock with reasonably priced flats—reasonably priced if one was doing well as a shopkeeper or a rising clerk, and if one was not, well, one could always find someone to share the flat with.

This was certainly the case with the gentleman who was about to interview the two young ladies who were outside a greengrocer's establishment. "Well," said Nan Killian, gazing across the busy street at the very unprepossessing front of a purely residential building. Tall and narrow, like most buildings in this part of London, it might have been the home of one of those single families, with a kitchen on the ground floor and servants' quarters in the attic, but it was, in fact, carved up into flats presided over by a landlady who resided on the ground floor and provided meals and charlady services to her lodgers. There were three flats; their goal was the middlemost one.

"Well indeed, and well enough," Sarah Lyon-White replied, flashing an impish smile at her tall friend. "Shall we go beard the dragon in his den? It would be a shame to have come all this way to show the white feather and run away, besides being a great disappointment to Lord A and Master M."

"*Mister* M can go stuff—" Nan began.

"*Nan!*" said Sarah, in pretense of shock.

"—his hat up a drainpipe for all I care," Nan continued smoothly. "But I would never like Lord Alderscroft to think we were too cowardly to deal with a mere mortal man. Even if, up until a few days ago, we thought he was merely a literary construction. All right then. On we go. After all, it's only an interview."

Suiting her actions to her words, Nan checked the oncoming traffic for runaway hansoms and inconsiderate carters and strode across the London street, with her much shorter friend Sarah half-skipping along beside her.

Not troubling to wait for the landlady to answer a knock, she opened the door to the narrow, tidy, but sparsely furnished entryway, and spotted the staircase leading to the first floor and flat "B." Still leading Sarah by a few paces, she ran up the stairs and knocked briskly on the door. It was opened almost immediately.

The gentleman in the dark gray suit who opened it raised one sardonic, heavy eyebrow. "Very prompt, I see. You would be—"

"Miss Killian. And this is Miss Lyon-White," said Nan, taking the open door as an invitation to come in, which she did. Sarah was right on her heels.

"Indeed. Would you take a—" the man began, but Nan strode across an untidy room packed with all manner of curious objects and smelling strongly of tobacco and faintly of gunpowder and chemicals, and threw open the window that overlooked the street.

"I hope you are not some manner of fresh air fiend, Miss Killian," the gentleman said, without showing a flicker of surprise that Nan had made so free with his window. "I am sorry to say that the air on this street is not the most salubrious."

"Not at all, sir," Nan replied, half-turning from the window. "But as you are well aware, Sarah and I are only half of the quartet you are to interview." A swiftly moving shadow flashed between the light and the window, and there was a sound of flapping wings as an African grey parrot suddenly landed on the sill. "Ah, here is the third of the party," Nan said calmly, offering a hand to the parrot, who stepped up onto it, then used it as a launching point to take a shorter flight across the room to come to rest on the back of the chair Sarah had taken at the invitation of their host.

A much larger shadow interposed in the next moment, and an enormous raven replaced the parrot on the sill.

"And here is the last of us," said Nan with satisfaction. The raven leapt ponderously to her shoulder with a flap of his wings and she closed the window again. With the raven balanced precisely on her shoulder, she took her place in the armchair next to Sarah's, closer to the fire. The raven transferred himself to the back of her chair. The gentleman took his own seat on the settle opposite them, and silence descended as they took stock of one another.

Nan knew what he would see as he looked at them; she wondered if it surprised him, amused him, or merely entered into his calculations. Two young women in their early twenties, regarding him with direct and unwinking gazes, as direct as if they had been young *men,* and not women. The shorter, Sarah, had the sort of face that could have graced a Professional Beauty, if she had cared to travel that route, surmounted by a slightly untidy coif of masses of blond hair piled up in an approximation of a pompadour hairdo. She wore no hat, largely because she had a tendency to lose them. As for Nan, she had a face that could charitably be called "strong" and which she privately thought of as "horsey," and her own hair was confined in a very tidy French Roll under a small, neat, unadorned round felt hat. They were both wearing gowns of dull colors—grays and blues for Sarah and browns for Nan—which might be described as "dowdy" (although Sarah could never look dowdy in anything). However, the knowing eye would recognize their gowns as Ladies' Rational Dress, a mode of non-fashion that allowed the wearer almost as much freedom of movement as if she were in a bloomer suit. Nan rather thought their interviewer had already recognized that.

And, of course, their interviewer could not possibly overlook the birds perched on their chairs, who were eyeing him with great interest.

As for Nan . . . well, she found herself facing a man no one could call "handsome"—but no one would ever forget, either. It was not his costume that made him unforgettable. Men, of course, could wear the same suits for decades—perhaps even wear the suits their fathers passed down to them—and so long as they were not visibly worn or shabby, they would pass muster virtually anywhere. So there was not much to be learned by studying his suit except that he was as neat and clean as a well-cared-for housecat, in surprising counterpoint to the untidiness of his sitting room. Then again, a man who makes his living by examining the clues other men leave behind or carry about on their persons was unlikely to leave many clues on *his*.

He was very tall, and very thin, so thin he seemed taller than he was. The neatly cut hair was very black, as were his bushy eyebrows. Sharp, piercing gray eyes gave the correct impression that he was taking note of absolutely everything. His thin, hawklike nose was of a piece with his thin face. He had very fine, graceful hands—the hands of a musician, which he was, although not professionally.

Observation was merely putting the cap on what he had already learned. Nan was perfectly sure that he had uncovered all sorts of information about *them* before they ever arrived here, though she was also fairly certain he had dismissed a good half of what he'd learned about them as "superstition" and "twaddle."

This interview was for one reason only, and it was up to Nan and Sarah to pull off a coup. To prove to him that his assumptions were wrong.

She lowered those mental shields that Karamjit had taught her so well how to put in place, and allowed herself to reach out to the gentleman's mind.

It was as tidy and orderly as his sitting room was untidy and chaotic, and as busy as one of the great factories where mills whirred and clattered and produced goods at a dizzying rate.

"You're thinking that I have managed to conquer my background as a street urchin to an astonishing degree. You're marveling at how there is no trace of the guttersnipe in my speech, and you wonder if I've lost the East End brat entirely, or just learned the Queen's English as if I was learning a second language." Her mouth quirked a little. "Oil roight, guv'nor, wat'cher thinkin' naow?" She continued as his eyes widened for just a fraction of a second. "Now you are thinking the world lost a talented actress when I declined to try the stage. Thank you for that flattery, but an ear for language is not the same as a talent for acting. I shall continue, with your permission." She didn't wait for it. "The last item you smoked before we arrived was your cherrywood pipe, your usual shag tobacco, although you had been considering a cigar, and now you are thinking I must have the same nose for tobacco products that you have; I assure you that I do not. To me they all smell alike. You were rereading some unsatisfactory letters from would-be clients as you were waiting for us. One was a tedious whinge from a gentleman who is certain his wife has taken a lover. One was a man who wants you to find his lost watch, another who wants you to find his lost hat, a third who wants you to find his lost dog and an attorney who wants you to find an heir. The only one that showed any signs of being interesting was the letter from the parents and fiancé of a missing girl; it is interesting to you largely because the young lady's sister is the operatic diva, Magdelena von Dietersdorf, and the missing girl had accompanied her sister to London, then apparently vanished. There are aspects of this case that were initially intriguing, but you are wondering now if it is worth your while; you have made some slight enquiries at the opera house to gather gossip, and Fraulein von Dietersdorf asserts that her sister ran off with a young man to Canada, not having the courage to dismiss her affianced to his face, and that seems more likely to you than a mysterious disappearance."

Now I have your attention!

She saw his right hand twitch a little, and she added, "Don't bother to look at the papers again. There is nothing in them that I could have gleaned about this case. *Fraulein* does not want a scandal to spoil her operatic debut here in London, and it seems she rules her parents, rather than the other way around. Nothing of this has been released to the press, and the parents have come to you rather than the police in order to keep things as quiet as possible. You have seen them in person once, since you first received their letter."

She glanced over at Neville, who was observing the gentleman with narrowed eyes. "Neville thinks you should take the case. He believes that the parents' instincts are correct."

The raven nodded gravely. So did the sylph who suddenly showed her dainty self just over the gentleman's shoulder, hovering in midair, wings vibrating so fast they were a blur. Nan ignored the sylph. The gentleman did not believe in them, and it was not in her best interest right now to mention the Air Elemental.

The gentleman had recovered his composure so quickly only someone like Nan would have known he had ever lost it in the first place. "These are clever conjuring tricks, Miss Killian," he said dismissively. "I get dozens of letters from tedious people with equally tedious problems they wish me to solve, most of them are alike, and it takes no great effort to imagine what those problems might be. And as for the Von Dietersdorfs—you could easily have read the first page of the letter from where you sit, as it is pinned to the mantelpiece with my pocketknife."

"But the second, third, and fourth pages, sir?" Nan retorted. "I think not. I got that information from your own mind. The Von Dietersdorfs wrote you from Berlin before arriving in London. The father's written English is excellent, and his spoken English nearly as good. You know Herr von Dietersdorf wrote this himself rather than employing a professional translator because he occasionally made the mistake of putting the verb at the end of his sentence, which no professional translator would ever do. The letter was written on stationery from the Hotel Berghof, which you yourself have stayed in, and know to be an establishment that caters to the wealthy merchant class. When you stayed at the Berghof last, which was about a year and a half ago, your room was on the west side of the fourth floor; you engaged it because it had an excellent view of a room directly across from it so that you could follow every movement of a man you were tracking, for purposes of your own which you did not divulge to anyone. Shall I go on?"

The slight dilation of the gentleman's pupils showed she had hit the mark squarely; *no one,* not even his closest friends, knew he had been in Berlin at that time, much less what hotel and what room he had stayed in, or for what purpose. He had, indeed, not told anyone *why* he had been there—or half a dozen other places that year.

"Either you are the most remarkable agent I have ever met, Miss Killian," he said, slowly, "Or—"

"I am not an agent of the gentleman you were concerned with, as you should know, since your brother sent us." She shrugged.

"*When you have eliminated the impossible, whatever remains, however improbable, must be the truth,*" she said, daring to quote him. "Improbable as it may be, the simple truth is that I have the psychical Talent for reading thoughts, and I have performed my part of our audition for you by reading yours."

She sensed a veritable torrent of questions cascading through his mind, then. Chiefest among them was the dreadful worry—*how many more like her are there?* That was paired with an even deeper concern—*and are any employed by my enemies? Especially—him?*

"You, sir, are uniquely gifted to prevent anyone from learning thoughts you do not wish them to know," she continued, answering the question that he had not asked, even to himself, yet. "Your will is uncommonly strong, disciplined, and well ordered. If you are in a position where you fear your thoughts may be overlooked, all you need do is concentrate your mind on something trivial and appropriate; a complicated calculation, perhaps, or a chemical formulation, or the complete route you took to arrive at your destination. Keep your mind focused on that, and that alone, and it will be as if you are shouting the information. It would take another Talent with a mind as sharp as yours to be able to discern any of your thoughts past that barrier."

Instantly, the gentleman's mind filled with a chess problem. She smiled. "Exactly like that, sir. Chess problems are ideal. Even when you are disguised, chess is a hobby that transcends class, race, and wealth. Oh," she added, "Do not concern yourself about performing these mental gymnastics at all times. A psychical receiver cannot easily discern the thoughts of an individual at any distance. It is not unlike trying to pick out a single voice in a theater audience. Even if you know the voice, even if you know the 'words' to listen for, once you are more than a few yards distant, the voice is lost in the general hubbub."

"But if one was alone—out on the moors, say?" he hazarded.

"Ah. Then you would have to take some care. But except between people who are both psychical and related by bonds of blood or affection, it is still intolerably difficult to sense thoughts at a distance of greater than half a mile." She nodded at the flash of relief in his eyes. "Also . . . while it is not unheard of, in general, anyone who is Talented in the way I am is either too empathic to function as a criminal or utterly mad. Not that the utterly mad could not be criminals," she added thoughtfully, "But they generally betray themselves in their madness."

He blinked a little at that. "Well then," he said, turning to Sarah. "Have you a similar demonstration to make?"

She shook her head slightly. "Not in the way you expect," she said candidly. "I am mediumistic, and there are no departed spirits hanging about you with whom I could converse."

A flash of humor lit his eyes, and his mouth quirked in a little smile. "Then you would be the first so-called medium I have ever encountered that has made that confession to me. Most of them seem to think that spirits are flocking about everyone like pigeons in pursuit of crumbs."

"Spirits have very little interest in the living," Sarah laughed. "Which is just as well. However, you do have a bit of a guardian. A 'watchdog' is more what I would call it. Besides being mediumistic, Nan and I are also able to see what your friend the doctor has tried to convince you actually exist—creatures we call Elementals."

Nan gave a ladylike snort. "I hadn't wanted to mention that, since I couldn't *prove* it to him."

"Well, I would be remiss if I didn't say something about it." Sarah shrugged. "Sadly, as an Air Elemental, it's not the most . . . reliable of watchdogs. It's a sylph, and they do tend to be rather flighty."

Out of the corner of her eye, Nan saw the sylph, a winged, half-naked little female about a foot tall, dart into clear view, stand up in midair with her wings beating furiously, stamp her tiny foot, put her fists on her hips in a gesture of offense, and then stick her tongue out at Sarah.

The grey parrot—named Grey—laughed. "She's angry!" Grey chortled. "Sarah! Be nice!"

"You can talk!" the gentleman exclaimed, far more interested in *that* fact than that there was an Elemental guarding him.

"So can I," Neville the raven croaked. "We can talk, can you fly?"

The gentleman sat straight up at that, and looked sharply from Neville to Grey and back again. Finally, he threw his hands in the air. "All right!" he growled, although he sounded as amused as irritated. "You can come out, John. The wretched girl is right. I have eliminated the impossible, and the improbable remains. Evidently my brother has not had wool pulled over his eyes by these young women. Consider them vetted."

A screen had been put up over by one window, and a man shorter than the gentleman interviewing them came from behind it. He was midsized, strongly built, with a square jaw, sandy hair, and a moustache, wearing a well-fitted black suit of the sort doctors usually chose. He was, in Nan's estimation, quite handsome, and his slight limp only added to the attraction. *After all,* she thought wryly, *What red-blooded girl doesn't like a fellow who needs just a touch of nursing, now and again?*

John was laughing. "When have you ever known Mycroft to have the wool pulled over his eyes about anything, Holmes?" he asked. "You've said more than once, he's more intelligent than you are."

"Intelligence is one thing," Sherlock Holmes grumbled, though still with a hint of amusement. "I've known highly intelligent men to be gammoned by little girls."

"*And* they have the blessing of Lord Alderscroft," John Watson went on.

"Who, for all I know, is as mad as a hatter." Holmes shrugged. "But if you are going to persist in gadding about, taking on the ridiculous cases I refuse to, I see no reason why Miss Killian and Miss Lyon-White cannot assist you. At least the psychical Talents of these young ladies have *some* basis in science, unlike your Elemental nonsense!" He snorted. "The discipline of deductive reason—"

"Adductive," corrected Sarah, before he could finish.

He was surprised enough at being interrupted that he stopped in midsentence and turned back to her. "Eh?" he got out.

"Adductive reasoning," Sarah said, quietly. "You *gather* all the facts in a case. You *add* them together. You do not *deduct* anything. You use *adductive* reasoning to *deduce* the answer, not *deductive* reasoning."

Nan held her breath, afraid for a moment that the famous detective would react poorly to being corrected. But instead, he slapped his knee and laughed aloud, then turned back to Watson.

"There, you see! I keep telling you this, Watson, and you persist in making the same mistake over and over in your prose. It's *adductive* reasoning, and a mere girl has shown you up!"

Watson's jaw firmed stubbornly. "But people like the phrase 'deductive reasoning,'" he countered. "It rolls off the tongue. 'Adductive' sounds wrong, particularly when paired with 'deducing' and 'detecting.' You leave the wordsmithing to me and Doyle, and I'll leave the clue-spotting to you."

But Holmes could not stop chuckling over something he obviously considered to be a major victory over his Boswell. "All right, all right. Miss Lyon-White, for that, if for no other reason, I give you two my blessing to go haring off after ghasties and ghoulies with John and his wife. Take them up to Mary, Watson. I shall make no further objections. You all have my approval, not that you'd have listened to me in the first place if I forbade this nonsense. If you four want to waste your time on airy nonsense, who am I to interfere?"

"Have I ever listened to you when you told me my cases were airy nonsense?" John replied, with a laugh of his own. He gestured to the girls, and they both rose, their birds hopping to their shoulders as they did so. "Come along upstairs and meet my better half."

They left the flat by the same door they had entered, and climbed the stairs to 221 C Baker Street. "When I was still a bachelor, our upstairs neighbor was a—thankfully—deaf old gent who lived alone. I say thankfully, because Sherlock is inclined at times to indoor shooting practice, and while Mrs. Hudson puts up with it, I doubt anyone who wasn't deaf would have. Nor with his violin playing at odd hours when he's in a fever of thinking. Sherlock came into some money and bought the old fellow out just after my wedding, and presented the flat to Mary and me as a wedding present."

"But—the stories—" Sarah ventured, as they all paused on the landing.

"It serves us very well to let others think we reside elsewhere," John Watson said gravely. "As Sherlock has pointed out, Mary and I are ready targets for his enemies. If the cost of keeping our place of residence a secret is that I have to sneak out by the servants' entrance to go to my practice and pretend to enter and leave a block of flats near it, so be it."

Personally, Nan thought that was a capital idea. It had occurred to her more than once that collecting enemies meant that those enemies would look for a weakness in your defenses—and being known to be fond of someone was a weakness.

The door to C was not marked by a nameplate; John inserted a key and opened it, waving the girls and the birds in before him. The sitting room that greeted them was as bright and tidy as Sherlock's was dim and messy. The room was painted rather than papered, in a cheerful yellow with the trimwork in white enamel; the drapes were a deep gold, a color that would stand up to the London soot. The carpets were unfashionable and sturdy. Pictures were good prints rather than bad originals, mostly of rural scenes. There was a homely scent of toast and cinnamon in the air. Nan felt at home immediately, for it was not unlike the Harton School when it had been in London; old furniture, slightly out of fashion, reupholstered in durable material. None of the fussy lace and furbelows most fashionable wives seemed to think was necessary. Everything was of good quality and meant to last, but not new; made for comfort and use, not looks. There were books; most of the walls were taken up with bookcases stuffed with books. There were two desks, and beside one of them was the sort of heavy bag generally carried by doctors. The focal point of the sitting room was the hearth, which featured the only really new thing in the room, a modern fireplace stove. Presiding over a nicely laden tea table by the hearth was a petite blond woman, her hair in a French Roll like Nan's. She was not pretty, but she had truly wonderful eyes. And when she smiled at them all in greeting, her face was quite transformed by the expression. She rose in greeting as they entered.

"And here are our new companions, Mary!" Watson exclaimed, and rubbed his hands together at the sight of the laden tea table. "I see you have provided us with a feast!" He directed the girls to a chocolate-colored settee on one side of the table and took his seat beside his wife on a mostly-matching settee on the other.

"I expected that after their interview with Sherlock they'd be hungry as hounds," said Mary Watson, gesturing that they should come help themselves as she poured out tea for all. She pointed to a spot where there were newspapers and four bowls waiting. "I spread newspapers on the carpet and put cups of water and saucers of chopped fruit on the floor there for your friends, if that will be all right?" she added, a little anxiously.

"Oi' druther 'ave yer *eye*, me ducks!" said Neville, and uttered a bloodcurdling laugh.

"*Neville!*" Nan exclaimed in sudden anger at her feathered companion. But then she saw Mary was laughing uproariously, and sighed with relief.

"Good heavens, he's like a feathered Penny Dreadful!" Mary exclaimed, and to her unconcealed delight, Neville flapped over to the back of the settee behind Mary and misbehaved his little heart out, alternately demanding she "Give us a kiss!" with threats to her eyes, liver, kidneys, and lungs. When he had her laughing so hard she had to put her hand to her side and could scarcely catch her breath, he finally stopped his antics, flapping down to the floor and stalking over to the papers protecting the carpet, and joined Grey at the feast.

Grey eyed him as he approached. "Show-off," muttered Grey, diving back into the apples and grapes.

"Jealous," said Neville, doing the same.

John settled next to his wife and handed her a handkerchief to wipe her eyes with as she finally caught her breath. "I don't think I have laughed so hard since the last time we were at the theater and saw that wonderful Gilbert and Sullivan production," she finally said, in a voice still rich with mirth. "How do you ever keep a straight face around that raven? Sugar?"

"Two please," Nan said, accepting cup and sugar lumps. "No milk, thank you. He usually is not that much of a cutup. I think he must have decided you were in need of a good laugh." The tea set was the one thing in the room that really *was* of very high quality; Nan fancied it was probably one of the few things that remained from before Mary had lost her fortune. As a consequence, she resolved to be very careful with it.

It felt distinctly unnerving to know as much as she did about Mary and John Watson, since technically she had never seen them before today.

I wonder if this is how Holmes feels about his clients? I wonder if this is how his clients feel about him?

"Well, I was very anxious that our mutual friend find you acceptable," Mary replied, handing Sarah her tea (one lump, and milk). "I know we could have gone right on without his approval, but it would have put a strain on our friendship."

Watson snorted. "Meaning he would be dropping his acidic little asides every chance he thought one would irritate me. And the worst of it all would be my knowing he was doing it with the best of intentions, which makes it ruddy difficult to get angry with him. *He* thinks he is being tolerant of my 'table tilting' and doesn't wish to hear anything that might persuade him that magic is real. Though I'll give him this, he's always happy to hear about the frauds we've exposed, and he never stints on praise when we've done so."

Nan looked from John to Mary and back again. "I'll confess that I find myself in the peculiar position of *thinking* that I know a great deal about you, when in fact, I might not. It's difficult to tell what in the fiction is based on fact," she ventured.

"Most of it," Watson assured her. "If anything, Doyle and I have left out the greater part of what goes on around here. As for our friend downstairs, bless him, Holmes can charm birds out of a tree, but only when he needs to do so. The rest of the time— and particularly with his friends—he sees no need to trouble with common politeness at all."

"I actually sympathize with him, a bit," Sarah put in, and grinned. "I've often wished I could get away with speaking my mind. Common politeness all too often covers thoughts that are anything but polite. There is a great deal of relief in being able to say out loud exactly what one is thinking."

Neville and Grey both laughed at that. Grey sounded just like Sarah when she laughed. Neville sounded like a pirate.

"Young woman, you terrify me," said Watson, helping himself to seedcake. "Common politeness is all that stands between us and anarchy. I shall next expect to discover you have been making bombs in your lumber room."

"No," said Sarah with a twinkle. "In the linen closet."

* * *

24

"When *did* you start taking the cases that your friend calls 'twaddle'?" Nan asked, when tea had been disposed of, the birds had eaten anything that was left, and the tray had been left on a stand on the landing for Mrs. Hudson to take away.

"A few months after I joined him on that initial case," John replied. "Sherlock sent a frantic young man off in disgust. I intercepted him before he got too far down the street and offered to help him myself."

Nan could not help but get some of the thoughts of their two new friends, so she knew that the young man in question had deceived a girl below his station and left her "spoiled." And she had been something of a Fire Magician, and determined to have revenge on him until he "did right by her."

And to his credit, when Watson untangled the mystery, he had seen to it that the young man did just that. Marriage was out of the question—not, in Watson's mind, because the difference in class between them, but because the young man would inevitably betray her again and again, and the whole situation would turn into a tragedy. No, Watson saw to it that the blighter settled enough money on the girl that she could set herself up in a little cookshop. "Make a success of this," Watson had told her, in the most kindly way he could, "And you shall have any man you choose. Good cooks are very much run after. Good cooks with an independent living are jewels, and an honest man knows that. And confine your magic to helping yourself in your work, if you please, or sterner men than I will come bring you to judgment."

That, in Nan's estimation, was the best thing he could have done. Evidently the girl had gone and done exactly that, as no more was heard from her.

"My parents and my native friends knew I was possessed of gifts when I was quite young, even before I really knew about them," Sarah said. "Mama and Papa knew they weren't Elemental Magic like theirs, but they knew I had *something*, and when M'dela told them *what* it was, they knew I needed to go where I could get better training than they could give me. When did you know you were magicians?"

"Oh, I think I knew from the moment I could reason," Mary said. "My earliest recollection is of playing with sylphs, or rather watching them in my crib as they played to amuse me. Mother and Father were also Air Magicians, so they quickly understood what was going on, realized I was a budding Air Master, and began training my magic as well as teaching me to speak and walk."

John chuckled. "You had an earlier start than I, my love. I knew I was an Elemental Magician from the time I was ten, when *I* began to see Water Elementals; my father, who passed the gift and Mastery on to me, made certain I got training immediately. Unfortunately, my elder brother did not share our gifts." His face darkened. "I sometimes wonder if that was what led to his—later problems. We never could convince him that the gift is as much curse as blessing."

Nan felt very sorry for him, as she got a flash of the beloved older brother, so promising a student, losing his focus at university, taking to drink, then slowly losing himself to it.

"It is very hard to persuade them otherwise," Sarah said sadly. "Not without taking them on expeditions which they are ill-suited for, ill-armed for, and would prove hazardous in the extreme."

"We've *done* that, actually," Nan added. "It proved to be so traumatizing that the friend in question distanced herself immediately, and we have not heard from her since."

John coughed. "Well, to get back to your question, I sorted out the first young fellow who was rejected myself, and that was my first case. It took less than two days to deal with *him*. The second was more of a puzzle. Sherlock was asked to investigate a haunting. Obviously he laughed in the poor man's face and sent him away. I intercepted him and undertook to solve the situation, once I realized that the symptoms of the so-called 'haunting' more closely matched the powers of an Air Magician. I discovered the perpetrator was a street urchin taking revenge on the fellow for knocking him down into the street, practically under the wheels of a cab, then shouting at him for 'being in the way' and calling a constable on him."

"Served him right, if you ask me," Mary said crossly. "I'd have done more than throw stones at his window and wake him up, blow his casements open during a rainstorm and soak his furniture, or drop random trash down his chimney to put out his fires. I've no patience for a man who treats others as if they were less than the dirt in the street. *Especially* children."

John chuckled. "Well, it did become a bit of a Dickensian adventure. Before I banished his 'ghost,' I made sure he was suitably contrite for his hard-heartedness, and I got the lad to someone who was pleased to take him as an apprentice." He glanced over at Mary. "I knew what Mary was the moment I met her, of course, just as she knew what I was." He coughed. "I'm just grateful to Divine Providence for arranging things the way they came out. It isn't often a man is blessed with the perfect partner in all things."

"Not *all* things, John," Mary chided. "You could not persuade me to help you in the surgery for anything."

"Not even that new hat?" he teased.

"Not even that," she said firmly.

"So what *are* you doing now, dearies?" asked Grey, causing all of them to stare at her. She gave an evil chuckle at their reactions.

"Just latterly, I was responsible for putting the little sylph as a guardian on Holmes," Mary replied first. "John wanted to, but it would have been useless to try, because he is Water."

"That's odd, isn't it?" Sarah asked, as Nan paid close attention to the give-and-take between the husband and wife, and was pleased to see that they were as close a couple as Memsa'b and Sahib Harton.

"It is," Mary acknowledged. "Physicians are usually Earth, but if he'd been Earth he likely would have found living in London to be intolerable."

"Not that living in London is easy for any Elemental Magician except Fire," John pointed out. "But Earth Magicians have the worst time of it. And it would have been no good putting a Water Elemental on Holmes, he's too far from water most of the time for one to have been of any use as a watchdog."

"Besides," added Mary, "The poor thing would wear itself to a droplet, trying to keep up with him."

It was Neville's turn now to remind the company that the birds were equal partners in all of this. "You need us, why?" he croaked.

"Too many of the obviously occult cases are things Mary and I can do little about," John explained, turning courteously to speak directly to the raven. "Real hauntings, psychical poltergeists, fraudulent mediums taking advantage of people—we finally asked Lord Alderscroft if he could recommend someone in London who could assist us, and he sent you, after consulting with Mycroft Holmes."

Nan furrowed her brow. "Why consult with Mycroft, when our business is with you and not his brother?"

Mary and John looked at each other and laughed. "Have you ever *tried* to keep a secret from either Holmes?" John asked. "The moment you started associating with us in any way, he'd have begun investigating you. In fact, he would have taken it on as a priority, regardless of whatever else he was working on at the time."

"And that might have ended . . . unpleasantly," Mary pointed out. "You two young ladies have had quite a number of adventures, and you are quite prepared to defend yourselves when you detect someone skulking about. And as for those servants of Memsa'b Harton . . . I am not sure even Holmes would be the equal in combat to three veterans of Indian regiments, much less when two of the three are a Gurkha and a Sikh."

"I wouldn't discount Selim either," Sarah said with a laugh. "Magically, he is the strongest of the three, and he does not hesitate to *use* his magic if he feels it is called for."

Nan thought that over a moment. "True, things could have gone badly," she agreed. "Karamjit, Agansing, and Selim may not be as young as they once were, but I do not think even Sherlock Holmes' formidable talents at singlestick, boxing, and Japanese fighting would help him if all three tackled him at once. And they would have; I do believe they miss the days when the Harton School was in London, and they got to run off ruffians on a daily basis. I think undergoing the trial-by-interview was the wisest approach."

"It was tempting to give him a comeuppance," John admitted, with a slow smile. "When he graces me with that patronizing smile and pulls the curtain away to reveal his legerdemain, and says condescendingly that even though I know his methods, I still cannot apply them, I often wish I could give him a taste of his own medicine."

"He needs his moments of applause, dearest," Mary pointed out. "The dear Lord knows he's earned them, he often doesn't get any other payment, and often can't get any accolade at all from the people he's helped. Never mind the cases he has lost, rather than won."

"True, and it's only Christian charity to let him have accolades in abundance." John nodded decisively. "He's certainly earned that charity. He'd hate me to say it, but the fellow is damned selfless when it comes down to the way he handles anything that comes his way that interests him. For every King of Bohemia, there's fifty people who can't pay him a penny, and many an impoverished innocent he's saved from prison or the gallows."

"Well, I have heard enough about Sherlock Holmes," Nan said decidedly. "We are not here to help him, we are here to help *you*. Have you anything on the boil you'd like us to tend?"

John filled his pipe, thinking for a moment. "Mycroft gave us to believe that you, Nan, are psychically receptive, and you, Sarah, are mediumistic. Is there anything more you can do?"

"Grey is an Astral Guardian, as is Neville," said Sarah. "Nan manifests on the astral plane as a Celtic warrior-woman, and she is able to read things about the past of objects by handling them. We both were permanently granted the ability to see Elementals by the Oldest Old One in England."

"The Prince of Earth?" Mary said in surprise. "The tricky fellow in *Midsummer Night's Dream*?"

"The very one," Nan confirmed.

The married couple looked at each other. "Number 10, Berkeley Square," John said, and nodded as their guests' eyes widened in recognition. "It's claimed another life. It's time to put a stop to this—thing—whatever it is."

"We've encountered it before," Sarah murmured, "But we were children at the time . . ."

"The place is ruinous, and I don't know that there is even an owner now," John told them. "It's killed a sailor off the HMS *Penelope*. His sweetheart came to Holmes, who dismissed her, of course. Mary and I looked into the case. He definitely died after he and three shipmates took a dare to stay there overnight. The official verdict is 'heart failure.' The girl says he died of fright. Of the other three lads, two said they suddenly felt absolute terror and ran, the fourth looked back over his shoulder and swore he saw a 'black spirit' chasing them. Holmes dismisses it all as drunken hallucinations caused by tainted gin; he feels sorry for the girl, but after he went to the house and found no clues, he dismissed it as 'twaddle.' It is true they were drinking, but there's more to it than that."

"It's very likely that being drunk opened them up to that thing, whatever it is," Sarah replied thoughtfully. "And if the house is as ruinous as you say, that's all the more reason to put the damned thing to rest. Anyone could break in. Children, even. It could even have claimed vagrants we know nothing about."

Mary sighed, with distinct overtones of relief. "I was hoping you would say that. Well, what do we do?"

"We need a battle plan," Nan said firmly, as Grey nodded and Neville *quorked* his agreement. "This is no ordinary haunt. Memsa'b was certain it was something that had been bound there. So the first thing we do—"

"Is our research," put in John Watson, putting down his pipe unlit and looking more than ready for the task.

"Preeeee-cisely," said Grey.

2

This was the first time that Nan and Sarah had been inside the Exeter Club. Mind, not even the patronage of Lord Alderscroft was going to get them into the sacred precincts of the "public" rooms, but he did arrange to smuggle the girls and Mary Watson up to the Hunting Lodge's archive room on the top floor via the servants' stairs. It was not the first time Nan and Sarah had made use of such a thing, and Nan was certain it would not be the last. Unlike the lushly carpeted, wide stairs used by the (exclusively male) members of the club, the servants' stairs were narrow, just painted wood without any carpet, and the treads themselves were narrow, poorly lit, and drafty. Had any of the three women been wearing fashionable gowns, they'd likely have trodden on each other's hems and probably killed each other in the subsequent tumble down the stairs. Fortunately Mary Watson was as fond of Ladies' Rational Dress as Nan and Sarah were, so they all climbed to the archives without mishap. John Watson, bless him, declined Lord Alderscroft's invitation to ascend via the "proper" stairs and came with them. Nan was glad he had, since if any of them *did* take a tumble, he was probably ready to catch them.

So, here they were, in a miniature library the size of the Watsons' sitting room, meticulously catalogued and cross-referenced, a compendium of everything about Elemental Magic that eight generations of Elemental Masters in London had managed to compile. It was a beautiful room, as suited the Hunting Lodge

31

of London; the bookcases probably dated to the founding of the Club and were substantial Georgian items, no-nonsense, sturdy articles the color of dark honey. They were not glass fronted; having glass doors would have prevented them from being set as closely together as they were.

"There's more books on Elemental Magic than we have here, of course," Lord Alderscroft said, as they wedged their way among the floor-to-ceiling bookshelves holding untold treasures. "There are all manner of handwritten books, passed down through the gifted families all over this country. And every time we can get someone to part with one long enough to make a copy, we do. But I would reckon there's ten times the number of books on magic and chronicles of Elemental Masters that we've no notion of out there than there is in here. And that's a conservative estimate." He led them to one particular set of shelves. "Fortunately, what we want and need is all right here." He indicated a line of books. "The Chronicles of the Hunting Lodge of the Exeter Club going back to its founding, before there even was an Exeter Club. I would suggest starting no later than 1650. Berkeley House was built in 1698, as I recall. There may have been strange activity at the site of that house before it was built."

"That sounds like a very sound plan," John agreed. "Thank you, Lord Alderscroft." They gathered up the books and took them to a table matching the bookcases at the front of the room, where they spread out their treasures. There was very good gas lighting here, which was just as well, since there was only one window. *The more room for books, I suppose,* Nan thought.

His Lordship merely smiled as they took their seats at the table. "You need not thank me. This is precisely why I brought you all together, although I must confess I am just as pleased you did not bring the birds."

"They are not to be trusted if they become bored while we read through dry tomes," Sarah confessed with some chagrin, selecting a book from the pile. "Unfortunately they have a great deal in common with precocious children. We left them with some puzzles containing their favorite treats, which can neither be hammered open nor pried open. They were greatly enjoying themselves when we left, and when they tire of that, Suki will bring them their tea and they'll nap."

"Ah, Suki! She'll keep them out of mischief." Lord Alderscroft chuckled. He had met Suki, an orphan with similar telepathic abilities to Nan's that the girls had found working as a kind of slave for a fraud of a fortune-teller. Suki had been so grateful to be rescued that there was nothing she would not have done for Nan and Sarah, and as another street brat, she had no compunction about wading into any potential threat, fists and feet flailing. She was fearless with the birds as well, and they were fond of her, so she had joined them in their flat as a sort of apprentice. She found going to school a great deal more onerous than serving as their maid, an affinity which occasionally exasperated Nan.

The flat they all lived in was paid for by Lord Alderscroft, who kept the girls on a sort of retainer to perform investigations for him. He had found it extremely useful to have them at hand when he needed someone whose talents were psychical rather than magical. Or someone who was female, and likely to be more overlooked than a male. *They* were grateful for useful employment. As they had both decided, the conventional life of a governess, a shopgirl, a teacher or a nurse was not something either of them was suited for.

"I will confess I feared for my books around those inquisitive beaks," he replied. "I will leave you to your researches, and I wish you great good luck in them."

"His books are the last thing he needed to be concerned about," Nan chuckled when he had left. "The birds know better now than to harm anything made of paper. It would be his *secrets* he needs to think about. Whenever they find that there is a hiding place for something, they are unrelenting about getting into it and discovering what is hidden there."

John Watson laughed. "I can think of one instance where they would have saved Holmes a great deal of effort."

With that, they all settled down to perusing the books. Many were handwritten, although there were some that had been printed. Nothing untoward was reported in the area where the Berkeley Square house now stood before the house was built, nor for many decades thereafter. Then Sarah, who was reading a volume that started about 1800, looked up with an expression of triumph on her face. "I think I may have it," she said. "The gentleman who owned the house when this book was written is said here to have had an interest in Roman antiquities of the English occupation. Around 1805 he went on several trips to excavate some himself. And in December of 1805, I find a mention of an *uncanny occurrence*. I think we may have pinpointed our culprit."

Nan's brows furrowed. "He certainly could have brought back something he shouldn't have," she admitted, "But wouldn't the artifact be long gone by now?"

"The size and danger of a haunting is in no way related to the size of the thing the haunting is tied to," Sarah replied with authority. "It *is*, however, related to the amount of power invested in the object."

"A ceremonial amulet, for instance?" Mary Watson exclaimed. "Something small and easily mislaid, perhaps even fallen in a crack between floorboards?"

"I would suspect you of having Nan's power of mind reading, you are following my thought so closely," Sarah replied. "An amulet, a piece of jewelry, or even a coin; all these are possible. If the object in question turned out not even to be Roman, but from some other culture, the gentleman in question wouldn't even miss it if it got misplaced."

Sarah and Nan exchanged a look. "If that is the case," Nan said, taking up the thread, "It's likely something inimical to the Celts. It was in trying to protect Sarah from it that I first manifested my persona of a Celtic warrior-woman."

John Watson drummed his fingers on the table. "Found in or near a Roman excavation but not necessarily Roman . . . inimical to the Celts, or at least something your—former incarnation?— would perceive immediately as an enemy . . . I think we need an expert on mythology. Or history. Or both, preferably."

Mary waved her hand at all the books. "We might be able to start here, in any event, now that we have a better idea of what we are looking for. After that, we might try the Reading Room of the British Museum."

But several hours later, they were about to admit defeat. There *was* an extensive collection of books about the Roman occupiers and the tribes of the time and their respective mythos. But there were so *many* possibilities that they had to give up. It was too hard to narrow the field.

"Well, now what?" Nan asked the Watsons.

Mary shook her head. But John Watson looked as if he'd had an idea. "I believe we ought to ask someone Lord Alderscroft doesn't precisely approve of." He laughed a little. "Neither does Holmes, for that matter."

"Who would that be?" asked Mary, just as curious as the girls were.

"Beatrice Leek. She and her family have been in the . . . less conventional occult circles for quite some time."

Mary began to laugh. So did Nan and Sarah. "'Less conventional'? Half of them are deluded, a quarter of them are outright mad, and the remainder I'm not quite sure of," said Nan, wiping the tears from her eyes. "Still, if you think there's a sane one, by all means. That's a good idea."

"Excellent." Watson pulled out his pocket watch. "As it happens, I know exactly where she will be at this hour." He rose. "Care for tea, ladies?"

"Perishing," said Mary. "Let's get out of this stuffy room and into the air. What there is of it. It *is* London, after all."

This was not a tearoom that Nan had ever been to before, nor likely would ever have found. It was in Chelsea, a district where she and Sarah almost never went, despite the fact that they had adopted the dress of the female artists who lived there. In fact, if it hadn't been for the sign on the door that *said* it was a tearoom, she likely would not have taken it for one, because most tearooms catered to ladies and only the occasional gentleman, and this place was crowded with both sexes. And in this tearoom, the Ladies' Rational Dress she, Sarah, and Mary Watson were wearing was absolutely unremarkable. In fact, the gowns worn here actually included bloomer suits, as well as Artistic Reform gowns, gypsy-like ensembles layered with fringed shawls and masses of bead necklaces, and even an Indian sari or two. Some of the men were almost as colorful, in paint-stained smocks, velvet coats in jewel tones, or scarlet cloaks.

There was hardly any wall showing. It was all paintings, and it was impossible for Nan to tell if any of them were any good, because having every square inch of wall populated by paintings just made everything confused, at least for her. She couldn't concentrate on any one of them, feeling overwhelmed by the visual cacophony.

As John led them past crowded tables and people sitting or occasionally standing and chatting at the tops of their lungs, Nan noticed that the tea services themselves were as . . . eclectic . . . as the customers. That was putting it kindly. To put it unkindly, it looked as if the owner of the shop had gone to every jumble sale in London and bought up every odd teapot, teacup, napkin, and tablecloth he or she could find.

At the back of the shop, there was a table set a little apart from the rest—or as much as a table could be, given the crowded conditions. There was a middle-aged woman there, holding court, it seemed, among a small group of incredibly serious-faced and fantastically garbed people. But when she spotted John coming toward her through the shop, she made shooing motions at them.

"Off you go, my chickens," she said genially, although their faces betrayed their disappointment at being sent away. "John and I have something serious to talk about." She looked from one to another of them with bright, sharp eyes. "Well, sit, sit. You never come to me, John Watson, unless you've questions to ask."

All of them took the motley assortment of vacated chairs. It appeared the jumble sale habit of the teashop owner extended to the furnishings. Nan took the opportunity to examine this person that John had brought them to see. She didn't look particularly prepossessing; late middle-age, plump, with a good-natured, round face, black hair put up in an untidy chignon under a black hat a-dance with jet ornaments. Her gown was black as well, an odd sort of outfit that seemed to be designed as an Artistic Reform tea gown, but instead of being made in fabrics of jewel tones with heavy embroidery, it was in black satin and velvet with jet bead embroidery.

"Number 10, Berkeley Square," Watson said without any preamble.

The woman pursed up her lips, and shook her head. "You're a brave boy, you are. You couldn't get me next or nigh that place if the last dollop of Devon Double Cream in the world was just inside the threshold."

Watson looked around at the four of them. "I think we can at least find out what's in there, and discover a way to lock it up before it kills anyone else."

The woman looked at each of them in turn, eyes narrowed. *Sizing us up,* Nan thought. *I think she's a magician of some sort.*

"That may be," the woman replied. "But I know when I am outmatched, and whatever is in there, it's too much for the likes of me."

"Beatrice, if anyone knows anything more than I've been able to discover, it's probably you," Watson said flatly. "We've determined that the hauntings didn't start until after the owner went on some expeditions to dig up Roman ruins and brought back artifacts. But that's all we know."

She tapped her index finger against her lip, her eyes lost in thought. "Well . . . there's a great deal of anger and hunger there, more than I've ever seen in a haunt in London." She glanced over at Nan and Sarah. "Ghosts don't do well in London; all the friction of so many living souls about tends to thin them out and they go to tatters."

Sarah nodded understandingly.

"Spirits *anchored* or *bound* to something, however, are another story. So it does make sense that your devilish thing is bound to something physical." She pursed her lips. "I do have a thought, Johnny. Buy me some teacakes, like a dear."

John Watson didn't even blink. He got the attention of a passing waitress and ordered the teacakes, and for good measure, some sandwiches and scones, for which Nan, for one, was very grateful. "I think we can take the time for a proper tea first, unless you can think of a reason for us to hurry, Beatrice."

"I can never think of a reason to hurry through teatime," she countered, and kept the conversation going on a lighter note, telling John and Mary stories about her circle of friends, which seemed to include everything from artists to gypsies, but mostly held occultists whose names were vaguely familiar to Nan, but only vaguely. Nan didn't mind being only partly involved in the conversation; she was too busy eating ham sandwiches and scones with currant jam.

But Beatrice did not touch the teacakes that Watson had ordered specially for her. Instead, she wrapped them in her handkerchief and put them in an enormous handbag, almost the size of a medical bag. Watson didn't seem at all surprised at this.

John paid the bill, and they all got up to leave. "Off to Berkeley Square, then," Beatrice said, with a sigh of resignation. "It's every bit of ten miles. . . ."

"Cab there, and I'll put you in a cab home," Watson promised, and went out to hail a vehicle that could carry all of them. Beatrice looked a bit more mollified.

"Well," the older lady said, when they were all settled inside an old-fashioned hackney carriage of the kind that had brought the four of them to Chelsea. "I suppose I should explain to you two youngsters that I'm a witch."

"Earth Magician," Watson said, with a weary sort of inflection as if he was used to making that correction.

"You call it what you want, dearie," Beatrice said, patting his hand. "I'll call it what my mam, and my great-grandmam, and *her* great-grandmam, and so on back to Ireland called it. We're witches. It runs in the family." She gave him a stern sort of look, silently admonishing him not to correct her anymore. "Now, the problem Johnny and dear Mary have is that nothing they can summon is going to be able to give them any advice about what's inside Number 10. But the creatures I can talk to might, if they're not too frightened. And Berkeley Square has enough clean ground in the park there should still be some in residence." She lifted her bag off her lap slightly. "I can't summon them, but I can call them, and they'll come for teacakes."

"Earth Elementals don't stray much from their homes, do they?" Mary asked.

Beatrice shook her head. "Not unless they are forced to. The ones there will have been there for several centuries at least, and the thing in Number 10 can't seem to go outside those four walls, so it's likely that while they are afraid of it, as well they should be, they won't have been forced to flee. They'll simply avoid Number 10 and the area around it for a good distance."

Nan knew enough about the Elementals by now to realize why neither John nor Mary had summoned their own creatures to give them information about Number 10. There wasn't enough water in or near the house for John to get any information from his, and the Air Elementals that Mary could summon were . . . flighty. They easily forgot things that had happened a mere month ago, and as for decades, well, that was out of the question. But Earth Elementals prided themselves on their long memories, and generally were happy to share information if they knew it.

"The thing in Number 10 didn't seem able to leave the four walls of the building," Sarah offered. "At least when we encountered it, once we were outside, we were safe. And I think if it *could* have followed us, it certainly *would* have."

Beatrice glanced at Sarah sharply. "Oh . . . so you two were *those* little girls." She paused for a long moment, biting her lip.

"Neither we nor Memsa'b and Sahib ever found out who was behind luring us to that place, either," Nan said crossly. "Though it might be just as well. I think Karamjit or Selim might have taken the law into their own hands if they had."

"Well . . . it was a long time ago," Beatrice said slowly. "And there's a lot that isn't mine to tell. But I can promise you that the person responsible for putting you children in deadly peril never got the opportunity to do that again with anyone, child or adult."

All four of them fixed their gazes on Beatrice, who just shrugged. It was clear she wasn't going to say anything more about it, so although Nan was curious, she decided that she wasn't *that* curious. *It's enough to know that nobody else fell victim to him.* And when she told them, it would satisfy Selim and Karamjit, who were still brooding over the incident.

Mary Watson immediately, and tactfully, changed the subject to the crowd that had been around Beatrice when they had first arrived at the tearoom. "I didn't recognize any of them," she said, tilting her head at Beatrice in invitation to say something about them.

So for the rest of the ride, they got a very entertaining description of the gaggle of young poets, artists, writers, and musicians who were "courting" her.

"They want me to introduce them to the occult, of course," she said matter-of-factly. "And I do my best to keep them occupied harmlessly without getting themselves into trouble."

"Better you than some," John Watson said darkly, and Nan nodded.

"Sahib and Memsa'b have extracted a few dilettantes from things they . . . regretted," Nan added.

"They're harmless little ducks for the most part. A few are terribly earnest, most are only terribly earnest as long as their interest lasts, which isn't long. They all want to *see* things, of course, and have delirious visions of things they can paint or write about, and when that doesn't happen, they go on to some other enthusiasm. Usually it's the Lake District. I try to encourage that." Beatrice shrugged. "Not a speck of our sort of Talent among the lot of them, of course, which is just as well. One never knows when the next fad might be hashish, opium, or cocaine parties, and mixing the occult and drugs is as dangerous as waltzing with tigers, if you don't know what you're about."

"That's an understatement," John Watson said darkly. "What about the one with the angry face? The one that was lurking within earshot, but not in the circle?"

"Oh, Alexandre." Beatrice waved her hands dismissively. "He has ambitions and driblets and drablets of ability. I said to him the other day when he came oozing about, talking about what he was 'about to' write, 'Alex, you don't want to write, you want to *have written.*' Oh, how he glared! He knew exactly what I meant, though it escaped the others."

"That he wants the laurels of being a writer without the work?" Sarah hazarded, which clarified things for Nan, who couldn't work out what Beatrice had meant, either.

"Exactly, my dear." Beatrice patted her hand. "He would love to be Oscar Wilde, but he hasn't a tenth of Oscar's heart, nor a twentieth of Oscar's talent. He also fancies himself a grand occultist, and as you might imagine, he's going at it through the application of drugs and *atmosphere.* I've warned the ones that will listen against him."

"And the ones that won't listen?"

"I can't be responsible for everyone," she replied philosophically.

"Beatrice, you should be careful about him," Mary Watson said, suddenly. "I've heard things about him. He's vicious, sadistic, and thrives on revenge."

"And *I* have my little book," Beatrice said, with a decided nod. "It's *my* version of The Woman's photographs. There are things I know about half of London, and proof of all of them. Why do you think I've never been run up before the judges on fortune-telling? No one wants me to start reciting what I know before a judge. But you're right, and I will be careful about him."

Mary relaxed. "Good. He may be a weasel, but a cornered weasel is the most vicious of his kind. The best thing you can do is make him decide you're not worth the trouble."

Beatrice pursed her lips, but nodded agreement.

By this time they had arrived at Berkeley Square; as directed, the cabby stopped the horses beside the park that made the square such a pleasant place to live. John got out and handed all the ladies out before paying the driver.

"Well, dearies," said Beatrice, the jet ornaments on her hat bobbing and shivering as she looked about the place. "Down there, I think," she continued, nodding at the nearer end of the cartouche-shaped park. "Under that big tree." The park was relatively deserted—too late for nannies and children, too early for evening strollers. Beatrice led the way down a broad gravel path with the air of someone who knows exactly where she is going and what she is going to do when she gets there. None of the few people walking, reading a newspaper, or simply enjoying the late afternoon air gave any of them a second look. Their timing could not have been more perfect.

There was a little group of wooden benches at the end of the graveled path, right under the tree, and Beatrice occupied the center of the middle one. "This'll do," she said, and closed her eyes with the air of someone about to perform some sort of task.

Nan didn't sense anything, nor see anything except a trio of red squirrels at the roots of another tree to their left that slowly, nervously, began to edge nearer. Although it was a little odd for squirrels to be so shy; normally, at least in her experience, the little rascals were as bold as ravens, and here in a park, you'd think they were used to approaching people for food. The pigeons certainly had begun to gather, cooing hopefully and eyeing Beatrice's big bag.

Nan wished Neville was here; he could have scouted for Elementals, or other hints of magic.

The three little rodents ran in short little spurts until they were all huddled together in the center of the path, facing the bench. Beatrice opened her eyes and fixed her gaze on the squirrels. She smiled encouragingly at them. "Ah, there you are, lads. Come on then, show your proper shapes for us." Now she reached into her bag and brought out the wrapped cakes, letting the handkerchief fall open so the squirrels could see the treat. "See what we have for you, dearies?"

If Nan had not been so used to magic by now, she knew she might have thought she was going mad. One instant there were three squirrels huddling together in the middle of the graveled path. The next—

They weren't squirrels. They were fauns. Goat-footed, handsome little boys with tiny horns peeking through their curly hair, goat eyes fixed nervously on the cakes in Beatrice's hand. "Come now," Beatrice cooed. "We've no intention of hurting you, and there's no Cold Iron about us. We just want to have a chat."

They were goat from the waist down, and unlike some fauns Nan had seen in the past, they preserved a vestige of modesty by wearing ragged loincloths. Otherwise they were completely naked. Then again, it wasn't as if they were in *need* of trousers. Or shirts, for that matter. None of the Elementals Nan had ever seen had ever shown any hint that they were the least inconvenienced by cold or heat.

"A chat?" bleated the one in the middle, faintly. "About what?"

"Have a cake first," Beatrice suggested. "Then we'll talk." She held out the handkerchief, and slowly, slowly, the little Fauns edged sideways toward her, one at a time, getting just close enough to snatch a cake, then dart back to a safer distance. There they crouched over their treats, stuffing their cakes into their mouths so fast Nan feared they'd choke, their eyes never leaving Beatrice's face. It was only Beatrice they paid any attention to. So far as the rest of them were concerned, the fauns didn't seem to think they were of any importance.

Then again, maybe the fauns thought the rest of them couldn't see the Elementals for what they were. Or, not being Earth Magicians, Nan, Sarah, Mary, and John weren't dangerous in the sense that they were not able to coerce creatures of Earth.

"Here now," Nan said, getting a bit impatient with their near-panic. "Look deeper into the millstone than just the surface, will you? My friend and I have leave under Oak, Ash, and Thorn to come and go and look and know—"

She was about to add something about the fact that being afraid of *them* was just silly, but all three fauns stared at her with eyes first rounded with alarm, then narrowed with concentration, then, suddenly, rounded again, but this time with awe.

"She has the hand of *him* on her!" the middle one bleated. "The Oldest Old Thing himself!"

Finally. This was not the first time that Nan and Sarah had to coax Elementals to speak to them, but usually they saw what Sarah called "Puck's Blessing" on the girls right away, which at least acted as a sort of passport to being considered trustworthy. So her impression had been correct; these three were so skittish that they hadn't even glanced at anyone but the single Earth Magician that had called for them.

"And look more. Air and Water Masters here as well, and none of us going to harm you," Nan continued, since she had their attention. They looked over at the Watsons, and all three nodded respectfully to the pair, then returned their attention to Nan, and to Beatrice.

Now they crept close again, still nervous, but more willing to trust. Beatrice offered them the rest of the cakes, (probably well aware, as Nan and Sarah were, that by accepting the treats, the fauns put themselves in the Earth Magician's debt).

When the last crumb had been eaten, the fauns looked up at Beatrice with a little more calm. "You wished to chat, mage?" said the centermost one, a faun with oddly piebald skin that matched his hairy goat legs and ivory-colored horn-buds that were slightly longer than those of the other two. Nan guessed that he was the eldest of the three. Maybe the de facto leader. He settled onto his haunches, and so did the other two.

"I need knowledge," Beatrice replied solemnly. "More than I have. I need to know of the Dark Thing, over yon—" She gestured in the general direction of Number 10.

The three fauns sprang together again and clutched each other, shaking, as they stared at Beatrice with their eyes starting out of their heads. "We cannot go there!" the middle one bleated in a panic. "Do not ask us! It is death! It is death!"

"Oh calm down, do," Nan said a little crossly. "No one is asking you to go there. We only want to know what you know about it."

Her matter-of-fact tone seemed to snap them out of their panic. They turned to look back at her. "Only that? And nothing more?" As usual it was the middle one that spoke. So far the only thing that had come out of the other two were frightened squeaks and bleats.

"Only that." When nothing was forthcoming out of them voluntarily, Nan decided to take the initiative and start asking questions. "Was it here when you first came to dwell here?"

All three shook their heads.

"And how and when did you come here?" Sarah asked. "And why?"

"We came with the Legions," offered their spokesperson, after looking at his two companions for a moment. "Our groves and forests were being cut down for farms. They loaded their ships with stones. We came with the stones and hid in the darkness. It was fearful, but losing our groves was more fearful."

"They must have come with the ballast stones," put in John. "But they aren't dryads, to be tied to the stones the way a dryad is tied to a tree. The stones must simply have given them something to anchor to, in order to make the crossing over so much water."

"Even so," agreed the Faun. "And we found here, where we are now, these groves near Londinium. It was a fair place, and so we homed. And the Black Thing was not here then. Sons of Adam came and went, but the trees remained, and so we stayed and stayed."

"If the Sons of Adam trouble us not, we will not leave," said the rightmost one, softly.

"When did the Black Thing come?" Sarah asked. "Did it come on its own? Is it a thing that perished here? Was it brought here?"

"By a Son of Adam, yes, it was brought," agreed the talkative Faun. "Five tens of years ago, thereabouts."

They all exchanged a look but Beatrice. "That accords with our research," Mary Watson said softly.

"And what is it?" Nan asked bluntly. That put the Fauns in a panic again and they clung to one another.

"It is death! It is death!" the middle one cried in desperation.

Nan resisted the urge to reach out and shake some sense into the creature. "We already *know* it's death," she said sharply. "We know it has killed Sons of Adam more than once. But besides that, what is it?"

They were still trembling, but at least they stopped making meeping sounds. "We . . . do not know. It is not of the Legions, though it hates them, and we can feel its hate when it thinks of them. It is not of the tribes the Legions drove away from here. It is not of the tribes that came here when the last of the Eagles left. It is not of the Druids, it is not of the Christians. It is not of the Winged Helms, nor any other invader. It is not a lost spirit, and it is not a dead thing. It feeds upon the living. It feeds upon fear. It would feed upon us, could it reach us. And it is old, old, old. It is a thing that was here before the tribes, but a Son of Adam plucked it from its proper place, where it at least slumbered, and brought it here, and the bringing awoke it."

Well, that at least gets us a lot farther along than we were when we started, Nan thought. *We know places* not *to look.*

"That is all we know," the little faun said, desperately, as they looked at each other in silence. "Truly, truly, truly."

"I believe you, pet," said Beatrice comfortingly. "You've earned your cakes. Run along."

One moment the fauns were there. The next, there were only a couple of stray leaves where they had been, and three squirrels running for another tree. They swarmed up the trunk and disappeared among the leaves.

It was pretty obvious from the utter lack of interest that anyone else was showing them that *they* were the only people who had seen the fauns for what they were.

"Oh!" said Mary Watson, suddenly.

They all turned to look at her, because the tone in which she had spoken that single syllable sounded as if she had had a revelation of sorts.

"What is it, my dear?" asked John, putting a hand on hers.

"I might know what it is," she said, a little breathlessly. "I never thought all that delving into Celtic legend was going to come in handy quite so soon. I think it might be a Fomorian!"

3

Nan waited for the proverbial "other shoe to drop." When it didn't, she sighed. "All right, what's a Fomorian?" she asked patiently. *Why is it that people who know something expect you to somehow pick it out of their mi—oh. Well, I could do that, I suppose, but it would be terribly rude.*

Mary paused a moment, gathering her thoughts. "Well, according to really ancient Celtic stories, humans weren't the first people here—certainly weren't the first people in Ireland, where you find most of these stories, although the Celtic stories from Britain often as not mirror the Irish ones. The first 'people,' if you can call them that, were the Fomorians. They were extremely powerful magicians. Most of them seem, at least in the legends, to be monsters of various sorts. Creatures with the bodies of men and the heads of animals and reptiles, or reptilian humans. Their leader, Balor, was a giant with one eye." Mary paused, as Nan frowned.

"That sounds familiar," she said.

"Like a Greek Cyclops," Sarah added.

Mary nodded. "It does, doesn't it? We all know that some of these legends have some basis in fact, and this may well be one of them, given that the Greeks and the Celts are not the only cultures to speak of one-eyed giants. But we can explore that at a later date."

"Right." Nan nodded. "So you were telling us what you know about the Fomorians." The sun was getting low, and Nan really wanted to be back in the flat before dark.

Mary's brows creased a little in thought. "The Fomorians were conquered by the Tuatha De Danaan, another nonhuman race, but not until after some really terrible wars that left the earth torn up and melted in places and the lakes boiled dry."

"Which sounds like a fight between Elemental Masters . . . or a fight between an Elemental Master and a very powerful Elemental." John pursed his lips. "Interesting."

"The Fomorians were supposed to be immortal. Although they *could* be killed, it was very difficult, and it was actually easier to imprison them somewhere. Under hills, in trees . . . or in objects." Mary glanced in the direction of Number 10 and shivered. "And if this thing is a Fomorian, whatever a Fomorian might actually be, I don't think we are *nearly* prepared enough to take it on."

"Not today, certainly." John frowned, but agreed, and Nan breathed a sigh of relief.

"There are old warriors, and bold warriors, but no old, bold warriors," Beatrice said philosophically. "And now that you have some semblance of a clue, I would very much like you to find me a nice hansom cab to take me back to Chelsea, John Watson. I fancy a bit of soup, and I promised one of my flock of chicks I'd read his sonnets before bed."

"And I would very much like to do that for you, Beatrice Leek," John replied, getting to his feet and offering a hand to Mary, then one to Beatrice. "You've been immensely helpful. I don't think we'd have gotten nearly this far, this fast, without you."

They all returned to the street, where John had the luck of hailing two cabs: a hansom for Beatrice and another hackney for the rest of them. He put Beatrice into the first, paid the fare in advance, and handed the rest of them into the second. "221 Baker Street," he told the cabby through the little hatch in the roof.

"Right, guv'nor," the cabby replied, and closed the hatch, and they were off at—an amble. This was a very stylish and quiet neighborhood, with the exception of Number 10, and one just did not send a horse into a noisy trot on this street. Which was fine with Nan; those sandwiches at tea were enough to keep her until dinner, and only Beatrice had actually expended any energy calling the fauns.

"I think more research in Lord Alderscroft's archives is in

order," Mary Watson said, as the cab turned onto a less refined street, and the cabby gave his horse the signal to go a bit faster.

Nan nodded agreement, as did Sarah. "Do you think there would be anything more about Fomorians in the British Museum?" Sarah asked.

But Mary Watson shook her head. "I embarked on a course of study of Celtic legends because they had become so popular," she explained, "And I wanted to be ready in case some fool accidentally invoked something. I've gone over every book they have on public offer, and I have checked the catalogue in the Rare Manuscript Room, but there is nothing of interest there. Most of what *is* there is analysis by linguists and other learned gentlemen who pay more attention to declensions of verbs than context."

Nan raised an eyebrow. "Do people *often* invoke things by accident? I thought magic was harder than that."

Mary shrugged. "Sometimes it's a matter of will and a smattering of Talent. Sometimes it's because whatever breaks through was trying very hard in the first place, and the person in question just managed to open a crack that it could exploit."

Sarah nodded sagely. "That happens with malign spirits, too." She sighed. "You just can't save fools from themselves, can you?"

"Would that we could," John replied. "That's one reason why Beatrice is here in London—well, Chelsea—rather than some place out in the deep countryside. She's trying to keep an eye on the artistic set, since that lot are the ones most likely to go into obscure religions and mysticism and get caught up in magic. As a magician rather than a Master, she's not quite as sensitive to the poisonous things people in town have done to the earth. If anything comes up that she can't head off, she's got the Hunting Lodge at her disposal."

"And the other reason?" Sarah asked, archly.

John smiled. "Because she's always been a bohemian herself. And she has a bit of a past among the artistic set as well. She posed for quite a few painters in her reckless youth, and—though a gentleman never pays attention to rumors—there are rumors she had more than a few amorous adventures among them."

"She may be a bit of a bohemian, but everything I heard out of her tells me she has enough good common sense to be able to keep a small herd of flighty artists out of trouble," Mary replied with some affection. Nan smothered a smile; it was obvious that Mary had warmed up to Beatrice immediately.

"That she does," John agreed. He regarded all of them soberly. "Do any of you feel that there is any urgency in taking care of Number 10? I'm not only asking about logic and reasoning; I am asking about instincts."

Nan leaned back in her seat and clasped her hands on her knee. Sarah got a faraway look in her eyes. "I'd like to ask the birds before we come to a conclusion," she said, finally. "But I'm not getting any sense that we need to move in the next—three or four days, at least. Sarah?"

Sarah shook her head. "No feelings of nameless dread here. And speaking logically—Doctor Watson, won't the police be doing their best to keep anyone out of Number 10 for a while?"

"It's been boarded up, and yes, whoever is patrolling Berkeley Square as his regular beat is going to be keeping an eye on the place to keep the curious out," Watson said in a decided tone of voice.

"Then let's do what we seldom get a chance to do," Mary Watson chimed in. "Let's do what *Holmes* does, survey the site, get the plans of the house, gather information on our foe."

"Speaking of Holmes, I wonder how he's coming with that missing girl case?" mused Watson. "Or if the raven was wrong, and it's too ordinary for him to care about?"

"I just hope he doesn't expect to dragoon you into it before we finish with Number 10," Mary said darkly. "I'll . . . I'll organize his case files if he dares."

"Mary!" John clutched at his chest in pretended shock. "You wouldn't!"

She looked mock contrite. "No, I wouldn't. But I *will* see to it that Mrs. Hudson burns all his toast."

"That, he wouldn't notice. He scarcely notices when his food is ice-cold." Watson snorted. "Still, we should look in on him on the way up. And we should decide if you are dining with Mary and me, ladies."

Nan answered for both of them. "I wouldn't impose on Mrs. Hudson's good nature without advance warning. Tomorrow night, however, we would be delighted."

On arrival at 221, the quartet headed straight up the stairs to B, opening the door to the strains of, "Watson! Bring the young ladies in! I need the feminine perspective!"

Watson's eyebrows rose, but he waved the women in ahead of them, and they all fitted themselves into the somewhat chaotic sitting room. Holmes was deep in perusal of what looked to be a thick packet of papers, his brows furrowed, as he waved them all to seats. "This case is . . . very interesting, Watson. On the face of it, it would be a simple elopement. However, there is nothing *simple* about it, once one gets past the surface. Take these letters, for instance. Here, take them indeed!" He divided the packet into three, and handed one third each to Nan, Sarah, and Mary. "These are not the originals, of course; these are translations. Read those over, and tell me what you think. You, in particular, Mary."

"Translated by whom?" Mary asked, accepting her packet. "You know what they say about translations . . . they can range from incomplete to inaccurate."

"By me, of course," Holmes replied. "These are part of my case notes. I promise you, I have been careful to reproduce the least nuance."

Nan read her letters . . . and at first, they seemed very commonplace. Addressed to the missing girl's parents, there was nothing in them to excite any sort of suspicion. In fact, they were utterly dull recitations of where the girl had gone and what she had done.

. . . perhaps, a little *too* dull.

No, a great deal too dull.

"Had this young lady ever been anywhere away from home before?" Nan asked, more sharply than she intended.

"Ha!" exclaimed Holmes. "I believe you have seen what I have! No, despite her sister's profession, Johanna had never been away from home for as much as a night. She had never traveled beyond the borders of her city."

"It's more what I *haven't* seen, Mister Holmes," Nan pointed. "There's no excitement here. She's never been outside of her home city you say, never been to a strange country at all, and yet, these . . . descriptions, if you could call them that, are like a particularly stodgy guidebook. She doesn't exclaim about things that surely must seem odd to a German. She doesn't go into raptures over a beautiful building, or a stained glass window, or even, for heaven's sake, the interior of St. Paul's. There's nothing of the personal in any of the letters you have given me. *Nothing* about fashions, and the first thing most young women would talk about would be fashion, because there are always differences in things we women notice between countries. Surely she should have been on the lookout for the Professional Beauties, and yet . . . there is nothing. *Nothing* about the new food she has been trying. Nothing about the opera other than the description of the opera house! And absolutely no sense of excitement in any of it." She frowned. "In fact, these are letters that are devoid of *people* as well. Didn't she meet anyone besides her sister?"

Sarah nodded agreement. "Wasn't she introduced to *anyone?* Surely, with her sister performing her London debut, there must have been all manner of nobility and notables swarming about, but you'd never know it from these letters. Nothing about the opera house dandies. Nothing about the artistic set. Nothing about musicians. She mentions no one, least of all this mysterious Canadian. He should have appeared somewhere in these letters at the beginning, even if she attempted to hide a growing infatuation by eliminating him from later missives."

Mary was frowning even more deeply. "Sherlock," she said sharply. "Even assuming that this girl was the dullest, shyest creature on the planet, there is nothing in here that shows me she was in love enough with a stranger to elope with him. A woman in love does tend to wax poetic and rapturous about even the smallest of trifles, if it can be related at all to the beloved. I would have *expected* poems of praise to any little thing that recalled him to her mind."

"Wouldn't she have been trying to conceal that?" Holmes asked, looking for all the world like a hound on the scent. "These are letters to her parents, after all. One might assume that the fiancé would see them, and she would not have wished him to learn of a rival."

"Trust me, Sherlock, a young girl is absolutely incapable of completely hiding an infatuation from the knowing eye," Mary replied. "It is a great deal like the analogy of 'seeing' a hole in a dark cave by lighting its edges. You might not be able to see the hole itself, but you can certainly intuit where it is. She *does not* avoid the existence of her fiancé; she refers to him several times in each letter, in the most commonplace way, and he would be the last thing in the world she would want to touch on, if she were in love with another. And there is a complete absence of anyone else, at all, other than her sister Magdalena. If I were to say anything about these letters, I would say for a certainty that they were not written by anyone madly enough in love with someone to fly with him."

"Ah!" Holmes settled back in his chair with contentment. "That was precisely what I thought, but I wanted to see if you ladies would come to the same conclusions I did. I tend to find the ways of the feminine sex . . . obtuse. But never let it be said I ever hesitated to consult with someone more expert than I, when my knowledge is lacking."

"I can't say I've ever been in love, but I tend to agree with Mary," Sarah told Holmes, handing over her share of the letters. "These are the letters of a dulled soul, not an enlivened one. A girl in love sees the stars everywhere. Whoever wrote *these* letters was staring fixedly at the ground, and never looked up."

Nan passed hers over with a shrug.

"Then there is the matter of the unheartbroken fiancé," Holmes continued. "And the now-unconcerned parents. You will recall I got heart-rending missives from the parents as well as the fiancé from Germany. I also interviewed them as soon as they arrived; the fiancé came the day after the Von Dietersdorfs. They were quite upset, not to say distraught. Then, today, they all returned *en masse* to tell me there was no further need for me to investigate. They told me, calmly, serenely even, that the matter was settled and I was no longer to concern myself about it. That Johanna had indeed run off with a young man from Canada, and that she would be fine. Now . . . I could imagine the parents having been convinced that this was the case—but the fiancé? Unless he was covering his injured pride and emotions with feigned indifference . . . no." Holmes' eyes glittered. "I generally am not prey to emotions myself, but I am by no means blind to their effects in others, and the young man—Helmut Reicholt—was as calm as if the girl *now* meant nothing more to him than the waitress at a café, and this was a young man who had been pleading desperately with me, in tones of woe, to find her and persuade her to return not half a week ago."

"I take it you are *not* giving up the case, then, Holmes?" Watson said sardonically.

"I can afford to indulge myself in an occasional case that is purely of my own interest," Holmes replied, with a brisk nod. "And this one . . . is interesting."

"I don't suppose you want to make use of *my* Talent on the parents or the fiancé, do you?" Nan asked. She was a little concerned, since that was bordering on the unethical, especially when there was absolutely no proof that there was anything more going on than a girl who had run away and a fiancé who was experiencing relief at getting out of an engagement he might not, perhaps, have been wholeheartedly happy about.

"No, no," Holmes replied, waving her offer away. "In a sense, that would be cheating. I prefer my own methods. But thank you for the offer."

At that moment, Nan wished she had the originals of those letters in her hands, because she had another Talent that she had only touched on to Holmes—the ability to trace where an object had been, its history, and something of the emotions of the latest one to have held it.

"In that case, Holmes, I will see the young ladies to a cab, and would you care to come up to dine with us?" Watson asked genially.

"Thank you, but I'm dining out," Holmes replied, standing up and reaching for his overcoat. "There are some musical friends I wish to speak to tonight, and the only way to capture them is to lure them with a feast. Good evening to you all, and I'll go out with you."

"Oi miss! Yer roight in time! Them birds been right good's gold!" said Suki, meeting them at the door to their flat. "An' Mrs. 'Orace on'y jest brought up dinner!"

"Excellent, my little imp," said Sarah, stooping over to kiss the top of the little girl's head. Or rather, the enormous bow that crowned it. Little Suki, having been dressed most of her short life in whatever her mistress picked up at stalls and rag-vendors, was inordinately proud of dressing well, in the neat little frocks Memsa'b had had made for her that looked as if they had come right out of the pages of a Kate Greenaway book. "We'll all have dinner straightaway, then. Did you have a nice tea?"

Suki nodded; she was an attractive little mite. Her hair was a tumble of short black curls, she had a pair of enormous, beautiful brown eyes, and if her dusky complexion made some people suspect she owed her dark coloring not to Italian blood but to an African race, they were too polite—and too wise—to voice that suspicion around Nan and Sarah. When she opened her mouth, she was pure Cockney, though she was trying very hard to "speak roight," so as not to shame the young ladies. "Oi 'ad a loverly tea," she replied. "Mrs. 'Orace give us all a curry." By "us all," of course, she meant that the birds had shared it. "She do a bang-up curry."

"Excellent!" Nan replied, hanging up her hat and shawl. "Now, what are we having for supper?"

"Lamp-chops," Suki said, forthrightly. "Lamp-chops an'—fixin's."

Nan whistled, and a moment later the birds came flying in from their own room. They had a room all their very own, which they knew they were supposed to remain confined to when Nan and Sarah were not about. It had an ultra-safe iron stove in the fireplace, good, heavy perches that would not fall over short of an earthquake, a bath pan for each of the birds, water and food dishes, and a multitude of "toys" of various sorts. And of course, when the girls were gone, Suki spent most of her time in there with them, keeping them company.

Neville landed on Nan's shoulder, Grey on Sarah's arm, and everyone went in to dinner together.

The flat was a very spacious one, above a bookshop also owned by their landlady, who had a smaller flat behind the bookstore. It had four bedrooms, one of which was the bird's playroom, a sitting room, a dining room with a pantry, and a real bathroom with piped-in water and a boiler for the bath. It didn't require a kitchen, for like Holmes and the Watsons, the widowed landlady, Mrs. Horace, provided breakfast and supper, and if arranged, luncheon and tea as well. All they needed was the little stove in the sitting room to provide hot water for tea and a place to toast bread. Lord Alderscroft paid for this highly agreeable arrangement, and the landlady understood that they were, unlike most young ladies, apt to be coming and going at all hours. Nan more than once suspected that Mrs. Horace at least *knew* about the Hunting Lodge and the Elemental Masters, even if she was not a magician herself, and assumed that Nan and Sarah were part of that establishment. Nan was perfectly content to leave her with that impression. It was near enough to the truth after all.

"Memsa'b senna note," the urchin continued, as they all took their places around the table. The birds joined them on perches, with their own food and water in cups fastened at either end. Grey got chopped fruit at this time of the evening, with a few shelled nuts. Neville got raw meat, the trimmings from whatever Mrs. Horace cooked for the girls. "She ast if I wanta come go t' th' Lunnon Zoo. She's bringin' th' school an' sez I could meet 'em there."

"When would that be?" Nan asked, taking the cover off the new potatoes and peas and helping herself, then passing the plate to Sarah. Sarah had taken a lamb chop and served first Suki, then herself, and was spooning out mint jelly from a bowl.

"Day arter termorrer," said Suki, her eyes on the spoon holding the sweet stuff.

"I'll send a note saying you may," Sarah told the girl, who looked up, grinning with glee. "Just remember that the birds in the aviary are *not* like Grey and Neville, so don't go climbing past balustrades and fences so you can get closer to them."

"Yes'm," Suki promised, taking bread and buttering it.

Supper was followed by Suki reciting the lessons that the girls had set her to do during the day, and a bedtime story. After Suki had been put to bed, and the birds settled onto their perches beside the hearth, Sarah stared fixedly for a while at the center ornament on the mantelpiece, which happened to be an enormous, and unusually fine, whelk shell, a gift from the Selkie-folk.

"What are you thinking about?" Nan asked, after a while.

"Well," Sarah said slowly. "I was wondering if there was any way we could ask that fearsome Celtic warrior you turn into now and again about the Fomorians. . . ."

"Huh." Nan considered that. "That's not exactly under my control, you know."

"Hypnosis? Or perhaps Memsa'b and Sahib know a way?" Sarah continued to look hopeful.

Nan smiled wryly. "I am sure Holmes knows hypnosis, but I am equally sure he would not be in the least interested in attempting to summon a Celtic warrior-woman out of my head. I'll tell you what, though, we can ask Mary and John and see what they say."

"I hope they know a way. Or that they know someone who knows a way." Sarah tilted her head to the side. "Do you think that it is a past life of yours?"

Now Nan laughed. "How should *I* know that? When it happens, it's as if a separate person comes and takes over my body, and we don't have anything to say to one another. I don't understand what *she* is saying, and I am fairly certain she doesn't understand me."

Sarah bit her lip. "You could try lucid dreaming. . . ."

Nan felt annoyed with herself. "Yes, I could, and I don't know why I didn't think of it myself. Good work, Sarah! This is why we are better as a team!"

Sarah flushed with pleasure, and they both returned to their books.

Nan and Sarah had been taught the technique of lucid dreaming, or "dreaming-to-order," when they were in their early teens. Memsa'b had said it was a useful technique when you were trying to remember something, or when you were working through a problem, but with proper precautions it was also useful when dealing with the occult. To be fair, Sarah used it more often than Nan; her mediumistic tendencies tended to attract spirits, and often they were too weak even to make themselves and their needs known to her when she was awake. So once every fortnight or so, she would deliberately set out to use lucid dreaming to see if there were any ghosts in need of her assistance. More often than not she didn't even bother to tell Nan of the result, because more often than not, it was the spirit of a child or an adult who had died unexpectedly; they were confused and only needed help to realize what had happened and be sent on their way. Only when the case was exceptional would Sarah say, casually, usually over breakfast, "I had a special visitor last night. . . ."

The first thing to do when one was about to attempt a lucid dream—at least when one was as well trained in the occult as Nan and Sarah were—was to *decide* that such dreaming would take place. Then, one simply relaxed and put the thought in the back of one's mind. The trained will would take care of the rest. So Nan concentrated on the book of Celtic myths and legends that she had providentially found in the very bookstore they lived above, and left the rest to take care of itself. She didn't make any special preparations, except that when she was in her own room, she made sure that the room was well warded and that all her shields were charged and intact.

Then she turned down the lamp and tucked herself into bed.

As most nights, she fell asleep immediately. As a child, before she had come under the protection of the Hartons and after her grandmother had died, sleep had been something she pursued only at her peril. In any season, drink took precedence over shelter for her mother; as long as the weather wasn't absolutely freezing, it was even odds whether they would sleep in a cheap room, often shared with others, or under a bridge or in an alley. In winter, at least, her mother would try to get a room, but a room in winter always meant sharing, and sharing meant sleeping with one eye open. There was no telling what any of the other inhabitants might try, from rifling through her clothing in search of valuables to trying to take what Memsa'b called "liberties." And never mind that she was just a child; to the minds of some men, that was an asset.

But after a year of living safely and securely at the Harton School, Nan had picked up the knack of falling asleep immediately, and staying asleep unless something woke her. She *still* had a hair-trigger reflex that brought her completely awake if there was any sound or movement she didn't expect. Completely awake, alert, and ready to act.

It was a nuisance sometimes, here in London, where even on their quiet street there could be unexpected noises, but she reckoned it was worth it. Just in case.

She was aware as she drifted off of Neville muttering a little from his perch on the headboard of her bed.

Then she was somewhere else. She was some*one* else.

The hair on her head felt tightly braided; glancing down at herself, she saw she was wearing a checkered tunic of brown and gold, brown trousers, and over it all a sort of armor-shirt of leather, with bronze plates riveted to it. This was held in at the waist with a thick leather belt, from which hung a sword, a dagger and . . . a stick?

She was squatting on her heels in a circle, with several other personages. Two of them . . . if the colors they had been wearing had been as bright as modern dyes could make them, their ensembles would have been eye-watering. The bearded, red-haired man wore a cloak of sorts striped in yellow and green, a long-sleeved tunic checkered in red and brown, and a pair of trousers checkered in blue and black. The woman also wore a striped cloak or shawl; hers was red and green, her long tunic was brown and blue, and her skirt was striped in black and yellow. There were also men in checkered or striped tunics and plain or checkered or striped trousers, but no one wore as many colors as those two. It was enough to distract her from the conversation for a moment.

Well, it was distracting *her*. It wasn't distracting the body she was riding around in. The personality in charge of this body was going right on with what she was talking about.

". . . fearsome black it was, but like a shadow, and not altogether of this world," she finished. Or rather, whoever was in charge finished. "I ran."

The two . . . brightly colored personages looked at each other. Something whispered to her . . . some bit of thought that came over from the mind of the person she . . . had been? Because now she got the distinct impression this had been her, Nan, a very long time ago. Memsa'b and Sahib—and Karamjit and Agansing and most of the Hindu and Buddhist members of the Harton School—wholeheartedly believed in being reborn. Reincarnation, they called it. Nan had held on to her reservations, thinking that the Celtic warrior she "manifested" as in times of danger was just something she'd cooked up in her own head, out of stories.

And right now, well, her reservations had just gotten chucked out a window.

At any rate, without any previous knowledge of the lives of early Celts, she knew that the person she *had* been knew these two as druids, because only druids and bards were allowed to wear clothing of six colors.

She kept her mouth shut, and listened to the druids and the other tribal leaders talk. And the more they spoke, the more convinced she became that, whatever the dark thing was they were about to battle, it *wasn't* a Fomorian. These people presumably knew what Fomorians were, and they never once referred to it by that name. They *did* call it "A Shadow Beast," and "An Ancient Shadowed One," and though she knew that the practices of these folk caused them to avoid speaking something's proper name for fear of invoking it, she thought they would have said the word once at least.

But they did nothing of the kind. And she felt herself drifting out of the dream—or the memory—in a state of intense frustration. Once again, it seemed they were at a dead end.

INTERLUDE: *VALSE TRISTE*

It had been surprisingly easy to slip into the unoccupied room below that of his target. No one looked twice in this fine establishment at a man dressed as he was, in expensive evening dress. Not even at two in the morning, since a man-about-town could be expected to be out as late as he pleased. None of the staff here would even *think* to question someone like him; if anything, the violin case he carried would make him appear even more trustworthy. The halls were quiet, his magical servants stood guard against anyone coming whilst he was unlocking the door, and the locks on these doors were no challenge to someone with his talents. Once inside, he did not, however, light a lamp. He didn't need one, and there was no point in alerting any staff who might be roaming the corridors. A boot-boy looking for shoes left out to be polished or a maid sent for chocolate by a restless guest should not see light under the door of a room that was supposed to be untenanted. They might assume that the gas had been lit and left to burn unwatched, both wasteful and dangerous.

Besides, there was enough light coming in the windows for him to see, once his eyes adjusted. He moved out of the sitting room and into the bedroom, laying his case on the neatly made bed.

He opened the violin case silently, and just as silently removed the bow and the instrument. Everyone these days, of course, knew that a fine violin crafted by the hand of one of a few blessed luthiers was needed to create the most truly exquisite music. Few realized that the bow was just as important.

In this case, it was more important. . . .

His fingers caressed the neck of his favorite instrument, the "Boissier" of 1713. A Stradivarius, of course. She was special, very special. Only on this violin could he, would he dare, combine music with magic.

She was already tuned and waiting, and he imagined he could feel her quivering a little at his touch, ready to serve him and his task.

He lifted the bow, which flashed white in the light from a nearby window. A beautiful bow, he had made it himself, and it shone like the finest ivory. The bowstring, too, was shining, a shimmering gold, even in the dim light.

This required the most delicate of touches.

He teased out the merest whisper of music; faint, but hardly faltering. The harmonics were complex, and the tune . . . no one would have recognized it, since it was his own, but one he would never play in public.

But it brought forth what he summoned.

For a moment, the apparition hung in the air before him, a shimmer, a glimmer in the dimness. Not enough to tell that it was anything other than an errant wisp of fog somehow gotten into the room past the closed windows. But he knew who and what it was, and he played for her, giving her strength.

Strength enough to call to her all the other unhappy spirits still in this hotel—for every hotel, if it is old enough, has them. The unhappy ghosts of the suicides, of the murdered, of the poor drudges worked to death and lying down for a sleep that turned out to be their last. And *she* called them, spun them around her in a slow, sad waltz to his slow, achingly sad tune. And when the music was over, he spoke a single word to them all.

"Go."

And they went. *She* would show them who to haunt, although they would lose their power to stalk the dreams and make the night restless at worst, and a horror at best, once their quarry left the hotel. Unlike her, they were bound to this place.

But he would follow the quarry to her next abiding place, and he would call the spirit of that new place forth with his music and his bow, and then the dance would begin again.

The room was empty now, and he packed up his instrument and slipped out, locking the door behind him, leaving no trace of his presence or his passing.

4

John Watson had insisted on dinner being served before Nan told them anything. The Watson's pleasant sitting room stood double duty as a dining room, and Mary had made a point of providing for the birds as well. They had to stand on newspapers on the floor by the hearth and eat and drink out of spare teacups, but they didn't seem to mind. As a child Nan had gone hungry more than enough times to appreciate a good meal when one was placed in front of her, no matter how she otherwise felt.

"Instead of focusing on what we do not know," said Sarah, when Nan had finished telling the group of her fruitless quest into lucid dreaming, "What can you remember that the druids *did* say about these Shadow Beasts? Because it seems to me they had a plan to deal with the one they faced."

"Oh, they did, indeed, have a plan," Nan replied, staring glumly at her new peas. "To board up the door and stop up the smoke-hole of the hut where it seemed to be focused, and burn the place down with everything in it. If we try that at Number 10, we are likely to find ourselves cooling our heels in the gaol."

"Burning the building down seems rather drastic to me," Mary Watson replied, mildly. "What were their reasons?"

Nan thought, trying to remember. One of the warriors had indeed objected to the drastic procedure, wanting to remove valuables first. "The druid said that they could not be sure what object the Shadow had been bound to, or had bound itself to.

He said that they were very good at concealing their presence."
She closed her eyes for a moment. "And he did say it was likely
to attach itself to something valuable, so as to excite greed, and
guarantee it would be taken and protected."

"Well, at least *we* know that whatever the object is, one thing
it *won't* be is commonplace and modern," Mary pointed out. "Did
they say anything else?"

"It can't abide sunlight, apparently." She pummeled her brain
for more facts, and sighed. "That's all I have. Except that once
the hut was burned down and everything left over exposed to
sunlight, which would drive the Shadow into its object, they were
going to take whatever was still left, put spells on it to seal it in
further, and bury it in a lead-lined box under a fairy mound. They
said the Fair Folk would guard it for them."

"Which likely meant that they were putting some Earth
Elementals in charge of guarding it," John Watson said firmly, his
tone making it quite clear he didn't believe in "Fair Folk." He
stabbed at a bit of chop to emphasize his point.

"It could," Nan admitted. "My Talent for reading thoughts
evidently didn't extend to reading theirs, whether it was dream or
past life, or both."

"Well, *they* were better equipped to destroy it than we are,
and the fact that they weren't even going to try suggests that
they couldn't." John drummed his fingers on the table, thinking.
"Perhaps we should follow their example after all. I'm getting the
shape of a plan. Let me think about this a while."

John still was not ready to discuss anything by the time they had
finished their meal, and before they could settle down to discuss
anything *else,* there was a knock on the door. Before Mary could
answer it, Holmes thrust his head in.

"May I—"

"Of course." Mary gestured to a free chair at the fireside. "I
don't suppose you need the female perspective again, do you?"

"Not precisely." He closed the door behind himself, took
the offered seat, and accepted a brandy from Watson. "I just
wanted to know if the latest development in my case seems as

peculiar to you as it does to me." He turned the glass in his long, sensitive fingers. "The fiancé is now affianced to the sister, Magdalena von Dietersdorf."

Nan blinked at him. She glanced at Sarah, who looked just as surprised. Mary looked more than surprised. "That . . . seems extremely odd to me," she said, finally. "Coming on top of all the other oddities. . . ."

Nan suddenly *knew* what was going on. Sherlock wasn't here because he wanted to know if they found any new aspects of his case peculiar. He was testing them. Testing her and Sarah, in particular.

"If this case were entirely in England," she said slowly, "I would go speak to the young man's friends, and find out if there had been reluctance on his part to marry Johanna—if it had something to do with inheritance, for instance, that the greater portion was being settled on the younger daughter because she had no brilliant future as Magdalena does. I would speak to Johanna's friends, and find out if she was lukewarm about her prospective husband. But with all those friends being in Germany, that does make things difficult."

Holmes nodded. She hesitated a moment. "I do have . . . another ability, although it is not as reliable as telepathy. If I could hold an object belonging to Johanna, I might be able to tell something about her, her emotions, her personality."

"Not where she is now?" Holmes asked, a little sharply.

She shook her head. "No, this is something that allows me to 'read' the past of an object. Once it parts company with someone, it's rather like being handed a diary someone has abandoned."

"Ah." She got the impression that Holmes was both satisfied and dissatisfied with her answer. *Maybe he's satisfied because it matches what he thinks is logical, that items can record impressions, but dissatisfied because it would be useful if I was something like a psychic bloodhound.* The image *that* conjured up was faintly amusing.

"Well, unfortunately, Johanna packed up all her personal possessions and took them with her. I am given to understand that these were not many, as she and Magdalena were of the same size, and shared a wardrobe." He raised an eyebrow at Nan. "I suppose offering you a bonnet they both wore would get the—er—'impressions' muddled."

"Definitely. Especially if Magdalena has the more . . . forceful personality, which Johanna's letters would certainly seem to have indicated," Nan replied.

"Well, if you want the *feminine perspective,* I honestly cannot imagine any young woman tying herself to a man who was marrying her only for her inheritance," Sarah said slowly. "Which . . . actually makes her elopement with this ghostly Canadian more likely, I suppose. And might account for how dull her letters were."

"Yes," Nan put in, "Except . . . if she was dull enough to submit to being married off to someone who was only marrying her because of her inheritance, how did she suddenly get the spirit to run off with this stranger? And if she had the wit and spirit to manage to escape undetected and run off with a stranger into the unknown, then why did she put up with being affianced to someone who was only after her money in the first place? Surely even in Germany, in this day and age, young women of spirit are *not* inclined to being handed off by their papas like that!"

"Unless she was very plain. . . ." Sarah said, suddenly uncertain. "Sometimes plain girls will marry the first man that asks because they don't think it likely they'll get anyone at all."

Nan snorted. "The more fools they. But you're right." She looked to Holmes. "So, was Johanna plain? Is Magdalena the one that got all the fairy gifts, and Johanna got none?"

"Actually, Magdalena is the plain one," Holmes replied. "It is her voice and force of personality that makes her remarkable. According to the mother and father, it is Johanna who has the winning personality and intelligence . . . and as for her looks, well, you may judge for yourself." He handed Nan a photographic portrait, Sarah leaned over to look.

What they saw was a young woman . . . very Germanic, with her round face, apple cheeks, broad forehead and wide mouth. Her eyes were probably blue, her hair very fair. By anyone's standards, a beauty. She looked directly at the camera with no hint of pretense, coyness, or shyness.

Nan handed the photograph back to Holmes. "I can imagine a girl like that running off with someone she was in love with. I *cannot* imagine her being engaged to someone she did not love. So if she was in love with her affianced, why did she run off with a stranger? And if she was *not* in love with him, why would she act contrary to her nature and become his fiancé in the first place?"

"All good questions, to which I should be seeking answers," Holmes said blandly, pocketing the photograph. "I shall go back to my case, and leave you to yours. I assume you have a case?"

Watson nodded. He started to open his mouth, but Holmes waved at him with a little irritation.

"Please, don't tell me, I'll only become annoyed at the superstitious twaddle," he replied brusquely. "Unless it's purely psychical in nature?"

"No," said Nan, before John could answer.

"Then I'd rather not hear about it," Holmes said firmly. "Carry on. I'll let myself out."

And with that, he did just that.

"You know," Sarah said, after a bit. "I had a thought that has nothing to do with Sherlock Holmes." She looked at each of them in turn. "I think we would be fools if we didn't ask Sahib and Memsa'b to help us with this."

The Watsons looked at each other, then back to Sarah. "Do you think they would?"

Nan and both birds laughed. "I think they would murder us if we didn't at least ask them," she said.

"Well then, let me take more time to formulate a complete plan," said John. "While you young ladies set up a time when we can meet with your fearsome guardians, and I'll have something more concrete to present to them."

Sarah laughed, probably at the idea of Memsa'b and Sahib Harton being considered "fearsome" by anyone. She confirmed that with her reply. "They're dears," she said fondly. "And they'd only be put out at not being consulted because they are concerned about us. Now Agansing, Karamjit, and Selim . . . *they* are fearsome." She looked thoughtful for a moment. "Would you object to a Gurkha, a Sikh and a Moslem being part of this party? It would be three more seasoned fighters, both in the conventional and the occult senses. And they were all involved the first time Nan and I encountered this Shadow Beast."

"I'd welcome a half-naked cannibal princess and her pet tiger if they could be relied upon not to eat *us*!" John exclaimed. "And here I was concerned that four of us might be too few and was trying to think of a way to persuade Beatrice and anyone else she could dragoon in."

"The addition of five more would make us nine, John," Mary reminded him. "And nine is a very auspicious number in the occult."

John nodded slowly. "So it is."

"Then let's take advantage of every bit of help we can get," said Nan, and Neville and Grey bobbed their heads in agreement.

The nine of them stood in the bright sunshine just before noon outside Number 10, in the deserted mews that served as a sort of back alley. Standing around at the front of the house had seemed like a dubious idea—they hadn't wanted to attract attention, and they certainly would do that as a group of nine people clustered at the front of the house. So John had obtained all the keys from the owner, and they had come, one at a time, down the lane that no one but the servants in these houses ever saw, and were now shielded from view by the buildings around them.

The first three days of the last week had been spent in careful preparation, working a little at a time, and one at a time, inside the old house. Most of the work had been done by Karamjit, Selim, and Agansing, who would not permit the others to undertake it. The remaining four days they had let the house stand empty and darkened. Darkened, because thick pasteboard had been carefully fitted over every window in the place, and every chink that could have let in light had been pasted over with thick paper and wallpaper glue.

John's idea had been to confuse the Shadow Beast by putting the house in full darkness *all* the time, hoping that it was not somehow sensitive to the rising and setting of the sun by some other means. "The worst that happens is it will not come out to our bait," he had said. "And in that case, we will have to try some other means to find whatever it is bound to."

Now they were ready to face it. All the women were wearing extremely practical gear, something they could run, and run fast in, if need be. "All right, then," John Watson said. "Let's get in place. Sarah, Nan, give us half an hour, then come in and go to the room you were locked into the first time you were here."

John and Mary Watson had performed some sort of business over themselves and everyone else except Nan and Sarah. Nan wasn't entirely sure what it had been about, but John had called it "shielding" and said that he thought that when he was done, not only would the others be protected from this creature, for a while at least, but it would be unable to sense them while they took their places. The result didn't look all that impressive to Nan—thanks to Robin Goodfellow, she and Sarah could see some magic, even if they couldn't use it. These "shields" looked like nothing so much as soap bubbles. But then again, maybe they didn't need to *look* like much in order to do what John and Mary wanted them to do.

Nan had a man's pocket watch she habitually wore, so she was the timekeeper of the two. She and Sarah had their birds on their shoulders; Neville and Grey were sitting so quietly they might have been stuffed.

This was by no means the first time they had gone into danger together, but it *was* the first time they'd had so long to prepare for it. Nan thought that was probably worse than just rushing headlong into a bad situation; you had so much more time to brood over what could go wrong. . . .

Sarah seemed calm, but Nan knew her well enough to know that was the face she put on whenever things were bad. *Then again, so do I.* Sensing her unease, Neville finally moved a little, leaned forward—and stuck his tongue in her ear.

"*Neville*, ye blarsted little barstard!" she exclaimed, reverting to her Cockney accent.

Sarah burst into a nervous giggle, which broke the tension.

"Devil in feathers," Nan grumbled good-naturedly, and reached up to scratch the back of his neck. Neville chuckled, and she looked at her watch.

The watch had reached the appointed minute, and she put it in her pocket. Taking that as the signal to move, Sarah went in the back door ahead of her. Sarah, after all, was what the Shadow Beast had been most attracted to the last time they'd come up against it, so Sarah was serving as the bait.

It was as black as pitch inside the door, and Sarah took out a little lamp of the sort that miners used, and Nan lit it with a lucifer match. By its faint light they made their way up the narrow, steep servant's stair; it was too narrow for them to go side-by-side, so Nan went up first, with Neville clinging to her shoulder for dear life. Feeling their way as much as seeing it, they ascended to the third floor, just below the attic and the servants' rooms, where they had last met the Shadow.

The room they entered hadn't changed much since they had last been there, around ten years ago. There had been a thick layer of dust on the floor, which was scuffed up, perhaps by the sailors who had last been here. Nan held the lantern higher. "Look," she whispered, pointing to where a couple of blankets were crumpled up in the corner. "That must be where those two idiots decided to spend the night."

"You shouldn't speak ill of the dead, Nan," Sarah chided. "They might still be here."

Nan shut her mouth. The paraffin lamps that had given an illusion that the room was tenanted were still here, miraculously unbroken, although she had no doubt they were empty. And there were still a few boards piled in the corner opposite the blankets, the remains of a bed from which she had wrenched a board as an improvised weapon.

Unprompted, Sarah walked over to where the window was, behind the pasteboard and paper, turned, and stood facing the door. Nan took her place behind her, with one hand on the improvised handle of twine at the top of the pasteboard window-cover.

"Well," Sarah whispered. "The next thing to do is . . . be frightened." She laughed nervously. "That's not going to be hard."

Nan wanted to pat her reassuringly, but that was the very opposite of what Sarah strongly needed to feel right now. They had to rouse that Shadow, make it think because of the darkness of the house that it was night, and lure it to where Sarah was—all without letting it notice where the others were. To do that, they had to make sure it was focused on Sarah.

That actually shouldn't be too hard, Nan thought. *I don't think it's been eating well. The police have been making sure nobody breaks into this place, and it's not as if this is Spitalfields or*

Whitechapel, where there are hundreds of people who wouldn't be missed. It must be ravenous by now.

Just as she thought that, the flame in the little lamp suddenly dimmed and burned blue. There it was, the same as last time. . . *lights burn blue when spirits walk . . .*

Nan felt a tingle go through her, and when she glanced down at herself, she was utterly unsurprised to see she was no longer wearing the practical bloomer dress she had walked in here wearing. Instead, she was clad in a tunic of bright red wool that came to her knees and a belt of heavy leather, her long hair in a thick plait that fell over one shoulder. Over the tunic, she wore bronze armor: armguards, a breastplate, and greaves. In her right hand was a sword that shone with its own light, bronze-gold as the sun. Neville on her shoulder was heavy, as heavy or heavier than an eagle might have been; well he was the size of an eagle now, and his wings spread protectively around her.

Unlike the first time this had happened, she was not chanting, nor was Grey. They had to make the thing approaching think that Sarah was helpless. But Nan could feel the words of the chant building in her mind, wanting to get out, as the temperature in the room plummeted until their breaths were puffing white in the dim blue light.

The darkness just beyond the open doorway somehow grew darker, stygian—it seemed to *negate* light. Ponderously, it moved toward them, not as if it could not move faster, but as if it was trying to induce still more terror by taking its time. This time she understood that the shadow hid a deeper shadow still at its core, something that could not be seen, but which sent out waves of terror to strike devastating blows on the heart.

And this time was different. This time the shadow-within-the-shadow opened its eyes. Two glowing, red eyes that promised horror and pain. It paused in the doorway, as if relishing their fear.

"*NOW!*" Nan screamed, and pulled at the handle of twine in her hand.

The pasteboard covering tore away from the window, and the bright light of the afternoon sun struck the thing full-on.

Nan clapped both hands to her ears—fruitlessly, since the dreadful howl the thing emitted was inside her head, not outside it. Then she gave a ruthless mental shove and grabbed for the mirror hanging from her belt as the creature turned and fled down the hall, looking for darkness.

But there was no darkness; Nan's signal had made the other seven people in the house pull down their window-coverings as well, and the Shadow was faced at every door by someone with a mirror, ruthlessly directing the sunlight right at it.

It sped for the door at the end of the hall and vanished inside.

"Selim!" John Watson shouted.

"I am unharmed," came the deep voice Nan knew so well. "And I see whence it has gone. Come!"

They all crowded into the room, to see that Selim was reflecting his beam of sunlight down upon one corner of the room. "It entered, and vanished through a crack in the floorboards," Selim said calmly. "I think there may be a hiding place there."

"Let me have a look," said Frederick Harton, getting down on his knees with a little difficulty. "Selim, Agansing, Karamjit, have you any experience in finding concealed panels?"

"Not I, Sahib," said Agansing. "Nor I," agreed Karamjit. But Selim relinquished his mirror to Sarah, and got down on his knees beside his employer, fellow mystic, and friend.

"I think I feel the outline of it here—" said Harton, sketching the lines with his fingers. "The question is where the catch is. . . ."

"Ah, I think . . . permit me, Sahib," said Selim, and withdrew one of his formidable daggers from his belt as the rest looked on, ready to combat anything that might emerge. He used the tip as delicately as a surgeon along the line of one of the floorboards.

Then he twisted the blade suddenly. There was a sharp snapping sound and a section of the floorboards lifted a trifle.

"Everyone please to back to the walls, and duck as low as you may," Selim said, calmly. "I am not anticipating a trap, but it is better to be feel foolish and alive than surprised and dead."

They followed his instructions; Nan and Sarah, accustomed to some of the wicked traps on objects in ancient tombs, curled themselves into tight little balls and shielded their faces. Nan looked cautiously over her shoulder, and saw Selim moving as far from the hiding place as he could and still lift the lid with the tip of his knife. With a single deft motion, he flipped the top of the hiding place open.

Nothing happened.

The room filled with the sound of nine people heaving a collective sigh of relief, and they all came crowding back around the now-open hole in the floorboards. All but Karamjit, who had the presence of mind to direct a bright beam of sunlight into the hole with his mirror, perfectly illuminating the small strongbox that lay inside.

It all but radiated cold, and evil.

And Nan got the sudden urge to wrest the thing out of the hole and wrench it open. From the sudden jerk that everyone else gave, she knew they must have been overcome by the same impulse at the same moment.

"*That* will be enough out of you," Isabelle Harton said firmly and dropped a thick piece of raw silk fabric over the top of it. Abruptly, the impulse vanished.

"Thank you, Memsa'b," said Karamjit, with feeling.

John Watson shook his head. "Whatever that thing is," he said, slowly, "It's no Elemental I ever encountered, or read about."

"And I, for one, am not at all eager to study it," Mary Watson said firmly. "If there are no objections, we'll proceed with our original plan." She looked up and they all shook their heads, Nan included. She pulled a pair of silk gloves out of her coat pocket and put them on, carefully wrapping the strongbox in the length of raw silk fabric that Memsa'b had provided. There was plenty to wrap it thoroughly. Isabelle had come equipped with several pieces of the cloth, which was used to bale the finer silks imported by her husband's trading company; silk was a potent insulator of magic, and it didn't matter if it was the slub-filled, heavy, raw sort, or the finest of near-transparent veils.

Agansing trotted downstairs while Mary Watson was wrapping the box in a silk shroud and returned with a heavy satchel. From it he brought sheets of lead—thicker than the foil that tinsel was cut from, perhaps as heavy as a sheet of thin cardboard. He laid one out, unfolded, on the floor, and Mary put the mummified strongbox in the center. Working deftly, but with great care, he molded sheets of lead around the box and its covering until it was completely encased in at least three thicknesses of lead on all sides. Then he took the pommel of his knife and burnished the seams down flat. When he was satisfied, he gestured to John Watson to take it.

"What do you plan to do with this thing?" asked Memsa'b, as he picked it up.

"I don't believe we dare try to hide it anywhere on the face of the earth," Watson said, slowly. "If I had *my* way—and if it was possible—I'd fire the damned thing into the heart of the sun. I discussed this with Lord Alderscroft at length, and we decided there are only two possible options. We give it to the Water Elementals to hide somewhere in the depths of the sea, or we give it to the Fire Elementals to drop into a volcano. We couldn't make up our minds, so he decided to leave it to us." He knelt there, the box in his hands, and looked around the group. "Everyone gets a vote."

"Volcano," Sahib said instantly, as Isabelle nodded. But Karamjit shook his head.

"I prefer never to dispute with you, Sahib, but what if destroying what it is bound to only releases the creature to work even more evil?" he asked. "If we could be sure the volcano was in Hell itself, perhaps but . . . we know it is contained now. And the Elementals of the Water will be aware it is dangerous and be sure to shun the place where they leave it."

"I too, think that the sea is the best place to leave this thing," agreed Agansing.

"But the efrits of Fire are wise. Surely they can combat this creature of darkness should it escape!" Selim objected. "I would send it to the fires."

"You know my vote would be Water," said Watson, and looked at Mary, who nodded.

"Volcano," said Sarah firmly. "It hates the light, and a volcano is full of light."

"It hates the *sunlight*," Nan corrected. "It didn't care at all about our lamps." She looked around the group. "Four and four, so I suppose I cast the deciding vote." She thought about this for a while. "I don't know anything about the Fire Elementals, but I know a lot about the Water." She looked at John. "Can you convince them that this thing is as dangerous to them as it is to us, if not more?"

"Easily," he said fervently. "If it escaped, it would probably devour them more easily, and more readily, than a mere mortal human."

"Then I think it would be safest at the bottom of the sea," she said. "And the sooner it is there, the better."

They made an interesting little procession, what with Sahib's three friends and employees being arrayed in slightly westernized versions of their native garb, Nan, Sarah, and Mary Watson in bloomer suits, and the Hartons, while in more conventional clothing, also bearing enough bags and pouches for an expedition to some exotic locale. And they wouldn't all fit into a single cab, so the group required three. London cabbies, however, are a race that has seen nearly everything, and good tips generally ensure that they are utterly incurious and completely polite about whoever and whatever they are asked to convey.

John Watson had, it developed, taken the precaution of engaging a boat—and since it would be going some distance out to sea, and not just down the Thames, it was big enough to hold them all. Mary Watson had had the forethought to make sure the boat had taken on hampers of provisions, which was just as well, since they were all as ravenous as starving lions after the excitement of the capture.

Nan and Sarah had been on quite a few seaworthy boats on their visit to the Welsh coast and their adventures with the Selch, the seal-folk, but the *Lively Lady* was bigger than any of them. Well, it had to be, seeing as it was carrying nine people, the captain, and a crew. They all went aboard, Nan being the last.

It was also beautiful, flying away toward the sea under full sail.

It would have to be a sailing boat; Water Elementals would never approach a boat with a great iron and brass engine in it. It was a lovely thing, the wood almost alive under Nan's hand, and when she looked up at the sails, she spotted sylphs playing among them. The captain was probably a Master, and likely Air; as such he'd always be able to guarantee a following wind. The crew were probably not Masters, but likely were a mix of Air and Water. They scrambled among the lines and canvas like a lot of monkeys, while the captain, after a few quiet words with John

Watson, went to the wheel and stayed there, for all the world like a fancy engraving come to life.

Nan and Sarah, out of experience, had spotted a place on the deck where all the passengers could sit comfortably together, share out their hampers, and not be too much in the way of the crew. So they had lugged everything there and set up, and the others (who fortunately *all* seemed to be devoid of seasickness) followed their leads.

So the trip out to sea was something of a celebratory party. Mary Watson did prove to be slightly imperfect however, because the hampers did not contain nearly enough cutlery and cups to serve everyone, so some of them were "forced" to eat with their fingers and drink out of bottles like a lot of Cockney holiday-makers. Nan and Sarah were two who made the choice to picnic like a couple little barbarians, going into fits of giggles every time Memsa'b looked at them and sighed.

The giggles, at least in Nan's case, were coming out of the release of terrible tension as well as out of amusement. Every time she glanced back at where the lead-covered strongbox waited in the bow, she was reminded about how badly it all *could* have gone. Her "memories," if that was what the dreams had been, told her that two extremely powerful magicians had barely been able to contain this thing, or something like it. If the day had suddenly gone overcast, they could very well have found themselves with a fight on their hands.

She ate a buttered scone thoughtfully, listening to the others talking. She was pretty certain the far-too-light conversation going on was covering the fact that everyone else was thinking the same thing. *Then again . . . I think this might have been the very first time so many people of so many mystical persuasions* and *with knowledge of modern science worked together against one of these Shadow Beasts.*

Still, she would be much happier once that box was gone.

The Hartons and the Watsons were nattering merrily away; they seemed to know a great many of the same people in the occult community—and in the rather larger community of people who were under the decidedly erroneous impression that they were the sole holders of Great Mystic Secrets. The conversation could very easily have been a sort of gossip-feast of laughing at the foibles of the latter folk. But in fact, it wasn't. As Nan listened, she quickly understood that the Hartons and the Watsons were exchanging information about which of these people were harmless, which were exploitive, which could get themselves in trouble, and which would be all too willing to get *other* people in trouble.

For her part, Nan put her face into the wind and reveled in the rise and fall of the ship, the smooth, warm wood under her hand, and the breeze that was rapidly pulling her hair out of its pins. If the truth were to be told, she missed being out in a little sailing boat with the Selch lad she'd passed some time with more than she missed the lad himself. Not that he'd done badly for himself, for once Nan and Sarah had made all their reports to Lord Alderscroft, another Water Master in Cornwall had heard of the colony of Selch and come to meet with them and brought his pretty daughters and . . . well, one thing had led to another, which had led to a double wedding. And Nan had greatly enjoyed every bit of her time there, though she was *not* sorry to leave before winter came again. Winter could be brutal on the seashore, or near it.

Grey sat on Sarah's shoulder, and Neville sat on Nan's, although they were both strong enough flyers they could easily have kept up with the boat if they cared to—or even flown ahead of it. They were used to boats now, just as Nan and Sarah were. They didn't *like* boats nearly as much as Nan and Sarah did, but they didn't object to being on them either. Nan was glad for the padded shoulders she had put in all of her jackets; Neville's grip was rather powerful as he braced himself against the wind, his wings slightly spread and his eyes half-shut.

The faintly putrid green algae smell of the Thames abruptly gave way to the cleaner salt air of the sea as they sailed out of the estuary and into the open ocean. And now was the first time the captain spoke out loud, as he called out to John Watson. "So, Master Watson! How far do you wish us to sail?" Nan liked his voice. It had a brisk, no-nonsense, yet friendly tone to it. It sounded like the voice of a man who laughed a great deal.

"Far enough out that we're not easily watched, and make sure we're out of the shipping lanes, then put out the sea anchor if you please, Captain Landers," Watson replied. "I've already sent out a messenger, and we should be met."

"Aye, Master Watson, that's easily done." He shouted out some directions, and his crew made some adjustments to ropes and sails as he moved the wheel slightly. By the sun, they had turned in a more northerly direction, more toward Belgium than France, which would certainly take them out of the shipping lanes between London or Dover and Calais. Watson looked satisfied, so Nan assumed this suited him.

When the two shores seemed equally distant to her and all the ships in sight were moving on a course that was at a right angle to their own, the Captain ordered the sails be furled and the sea anchor dropped. The sea anchor was nothing more than a stout rope with some boards and canvas at the end of it, but as soon as it had been dropped in the ocean and the rope went tight, Nan immediately understood what its purpose was. Not to keep them in one place, but to keep the bow of the ship heading into the waves.

"And now we wait," said John Watson, who seemed in no hurry now that they were out here. Mary appeared to be perfectly content to lean back against her husband and turn her face up to the sun. Nan looked at the others, and Memsa'b shrugged and got a book out of her bag. Sahib read over her shoulder, and Karamjit, Agansing, and Selim took out their various edged weapons and began sharpening them.

Grey hopped down into Sarah's lap and demanded a scratch. Nan raised an eyebrow at Neville. "I don't suppose you want to be cuddled, do you?" she asked.

Neville made a noise that was a reasonable imitation of a human snort then flew up the mast to chase off some curious gulls who were gathering to see if the boat had any fish they could steal. Neville very much enjoyed bullying the bullies.

It was just about the same time that Neville had routed the last of the would-be fish thieves that one of the crew shouted, "Sail ho!" and pointed northward. That roused everyone; Neville came back down to Nan's shoulder, and Nan shaded her eyes and peered in the direction the sailor had indicated. All she could see at this distance was a dot, but the dot rapidly grew to a tiny triangle of sail, and then to a triangle with a sliver of boat beneath it, and then to a recognizable shape. It was a small fishing ketch, one that could be handled by a single man, or a pair, exactly like the one that Rhodri had sailed back in Wales. . . .

Then Nan jumped right up and began waving her arms, and so did Sarah, because it *was* Rhodri, skillfully sailing his craft toward them. There was no mistaking him in the garb typical for a Welsh fisherman: waterproof boots, plain trousers, linen shirt, waistcoat, and jacket, but with the unusual touch of a sealskin cloak thrown over one shoulder. His curly black hair was a bit longer, but he was still clean-shaven, as Welsh fisherman tended to be until they were old and gray-haired. Neville gave a great quork and flew laps between their boat and the ketch until Rhodri had brought it up alongside theirs. Grey kept giving wild whistles as Neville flew. Rhodri tossed two ropes to the crew, who tied them up, bow to stern and stern to bow.

Then he stood in the stern, and gave them all a looking over until his eyes fell on John. "Water Master," Rhodri said, with a little bow to John Watson. "The sea-lords say you have a thing you wished disposed of. When I heard you had our friends with you, I said I would cross to the Middle Earth to take your task." Then he winked. "And hello, Nan Killian, it is fair to see you, and you, Sarah Lyon-White! Sally Anne sends her love."

"John, this is Rhodri, of the Selch," Nan said quickly. "Rhodri, this is John Watson. We met Rhodri and others of his clan when we were doing a bit of work for Lord Alderscroft in Wales."

John didn't smile. "This is a dangerous thing we are asking you to handle, Rhodri of the Selkie. Dangerous to your kind as well as ours, perhaps even *more* dangerous to your kind."

Rhodri merely nodded, intense, blue eyes unwontedly sober. "So the sea-lords say. I am but the courier. The sea-lords will have the disposing of it. Perhaps even Lyr himself. He is no friend to the sons of Adam, but no enemy either, and a thing that is dangerous to all is safe in his hands."

"Come then, and let me explain," said John; Rhodri leapt over to their deck, and the Watsons explained as briefly as they could what they all *thought* was in the box, how it had acted, and how they had contained it. Rhodri listened closely with his black brows knitted with concentration.

"So, it must go somewhere it is not likely to be damaged, and somewhere no one is like to haul it up by accident." The Selch nodded decisively as the wind ruffled his hair. "It's not for me to say, that will be up to the sea-lords, but I expect it will be taken to the deepest part of the ocean, where light never comes, and tucked deep inside some crevasse or sea cave. Then a watch will be put on it. Or, it may be we'll lay it in the path of lava from a sea volcano, for there are such things, and let the lava cover it up and encase it forever in stone, and a watch will be set on it. Either way, the wisest heads will see to it that it does no more harm."

John heaved a sigh of relief, and his face relaxed into a smile. "Then that is exactly what I had hoped. Thank you," he added, and gave a little bow of his own.

Rhodri and Watson got the heavy, lead-sheathed strongbox over to the bow of Rhodri's ketch—no need to worry about the safety of it, in a possibly magical ketch steered by a Selch!—and secured it there. Then Rhodri spent a little more time exchanging news with Nan and Sarah.

"Gethin is mellowing, now that my Sally Anne is expecting, and Idwal and Mari are as well," Rhodri told them. "More Selch for our clan, of course, and with Water Magic blood in them as well, and once in a great while he admits that your mortal meddling was a good thing after all. He can't lift the banishment on Idwal and Mari until the full seven years is up, and he'll never admit to forgiving her, but I think he'll pretend to forget to renew it, and take care never to be about when they visit our clanhold." His eyes sparkled with amusement at that, and Nan grinned. "I'll tell you more one day soon. For now, it's best I be off. The sooner yon package is in the hands of the sea-lords, the safer we'll all be."

With that, he hopped back into his boat; at his signal, the crew from theirs cast off the ropes. A moment later, he was sailing past them, going south, heading across the channel and to the sea.

"And that is a good day's work, my friends," John Watson said, into the silence Rhodri's leaving had cast on them. "Time for us to return, my good Captain Landers to be paid, and I think a celebration is in order."

"I'll drink to that!" said Grey.

5

It was long past teatime when Nan and Sarah returned home in a hansom cab. The Watsons' idea of a celebration had been to go to a pub, which was not a good place to get what Nan and Sarah considered to be a proper tea, so after a couple of sherries, they had left the Watsons, the Hartons, and the captain and crew of the *Lively Lady* all toasting one another, and headed home. The birds were just as happy to leave the pub; they didn't care at all for the tobacco smoke, and truth to tell, neither did Nan or Sarah.

They were a little surprised to see another cab standing in front of their landlady's door as theirs stopped to let them off. They were even more surprised, as they opened the door, to discover someone waiting on the little bench in the entry, a young boy dressed in the livery of the Langham Hotel, who jumped up at their arrival.

"Beg pardon, but would one of you ladies be Miss Sarah Lyon-White?" he asked, with a nervous glance at Neville and Grey and a dubious one at their bloomer dresses. Nan was amused; the sailors on the *Lively Lady* hadn't given their gowns a second look, nor had the denizens of the pub, but this lad looked scandalized.

Nan and Sarah exchanged a look, silently asking each other if they should just send the boy away unsatisfied, or admit to their identity. *Well, what can it hurt to find out what he wants?* Nan nodded slightly.

"I would be Miss Lyon-White," Sarah said, with all the

imperiousness of someone born to a coronet—a tiny bit of a snub for the dubious look he'd given her gown. "Might I inquire as to your business with me?"

For answer, the boy flushed, sketched a bow, and handed over a folded, sealed note. "I'm to wait for an answer, miss," he said, cowed by her manner—which he probably experienced on an hourly basis at the Langham.

Sarah broke the seal and unfolded the note, which was on the Langham's stationery. She and Nan put their heads together and read it.

To Miss Sarah Lyon-White: I have been given to understand by Mrs. Beatrice Leek and others that you are the most expert person in all of London in dealing with and banishing unwelcome spirits. I am being persecuted nightly by such spectral visitors. At first I could ignore it, but they strengthen with every passing day. This has become a torment I can no longer bear. I beg you to come and assist me. Whatever remuneration you require I will supply. Magdalena von Dietersdorf, Room 1004, Langham Hotel.

Nan kept herself from showing her shock with effort. *Magdalena von Dietersdorf? The sister of the missing girl Holmes wants to find? Is this some kind of trickery?*

Sarah folded the note when they had both read it. "Tell the lady we will come speak to her on her matter in two hours," Sarah said. "Neither of us are in any fit state to call."

The boy looked as if he would have liked to protest but did not dare, not with both women *and* two formidable-looking birds staring down at him. "Very well, miss," he said, touching his hat and making a reluctant exit. A moment later the cab clattered away, leaving them standing alone in the entry.

With unspoken consent, they ran up the stairs without discussing things until they were in the privacy of their rooms. For all that they *suspected* their landlady knew something of what they were engaged in, until she said something, neither of them cared to talk about it where she could listen.

Suki met them at the door, as she always did, and the birds flew to her outstretched hands. She looked as adorable as a little doll today, all in pink and white. "Boy come here, lookin' fer Miss Sarah," Suki said, with a touch of self-importance. "I tol 'im 'e could just wait in the 'all." There was nothing Suki enjoyed better than putting people who had once looked down their noses at her in their place. It didn't matter to her in the least whether the person she gave the set-down to was someone who had wronged her in the past. All that mattered was the chance to deliver a blow to their class.

"Absolutely correct, Suki, thank you. Did Mrs. Horace bring up tea?" asked Nan, as Sarah headed for her room to change.

"On'y just, since yew tol' 'er yew was like to be late. Yew an' Miss Sarah goin' out agin?" Suki asked, heading for the birds' perches next to the table, where their food awaited under covers to keep it warm.

"After tea." Nan decided to wait until after she had eaten before changing. It would be easier to do Sarah's hair once she'd changed. Sarah came out in a remarkably short time wearing one of her more opulent Artistic Reform gowns, her hair combed out and not put up, but otherwise suitable for a visit to a noted operatic diva at the Langham Hotel. They both ate Mrs. Horace's very fine Irish stew quickly, then Nan put Sarah's hair up and changed herself into a similar gown, not omitting a touch of jewelry. While Nan was changing, Suki ran out on Sarah's request and secured a cab. By the time the sun was setting, they were on their way.

The Langham was one of London's Grand Hotels, and a popular destination for musical and literary notables, which meant it catered to a wealthy, but still slightly bohemian set. As such, the girls' gowns were not at all extraordinary; as they entered the lobby, there were several other women present wearing some form of Artistic Reform costume. It was not yet dinnertime, and most of those in the lobby itself were either meeting friends before going out to dinner, waiting for dinner to be served in the hotel's famous restaurant, or coming in to meet someone, as Nan and Sarah were, or to go up to their own rooms. There were enough people crowding the opulent crystal and cream-marble lobby that two unescorted ladies did not cause any comment. In fact, they were completely unnoticed, and they sailed past the busy front desk as if they were on their way to their own rooms.

The hotel boasted elevators with a trimly uniformed attendant, who whisked them up to the tenth floor with no comment except to politely ask which floor they wanted. They knocked on the door of 1004 without having encountered any attention or interference whatsoever.

A dark-haired teenaged girl in a black and white maid's uniform and white lace cap opened it immediately. "Please inform Miss von Dietersdorf that Miss Lyon-White and Miss Killian are here at her request," said Sarah, before she could open her mouth to say anything.

The maid dropped her eyes and sketched a curtsey. "Very well, Miss. Will you come in, Miss?" She opened the door for them, and they entered a lushly appointed sitting room, all in cream brocade and gold, with a plush Turkey carpet over polished wood floors. There was a magnificent sable cloak flung over the back of one of the chairs, although Nan would have thought it was too warm for furs. They both took a seat on a small cream-colored sofa, opposite to the matching chair they expected the diva would prefer to sit in, a fainting couch that might have been designed on purpose for dramatic poses.

It was several minutes before the lady herself entered. Her cream brocade gown was, if Nan was any judge, by Worth, and suggested that either Magdalena was being paid an extraordinary amount of money (possible) or that she had some extremely wealthy "admirers" (also possible). Or both! She was dressed for dinner, and arrayed in a gold and garnet necklace with matching earrings and hair ornaments. Her blond hair had been done up expertly in a pompadour style. Unlike her sister, she was not beautiful; her features were too strong for beauty. But she was striking. The first impression that Nan got from her was *this is a woman who will stop at nothing to get what she wants.*

Then again, that was *de rigeur* for anyone who wanted to rise in the world of opera or the theater. One certainly could not describe the Divine Sarah Bernhardt as a shrinking violet!

Sarah spoke first, as the lady hesitated for a moment, looking between them. "I am Sarah Lyon-White, come as you requested," Sarah said. "This is my companion and coworker in the occult, Miss Nan Killian."

"Oh! Thank God you have come!" the lady replied, casting herself down upon the fainting couch in a dramatic pose—

precisely as Nan had thought she would. "The persecution is unending! I have changed rooms *twice,* and still the spirits follow me! And of course, no one sees or hears them but me! It is *unbearable*! I cannot sleep! I cannot rest!" Her hands fluttered, as if she could not find words to properly express herself. Her voice had very little trace of a German accent, but then she must, as an opera singer, have a good command of at least French, Italian, and English, in addition to her native tongue.

"Perhaps if you begin at the beginning?" Sarah prompted. "When did this persecution begin?"

"Some time after my sister Johanna ran away with that Canadian adventurer," Magdalena replied, and pouted a little. "Johanna! What a scandal! Thank God it did not reflect on me! I told *Vater* he should wash his hands of her! He kept asking me why she would run off like that! *I* do not know why she would have done such a thing, except that she did not truly love poor Helmut, and he would not, in respect for her reputation, end the engagement himself, so perhaps this was her way of ending it herself."

What an odd thing to say . . . Nan decided at the moment it would be a very good idea to do a little thought reading. After all, this was one of the big questions, wasn't it? And if she had the answer to that one, she might be able to give Holmes the information that would put him on the right footing in *his* case. But surprisingly, Magdalena's thoughts were so shielded that it would have taken a great deal of effort—and the risk that Magdalena would sense something—in order to read them. Nan curbed her impulses and went back to less occult means of observation.

She also reminded herself that, so far, Magdalena had only shown herself to be self-centered, which, given her profession, was rather to be expected. It wasn't *that* unusual for people to have natural shielding on their minds, after all, and having such did not imply anything sinister.

In fact, if Magdalena was, indeed, plagued by ghosts, her mind might naturally have sealed itself off in an effort to protect itself.

"But when, more precisely, did you first notice anything unusual?" Sarah asked.

"It was just after my parents and Helmut arrived to see if—" Magdalena paused. "Well, I think they did not believe that my outwardly gentle and compliant sister would do something so reckless, even if her engagement with Helmut was one that suited my father, rather than Johanna. They thought her to be meek and utterly obedient. They did not know her as I did."

"Parents are often deceived," Nan murmured.

Magdalena cast her a sudden, slightly suspicious, look, then returned her attention to Sarah. "My sister was . . . romantic," she said, knitting her perfectly shaped brows together.

"And you are not?" Sarah said, blandly.

Magdalena laughed. Strangely, it was a sound with very little humor in it. "One does not rise in the theater without learning that *romance* is not unlike a stage backdrop. It might appear real and enticing, but when you draw near to it, you find there is nothing but painted canvas, air, and nothing of substance. But Johanna still believed in *maerchen*. Fairy tales, I think you call them."

Oh yes. Fairy tales. Where eyes are scratched out by thorns, girls are poisoned by their stepmothers, or men are sent to cut out their hearts . . .

"And Johanna was able to keep her secrets close. Even I knew nothing about this man until the day the maid awoke me and gave me her farewell letter." Magdalena shrugged. "But that has nothing to do with why I wish your help, Fraulein Sarah. I am dying for lack of sleep. These haunting spirits will not allow me to rest! I no sooner close my eyes than I am awakened by them!"

"Ye-es . . ." Sarah said, slowly. "That was something I wanted to ask you about. You never are disturbed by them until *after* you have fallen asleep?"

"Exactly!" Magdalena was pleased. "That is precisely what happens!"

Sarah nodded gravely. "Then I must tell you, it may not be . . . spirits. It may only be a . . . sort of waking dream. Many people have these attacks, and mistake them for—"

"*No!*" Magdalena sat straight up, and even stamped her foot on the floor. "I am telling you, this is *not* something I have dreamed! It is *real*! These are *spirits*!"

"Calm yourself, *fraulein*," Sarah said hastily. "I know that these waking dreams can feel absolutely real, and unfortunately if *that* is what you are suffering from, I cannot help you, although a physician may advise you on sedatives that will allow you to sleep." She made a point of looking around. "I neither see nor sense any spirits here now."

A look of absolute fury passed over Magdalena's face. It was so violent that Nan felt a brief moment of fear.

But the expression was there and gone in a flash, and the only outward signs of the diva's anger were the hands clenched in her lap. "They never appear until after I have fallen asleep," she repeated. "I tell you, this is not some waking dream, they are real, and they are horrifying. You must help me. I will pay you any amount you require. If you require something other than money, I will obtain that." Her mouth twisted wryly. "At least you are more honest than the charlatan I first consulted, who claimed to see spirits infesting this suite in the light of day, and said nothing about . . . waking dreams."

Sarah nodded slightly. And under the cover of her skirts she poked Nan's foot with her own. That meant, in their private code, *follow my lead.*

"Well, what, exactly, is it that you want me to do?" Sarah asked patiently.

Magdalena waved an impatient hand, and reclined again. "Whatever it is you do! Remain here in my suite. Confront these spirits when they appear. Banish them! I will pay whatever it takes to be rid of them! Only tell me how much, and what else it is that you need."

"Tonight?" Sarah asked, a little startled by the imperious order.

She threw up her hands with impatience. "Of course, tonight, and every night they plague me! How am I to perform if I cannot sleep?"

Sarah bit her lip. "I need to talk this over with my companion," she said firmly. Very firmly, her tone saying that this was *not* negotiable. Magdalena looked as if she was about to object, then shrugged, waved her hand at them, and turned to the young maid and ordered wine.

Sarah got up and moved to the back of the sitting room; Nan came with her. "Do you really want to go along with this?" Nan whispered dubiously.

"Well, we've finished the only job that John Watson has for us at the moment," Sarah pointed out. "And . . . I might be able to find more for Holmes about the sister if I stay."

Nan glanced over at Magdalena, who was sipping a glass of champagne. "Do you really think she's being haunted?"

"I've no notion. The only way to find out is to spend the night here. I can sleep during the day at home." Sarah made a little face. "I don't much *like* her, but I don't have to like her to want to help spirits trapped on this side. Maybe it's the fact that she's made herself a focus of envy that has attracted them. Maybe it isn't ghosts at all, but the actions of an Elemental Magician, in which case the Watsons and Lord A should be told. And maybe it's night terrors, in which case I will wash my hands of her and suggest Watson come treat her; he *is* a doctor, after all."

Nan sighed, but she knew Sarah in this mood, and there was no changing her mind. "All right, stay the night. But charge her something absurd. If she is going to make you lose a good night's sleep, she should be prepared to pay for the privilege."

They returned and took their seats on the couch. "I am prepared to spend at least one night to determine if you are indeed haunted, and do what I may about it if you are," Sarah said, steadily, and held up a hand to keep the diva from saying anything. "This is a considerable inconvenience to me. I will require ten guineas for this single night. If, after tonight, I determine that you *are* the subject of hauntings, we will discuss further fees."

The amount, which was enough to pay the rental on their lodgings for the better part of a full month, scarcely seemed to faze Magdalena. Instead, her face only registered satisfaction. "Excellent! You need not remain here all evening. I am about to leave for the opera house; I will return at midnight. Alicia will let you in, if you come at that time. Alicia, my box, at once."

The maid hurried to another room, and came back with an elegant inlaid box, which Magdalena opened with a key she took from around her neck. She counted out ten guineas, and leaning forward, placed them in Sarah's hand. "I shall see you at midnight, then. Alicia, have my usual supper, laid for two, at that time."

Well, she's generous, I'll give her that.

Now Magdalena rose, and perforce they did, too. She took Sarah's hand, briefly. "Thank you again. The torment I am undergoing nightly is taking a toll on my art. If you can free me from it, you will not only earn my gratitude, but that of every music devotee in the world."

"I'm sure I shall," Sarah said, and Nan could tell she was hiding her amusement at the diva's enormous ego. "Until midnight, then."

"Until midnight. Alicia, see them out. Then get my cloak."

The maid showed them to the door; Nan could not help but notice that the diva had taken as little notice of *her* as possible. *Probably because she thinks I'm just some sort of hanger-on to the great medium,* Nan thought with amusement—and irritation.

Sarah put the fee in her purse as they walked to the elevator and summoned it. They stood there, waiting, listening to the sound of the motor as the cage crept its way up to them. "Well . . . that was interesting. What do you think?"

"Other than that she has a very high opinion of herself? I don't know." At that moment, the elevator door opened, and Nan switched subjects slightly. "I wonder if our friends have gone to see her perform at the opera. I know John's neighbor is fond of violin music, do you have any notion if he likes voice as well?"

The elevator arrived, and they nodded at the attendant and stepped into the cage beside him.

"If he does, I never heard about it. But we've never gone to the opera, even though we both like music. I prefer the ballet myself," Sarah replied lightly.

"I know," Nan replied, amused again. "I've suffered through ballets often enough with you. Well, don't tell anyone, or I'll lose all respect, but you can give me a good old panto over either anytime," Nan continued in a conspiratorial manner, which made the elevator attendant smile.

The lobby was less full now than it had been when they arrived; the restaurant was open, and those who had been waiting to be seated had gone in. But now they were two unescorted ladies *leaving*, rather than arriving, and since they were well and modestly dressed, though people did notice them, they did so discreetly.

The doorman got them a cab, and they headed back to their lodgings. As they got out, Sarah got the attention of the cabbie. "Sir?" she said politely, as he looked down at her from his perch and accepted his fee. "I'm going to need accommodation back to the Langham at midnight; do you think you could arrange to be here to get me there in time?"

As she had added a generous tip to their fare, the cabby tipped his top hat and replied, "Ye can be certain of it, miss, sure as my name's Freddy Smart." Nan felt an instant liking for this man; he had none of the signs of a heavy drinker about him, an all-too-common trait in cabbies, and his horse was well groomed, glossy, and clearly well cared for. He was in late middle age, with a wedding ring on his finger, and from the carefully cleaned state of his top hat and coat, he was as well tended as his horse.

"Thank you, Mister Smart, I greatly appreciate it." She paused, and then added, "It is possible I may be making nightly trips there at the same time for a while. Would you be available for them, and if so, how can I reach you tomorrow night if it is necessary?"

"I'll tell ye what. I'll just trot by here at half past eleven tomorrow, and you can wave to me from the winder if ye needs me." He twinkled at her, and the skin at the corners of his eyes crinkled with his smile. "Missus Smart'd put me eyes out if I let a young thing like you take 'er chances with whatever cabby comes by at *that* time'o night."

"Thank you, sir!" Sarah said, relieved. "That will be perfect!"

"Thank *you*, miss. It'll be getting me a good fare, and taking me to where I'll get another good one. The Missus'll like that. Hup!" he said to the horse, who moved off without needing a touch of the whip he kept in its socket beside him.

"Well, that was sorted nicely. I was a little worried about your finding a way to the Langham tonight." Nan took the door key out of her purse and let them both in. Mrs. Horace poked her head out of her own door when she heard the outer door open.

"Ah, there you are! I've been keeping your dinner warm in the oven! It will be up in two shakes of a lamb's tail!" their landlady said, and ducked back inside.

Suki had heard voices and opened the door at their landing. "Table's set, Mrs. 'Orace!" she called, and ushered them both inside, like a fussy hen chasing in two chicks.

After they were all settled around the table and Mrs. Horace was back downstairs, Suki peppered both of them with questions about the opera singer, what she wanted, and whether or not Sarah *believed* her story about being haunted.

"Well, that's difficult to say, Suki," Sarah said, as they finished the last of an excellent white bean cassoulet and Nan passed around the treacle tart. The birds both begged for some, and got it. "The lady is an artist, and has an artistic temperament."

"Ye means t'say she's barmy," Suki replied wisely.

Nan laughed. "Not exactly. But she's very likely given to exaggeration and drama. It would do her reputation no harm at all if she could claim to be haunted; people do love a good ghost story, after all." She cast a glance at the birds. "I wish we'd been able to bring Neville and Grey; they are both quite good at telling when someone is trying to gammon us."

"On the other hand . . . I'm not so sure I want them there," Sarah said slowly. "They are birds, and they are more delicate than you'd think. I don't believe Magdalena von Dietersdorf likes animals *at all*. Normally these artistic women have pampered little dogs, or the occasional elegant cat. Sarah Bernhardt is said to travel with a cheetah! But Magdalena has no animals about her, and there is nothing in her rooms to suggest she would welcome such a thing."

Nan and Suki nodded. *Now that I think about it, Sarah is right. In fact . . . I don't think I want the birds anywhere around that woman.*

"It might be that she is subject to night terrors—you know what those are, Suki, you used to have them." Sarah took a bite of her tart as Suki nodded. "I find it very hard to think of a reason why she should be haunted in the first place. She says she has moved rooms twice, and the spirits follow her—as you know, spirits are usually bound to a place, and seldom follow a specific person about. She is a stranger to London, so there seems no logical reason why a spirit should choose her to show itself to. And yet . . . although there is a great deal about her that reads false to me, I am bound to say I think she is speaking the plain truth."

"She seems willing to pay almost anything to be rid of her haunts," Nan observed. "Which is a refreshing change from our non-paying clients!"

Suki laughed.

"Well, if she's a-payin', might as well see, eh?" Suki nodded, her curls bobbing enthusiastically.

"Exactly. So I am going to sleep a little and rejoin the lady when her performance is over. I will be there all night and return in the morning." Sarah smiled apologetically to Suki. "Nan will have to help you with your lessons, tomorrow at least."

Suki waved that away as unimportant. "Th' lady's payin'," she said, making it clear *that* was of primary importance in *her* mind. "'Sides. Miss Nan allus tells me the horripilatin' stuff *you* won't."

Sarah felt very . . . alone . . . as she got into Freddy Smart's cab and the horse trotted briskly away from the house. It felt strange to be doing anything without Nan and the birds. Wrong, even. But they had discussed this over dinner, and it had been quite obvious to both of them that Magdalena had issued her invitation to Sarah, and Sarah only.

Neither of them could think of any good reason for her to refuse to go alone. The Langham was the most respectable hotel in London. Magdalena might be a respected singer, but she was also a foreigner, and her debut could be utterly ruined by even a breath of scandal. And although the lady was taller and heavier than Sarah, it was not possible that she was stronger. Ever since they were children and first came into the Harton School, she and Nan had been instructed in many ways of self-defense by Karamjit, Agansing, Gupta, and Selim. Although normally Nan was the "warrior," Sarah was perfectly capable of defending herself, and she had several items secreted on her person to enable her to do just that.

But as the cab pulled up to the hotel, she still found herself wishing for the tall figure of her friend beside her and the gentle grip of Grey's talons on her shoulder.

The diva had not yet returned from the opera, but the maid Alicia let her in immediately and presented her with glacéed fruit and champagne. Sarah thanked her, but asked for iced water instead. If Magdalena *was* haunted, she needed to keep her senses sharp and her mind unclouded.

Alicia retired to a chair beside the door, sitting there as stiff as a doll. Sarah wondered if that was what she did every night. Possibly. Women like Magdalena thought nothing of keeping their servants up waiting till all hours of the night, then demanding they be up at the crack of dawn.

There was a dinner laid out, with the food under covers, on a small table at the window of the sitting room. And as Magdalena had ordered the table was laid for two. About fifteen minutes after Sarah had settled onto the sofa by the fire to wait, there was a commotion in the hall. Alicia leapt to her feet and flung the door open, and Magdalena sailed in like a royal barque, wrapped in furs, in a cloud of rose scent, bidding farewell to someone over her shoulder. She flung the magnificent sable cloak aside carelessly—Alicia was right there to catch it—and turned to see Sarah waiting at the fireside.

"Ah, you have come on time! Come, come and join me for a little supper. I never eat before a performance. I was singing *Tosca* tonight. I am famished!" Without waiting for Sarah's answer she sailed over to the table—Alicia was right there to pull out her chair at the right moment—and settled down.

Well . . . I am hungry, but I had better not eat much. If there are ghosts haunting her, I need to be wide awake, alert, and not bogged down with food. She joined Magdalena at the table—Alicia did not pull out *her* chair, as she was too busy serving Magdalena—and settled down.

Sarah waited until Alicia had finished serving the diva, then indicated what she would like. Her plate was about half-full compared to Magdalena's; the singer really *was* famished.

Magdalena was not inclined to conversation, at least not at this meal, so Sarah was able to study her covertly while she nibbled. Some actresses could be careless about removing their stage makeup; not Magdalena. She had no more than a dusting of powder on her face and a reddening of her lips that might merely have been staining from the stage lip-rouge. In contrast to the perfectly coiffed hair Sarah had last seen her wear, she sported a very loose pompadour from which a few strands had escaped. Sarah studied her features, trying not to be critical, but read what she could without judgment. There was a set to her chin and her mouth that suggested she was not to be trifled with when someone stood between her and what she wanted. But then . . . actresses and singers often had to be ruthless; dancers, too, but brilliant dancing talent seemed to be rarer than brilliant singing or acting, and one could get by appealing to the audience.

Finally Magdalena patted her lips with her napkin and indicated to the maid that she was finished. Sarah had finished several minutes before and waited with her hands folded in her lap for the diva's instructions.

Surprisingly, however—surprising because Sarah had gotten the distinct impression that Magdalena always ordered things to go *her* way, and was never disappointed—it was the singer who looked hesitantly to her. "Alicia will help me to get ready for bed; this will take perhaps an hour. After that, I will endeavor to sleep. Will you need to be in the bedroom, or—"

"If it would be more comfortable for you, I can certainly work from out here," Sarah assured her, not really wanting to be in the same room with Magdalena while she slept. "If there *are* spirits, they will certainly come to me here as soon as they sense me, rather than plaguing you. If there are not . . . then I may enter your room to see if you are suffering from night terrors. If so, I will awaken you to rid you of them, and in the morning I will suggest a physician who might, and I stress *might,* be able to help." She shrugged. "We still do not know what causes night terrors, but he has effected some cures by some of his suggestions."

"That will be quite satisfactory," Magdalena said. "You will never need to come into my room; there *will* be ghosts."

Sarah could not help but notice that poor Alicia looked utterly terrified. She did *not* like this idea, but she did not dare protest it. Sarah resolved to speak to her after Magdalena went to bed.

"Have you some means of amusing yourself?" Magdalena continued, a little doubtfully. "The only books I have are in German—"

"I brought a book. Just send Alicia out to tell me when you have gone to bed, and I will make my preparations so that the spirits come straight to me instead of coming to you." "Preparations" were not exactly what she was going to do, but Magdalena didn't need to know that.

The truth was if there were active spirits, they tended to be drawn to a medium like moths to a flame, because if there was anything that an earthbound spirit wanted, it was to have someone to hear its story. There just generally were not that many active spirits about. Most people passed on directly to whatever afterlife they were bound for. Some stayed because they didn't realize they were dead—those were mostly people who had died suddenly, or in a state of intoxication, or children. Some stayed because something held them here, which could be anything from a message to impart to a terror of what punishment they were bound for. But *all* of them were subject to attenuation and fraying, and the longer they stayed, the more frayed and faded they became, and the less they remembered. That was why there were no ghosts of Romans haunting London, nor early Saxons, nor the Vikings who had raided here—most haunts were people who had died within the last hundred years. *Most*. Because there were always exceptions, and the more powerful the personality, the stronger the will and emotions with which they held to earth, the more they knew of magic, and the more powerful their reason for remaining, the likelier they were to create a long-lasting haunt if they so chose.

Satisfied, Magdalena retired to her bedroom. Sarah settled onto that comfortable fainting couch with a book by Dickens.

At length, she heard a footstep and looked up; Alicia had closed the bedroom door and was turning around. Seeing that Sarah was looking at her, she hurried over.

"Mistress has gotten into bed, miss," Alicia said, looking over her shoulder nervously. "It will take her a half hour or so to fall asleep."

"Then you go to bed too, Alicia," Sarah said, trying to make her voice as kindly as possible. "I promise, I will keep any ghosts here, far away from you. Just stay in your room unless you are rung for until your usual hour of rising."

"Will you be all right, miss?" Alicia asked anxiously. "The necessary room is just there—" She nodded at a door in the same wall as the door Magdalena had gone through earlier. "It has a door into here, and one into Mistress's room."

"Then that's all I need," Sarah assured her. "Go to bed."

With a look of infinite gratitude, she hurried off to her own little room, probably just big enough to hold a narrow little bed. Sarah put her book away in her purse, went around the room turning the lamps down or putting them out entirely, and then sat down straight on the couch, hands folded in her lap, facing the side of the room where Magdalena's bedroom was, waiting.

To be honest, she really expected to discover Magdalena was prone to night terrors. That would be in keeping with someone who kept the hours she did, ate a heavy meal before going to bed, and probably drank a little too much.

So she was a little shocked to see the wispy shape of a thin, haggard-looking girl forming just above the floor, halfway between herself and the wall.

She looked like a sketch done with white pencil on black paper, though everything on the far side of the room was visible through her. Her feet were not visible; what there was of her dress looked a little like something a scullery maid might wear, and like a scullery maid, her hair was hidden beneath a cloth cap that was much too big for her.

The girl looked utterly pathetic, painfully thin, and frightened, and Sarah felt a moment of contempt for the diva, if *this* was the sort of spirit that "made her nights a terror." She held out her hand, coaxingly. "I can see you my dear," she said, aloud and in her mind. "Come and tell me what you need."

The revenant drew nearer, looking as if she would burst into tears at any moment. *"Sick,"* she whispered into Sarah's mind. *"Sick, so sick. Then lost . . ."*

"Then I will show you the way home," Sarah told her gently. She closed her eyes and . . . well, there were no adequate words for what she did then. "Opening the door," she called it; it was something it seemed she had been able to do since she began seeing spirits. And sometimes she saw the result, a kind of shining opening hanging in midair, and sometimes she didn't. This was one of the times she didn't—but the ghost certainly did; her face, what Sarah could see of it, was utterly transformed with an expression of disbelief and joy. She moved toward Sarah, and when she was about two feet away, she just vanished.

And that was when the horde arrived.

6

The temperature in the room plummeted. The lights dimmed, then burned blue. The fire in the fireplace all but went out, and a chill that had nothing to do with the physical cold came over her. She braced herself, knowing that this meant that there was not one ghost here. As Magdalena had claimed, there were many.

They began to form all around her, in a circle about twenty feet across with her at the center, at first nothing more than faint wisps, thin threads of light, and then threads became outlines and the outlines took on shape and tenuous substance. Two, six, a dozen . . . glowing and shifting in the now-dim light of the three lamps still alight and the dying fire.

This was a larger group of spirits than she had ever seen in one place at one time before, and there were more forming even as she watched. Her heart began to beat faster, and her breath quickened as a trickle of fear threaded its way down her spine.

Carefully, so as not to startle them into action before they had decided to actually do something, she slid her hand over to her purse, then inside it. She had brought Puck's talisman, something he had given her before she and Nan had left Criccieth in Wales. She had done so not really thinking she would need it, but just on the grounds that it was no great effort to bring something so small along, as she had so many times before. She hadn't taken it with her when they'd trapped the Shadow Beast at Number 10 because she had been afraid that it would sense Puck's magic and not come—but for this, well, it had seemed like a good precaution.

She felt a thrill of relief as her fingers closed on the little package of twigs and iron and she drew it out concealed in her hand. Just holding it made her feel bolder, and better protected. She brought both her hands together in her lap and cupped the empty one over the one holding the three twigs and a horseshoe nail, tied up with a bit of red thread. Who could have guessed there would be so much powerful magic bound up in something so ordinary?

"An iron horseshoe nail?" she had said, holding the thing in her hand. "I thought that magic creatures didn't care for iron, or salt, or—"

"Piff," he had snorted, tossing it from one hand to the other. "I am the Oldest Old Thing in all of Logres, and little things like iron and salt trouble me not in the least." Then he gave it to her. "And this will ward you from those things that cannot read my hand upon you."

The spirits had formed up into a silent ring all around her. Most of them looked "recent," that is, they were recognizably human, if wispy and transparent, and any obvious clothing looked relatively modern, so they must have died within the last fifty years or so. How long had the hotel been standing here? Twenty or thirty years, certainly. It was the largest hotel in London, with five hundred guest rooms and suites; that meant, just by the odds of such things, that there were more than a few guests who would have died here over that time period. There were probably hundreds of maids and other servants who worked here, and a goodly number of *them* had likely died on the premises, too.

And there were workmen who certainly would have died here while the hotel was being built. Every great building in London had had its share of accidents and deaths.

With so many people coming and going, living and working, it would have been odd if the Langham had not had its share of restless spirits. Guests died, though no hotel wanted you to know that; of old age, sickness, suicide, and murder. Servants dropped dead at work, poor things; no servant could afford to take days off for illness, and unless they had uncommonly kind masters, few were sent to their beds when ill. The response of a hotel manager to a sick maid would have been, "Get your work done and stay out of sight of the guests."

Most of those would have moved on, but there was plenty of time to have accumulated dozens of displaced haunts. And what had been on this site before the Langham? *Langham House and Mansfield House, I think.* More chances for haunts, for both had had heavy populations of servants, as well as their aristocratic families.

These all seemed bewildered, as if they could not imagine why they were facing *her,* and yet were irresistibly drawn to her. Some were barely recognizable as human beings, they had become so thinned out by time. Most, like the first wraith, were like white pencil sketches on dark paper. A few were so clear and crisp they were almost like white-on-black photographs of their former selves. Sarah began trying to categorize them, in an effort to sort out which of them might need her help the most urgently.

That was when *it* came screaming out of the dark at her, a raging, maddened thing, all tangled hair, eyes and claws and a frothing mouth, flinging itself at her as if it intended to rip her throat out! She gasped, and clutched Puck's talisman, the thing he had said would always keep her safe from "ghosties and ghoulies and things that howl in the night," and the creature *slammed* into an invisible barrier no more than three feet from her face.

Sarah—and it—were both frozen in a kind of shock. She recovered first.

Seemingly stunned, it hung there in midair for a moment . . . still scarcely recognizable as a human being. And then she saw, as she caught her breath and convinced her racing heart to slow, that there was another revenant with it, a weeping female in rags, far more human-looking than her companion. The woman was bound to the creature with a kind of silver cord that went from her navel into somewhere within the mass of tatters that comprised its body.

In a moment, the thing had gotten over the shock of slamming into Sarah's protective barrier and began circling around her, raving and clawing at her protection the entire time. It seemed to be testing the strength of what kept it away. Sarah had perfect faith that it would never break through something that a Great Elemental had set in place, but until she could get rid of this thing, she would not be able to help the other spirits here.

She looked at them, and they gazed at her despairingly. She licked her lips, and thought. The barrier would protect her, but *she* had no ability to affect a ghost, except to give it a way into the next life. *She* could not do anything to control this insane haunt.

But they could. Ghosts could affect other ghosts, as the living could affect the living.

"If I am to help you," she said quietly, but firmly, ignoring the insane *thing* that still prowled around and around her, dragging its prisoner behind her. "You need to help me first. *That* thing must be dealt with." She pointed at the mad spirit, who didn't seem to realize she meant *it*. "I can do nothing without it being restrained and controlled. And the living cannot control the dead."

That was not *entirely* true. There was a kind of magician, called a "necromancer," who could control spirits. But she wasn't one of those, and honestly, even if she'd been given the chance to be a necromancer, she wouldn't *want* to be one.

The remaining ghosts stared, first at the raving creature, then at each other. And then, without a word that she could hear, they swarmed it.

It had *not* been expecting that, and they took it entirely by surprise. They flung themselves all over it, stopping it in its tracks, and binding it in what appeared to be yards and yards of their own wispy substance, though so far as she could tell none of them got any weaker for binding it. After a few minutes of furious, utterly silent activity, they parted, revealing it to be bound up like a mummy, with only its eyes still uncovered. Then they waited, in a patient group, to hear her reaction.

"Well done," she said, and turned to the weeping revenant cowering in midair beside the creature, where she had fallen when the others had stopped the mad one. She was still sobbing into her hands as if she had no idea what the others had just done. "You, girl—what is your name, and why are you tied to that horror?"

The female spirit started and sat up to stare at her, as if she had not imagined Sarah could see her, much less speak to her. But instead of responding, the ghost simply stared at Sarah, her face half-hidden in a cascade of ghostly hair.

"She loved 'im, an' 'e killed 'er."

Sarah turned her head in the general direction of the faint

whisper of a voice, and saw one of the other spirits, a thin, malnourished-looking waif in a ragged Mother Hubbard gown too big for her, nodding at her. "Is that so?" she whispered back, and held out her hand. "If you mean me no harm you will not be hurt by coming to me."

The waiflike spirit ventured nearer, one cautious step at a time. Encouraged by passing the point at which the mad one had been stopped, she came even closer, peering at Sarah as if she was trying to see through fog. *"She loved 'im,"* the waif repeated. *"An' 'e murderated 'er."*

"Then that would be why she is chained to him," Sarah said softly. "Thank you. When I am done with them, you and I will speak next."

She turned back to the captive female. "Listen," she said, urgently, staring into the revenant's wide eyes. "He has to pay for what he did to you, and he is holding you back from where you must go. I know that you loved him once, but you must let go of that love, or you both will continue to be bound here together, in a terrible state of unlife."

She reached deep within herself and called up the "door" again. She still could not see it.

But the spirits could. There was a faint, collective gasp of horror as they all concentrated on a spot just past where the mad thing stood, bound.

The woman to whom it was tied gasped as well, and shrank back. Sarah reached inside herself again, and opened a second door, for her.

The revenant started with surprise, one hand going to her mouth, her eyes growing so wide they practically filled her face. But not with terror.

With longing.

"If you want that door—you must let go of him," Sarah told her quietly. "That love you have is one-sided, it binds you to him, but not him to you. Let it go. Let him go. Save yourself. You could not save yourself then, but you can now."

The spirit turned her face back toward Sarah, and now her eyes streamed tears. She mouthed two words; Sarah could not hear them, but she knew what they were.

"Yes," she replied firmly. "You must. Do not let him hold you here. He is not worthy of you. He never was. In life, you bound yourself to a dream that never was. Do not allow yourself to be so bound in death."

The spirit cast her head back in agony, though no sound emerged from her mouth. For a moment, Sarah feared that she would not be strong enough to free herself.

But then, the silver cord began to unravel, to thin into mist, and then . . . to vanish.

The wraith turned her back on the thing she had been bound to; the creature began furiously struggling, but she paid it no heed. She drifted forward in the direction she was looking, brightening the entire time until she became almost to too bright to look on.

And then, she disappeared in a burst of light.

The amassed spirits, and the child at Sarah's knee, gave out a collective sigh.

And then . . . as one, they moved on the bound thing, determination in every face. They moved on it, and shoved it, despite its increasing struggles, until suddenly, it too vanished.

Then, they turned to Sarah.

She smiled. "I promised I would begin with this one," she whispered, and turned toward the waif.

This is going to take a very, very long time.

Sarah cradled her face in her hands and eased her aching head with fingers that were very cold. It was taking a long time to warm up after the preternatural chill that had suffused the sitting room of the suite as long as the ghosts had been there. She accepted a glass of cold water that Alicia brought her and smiled as the maid hovered anxiously at her elbow.

The spirits had faded away at the first light of dawn, but not before she had promised those who remained that she would be back until she had helped them all. Alicia had appeared in her uniform, anxiously peering around the door, not long after that. On seeing Sarah sitting there, unharmed and alone but obviously very tired, the maid hastened to get her water, gasping a little when she realized the temperature of the water in the cut-glass pitcher on the sideboard was barely above freezing.

"Are you all right, miss?" Alicia asked, timidly, after waiting for some sort of further orders from Sarah. Obviously she was used to the constant demands of Magdalena. "Shall I order you some breakfast? The kitchen will be staffed by now, and ready to take orders." Unspoken was the fact that while it was unlikely her mistress would be awake any time soon, there were plenty of guests in this hotel that kept the same hours as working folks. Men of business, for instance, who could not afford to loll about in bed.

Sarah realized at that moment that part of the reason for her aching head was that she was utterly famished and accepted the offer gratefully. "Get breakfast for both of us," she insisted, making sure Alicia realized she would be rather put out if the maid did not share in the meal.

After anxiously inquiring three or four times if she would be all right alone, the maid left—presumably to order a meal somehow; the exact means by which the wealthy patrons of the Langham obtained room service was something of a mystery to Sarah. The only time she and Nan had stayed in a fine hotel had been in Wales, and there one placed an order for breakfast when supper came up, for luncheon when breakfast came up, for tea at luncheon, and supper at tea.

However it was done, Alicia accomplished the task in a few moments, and the service was prompt. Within an hour, her head was easing, and she had put the better part of a good, solid, English breakfast inside her.

She had made sure to insist that Alicia join her when it appeared the girl was only going to eat after she had finished, and after a weak protest the little maidservant had. Now the girl sat beaming at her proprietarily. "It does me heart good to see you eat like that, miss," she said. "It truly does. The Mistress won't eat no more than a bit of toast and drink a lot of coffee when she first wakes up. That can't be right."

Sarah shrugged. "If one goes to bed on champagne, one often doesn't feel up to facing real food in the morning," she pointed out. "Speaking of which, when *does* your mistress generally awaken?"

"Noon, not a bit earlier, even when she wasn't getting

haunted," Alicia said, promptly. "But to be fair now, she's working hard doing that singing, and don't get to bed before one or two. Sometimes later, if some gentleman takes her to supper after."

Sarah nodded. That seemed reasonable, put that way. "And when does she receive visitors?"

"Around about four? Teatime. She quite likes a proper tea, though she drinks more coffee, not tea, or sometimes chocolate. I guess they don't have teatime in German-land," Alicia replied. Sarah sighed with relief. Good. She'd be able to get a decent round of sleep before coming back to consult with the diva.

"Then I'll return about then. Wait a moment, and I'll write a note you can give her." Sarah stuffed the sheaf of notes she had taken on hotel stationery into her purse, then found a clean sheet and jotted down a few lines.

Fraulein von Dietersdorf; you are indeed the unhappy recipient of spirit-visitations. I will return about the time you normally receive visitors to explain at length. I believe you spent last night untroubled, and I believe I can disperse your visitants, although, as there are many, many more than I would have thought, it will take more time than I had expected. Respectfully, Sarah Lyon-White.

This she slipped into an envelope and handed to Alicia. "I'll have the concierge find me a cab. Thank you for your kindness, Alicia. I will see you later this afternoon."

The maid saw her to the door, and Sarah made her way down the utterly silent corridor to the elevator. Evidently the rest of the people who inhabited this part of the hotel were not the sort to rise early, either. The concierge quickly got her a cab, looking a little surprised to see a young lady awake at such an early hour.

A gratifyingly short time later, she made her way up the stairs to the flat, feeling every single minute of her ordeal and looking forward to falling into her bed. Nan and Suki must have heard her footsteps on the stair, for the door flew open, and Nan reached out to pull her inside.

"You look like you've been through the wars," Nan said bluntly. "To bed with you. You can tell us more when you've had a decent sleep."

She barely remembered Nan and Suki helping her to undress

and getting her into her nightgown. She definitely did not remember falling into bed, only the graceful wings of sleep closing around her.

"So," Nan said, pouring tea and adding milk and sugar. "To sum up everything you've told us, you are in for a long job of work. It's definitely more than you bargained for."

"More work, certainly," Sarah replied. "Nothing nasty or dangerous, other than the revenant of that murderer—I'm not certain I really want to know that particular story—but a great deal more work than I had reckoned on."

She tapped the pile of notes on hotel stationery she had taken from her purse. "Most of these spirits seem to have a great deal of unfinished business. Just three of the seven that I passed over last night dictated *that* much to me."

"Well, I can easily transcribe it," Nan replied, picking up the pages and leafing through them. She blinked, reading one part that went on for several pages. "Great Caesar's ghost, what is this, a legacy?"

"That's exactly what it is," Sarah agreed. "That one took the longest. It was a businessman who has a great deal of money hidden away in an extremely convoluted fashion. He was extremely anxious that his wife get all of it, but it seems that accessing it all will require her to go to solicitors and bankers all over London and indeed, outside of London, with her marriage lines and his death certificate, and in some places offer various pass-codes. He had intended to write all of this down in his will but—"

"Of course, I can guess, he dropped dead in the Langham before he got the chance." Nan shook her head. "Well, good news for her, anyway. The rest of these seem to be letters and addresses from your other two spirits. They're clear enough. I'll write them up properly for you and post them off. That's one thing less on your plate."

Sarah sighed, her face suffused with relief. "Bless you."

Nan did not ask what she dearly *wanted* to ask—which was how much longer this was going to take. Sarah couldn't possibly know that, just as she couldn't possibly know how many more ghosts had yet to appear. Nan didn't *like* any of this, but she could scarcely forbid Sarah to do it, especially now that Sarah knew how many spirits actually needed her help.

"It looks as if you are going to be taught your lessons by me for a while, Suki," she said to the little girl, who only grinned impishly.

"Oi don' mind." Nan knew very well why Suki didn't mind. Nan was far more likely than Sarah to offer a bit of sweet as a reward for a lesson done well.

"Nan, I am doing this for the sake of the ghosts—I've never seen so many trapped in one place before," Sarah said, leaning over the table earnestly. "But of course, there is Holmes' little mystery as well, which has only become more mysterious. Because she was not aware that I knew anything about Johanna, I have already learned from Magdalena that she had no great affection for her sister, which makes me wonder *why* her sister came with her in the first place."

Nan pursed her lips. "That is a good question. Was it the parents' idea? But *why,* if Johanna was engaged to that young man? I would have thought that they'd be anxious to get her married once Magdalena was launched on a successful career."

Sarah tilted her head as a nearby church clock struck the hour. "I need to go. I'll be back within two hours or so. Perhaps we can manage a visit to the Watsons before I need to go back at midnight."

"Possibly. Meanwhile I'll help Suki with her lessons while I transcribe your material." Nan grinned suddenly. "And you *knew* I would do that, didn't you!"

Sarah sighed dramatically. "Your hand is much clearer than mine. If we need to pass those letters off as being done by a secretary, it will be more easily accomplished if they are actually legible to someone other than you and me." She picked up her purse and went out the door.

Sarah was beginning to appreciate Freddy Smart and his gelding Crumpet. Freddy kept his cab absolutely immaculate, and Crumpet had the instincts of a polo pony for finding his way through crowded traffic. There was mud on the floorboards of this cab, by contrast, and the horse seemed tired, moving along at a discouraged amble. *I should be grateful there is no worse than mud in this cab,* she decided. Right *now* Magdalena was pleased with her, but she sensed that the least little misstep could alter the diva's temper in a flash.

But when she was admitted to the singer's suite again by Alicia, the maid gave her a little smile, and Magdalena welcomed her from her seat on the fainting couch with a triumphant cry.

"Miss White! I passed the night *completely* undisturbed! I read your note the first thing upon awakening, and you *must* tell me what happened!"

Encouraged, Sarah seated herself opposite the singer, who was arrayed in yet another expensive and gorgeous tea gown, this one the color of a wild rose, and related briefly what had happened, omitting the fact that five of the seven spirits she had dealt with last night had been quite lower class. She sensed that Magdalena would be appalled to discover that she was being haunted by the likes of scullery maids. The diva listened to the descriptions, nodding when Sarah said something she seemed to recognize.

"Yes, yes, that . . . screaming thing, and the creature it was tied to, I have seen that one, though only glimpses. I am not brave when it comes to spirits, one look and I cowered beneath the bedclothes like a little child. And the young girls who stared and stared, I remember those too. And the old man. The old man moaned and made motions at me. There are others, many others—"

Sarah sighed; the fact that Magdalena had seen all of these spirits for herself made things easier. "Yes, that is what I was coming to. It seems, for some reason, you have become attractive to every spirit that haunts the Langham and the ground it was built on. Sometimes that happens, though I have never seen it to this extent. I don't know why—" she said, forestalling any questions on that head. "It may be your sensitive artistic temperament; that allows you to see them, and because they know you can see them, they are drawn to you." Privately she thought that Magdalena was about as sensitive as an ox, but she *could,* without a doubt, see these haunts, and that might indeed be the reason they had come to her. When ghosts knew someone could see them, they often leapt to the conclusion that person could, or would want to, help them. "The cause really doesn't matter. What is important is to rid you of them. And . . . there seem to be a very great many of them. . . ."

Here she hesitated, because she had no intentions of doing this for free, and yet, she was uncertain how Magdalena would react to being asked to match that first fee, night after night.

"Oh blessed God! If this is as you say, any other hotel will be *just* as bad, and no other hotel in London is a match for this in comfort—please, Miss White, I will gladly pay the same fee every night you need to be here until they are gone!" There was no artifice there; Magdalena was truly afraid, and truly frantic to be rid of the hauntings. "What good is money if I cannot sleep for terror?" She clutched her hands together in an attitude of begging then stretched them out to Sarah. "Say yes, I implore you!" Her voice rose with the last sentence.

"Calm yourself, of course I accept," Sarah said quickly. "I will be here every night until I believe I have rid you of the ghosts. And if any new ones come after that, you have only to send for me."

Magdalena flung herself back into the embrace of the fainting couch with the air of someone who has just been saved out of all expectations. "A thousand blessings on you! Can you come at midnight again? We can share supper, as we did before." Then she sat up, suddenly. "Would—is it likely they would follow me—elsewhere? If I was to be asked to a private party after the opera—"

Hmm hmm. Private party. Well, she is getting those gowns and jewels and the guineas she is paying me with from somewhere, and it isn't the management of the Royal Opera. And I doubt her fiancé has any inklings of this, which is probably why she sent him packing as soon as she could. "The spirits here are more or less bound to this place," Sarah assured her. "They cannot follow you, not unless they happened to be tied to some object you were in the habit of carrying with you rather than this hotel, and from all I have seen that is unlikely. As long you only stay a few hours, I doubt very much that any ghosts resident where you will be will sense your presence. Besides," she added, trying not to sound sly, or worse, give Magdalena the hint that Sarah knew very well about her wealthy patrons. "They only plague you when you enter that half-world between sleep and waking, and I very much doubt you would be trying to sleep at a private dinner party!"

Hmm hmm, and this will keep you from ornamenting some

gentleman's bed for longer than it takes to satisfy him.

Magdalena laughed weakly. "Well, some of the guests can be dull enough to send one to sleep," she said. "But you are probably right. If I am not here, will the spirits come anyway?"

"They will, as long as *I* am here," Sarah told her firmly. "Remember, they want help, and they already know I can give it to them. I've no objection to working here if you are detained and sending them away, in your absence." *It might even be easier.* "All that will happen if you come in later is that they will be startled and leave, but they will return as soon as you have settled back into your bed. I can begin arriving at midnight and leaving at dawn, starting tonight."

"Alicia, fetch my cheque book," Magdalena commanded, then turned back to Sarah. "My lo—I intend to perform here for some time, so I arranged to establish a bank account here. A cheque will be easier and safer for you than a purse full of money."

"Much," Sarah agreed fervently. *Yes, your lover—or lovers—have set you up with an account, to make it convenient for you to buy whatever your heart desires. And I will politely pretend I have no idea that any such thing has happened.* She did wonder, though, what the fellow would think about the cheque to Sarah. *Likely, Magdalena will pass me off as a dressmaker. Heaven knows simple alterations or repairs to some of those gowns would easily cost ten guineas.*

Alicia brought the cheques, pen, and ink, and Magdalena made out a cheque swiftly, waving it in the air for a few moments to dry it before she passed it to Sarah. Sarah managed not to goggle at the amount as she took it, folded it neatly, and put it in her purse. *And I will be stopping at* my *bank on the way home!*

"I am sure you have a thousand things you must do before your performance tonight," Sarah said, giving Magdalena a graceful out. "And now that I know what I am facing, I have preparations to make as well." She smiled a little. "After all, I can't be using up all your stationery, taking notes of the pleas of desperate spirits! I shall come better equipped tonight."

She rose, and Magdalena beamed at her. "You are very much my savior, Miss Lyon-White. I am, and shall be, eternally grateful to you. I will see you tonight. I hope you like squab *demi-glacé*."

"I am very fond of squab," Sarah replied, though she would have said the same if she loathed the dish. "Thank you for your hospitality."

Alicia showed her to the door, and once down on the street, she was thrilled to see Freddy Smart lined up with the other hansoms waiting for people to emerge from the hotel. She waved to him, and he waved back, much to the disappointment of the other cabbies, who had been hoping for a fare. As he helped her up into the cab, he grinned. "So, now ye got me curious. What's your business, if ye don' mind a nosy parker askin'?"

"Séances for an opera singer," Sarah told him, since that was *almost* the truth. "I satisfied her last night that I can contact the spirit she wishes to speak with. So for the next several nights I will definitely be needing your services. She wants me to arrive at midnight, which is when she returns from the opera."

"*Séances?*" Freddy gaped at her. "Gor blimey! Yew must got nerves of steel!"

She was just grateful Freddy didn't scoff at her—or think she was a charlatan. "The lady pays very well, so I will need to stop at Barclay's on the way home."

"Right yew are!" Freddy said cheerfully, probably thinking happily of the substantial tips she had given him on the last rides. "Let's get yew there, then!"

With supper over, Sarah gave Nan the good news about the latest fee Magdalena had paid her. Nan goggled at the sum on the deposit slip as Neville peered over her shoulder, then, finding nothing to interest him, hopped back down to the floor and went back to his dinner of bits of raw meat. "I think this would impress even Lord A!" she said. "Speaking of whom—I sent him a note this morning that we—or rather you—were going to be engaged in this enterprise for an indefinite time. Here's his reply, it just came in the last mail."

She handed over the note, and anyone who knew stationery would immediately be aware that the writer was . . . very well off. It was beautiful vellum with the texture of cream, very heavy, and with Lord Alderscroft's crest embossed. Sun pouring in the window only emphasized how rich the paper was.

Sarah slid the penknife under the scarlet wax seal, opened it, read it quickly, and grinned. *"My dear Sarah,"* she read aloud. *"May I congratulate you on your good fortune. The lady in question has several admirers who are spending obscene amounts of money on her, and she can quite well afford your help. I am extremely pleased that you are doing so much good at the Langham, as it has the reputation of being the most haunted hotel in London. The fact that you are profiting as well is marvelous. I do not need your assistance at the moment, and I believe that the Watsons will be able to continue with the help of Nan alone for as long as the spirits require your aid. Good hunting! Lord A."*

"'The lady in question has several admirers who are spending obscene amounts of money on her,'" Nan quoted, furrowing her brows. "How does he *know* these things?" She looked up at Sarah, who shrugged.

"Agents everywhere, I suspect. He's friends with Mycroft Holmes after all; I don't doubt they pool their resources and information." Sarah put the note back in the envelope and tucked it with the bank receipt in a little file box they kept for important papers that would need to be put away properly later.

"Do you think you should get another nap?" Nan asked, but Sarah shook her head. "Well, then, what would you like to do between now and eleven?"

"I'd like to go talk to the Watsons. We should tell them ourselves what I'm going to be occupied with for a while, it's only polite." Sarah glanced at the window. "We've plenty of time."

"Want to go!" said Grey from her perch, after carefully wiping the curry off her beak onto the side of the cup. Neville tossed back the last bit of raw meat and nodded that he wanted to go, too.

"I don't see any reason why not, Mary Watson likes you two." Nan glanced at Suki. "Will you be all right alone here for a few hours? Your lessons are done, so you can do whatever you like. I know we can rely on you to keep everything safe, but I'd hate for you to feel lonely. We can light all the lamps before we go."

Suki nodded, looking very pleased that Nan had stated their trust in her. "Got lots to do," she said. And it was true, she did. Nan and Sarah had made sure she had plenty of books, and

Lord Alderscroft spoiled her with new toys every time he came by. She had a china doll, which was probably the equal of any in Queen Victoria's collection, with an extensive wardrobe, a toy theater, a telescope with which she could spy on the street and in the neighbors' windows, a kaleidoscope, a top, plenty of drawing pencils and watercolors and the paper to use them on . . . and other toys as well, but most of those were better suited for playing outdoors. For a child who'd had *no* toys until she came to live with Nan and Sarah, this was a dazzling array of riches. She took exquisite care of everything she was given, and the satisfaction in her eyes whenever she surveyed her treasures always made Nan smile.

"If you spy on the neighbors, make sure they can't see you," Sarah cautioned. "It's good practice for when you will be able to come help us."

Suki puffed out her little chest at the thought that she would one day soon be able to help in the "adventures." "I will, Miss Sarah," she promised. "And if I see anythin' rummy, I go tells Mrs. 'Orace, an' she gets a Bobby."

"Exactly right." Nan, Sarah, *and* both birds nodded approval. "All right then," Nan continued. "Birds, we'll bring you in the carriers, so go hop in." The birds jumped down off their perches and ran to their own room, where their special carriers waited. It was safer to take them in their leather carriers at night; they didn't see well in the dark, and if they were startled into flight they could easily come to grief.

"I'll get the notes—and your transcriptions for the widow of the late Mister Hopkins," Sarah said. "I think perhaps I'll ask John Watson if he can help us with that particular task."

The cab ride was utterly uneventful. They carefully timed their arrival at 221 Baker Street to avoid interrupting the Watsons at dinner, and sure enough, they passed Mrs. Hudson in the entry hall bringing down the tray of dishes. They ran past Holmes' door, up to C, and tapped on the door. Mary Watson opened it immediately, with a look of surprise on her face.

"Come in, please!" she said, looking happy to see them. "John and I were just settling in with the evening papers and some tea. We heard footsteps but thought they were for Holmes."

Nan was very glad that John looked as pleased to see them as Mary; she was a little uneasy about just dropping in on them without warning. She and Sarah took their seats on the same sofa they had used last time and freed the birds from their carriers. Grey went to Sarah's shoulder, but Neville went straight to Mary, jumping onto her knee and lifting his beak to her face.

"Give us a kiss, love," he crooned, and Mary, laughing, gave him a peck on his formidable beak. Satisfied, he lofted back to Nan, who took him on her arm and scratched his head.

"Am I going to have to be jealous, now?" she asked him. He chortled.

"Well, Lord A sent us a message about Sarah's hair-raising adventures with our opera singer," Mary said, opening the conversation *immediately* with the subject that was on all their minds. "But not in any great detail. So! Tell!"

For a moment, Nan was puzzled. *How did he—oh, of course. He probably sent the message either by Elemental or by some other magician's trick. That would certainly come in handy; too bad we can't learn it.*

Nothing loath, Sarah did. "And now I'm to clear ghosts away for her until they leave her alone," Sarah concluded. "The only nasty one was the murderer, and thanks to Puck's charm, he couldn't hurt me. The ghosts seem to be the usual mix of lost souls and those who have things they need to do. Two of them had a number of things they badly needed to say to several people who had been important to them, and one—well, John, that is the reason why we're here." She took out Nan's transcription. "I have an extremely complicated set of instructions from a Master Nigel Hopkins to his wife." She handed the pages Nan had transcribed to John and Mary. John raised his eyebrow over the sheaf of paper. Mary just shook her head, and the two of them bent over the careful transcriptions in Nan's neat, clear handwriting.

"Why on earth would anyone hide his money in this way?" Mary asked, after they had perused the first two pages.

"I suspect he has been asking himself the same question ever since he died," Nan said dryly. "I know some people mistrust banks, and they do have reasons to, but this was quite past simple *mistrust*. And here is the problem. Mrs. Hopkins might not believe a strange woman coming to her out of the blue with this . . . well, it looks like errant nonsense. I was hoping you would help us with a way to approach her, and how to explain this without bringing ghosts into it."

"First we would have to concoct a good story as to how you came by all this information," John pointed out. "Ah, which of you would be approaching her?"

"Me, probably," Nan volunteered. "Sarah is likely to need to be asleep during the day, you see."

"Good. Well. You could easily pass for a secretary, Nan. And this fellow seems to have patronized a great many solicitors, so you could be a solicitor's secretary." John shuffled the papers in his hands, then passed them to Mary, who put them in order and handed them back to Nan. "Sarah, he did say he was intending to put this in his will?"

Sarah nodded. Mary put her head to the side, as John pulled on his moustache a little.

"Then, let's say when he checked into the Langham, he sent for a solicitor we will just make up out of thin air. He *intended* to make all this a codicil to his will, so you say. Well, let's just allow his widow to assume that on his trip into the City he had had an inkling of his imminent demise and called this fictitious solicitor to his hotel room, then dictated all this to him." John chewed on his lower lip thoughtfully, his brows furrowed.

"The solicitor would know this was supposed to be a codicil to his will," Mary pointed out. "You can certainly say that he said that."

"Yes, but why wouldn't this solicitor have gone ahead and *done* that, had the codicil written up properly and delivered to Hopkins' regular solicitor? Especially as he'd have found out Nigel Hopkins had dropped dead the next morning?" Sarah objected.

"Because *he* dropped dead too?" Mary Watson hazarded, sounding uncertain. "I suppose it could happen. . . ."

"That does seem rather . . . unlikely," Nan pointed out. But Sarah laughed.

"And is the truth any *likelier*?" she retorted. "We've all agreed we can't go talking about spirits and ghosts, and if our imagined solicitor was an old man, an unexpected trip to a stranger's hotel room in the middle of the night might set *him* off, too. All right. So Hopkins drops dead, and so does the solicitor, so the codicil never got written and sent. But why were the papers only found now?"

Throwing all caution to the wind, Nan added to the tale. After all, why not? "Because they fell behind the desk, between the desk and the wall. I was in charge of dealing with everything to do with the office. The papers were only brought to my attention when the office was being cleared for a new tenant and the desk was moved out," she declared. "And as I was the late lamented solicitor's secretary, I was the one put in charge of trying to find Mrs. Hopkins and give her these details."

They all looked at one another. "Well. . . ." Mary ventured. "There is certainly one piece of information that will make all of this seem not only likely, but commonplace. That you, Miss Killian, came to see the great Sherlock Holmes to seek advice and discover the whereabouts of the widow. The great Sherlock Holmes made quick work of locating her address, and John has been entrusted with the task of seeing this to the end." She smiled broadly. "Just think how excited the widow will be to hear she was the goal of a Sherlock Holmes investigation! After that, you could tell her whatever you liked, and she would believe it."

"You're right," said Grey.

"Wisdom from the beaks of birds," chuckled John. "But, yes, I can see that. And for once I don't mind trading on my connection with Holmes to give something verisimilitude." He examined the address. "Slough. That won't be too difficult. We can take the train and then probably walk from the station. Tomorrow morning, then, Nan?"

Nan glanced at Sarah. "Once we get this started and get the first lot of money into the widow's hands, Nigel Hopkins will probably be ready to cross over," Sarah put in. "So it can't be soon enough for me."

Nan shrugged. At least she was *doing* something, even if it was just to serve as Sarah's hands and feet. "Sarah will be sleeping, and I can trust Suki to at least do those lessons that involve reading. Tomorrow morning it is."

"We'll meet at Paddington Station," John said. "Under the

clock, at seven. I'll get the tickets, that will mean one less thing for you to do."

Sarah reached for her purse and extracted more than enough money for two tickets, placing it firmly in John's hand before he could object. "We are paying," she said firmly. "With the obscene amount of money Magdalena is paying me, it is the least we can do."

Nan met John Watson promptly at seven in the morning; she had waited for Sarah to come home then taken over her cab to go to Paddington. The day was overcast, damp, and threatened rain. Beneath its arched roof of iron and glass, the station was noisy, crowded, and no one seemed particularly happy to be there as they hurried, bent over, to and from railway carriages. Nan *was,* but then, she enjoyed train rides. Before she'd been taken in by the Hartons, depending on where she and her mother were living, if there were tracks near, she would find a perch overlooking the train tracks and daydream about where those trains might be taking people, daydream herself into one of those coaches. Suki was the same; the child had sighed with disappointment at not being allowed to come along, and Nan decided she'd buy a penny chocolate bar for her from one of the machines at the station. Somehow, railroad station chocolate had always meant something special to her, and it did to Suki, too.

It's not as if I'm going to find something labeled "Souvenir of Slough" . . .although you never know. Suki had a little collection of such things; thimbles, teacups, embroidered pillows, seashells, paperweights. Nan was looking forward to the day when the child would be old enough to help, if only to relive *her* own excitement at travel through Suki's eyes.

The next train to Slough and beyond left at 7:15, which left plenty of time for the two of them to stroll to their platform and their carriage. John had thoughtfully bought newspapers, so they sat together in the carriage and passed the time tolerably enough, with Nan spending more time looking out the window than John did. She was rewarded with a fine view of Windsor Castle as they approached Slough. When they arrived at Slough Station, which was rather fine, Nan waited while John consulted with a local porter about the address of Mrs. Hopkins.

"It's farther than I care to walk," he said, on returning to her side. "You would probably think nothing of it—"

"On the contrary, it's looking like rain, and *I* don't fancy a soaking," Nan corrected. "If there is anything more miserable than soaking wet skirt hems, I don't know what it is."

"Cab it is then," John agreed, and went to hail one.

The cab let them out on a street of pleasant, genteel houses, mostly brick and stone, with neat little front gardens and some young trees, exactly the sort of suburban houses prosperous businessmen might buy. The rain had not yet begun, so after asking the cabbie to wait, they approached the door of a three-story brick home that looked very well cared for and John used the door knocker.

Given the size of the house, they expected the door to be opened by a servant, but instead, it was answered by a slight, gray-haired woman in deep mourning; her hair was parted in the middle under an old-fashioned flat cap. She peered up at them, a little shortsightedly. "May I help you?" she asked, uncertainly.

John immediately removed his hat. "Have I the honor of addressing Mrs. Nigel Hopkins?" he asked diffidently.

Now she looked a little startled. "Well, I would not say it is much of an honor, young man, but yes, that is I," she replied. Her hands, clasped together, rose to the level of her chest, and Nan saw she was wringing them a little, as if expecting bad news. "Might I ask why it is you wish to see me?"

"Mother?" came a male voice from inside the house. "Is it a—"

"Mrs. Hopkins, may we please come in?" John asked, putting on his most charming smile. "I promise you, we have come to bring you good news, rather than the opposite."

At that point, a ginger-haired man in, perhaps, his midtwenties appeared behind the woman. "Listen, my man," he said, putting on a brave front. "If you are here to collect for someone, I assure you that there is nothing *to* collect, but we intend to—"

"Not at all!" John cried, holding up his hand. "We are not here to collect, but to give. Please, may we come in and explain?"

"Let's have them in, Neddy," the woman implored. "What harm can it do?"

117

Neddy seemed uncertain, but he bowed to his mother's will. She conducted them into a very pretty parlor decorated in gold and brown. Or it would have been pretty, if everything had not been draped in black. Prominent was the black-draped picture over the mantelpiece of a middle-aged man and what looked like the middle-aged version of their hostess. She offered them seats on a horsehair sofa, which they took; she settled herself in a chair across from them, while Neddy stood protectively behind the chair. Nan had already decided, as they had planned, to let John do most of the talking, at least at first; they'd listen to him, and they might not to her.

"First of all, I beg you will allow me to introduce myself," John said. "I am Doctor John Watson."

"We don't need a—" Neddy began, but his mother interrupted him, her eyes wide and her cheeks flushed, one hand upraised.

"Not *the* Doctor John Watson!" she exclaimed. "The one in the stories! The—" She stopped, overcome.

"Yes, madam. The associate of Sherlock Holmes." He smiled as her eyes went even wider. "And it is in that capacity that I am here. You bring us to the end of a somewhat more pedestrian tale than Mister Doyle generally writes up for me. Miss Nan Killian was the secretary to the Honorable Henry Smith, a solicitor of London. And she has a story to tell you."

Now that she had their attention, Nan quickly and efficiently told out her false tale. "I was empowered to contract the services of Sherlock Holmes to locate the lady—you—named in these documents," she finished. "Needless to say, Mister Holmes made short work of the task, and arranged for the good Doctor to accompany me so that you would hear me out. Here are the instructions intended for you, as they were dictated to my employer in the Langham Hotel and transcribed by me."

She handed over the notes to the widow and her son, who examined them with a great deal of bewilderment. "None of these are dear Nigel's bank—" she said, faltering. "Nor his usual solicitor—"

"We apprehend that he may have had a mistrust of banks, and did not wish to leave too much of his savings in any one place," Watson replied. "I understand he had business over much of this part of England; another explanation is that perhaps he felt uncomfortable carrying about cheques that were too large, or large amounts of cash money, and so he used banks local to the places he was doing business with."

"Well—what should I *do*?" she replied, now clearly overwhelmed.

"We have laid out a simple plan," Watson assured her. "We would like to accompany you—and your son as well, if he cares to come—to the nearest bank on the list. If you see here"—he pointed at a listing halfway down the first page—"we will first need to visit this solicitor and obtain a safety deposit box key. Then we will visit the bank itself. I am uncertain what will be in that box, or if Mister Hopkins also had an account there, but it is not that far, and I have the cab waiting. You will see from the notes, you will need to bring your marriage lines and the—other document. Shall we?"

It took a little more persuasion, and then some hunting for the documents, but eventually they were on their way, stopping at a small solicitor's office in the business center of Slough. There, John simply took over, forcefully getting past the clerk to the solicitor himself.

"This is most irregular," the gentleman said with some irritation. "You should have made an appointment—" But he let them into his private office and shut the door, going to sit behind the desk, waiting for an explanation.

"I believe you had—briefly—a very unusual client," John said to the stone-faced gentleman, once they were all safely in his office. "His name was Nigel Hopkins, and he left you in charge of a key. This is his wife, now his heir. Here are her marriage lines, here is the certificate of his death. And the password for the key is *muttonchop*."

As soon as the password left John's lips, the solicitor's demeanor changed. Suddenly he was all sympathy, solicitously patting Mrs. Hopkins' hand, making sure she had a comfortable chair, and then retrieving an envelope from a file cabinet. "I have been wondering if someone would come for that key every day for the last twenty years," he said, putting it into her hand. "It's preyed on my mind, it has, the fear that he forgot it, and someone who deserved it would never know of it."

"That came nearer to the truth than we care to think," John

said, as the good man showed them out. "Thank you for your faithful service."

Mrs. Hopkins was practically speechless at this point, and her son was clearly dazed. Not a word passed from either of them during the short cab ride to the bank, where once again, John moved them smoothly past clerks and tellers and secretaries to the bank manager's office, where once again the documents were presented, and Mrs. Hopkins handed over the key with a hand that trembled.

"My dear lady!" the manager exclaimed, "Please, sit down. Yes, I remember Nigel very well. He made regular deposits here, and I am saddened to hear of his sudden demise! Franklin—get the lady's box. I'll get the accounts—" He hurried off himself, leaving an astonished Mrs. Hopkins sitting in the chair across from his desk, her son, just as dumbstruck, at her side.

It was not more than a few moments before Franklin and the manager returned—the clerk with a safety deposit box, the manager with a ledger. Rather than actually say anything, the manager simply opened the ledger to the relevant page, and pointed to a total on the bottom. "There is the total of his account in the bank to—" he began, when Mrs. Hopkins went white, then pink, and uttered a cry, as her son clutched the back of her chair, clearly stunned.

"Neddy! Neddy!" she cried out, and broke into tears. "Neddy, we are saved!"

The bank manager managed to hold on to his dignity, although it was clear that a weeping woman in his office caused him some distress. He sent Franklin for water, fetched his own handkerchief, and did his best to comfort her, as her son was too thunderstruck to undertake the job himself.

It was Nan who came to the rescue of all those poor bewildered men, going to the old woman, embracing her, and patting her back. "There, you see, your Nigel always meant for you to be taken care of," she murmured. "I'm only sorry it took so long."

After a few more moments, the lady murmured her thanks into Nan's ear; Nan took the hint and stood up, returning to her chair. Mrs. Hopkins dabbed at her eyes and blew her nose and regained some of her composure. After a sip of the water, and another dab at her eyes, she looked up at them all. "Things have been . . . difficult," she managed, clearly embarrassed to have to admit that her husband's death had left her in what must have been, by her reaction, very straitened circumstances. "All I had was what was in the household account. There were so many bills to pay . . . we had to dismiss the servants . . . we were trying to find lodgers, but no one answered the advertisements . . . I thought we would have to sell the house. . . ."

She broke down again, but this time it was to bury her face in the handkerchief. The bank manager took the key from Neddy's nerveless fingers and opened the safety deposit box.

It was full of papers.

Since Neddy didn't seem capable of reaching for them himself, the bank manager took them out and began opening unsealed envelopes to see what was inside. "I do not think you will need to worry, Mrs. Hopkins," he said slowly. "These are shares of stock in some very prosperous companies."

Now Mrs. Hopkins looked up, bewildered. "Shares? What does that mean?"

The bank manager slowly, and carefully, explained to her what shares of stock were, and how she could expect regular payments from them quarterly. "I can see what Nigel had been doing," he continued. "He put his stock dividends back in his account in this bank as deposits."

At that moment, John nudged Nan with his elbow, and raised his eyebrows at the manager. Taking the hint, Nan closed her eyes and opened her mind.

Neddy's surface thoughts were still . . . mostly blank. He was completely gobsmacked and hadn't recovered from the sudden reversal of the family fortunes. Beneath that was a vast well of love and concern for his mother, and still-raw grief over his father. Nan shied away from Mrs. Hopkins—Agatha. The open wound of her loss was enough to have brought tears to the eyes of a statue, and even finding herself possessed of enough money to live comfortably again was not enough to take even the edge off that grief. Nigel had truly been the love of her life and the center of her universe.

No wonder Hopkins was so insistent on dictating all this to Sarah.

Nan quickly turned her attention to the man John wanted her to examine: the bank manager, Trevor Howard. What she found there made her open her eyes quickly and nod to John Watson with a tiny smile. This was a fundamentally kind and painfully honest man. He might be next to helpless when it came to emotional situations, and more than a bit stodgy, but he could be absolutely trusted.

Which made her accede to his request when he asked to see the notes. He looked through them, carefully, then said to Franklin, "Send in my son, would you? And bring another glass of water for Mrs. Hopkins."

When Franklin appeared with a man who could have been the younger version of Trevor Howard, and to Nan's reading was the near twin of his father when it came to integrity, Howard sent Franklin out and reached over the desk to take Mrs. Hopkins' hand.

"I would like to propose something, dear lady," he said, speaking quietly, as if to calm a small child or a dog—which actually was the right tactic to take with the poor woman at this moment in time. "There are many banks and solicitors on this list of yours, a dozen at least. Doctor Watson and Miss Killian here cannot be expected to go with you to all of them, and you will need a trustworthy and steady fellow to accompany you. Now, I will not try to conceal the fact that I hope you will keep this account with my bank, and that indeed, I hope you will consolidate everything else you retrieve here as well. But whether you do that or not, I feel I must offer you the services of my son to accompany you. He is the assistant manager here. He can speak with authority, and if need be, some force, on your behalf. He will see to it that you are not cheated or put off in any way, and will make sure you and whatever you bring back come home safely. Would that suit you?"

Neddy finally shook off his shock and patted his mother's hand, still being held by the bank manager. "I think that's a capital idea, mother. They might try funny business with you and me, but they'll never dare do so with Mister Howard along."

The son smiled, and murmured, "Alan. I'd be pleased if you'd call me by my Christian name."

Neddy held out his hand to Alan, who shook it. "Thank you,

Alan. I'm Ned. And I cannot thank you enough for your kindness."
He looked over to the father while still shaking the hand of the
son, "And I see every reason why consolidating everything *here*
would be another capital idea."

"I cannot say that I think you'll find equal sums in those distant
accounts," Trevor Howard warned, "But I believe, given what I
know of your late father's business from his dealings here, that
your mother will be able to live in comfort and ease from now on."

There was more business talk—between the men, of course.
Mrs. Hopkins had clearly been brought up in an age and a
household where women were not expected to concern themselves
with business. It was arranged that the bank's own stockbroker
would take charge of the shares and any more such items that
surfaced in the course of retrieving what was in deposit boxes.
Nan would have been more than a trifle irritated by the men's
easy dismissal of the two women in the room as inconsequential
to this discussion, but she was just too relieved that her job had
been so easily discharged to really care.

But it was when she was looking in the box to see if there
were any more papers in it, that she moved an empty envelope
in the bottom and discovered a small, black, velvet-covered box.
"There seems to be something else here," she said, handing it to
Agatha Hopkins.

The widow opened it, hesitantly. "It's a gold locket!" Nan
exclaimed, recognizing the shape instantly as being nearly identical
to one she herself owned. "Open it—"

Inside was a small picture of what must have been Nigel
Hopkins—probably taken not long before his death. And inscribed
on the other half of the locket were two simple words that made
Agatha burst into tears again.

Love, always.

INTERLUDE: *DANSE MACABRE*

The room was shrouded in darkness, with only a single candle providing a faint illumination. The musician was playing from memory; he didn't need to consult with sheet music, as his ivory-colored bow swept back and forth across the strings of his instrument. The music was melancholy, gentle, yet insistent. He repeated the tune over and over, tirelessly, for at least an hour before he was answered.

A shimmering, transparent, slender white figure, seemingly made of mist, coalesced out of the darkness, just out of the reach of the candlelight.

The musician ceased to play, and rested his violin and bow in his lap. For a long time, he sat there, motionless, head cocked slightly to one side, brows furrowed in concentration. At length, he sighed.

"This is not what I intended," he said to the white shape that hovered in the darkness. "I did not anticipate such interference. I shall have to make other plans."

Again, he took on an attitude of listening.

"Yes," he replied. "I believe that you should. No, I believe that you *must*. Perhaps you will stir into life something too formidable for this meddling girl. As for me . . ." He smiled. "I believe I have an idea. My quarry will find *this* revenant much more difficult . . . and much less sympathetic."

He stood up, and put the bow and violin back in the case. "You may go," he told the misty figure, which promptly faded away.

He stood looking into the darkness after it had gone. Finally he let out a long breath. Not a sigh, but as if he had made up his mind.

"She shall not escape," he said, as if making a pledge. "I swear, she shall not escape."

7

Nan sat quietly with a book she was having trouble concentrating on. The window was closed against the dust and noise from the street, but the sun outside showed it was a pleasant, if cool, day. Three days had passed since the excursion to take Agatha Hopkins her "legacy," and Nan was beginning to get bored. Normally, if she and Sarah were not on some errand of Lord Alderscroft's, they were sitting right here at the table where she and Suki were now, transcribing old *grimoires* or histories that Lord A had borrowed from other Elemental Masters. When Suki needed help with her lessons, they'd take turns giving her a hand.

But Sarah was fast asleep right now in her bedroom, Nan didn't *have* any arcane volumes to transcribe, and she was in the position of being Suki's sole teacher.

It is a very, very good thing that Suki sees learning as a privilege and for the most part not a chore, or I should likely be screaming at her at this moment. From somewhat unfortunate experience, gathered when she had tried to fit herself into the position of "teacher" at the Harton School, Nan knew she did not have the patience or the temper to try to drive knowledge and information into the skull of a child who wasn't interested in learning. Suki, however, was the opposite, which at least made teaching her a task that was merely tedious, rather than maddening.

"Miz Nan? What's this word?" Suki said, interrupting her slightly sullen thoughts. She craned her neck around to see the word Suki's thin little forefinger was pointing at. This was a history lesson on Henry VIII, which would be followed by one on his son Edward, several more on his daughter Mary, and a great many on Queen Elizabeth.

"Elephantine," Nan replied. "What do you think it means?" She generally made Suki try a couple of guesses on her own before supplying an answer.

Suki grinned. "Tha's easy!" she scoffed. "Big's a nelephant!"

"It can also mean *fat*, or *bulky*," Nan reminded her. "Now, read me the sentence and tell me which meaning you think it has."

"*By this time, King 'Enry's body 'ad bloated t' el-e-phan-tine pro-por-tions*," Suki read, and furrowed her eyebrows. "Must mean fat, cuz I saw a pitchur of King 'Enry, an' 'e weren't big's a nelephant." She scratched her nose thoughtfully, "'E were purdy big, though."

"Very true; by the time he married his fifth wife he was very, very fat," replied Nan. "So fat it took six men to move him to the bed where he died." Suki's eyes went very round at that idea, and small wonder. In her world, or rather, the world from which Nan and Sarah had plucked her, people did not have enough money to get fat, much less grossly obese.

"There ain't 'nuff food in the worl' t'git that fat!" she declared, which led Nan to bring out an historical novel, where one of Henry's typical feasts was described.

"The first course consisted of a civet of hare, a quarter of stag which had been a night in salt, a stuffed chicken, and a loin of veal. The two last dishes were covered with a German sauce. There were two enormous pies, surmounted with smaller pies, which formed a crown. The crust of the large ones was silvered all round and gilt at the top; each contained a whole roe deer, a gosling, three capons, six chickens, ten pigeons, and one young rabbit. With the course came a stuffing, a minced loin of veal, two pounds of fat, and twenty-six hard-boiled eggs, covered with saffron and flavored with cloves."

Suki's eyes went round, trying to imagine all that food. Nan continued. "The second course was a roe deer, a pig, a sturgeon, a kid, two goslings, twelve chickens, as many pigeons, six young rabbits, two herons, a leveret, a fat capon stuffed, four chickens covered with yolks of eggs, and a wild boar." She looked up and smiled. "The third, fourth, and fifth courses are not quite that much. The third course is biscuits and an enormous jelly, the fourth course is spiced cream, sweetened cream, and fruit, and the last course is wines, nuts, fruits, and pastries. But King Henry loved to eat more than anything, and you can see how easily he could get fat, if all he did was have a mouthful or two of everything that was served."

"Did 'e, though?" Suki asked, her brow wrinkling. " 'Ave a bit of ev'thin', that is?"

"Very likely not everything, although he would definitely be offered everything. Heron, I am told, is rather nasty; it was more to show off the fact that you had goshawks who could take them down, rather than something most people would want to eat." Nan shook her head. "It is true, though, that Henry would have wanted to try almost everything, and it is true he never left the table until he couldn't hold another bite."

When Suki's curiosity was satisfied, she went back to her history lesson and Nan went back to her own rather unsatisfying book.

The problem was, not only was Sarah *doing* something and Nan wasn't. Now the nightly routine had stabilized to quite polite ghosts quietly lining up to air their grievances, tell her how they had *really* died (murder, usually), or dictate letters Nan would later transcribe and send off anonymously to their intended recipients. It was tedious, so Sarah said, because it was hard to hear them. Their voices faded in and out, and the older they were, the less they remembered unless they worked very hard at it. So tending to the needs of four to six spirits generally took all night. That was fine, Nan could understand that—but what was . . . irritating . . . was that Sarah was being made quite the pet of by Magdalena.

There were those delicious late night suppers at which Sarah was tasting things Nan had never even heard of—and equally tasty breakfasts that changed every day. Mrs. Horace was a good plain cook, but her imagination did not pass beyond what was typical for a solid English breakfast or oatmeal. And the Sunday roast tended to get stretched out to cover as much of the week as Mrs. Horace could possibly manage. It appeared in its magnificence on Sunday, reappeared Monday as sliced meat and gravy, made a new appearance Tuesday as an Irish stew, Wednesday as a shepherd's pie. By that time, Nan was getting rather weary of the mutton or beef or pork of the original. Suki wanted to hear about the suppers and breakfasts, and Sarah was only too happy to tell about them, but in contrast to what they'd had . . . it was hard not to feel a bit poorly done by.

But on top of that, last night Sarah had been asked to arrive at the hotel much earlier than usual, because Magdalena had taken the fancy to have her come see the opera. After hearing Sarah's description of the gorgeous spectacle when she'd come home this morning, Nan was convinced it was far superior to the panto, and been consumed with raw envy, and now. . . .

I'm jealous, she admitted bleakly, staring at the page of her book. *I'm just jealous. I'll never get invited to these things. No one is ever going to grace me with a champagne supper, or put me in a private box at the opera. So far as Magdalena is concerned, I'm probably nothing more than the erstwhile chaperone and occasional companion. And . . . just not posh enough.* And it didn't help that Magdalena was clearly going out of her way to be utterly charming to Sarah—who was, in Nan's estimation, falling for it.

And I don't dare say anything, because I know I'll be snappish, and then Sarah will just say I'm jealous, which I am, and completely disregard the fact that I think the woman is up to something. Of course, that *something* might be no more sinister than a plan to get Sarah's full-time attention as her own private little ghost-banisher, because if she really *was* somehow attracting spirits, until Sarah discovered *how* she was doing so, Magdalena was going to need something of the sort. But why should that be Sarah? Let her find her own minion!

It wouldn't be so bad if Nan just had something to *do*—

"Miz Nan?" Suki said, once again interrupting Nan's brooding. "Kin we go t' th' Tower? We niver could afore, on account'a Miz Sarah, an' all the ghostes. But you an' I kin go, aye?"

Nan's head came up, and she smiled at Suki. "Yes, we can. In fact, I think that is a capital idea. Get your hat."

Neville looked up from the toy he was playing with, a long piece of cord he was threading around an open basketwork of wire. *"Ork?"* he said, inquisitively.

"Yes, you can come along too and visit your relatives." Nan flung open the window, and Neville hopped up onto the sill. "Off with you. We'll meet you at the Tower. Don't steal too much of their food."

Neville laughed wickedly and lofted away. Nan turned to Grey, who was playing a game of her own with beads and straws. "You don't want to go, do you?"

Grey made a rude noise, and shook her head.

Nan had to laugh at that. "Well, yes. Neville's relatives aren't half as intelligent as you. All right, if Sarah wakes up, tell her where we've gone and we'll be back before supper."

"Nan and Suki went to the Tower. Back before supper," Grey said.

"Excellent." Suki ran in at that moment with her hat; Nan seized her purse, pinned her own hat to her hair, threw her shawl over her shoulders and took the child's hand. "Watch over Sarah while we're gone, Grey."

The parrot chuckled happily and bobbed her head, then went back to her game.

Well, Nan thought as she stopped long enough at Mrs. Horace's door to let their landlady know that there was only to be lunch for Grey and Sarah, *This is certainly better than brooding.*

Nan was happy to take Suki all over the Tower, and coaxed the guide to tell them the most bloodcurdling stories he could manage. The man was nothing loath when he realized that absolutely *nothing* he told them would frighten the sweet-looking little girl with Nan. He told them about Ann Boleyn and how the executioner took her head off so quickly with his sword that her eyes were still blinking and her mouth moving as the head rolled on the grass. He told them about Prince Edward and Prince Richard, the two little boys who were smothered in their sleep in the Tower by King Richard III. And he told them about many of the ghosts who were supposed to haunt the Tower: Ann Boleyn with her head under her arm, the spirit of Margaret Pole running screaming from her executioner as he hacked her to bits, the two little boys in their nightgowns clutching each other, and Henry VI pacing in Wakefield Tower. How no one, not even the Yeoman Warders, would go in the Salt Tower at night for fear of the invisible hands that would try to strangle them. Suki adored it all. But then again, Nan reflected, when the ordinary conversation over the breakfast table consists of deciding how to approach a widow with the detailed instructions of her dead husband, Suki was unlikely to be frightened by any reference to spirits.

The Ravenmaster recognized her, of course; he allowed them right into the raven mews, where his assistants goggled at the way the Tower ravens, which *they* could only handle wearing thick leather falconry gauntlets, acted as sweet as doves around her. They goggled even more when the same happened with Suki, ravens coming up to both of them to be scratched and made much of, making little happy chuckling sounds the entire time. Neville wandered among them, the only one with unclipped feathers, and seemed to be holding court among his relatives.

After that, of course, Nan and Suki got quite special treatment indeed, being taken to places where most visitors were never allowed, and eventually having tea with the Ravenmaster and his wife in their little flat within the Tower itself. Neville behaved himself beautifully, saying "Thank you" very nicely when presented with biscuits soaked in blood, a chopped boiled egg, and fresh fruit to eat. "It's what we feed the others," the Ravenmaster said. "That, an' plenty of fresh meat."

"I *know*!" said Neville, with such enthusiasm that they all laughed.

"Neville gets almost the same with us," Nan told him. "Though we've given him things like fish, too, when we're at the seaside, and he quite likes that."

"Mmmmm fish!" agreed Neville. Nan reflected that he was truly showing off his vocabulary for the Ravenmaster, who had been Ravenmaster when Neville had first flown off to be with Nan.

After tea, they all took their leave of the Ravenmaster and the other Yeoman Warders, and at a little shop across from the Tower, Nan indulged Suki's passion for souvenirs by buying her a very pretty printed paper fan with views of the Tower on one side and pictures of the Yeoman Warders and the ravens on the other. Suki played carefully with it all the way home on the 'buses, opening and closing it and admiring the pictures to her heart's content.

"Since you're studying the Tudors in history now," Nan said, as they got off the last 'bus on the corner and walked to the flat, "I think I should take you to Hampton Court Palace, which Henry stole from—" She waited for the answer.

"Cardn'l Woolsey!" Suki said immediately.

"Well done! It will be an all-day excursion, and Neville will have to stay home, I am afraid." She felt both a twinge of self-satisfaction and a twinge of guilt. She and Sarah had visited once, and Sarah had said several times she would like to go back. *But Sarah is getting lavish dinners and opera performances. I think we're due some cheap fun.* "But we will certainly take the train!"

"Coo!" Suki exclaimed, truly excited now.

They came in the door to find Neville there ahead of them—not a great surprise, since he didn't have to take several 'buses to get home but could fly direct. Sarah was still in her dressing gown with her hair down, drinking a cup of tea at the fire and reading over some papers in her other hand. She looked up at them and smiled as Suki ran to show her the fan.

"Did you get to talk with the Ravenmaster?" she asked them both.

"Better than that, he took us to the raven mews, and then we had tea with him and his wife. They spoiled Neville outrageously," Nan replied. "Digestive biscuits soaked in blood, if you please! Now he's going to be wanting them here!"

"Might," said Neville, giving a toss of his head.

Anything else they might have said was interrupted by a knock on the door. Sarah squeaked with embarrassment at being caught in her dressing gown so late in the day and ran for her room. Nan waited until she was safely inside before answering.

"Just the person I wanted to see!" said John Watson, looking particularly dapper in a very handsome dark suit and a school tie. "Holmes would like to make use of your special Talents, Nan."

Nan blinked at him in shock. Since when did Sherlock Holmes have need of "occult" abilities? "Holmes? Surely not—"

"Oh I assure you, he is entirely serious. May I come in and explain?" John asked, making a little gesture at the sitting room.

"You can at least listen to me and decide if what Holmes wants from you is practical or not."

Nan stood aside and waved him in. "Take any seat, Doctor. Sarah will be out shortly—as you know, she is dealing with the spirits haunting Magdalena von Dietersdorf, and that can only be done at night, so she has been sleeping by day."

"Well, as I said, it is you I wish to speak to principally," Watson pointed out. He took the seat Sarah had been occupying until her flight to the bedroom. "Holmes wants to know something of the limits of your Talent, and whether or not you could use it to learn something of great importance to an exceptionally dangerous case. And he would like to discuss this at length with you."

"Tonight?" Nan asked, startled. "Now?"

"If possible. He's under a time constraint, I fear, and *if* you can do what he needs, the opportunity to utilize your abilities on his behalf will come very soon and may not come again." If she had any doubts that this was some whim on Holmes' part, they were immediately dispelled, both by the expression on Watson's face and the anxiety in his thoughts.

"But Magdalena has asked me to come to the opera again tonight," Sarah exclaimed in dismay as she came out of her bedroom, now properly dressed. "And I told her I would. That would leave Suki alone for the better part of the night—"

A flash of anger passed through Nan and she kept from snapping at her friend with the greatest of difficulty. *There is nothing important about going to the opera performance!* she thought with outrage. *This is work! Why is it that Sarah's pleasure should interfere with an important request?*

But Watson was holding up a hand. "This won't take long. If Nan can run out now, I'll have her back before nine, ten at the most. Surely your landlady would be willing to look after Suki for an extra shilling or two for that long?"

"I don' need no lookin' arter!" Suki exclaimed rebelliously, but Sarah at least had the grace to blush and look discomfited.

Wasn't she just boasting about the obscene amount of money Magdalena is paying her? Surely she can spare a few shillings out of that! Nan thought resentfully.

"Of course; what was I thinking?" Sarah said contritely. "I'll run down and ask her, but I am sure she will say yes." Before Nan could say anything, Sarah had snatched up the small purse in which she kept the money she used for cabs and the like and was out the door.

"Well," Suki said thoughtfully, looking at the closed door. "Mrs. 'Orace do make sugar-biscuits sometimes when she's mindin' me. . . ."

Sarah was back within a few minutes. "Run on down to Mrs. Horace, Suki," she said as soon as the door was open. "She'll give you the birds' suppers. You're to feed them, make sure they can get to their night perches and leave a single gaslight burning here, then you're to have supper with her and make gingerbread afterward. If Nan is not back by bedtime, you are to nap on her sofa until Nan comes home."

Suki gave a whoop and ran down the stairs. Sarah picked up her shawl, put her coin purse into the larger reticule, and pinned on her hat.

"I'll just leave a little early," she said and, with a smile, before Nan could say anything else at all, she did just that, putting on her shawl as she closed the door behind her.

Well . . . that was odd.

Neville and Grey had flown to their feeding perches and gazed quizzically after her. Then they both turned to look at Nan. Birds did not have facial expressions as such, but Nan sensed they were as puzzled by Sarah's behavior as she was.

Nan throttled down her annoyance, and turned to John Watson. "Well," she said. "That's that. We might as well go."

"Excellent." He stood up; she gathered her things and they left together. *But there's going to be something said if this goes on much longer . . .*

Holmes was pacing when they arrived, and by the scent of gunpowder in the air, he had been making additions to his "VR" design picked out in bullet holes in one wall. Nan mentally shook her head as they came in. *Mrs. Hudson is far more tolerant than virtually any other landlady in London. Holmes must be paying her a fortune for the privilege of living here and doing as he pleases.* Then again, given that he performed services for crowned heads, he could probably afford to pay a fortune.

He flung himself down in his favorite chair as they took their seats. "I am sorry to have brought you out with so little notice, Miss Killian, but I am in a position of some urgency. I am . . ." He hesitated; his long face betrayed no emotion, but she understood he was wrestling with how much to tell her. "I have been in pursuit of a very dangerous man for quite a long time. I can trace his actions, but so far, I have been at a loss to discover exactly who he is. Until now, however. I am now in a position to identify him absolutely—*if* you think you would be able to see into a person's thoughts from, say, a distance of a hundred feet or so."

I am very glad I was able to demonstrate my power to his satisfaction! The notion that *she* would be able to provide real assistance to Sherlock Holmes was . . . rather heady. And it went a very long way toward salving her hurt feelings at being left on the sidelines. "I think I can do that," Nan said cautiously. "Provided he does not have some form of protection on his thoughts."

"Protection? As you instructed me to produce?" Holmes replied, tilting his head a little, and raising an eyebrow. "Or did you mean something else entirely?"

"Well, there are several kinds of protection that would make it either difficult for me to read thoughts, or dangerous," Nan said slowly. "For instance, if he suspects, or actually *knows,* that such a thing as telepathy exists, and suspects there may be a telepath about, he could do as I taught you. If he himself is a telepath, he will *always* protect his thoughts, as a side effect of having to protect himself from being bombarded constantly by the random thoughts all around him."

Holmes had opened his mouth as she got to "if he himself is a telepath," but had not interrupted her, and now gave her a quizzical look. "Really?" he said instead.

"The control of this ability begins with locking others *out* of one's mind. When the Talent begins to bloom, the first thing that happens is that you are aware of the strong thoughts of those around you. Then their weaker thoughts. Then the thoughts of those farther from you, until there is a veritable babble in your head, like being in the middle of a huge crowd of people all the time. There are a great many natural telepaths who never had the training I did, and who are locked up in madhouses for that very reason," Nan said with a sigh. "They cannot keep out the thoughts of others, and eventually they cannot tell the difference between their thoughts and those of everyone else."

Holmes pondered that for a moment. "That is entirely logical," he said. "A logical consequence of having the ability itself—but go on. How else could thoughts be protected?"

"Do not bark at me—but magicians like the Watsons can also protect their minds from being read, if they are protecting themselves from magic. And *they* have the ability to protect others as well. So." She clasped her hands in her lap and looked down at them for a moment, before looking up at him. "Do you have any reason to believe the person you want me to read would come under any of those categories?"

"No," Holmes told her. "I believe him to be nothing more than an uncommon criminal. Clever, extremely careful, methodical, resourceful, intelligent, dangerous, and ruthless. But I have never seen anything to make me believe he is anything more than that. He is very high in the service of the man I wish to identify; very possibly one of the highest of his trusted lieutenants. He does not know that I know this. I am going to be able to approach him on another pretext entirely, but I will, in the course of our conversation, ask him several questions that I calculate will bring the thoughts of his master to the surface, even though those questions will superficially have nothing to do with the man. Those are what I hope you will be able to read."

"I will certainly give it my best effort," Nan told him. "And given what you have told me, I should be able to do as you request. When will this be, do you know?"

"My meeting with him will be the day after tomorrow," Holmes replied. "I will have you in place before I arrive; I will take my place, and he will approach me. We are to meet at the British Museum Reading Room, where you will certainly have no difficulty in looking busy." His mouth quirked in a sardonic smile. "I cannot imagine that you and Sarah do not have passes to the Reading Room, but if you do not, Mycroft can certainly procure them for you tomorrow."

"We have passes. I am in greater danger of being distracted by my books than of being unable to look busy," she admitted. "Tell me where you are to sit; I can arrange to be completely out of sight and out of earshot."

Holmes sighed a little in relief. "That would be highly desirable. I do not wish him to connect you with me in any way. I am not exaggerating the danger, Miss Killian. The nearer I come to identifying this fiend, the more danger accrues to myself and to anyone associated with me. It is why Watson invented the ruse of living elsewhere, for he is known to be my friend and confidant, and if this monster thinks I am close on his heels, he will not hesitate to strike at my friends. If Mycroft had not given me his assurance that you are as brave as a lioness and just as capable of defending yourself, I would not put you at hazard in this venture, at all."

Nan inclined her head in acknowledgement, but smiled inwardly. So, Sherlock Holmes himself gave her the compliment of being "brave as a lioness!" And even more important, he acknowledged that she could defend herself. "So. British Museum Reading Room. Where?"

"I am to meet him at the absolute north, at nine in the morning," Holmes replied. "By which I am sure he means to be at the desk nearest the circumference of the room at due north by the compass."

Nan knew the Reading Room well; the walls of the great, round room were floor-to-ceiling bookshelves, and divided study desks ran like the spokes of a wheel from the double circular hub of the catalogue cases and the librarian's desk almost to the shelves.

"Then I will set myself up no later than eight within easy . . . let us call it eavesdropping distance. If he will be due north, then I will try for north-northwest. You might not recognize me, Mister Holmes, as I shall be in my most formidable bluestocking guise." She smiled a little.

"All the better. Miss Killian, I am in your debt." He reached across the space between them to shake her hand. She was pleased that it was the sort of good, solid handshake a man could have been expected to give a man, and she returned it in kind.

"Just leave your surface thoughts open to me, by concentrating on him," she said. "I will be able to tell who it is you are meeting from that, and I should be able to find his mind in that way, if I have not already sensed him because he is thinking of you."

"Logical. This Talent of yours follows good, sound logic." He did *not* add, *Unlike your messy, ridiculous magic, Watson,* but she had the notion he was thinking it. He was, at the moment, literally guarding his thoughts, as she had taught him to. That was just as well; she had the uneasy feeling that there were a great many things she did not want to know tucked away in his head. Not about *him*—about some of the sort of cases that Watson would never even hint about to Conan Doyle.

She hesitated a moment. "Mister Holmes . . . allow me to offer my services in this way indefinitely. I am sure you are perfectly capable of telling when a man is lying, for instance, but *I* can tell you what he is thinking at the time he is lying. If you are interviewing him, I can tell you what he is not revealing to you. I could be useful in similar ways."

"Miss Killian, you surprise and gratify me," Holmes replied, releasing her hand. "I thought that you and Miss Lyon-White were inseparable."

"We have on occasion divided our forces," Nan said with a shrug. "And at the moment, she is . . . de-haunting Magdalena von Dietersdorf. As well as undertaking a closer examination of that lady, which may come in handy for you at some later date, if you are still pursuing the case of her missing sister."

"I am," Holmes replied. "And anything Miss Lyon-White can tell me will be exceedingly useful. But I am surprised you are not assisting her."

"The ghosts, bar one or two, are proving more tedious than troublesome to send on their way." Nan picked her next words with care. "The diva has made it quite clear that she has no need of *me*, so I have been dispensed with, and would just as soon find more occupation than merely serving as a tutor to our young ward."

Holmes had snorted at the mention of ghosts, but nodded at the rest. "Then I think when Watson does not require your aid—" He glanced at Watson.

"Oh, I will. But I am a generous friend, and am willing to share," Watson chuckled.

"Then there are quite the number of occasions when you could be of great assistance to me. But let us get this little adventure out of the way first." Although Holmes spoke of it lightly, Nan could tell he was not *taking* it lightly. He was concerned, and clearly considered this as dangerous as any venture in which he would have instructed Watson to bring his pistol.

"Then I will *not* see you in two days' time," she said. "Might I suggest, since you are worried, that you come to our lodgings at around noon in one of your disguises? That way if your quarry has *any* suspicion that you are close to identifying him, he will not connect the two of us."

"Excellent. I shall be a curate; an entirely harmless country curate. You *do* entertain curates from time to time?" He asked the question as if he truly expected her to say "no."

"You would be astonished to discover that psychical Talent and wearing the cloth are not mutually exclusive," she replied with another smile. "Nor are magic and the clerical collar."

"I am relieved to hear it. Until then?" He stood up, and so did she.

"Until then, Mister Holmes," she replied, and once again shook his hand, with that same firm handshake. *I think I would ask him to play chess with me some time, except that I know he would play only to humor me, and probably trounce me within a few moves.*

John accompanied her out to the street and obtained a hansom for her. "I was serious about needing your services," he said as he handed her in. "I'll come along after this business is concluded, and we'll discuss it."

"Thank you, Doctor Watson," she said, but had no time to say anything else before the cab rolled away.

Checking the watch around her neck, she was relieved to see it was not yet nine. She would be home well in time for Suki's bedtime; in plenty of time to read her a story, in fact. *Is Suki old enough for that amusing American, Mark Twain? I think she might be.*

Nan bent her head over the volume of poetry by Thomas Wyatt, making notes in a leather-bound notebook next to her. She had several more volumes of work by much more obscure Tudor poets next to her; if anyone asked, she was working on a theory that some poetry attributed to others was, in fact, by Wyatt. She had been at this practically from the moment the Reading Room had opened. She and Sarah had passes, of course; thanks to Lord A, that had been one of the first items they'd obtained after they had settled in to the flat. Holmes and Watson *obviously* had passes as well; it would have been absurd of them not to, given how often Holmes must need bits of obscure information that could not be found in his own archives. As for their quarry, well, if he was as ruthless and clever as Holmes said, he could have gotten a pass any number of ways, including quite legitimately.

Today she had costumed herself to be completely unapproachable, and was dressed in such a severe style that several young female scholars had settled next to her for protection, like more timid hens around the matriarch of the yard. She wore an absolutely plain dark gray skirt without even a hint of bustle, a jacket in the same color cut in almost mathematical proportions, and a blindingly white blouse with a plain gray stone brooch pinned precisely at her throat. Her gray hat was a masterwork, absolutely designed to put off any suggestions that it might be "pretty" or "becoming", and she had wire-rimmed glasses with plain glass lenses anchored to her face. Her hair had been ruthlessly scraped back and contained into a tight bun at the nape of her neck, rather than the soft pompadour she usually sported. Her boots were absolutely sensible, and were, in fact, a pair she had used to hike down country lanes.

What could not be seen was that if, for some reason, from fire in the Reading Room to the attempted murder of Holmes, she needed to run, the severe skirt was split for just that purpose. That jacket had been made of fabric cut on the bias, which would stretch and give her as much freedom of movement as her bloomer suit, and her umbrella was of the same style as that of their formidable friend from Egypt, solid enough to knock a man unconscious, with a sharpened ferrule that could, at a pinch, be used to stab someone.

She had not thought it advisable to bring her pistol in her stout black handbag, although she had considered it.

She was sitting rather nearer to the north than she thought

Holmes would have been comfortable with; in fact, she was a mere two desks away from the one pointing due north, but that could not be helped. She had not been the only early scholar here, and it had appeared that several readers had particular places they "always" set up in, and this was the best she could do. At least she had her back to the relevant area; that should ensure their quarry would assume she was not there to spy on him.

So she made her notes on the poetry of the Tudors and kept her mind open, just brushing the thoughts of those around her. Mostly the background murmur was pleasant; the well-regulated brains of eager seekers of arcane bits of knowledge. People who knew what information they wanted and how to find it, if it existed at all.

Not *everyone* was here on scholastic pursuits, however. It turned out there were a couple of rather embarrassing minds she shied clear of; it seemed the Reading Room was also a hotbed of assignation for the bohemian set. Not all the passion in this room was held between leather covers!

Miss Killian. I am approaching the desk.

The thought blazed across her mind as clearly and sharply as if Holmes had spoken it aloud. She put down her pen and frowned, placing her index finger beneath a line as if something in it puzzled her, and let her thoughts join with those of Holmes.

She didn't dare delve beneath the surface thoughts; there was so *much* going on under the surface she knew she would get lost if she did. She was quite used to being one of the more intelligent people in a room; she knew at that moment that Holmes cast her quite in the shade. It seemed impossible that he should be able to think about so many things at once.

Holmes moved into place without spotting the man he was to meet, but the desk next to his was empty, and from his surface thoughts she knew he assumed the fellow was waiting for *him* to sit down before he himself made his appearance.

And so it was. Holmes had taken the precaution of bringing a magazine from the periodical section so as to appear as if he was *not* waiting for someone. He had leafed through about a quarter of its pages when he was joined by a tall man who sat at that empty desk.

Nan had had *no* trouble picking him out of the crowd as he'd approached Holmes; his mind was full of Holmes' face. But he did not know Holmes by that name; Holmes was in one of his thinner disguises; wearing his own face, but a suit that was several years out of date, a bit shabby but painfully clean, with a shirt with slightly worn collar and cuffs, and an absolutely plain, unpretentious tie without even a stickpin.

Nan surveyed the quarry through Holmes' sidelong glances. The newcomer was tall, as tall as Holmes. He was what Sarah would have called a "natty" dresser; a very modern brown suit just on the correct side of "showy," demonstrably expensive. He wore a trilby rather than a bowler that precisely matched his suit, and there was a gold watch chain crossing the front of his vest. Either his hair was very short or he was partially bald; what little of it there was seemed to be a mousy blond.

His face was remarkably bland. In fact, he looked a bit like a waxwork statue with a faint smile sculpted into the lips, a smile that did not reach his eyes. But the thoughts beneath . . . after one look, Nan kept herself to the surface thoughts. First, she was not altogether sure he *wouldn't* sense something if she went deeper, because his thoughts were those of a great predator, and every little external signal caught his attention until he could dismiss it as harmless. And second . . . she would have to have a much better reason than helping Holmes to delve into that cesspit of a mind.

"So," the quarry said, in exactly the sort of low, soft voice that was permissible here in the Reading Room. "You'd be Mister Meier, then?"

"I would, indeed, good sir," said Holmes. His voice had taken on a Germanic accent, a good bit thicker than Magdalena's, with a coloring of hopeful cheer. "It is my hope that we can do business together. I have brought sketches of products of the sort you requested."

Holmes slid over two or three pieces of paper; through the man's eyes, Nan saw that they held several sketches of what appeared to be common items of furniture—except that each of them had a secret. There were one or more hiding places concealed by sliding panels or false bottoms in each of them.

"Those are our regular line, sir," Holmes went on. "But if you have something specific in mind, or wish something exclusive, we have draftsmen and craftsmen who can design and build whatever you require."

The man looked over the pages of sketches. *This fellow's work will suit the boss very well,* he thought, and "the boss's" face flashed across his mind. "We'll need exclusives," he replied. "Our clients are very particular, and they wouldn't be happy to see a piece that they owned duplicated in someone else's study."

He speaks like a gentleman, but he has to think out everything carefully before he says it. Well, that suggested his origins were no higher than Nan's. And when he was carefully choosing his words, behind that, he was still thinking about "the boss," and again, the man's face, though not his name, flashed across his mind.

"Our draftsmen have learned their mastery from Chinese and Arabic craftsmen," Holmes said, with just a hint of servility in his tone now, the sort of thing calculated to appeal to someone who had money and was willing to spend it. "We can put a concealed space anywhere in a piece that you wish, and use a variety of hidden openings. Whatever your clients require, we can furnish. Whatever they wish to keep concealed will remain so, to the most thorough examination."

The man again thought about how pleased "the boss" would be with this. "May I keep these?" he asked, not giving them back.

"I brought them with that express intention," replied Holmes, again, groveling just a trifle. "We would be honored to take your commissions."

The man folded the sketches in half and tucked them into the front inside pocket of his coat.

"We'll be in touch," the man said, and offered his hand to Holmes, who shook it. "Thank you for meeting with me here, rather than at your shop." *Because the boss wants no direct contact between the maker of these cabinets and any of us. Good thing for us, he's ready to turn himself inside out to make a sale.*

"Not at all, sir, not at all. I come here often, it was no trouble." Holmes did not rise when the man did; and at that moment, Nan had to suppress the urge to shout at Holmes not to move. Because as the man strode away, there was another flash of thought.

Exactly what he would do to Holmes if Holmes made any attempt to follow him. Nan was glad she was already bending over her "work," because the pure, cold, calculated violence was enough to make her feel faint. That *anyone* would not only consider doing that to another human being who merely *looked* as if he was following but go so far as to plan out the exact moves and timing was enough to stop her heart. And she was only too glad to detach herself from the man's mind and wall herself away from everyone else.

As she had told Holmes she would, she stayed another half an hour by her watch, then got up and returned her books to the return cart at the end of the row of desks—in the Reading Room, mere mortals were not permitted to return books to the shelves, as they could not be counted upon to put them in their proper places. When she glanced over to the desk where Holmes had been, he was already gone.

It was not as difficult as it might have been thought to obtain a cab wearing this guise. She had but to fix her chosen cabby with a gimlet eye, and, cowed, he brought his rig in to the curb for her to enter. She took her place in the middle of the single seat, and although a strange man hurried up to try to join her, another steely, forbidding look made him apologize and run to catch another rig.

She was very glad to get home, and, inside the shelter of her bedroom, take her hair down and put it back up in a more comfortable style. Pulling it back that tightly threatened to give her a headache after too long. She was also glad to change into a more comfortable tea gown.

Sarah, of course, had been fast asleep for hours. The birds were in their own room, playing with their toys, so the flat was quiet except for the sounds of Mrs. Horace doing her housework and the traffic on the street outside.

Once changed, she joined Suki at the table, and together they went over her arithmetic work. Neither of them enjoyed it—but both of them knew it had to be done. On some days, Suki was sullen and resentful when presented with a page full of problems to work, but today, perhaps sensing Nan's growing irritation with Sarah, she worked dutifully at her task.

Eventually, she got the entire page right, and Nan rewarded her with a drawing of fairies to color. The little girl was still carefully filling in the flower-dresses with bright pink and blue when Mrs. Horace came tapping at the door.

"Miss Nan?" their landlady said, "It's nearly luncheon, but there is a Reverend Tellworth here to see you. Shall I hold luncheon and show him in, or show him in, bring luncheon and bring up enough for three?"

"Show him in, and we'll entertain him, thank you," Nan replied. "Curates are always hungry."

Mrs. Horace giggled. " 'Deed they are, miss," she agreed, and trotted down the stairs.

A moment later, Holmes tapped at the door, and Nan rose to let him in. And if she hadn't known it was Holmes, she never would have recognized him. The man stood with a stoop and seemed to be several inches shorter than Holmes. His cheeks were sunken, his nose had a long hook in it, and he peered out at her, not only from beneath his clerical hat, but from beneath a solid bar of bushy gray eyebrows.

But as soon as he got inside, he stood up straight—and there was Sherlock Holmes, in a crisp black cleric's suit with the proper dog collar, giving her just a hint of a smile. She smiled back. "Suki, clear the table, it's time for luncheon. Sir, if you'll take a seat?"

Holmes nodded and took one of the chairs as Suki removed her schoolbooks and drawing materials. No sooner was the table cleared than Mrs. Horace appeared at the door with a laden tray. There were a few moments of setting things to rights on the table, then Mrs. Horace was gone, and Holmes finally spoke.

But not to her.

"You would be Suki, I believe?" he said, offering his hand to the child. "I am Sherlock Holmes."

Suki actually squeaked with excitement. She knew who Holmes was; Nan and Sarah had read some of Doyle's stories to her. "Gor blimey!" she said, then, remembering her manners, shook his hand gravely, and said, quite properly, "Pleasure t'meetcher, Sir."

"Suki shares my abilities, Mister Holmes," Nan told him. "She's not ready to show her paces yet, but in a few years we think she will be sharing our ventures."

"Then perhaps in a few years you might consider working with my Baker Street Irregulars, Suki," Holmes said. "You sound as if you know your way about the streets, and there are times when it would be very advantageous to my young scallywags to have someone with Miss Nan's Talents on hand."

"Cor!" Suki said with enthusiasm.

"She passes very well for a boy now, which is what I have her dress as when she goes out to play," Nan told him. "If she was to do work for you, away from an adult, you should probably let your Irregulars believe that she *is* a boy. But that isn't why you are here." She ate a bite of the chicken sandwich Mrs. Horace had supplied them. Sunday's fowl would not stretch as far as a Sunday roast would, but there were always sandwiches out of it on the Monday, and the bones would be the basis of supper's soup. "Your quarry did not think of his superior's name, and I am inclined to believe he does not actually know it. The man in question is only known as 'The Boss,' as far as I could tell. But I would know his face in a thousand; there were memories of The Boss in several situations and settings, and several partial disguises."

"Well, that does complicate matters a trifle, but it is nothing I did not anticipate," Holmes replied. He had brought with him the sort of leather document case that lawyers—and men of the cloth—often traveled with, and had placed it at the side of his chair. Now he bent down to reach inside and emerged with a thick stack of paper. "If you would be so kind as to interrupt your luncheon while I display some photographs to you?"

"Not at all," Nan said, and set aside the sandwich while Holmes laid pictures down on the cream-colored tablecloth between them, one at a time.

Some were actual photographs, both posed and candid. She wondered how he had gotten *those*. Some were photographs cut from magazines or newspapers. Some were newspaper sketches. She identified the third one he displayed as being of their earlier quarry, earning herself the accolade of an eyebrow lifted in obvious approval from Holmes. All had one thing in common; they were of men who were, outwardly at least, highly respectable.

Which would only make sense if this criminal genius was managing to work his wiles completely undetected by anyone but Holmes.

It had crossed her mind that this . . . obsession of Holmes . . . might be some figment of his own highly colored imagination, seeing a conspiracy where there was none. But Watson had not warned her against this, and she rather thought he would have taken her aside if *he* had not been convinced that Holmes was on to something.

"I should warn you," Holmes said abruptly, as he laid down another picture for her examination, "That absolutely no one shares my view about the existence of this criminal genius except for my brother Mycroft, John and Mary Watson, and, I believe, your Lord Alderscroft. And even Mycroft has his doubts. I have not ventured to voice my theory too often, because if the possibility is ridiculed before I can bring the proof, a very dangerous man will have been alerted, and will find means to thwart me."

"And . . . people already regard you a bit askance, I suspect," Nan observed. "Such an assertion that an all-powerful master criminal was behind a great deal of the criminal activity in England would likely be taken as a sign that your mind had finally snapped."

Holmes sighed. "That would be more amusing if it were less true." He laid down the last picture. "So . . . the 'Boss' was none of these?"

She shook her head. "I am sorry—"

"Do not be," he interrupted. "I was saving the least likely— and yet, in my mind, the most likely—for last." He removed a slim, leather-bound book from the case, replacing the stack of photographs inside. She saw it had the unlikely title of *The Dynamics of an Asteroid*, although Holmes opened it too quickly for her to discern the name of the author.

He spread it out at the frontispiece, which was an expensively printed photograph of a gentleman standing beside a book-laden desk, hands clasped in front of him, looking straight into the camera lens. If the rest of the men in those pictures could have been described as looking "respectable," this man was positively a monument to proper breeding and upbringing.

There was just one problem.

Nan had not one speck of doubt that *this* man was the one she had seen in their target's memory. The one that a violent murderer thought of as "The Boss."

"This is he," she said immediately.

"You have no doubts?" Holmes replied.

"None whatsoever. This is he. And I can tell you that even as the man who met with you is absolutely the most cold-blooded killer I have ever had the misfortune to encounter, he looks up to *this* man as being even more cold-blooded and deadly than himself." She tapped her finger on the page. "The man you met today, Mister Holmes, fears *this* man as he fears no one and nothing else on earth."

Holmes regarded her gravely. "And yet only you and I, and his lieutenants, would ever believe that Professor James Moriarty is anything but a highly respected professional educator and a genius mathematician."

8

Holmes was long gone by the time Sarah woke up near teatime, and at that point, Suki and Nan had finished the lessons early. Wrapped in a white cotton dressing gown with blue trim, she joined Suki and Nan for tea.

Weary of hearing about the fine suppers Sarah was enjoying, Nan had gone out after Holmes left and made a few purchases, so today's tea was rather generous, with purchased tea cakes of a sort Mrs. Horace was not comfortable attempting, salted nuts, Turkish delight, chocolates, and candied fruit. The chicken made a final appearance as a salad in the sandwiches, but instead of only the one sort of sandwich that they generally had at tea, Nan had gotten enough good things that Mrs. Horace had added jam, egg, and ham sandwiches for more variety. And Nan had gotten proper clotted cream to go with the scones. She'd told Mrs. Horace to have some of the bounty herself, of course. It wasn't fair to pass all that under their landlady's nose and not share.

Suki was in heaven. Sarah blinked a little at the amount of food, but did not hesitate to join in. The sandwiches disappeared, and very soon they were making serious inroads on the savories and sweets.

But then, breakfast was a long time ago, she didn't eat any luncheon, and it is going to be a very long time between now and when she has that fancy supper tonight.

She was not as full of details about last night's opera

performance, since it was a repetition of the one she had already seen the night before. For her part, Nan elected to remain silent on exactly what Holmes wanted her for. She couldn't keep the fact that Holmes had visited a secret, Suki was too full of excitement that the great man had said she might one day help him. But when Sarah asked what she had been doing, she simply shrugged, and said, "Nothing like as fascinating as what you are doing. Holmes wanted me to help him determine whether or not someone was telling him the truth—and what they were not telling him. He brought a fellow to the Reading Room and talked a while, and I told him what I had learned when he came by here." That was entirely true. Holmes *did* want her help with exactly that. He just hadn't wanted that sort of help today. "And he and I looked through some photographs to see if I recognized anyone I saw there." Also true.

Thank goodness Suki isn't old enough to be interested enough in what we said to remember it and contradict my version.

"At any rate, I'll be spending a quiet evening here at home with Suki," she continued. "Are you going to the opera again?" She tried very hard to keep her voice indifferent, and her temper in check. The longer this went on, the more unfair it seemed. And Nan couldn't help but resent the fact that Sarah was in that private box all alone—a private box she could have invited Nan to share without Magdalena being any the wiser. Mrs. Horace could have looked after Suki again, and Nan could have come straight to the opera house by cab and home the same way after the performance was over.

"I think Magdalena is lonely and misses her sister, even though she pretends otherwise," Sarah said, apologetically. "Her sister used to sit in that box, every single night, and I think it makes her feel a little better to look up and see that it isn't empty anymore."

It appeared that Sarah was becoming very sympathetic to Magdalena's situation. *Well, good. Perhaps Sarah can get more information out of her that way.* "Did her sister attend the opera every night back in Germany as well?" Nan asked.

"When Magdalena was singing leading roles, yes," Sarah said. "The whole family attended when they could, but her sister was always there, faithful, and making sure to start the applause."

Odd. That doesn't quite fit with Magdalena's indifference when her sister eloped with that young man.

"And her fiancé didn't object to her going out every night without him?" Nan asked archly.

Sarah shrugged. "I suppose he was not a great admirer of opera. Some people find it unbearable. Or maybe he didn't care as much for Johanna as for her father's connections. Herr von Dietersdorf is not very political himself, but he knows a great many important political people, and I gather the young man has political ambitions."

So it wouldn't matter to him which sister he married. It might even be advantageous to be married to someone like Magdalena. She is unlikely to care about anything but her own career, so the last thing she would do would be to meddle in politics herself.

"At any rate," Sarah continued, "I suppose having a great artiste for a wife could do a young politician a great deal of good, so long as when she is off the stage, she is content to be ornamental and be much admired. Being a musician is quite respectable, not like being an actress, especially, I gather, in Germany. If Magdalena gets to the same level of fame as, say, Adelina Patti, she will be regarded as a national treasure."

"I can imagine she would like that," Nan commented, trying not to sound cynical. "The respectability of a *gut hausfrau*, without having to actually *be* a *hausfrau*, with plenty of adulation and politicians anxious to become acquainted with her."

She did not mention it might be difficult to maintain that respectability if she was going to entertain wealthy admirers . . .

Then again, if Lord A's stories are to be believed, half of the upper crust spends all their time running in and out of bedrooms that aren't theirs at weekend house parties, and somehow they all manage to keep a veneer of respectability.

"Well, being the ornament at political gatherings would probably be restful for Magdalena, when you think about it," Sarah pointed out. "It would be very much like being on stage, without the work of learning music and doing all the performing. I think she would be very good at it. And certainly there is a lot to be admired about her."

"Sarah, Suki and I were thinking of visiting Hampton Court

Palace while she is studying the Tudors," Nan said, getting a little tired of hearing Magdalena's praises sung. "It would be an all-day affair, which would leave the flat quiet for you to sleep; I think it would be possible to take Neville, unless Grey would be lonely without him."

Neville and Grey exchanged a long look. Nan heard a kind of whispering in her mind, like conversation too far away to make out. "Stay," Neville said, with a very definite nod. And she got the very strong image of the time she and Neville had gone to a tea shop, where, although she had eaten at one of the outside tables, the waitress had made a great nuisance of herself, trying to shoo him away.

"All right. I'll make sure you both get something special, and some new toys to play with," she promised. "If I can convince Mrs. Horace to soak digestive biscuits in blood for you, you shall have that. And I'll make sure to get Grey some grapes and nuts."

Neville made an approving, purring sound, and Grey bobbed her head with excitement.

"I wish I could go with you," Sarah said wistfully.

Well, now you know how we *feel, being left out of all your fun.* Nan couldn't help it. It probably wasn't a very nice thing to think, but . . . *Well, at least I didn't say it out loud.*

"Wisht ye'd go with us," Suki replied, also wistfully. "It ain't gonna be the same without you."

For one moment, Nan thought Sarah just might give in and "sacrifice" a day of Magdalena—

But, no.

"I'm sorry, Suki," she said, leaning over to kiss the little girl. "Another time. Right now Magdalena needs me."

Suki sighed, but didn't indulge in a fit of temper as some children might have. "Jes' 'member we needs ye too," she said, "Kin I be 'scuzed?"

Sarah gave her permission, and she retired to her room to play. Nan reflected that, for a child who had had such a terrible beginning, she was positively angelic most of the time. *Someone* must have given the little mite the love and affection children needed in order to learn to show love and affection in return. The period of nightmares and panic fits had finally passed, but then again, she had two adults she trusted who were able to see and understand her nightmares and knew exactly what had to be done to wake her out of them and soothe them away.

Nan gazed thoughtfully at the door to Suki's room. "Do you think we ought to send her to Memsa'b?" she asked.

"Suki? That is a very good question." Sarah pondered it, and Nan savored a moment of inner rejoicing that she had *finally* found a subject that would take Sarah's mind off the opera diva.

"She has a quick mind, and has been asking me questions that I frankly cannot answer," Nan continued. "About the stars and the moon, for instance, and she doesn't want fanciful answers, she wants the scientific ones. When she first came to us, it was out of the question, of course."

Sarah nodded, remembering Suki's night terrors. "Memsa'b would love to have her. And we can afford to *pay* for her schooling, or rather, Lord A can, which would not come at all amiss. It would do the other children no end of good to have someone from her class among them."

Nan had to laugh at that. "It would, wouldn't it! Some of the ones that are slacking would start putting some effort in, seeing a little street Arab excelling while they fell behind."

"And you know there are always some who put on airs; Suki would put them right straight in their places." Sarah giggled. "Remember when you told Arabelle that she needn't put her nose in the air, because if she ever went outside, you knew pickpockets that would take one look at her and laugh at her for being such a know-nothing, pompous little ass."

"And they would have, too," Nan agreed. "Let's ask Suki about it. I'll abide by *her* decision."

Rather than call the girl in, they went to her room, by way of emphasizing that she had as much to say about this as they did.

Suki listened gravely to what they had to say about going to live at the Harton School, both the advantages and disadvantages. "The chief advantages, really, are that you will get much better teachers, and there will be other children there to play with," Sarah concluded.

"But what if Mister 'Olmes wants me ter run wi' th' Regulars?" Suki wanted to know.

"That will not be for at least three years," Nan told her firmly. "And the reason for that is that we want you to learn how to fight just as Sarah and I can. The best people to teach you that are Karamjit and Agansing. If you are going to be doing the sort of dangerous tasks the Irregulars sometimes do, we want you to be able to defend yourself."

Suki thought about that, and nodded. "Kin I come live 'ere on the 'olidays?"

"We would be very put out if you didn't want to!" Sarah exclaimed. "And actually, since the summer term has already started, you would not be joining the school until September."

The little girl sat there, her doll resting in her idle hands, thinking it out. "Oil roight," Suki said, finally. "On account'o I wants ter learn t'fight, an' I wants ter learn 'ow t'speak proper, an' I wants ter learn the stuff yer says yer dunno."

Nan grinned at that. "Memsa'b can teach you all about your special abilities, too," she pointed out. "And she will be able to tell if you've got even more that we don't know about."

"Cor. Could I fly, mebbe?" Suki asked hopefully.

They both laughed. "I don't know of *anyone* who can fly, lovie," Sarah said, still full of mirth. "But there are many other useful abilities you might have."

"Oil roight." Suki nodded. "Yer wanter play ther Puck play 'till Miss Sarah has ter go?"

"That sounds like a fine plan to me," Sarah said, getting up to fetch the toy theater from its shelf. "Which part do you want?"

Suki grinned. "Puck! An' Bottom, an' Titania, an' The-sus."

"What, not Hermia or Lysander or—"

"No," Suki replied, wrinkling up her nose. "*You* gets tha goose-parts."

When Sarah left, a few hours later, Nan had managed to forget her irritation with her friend's—well, call it what it was—*infatuation* with Magdalena. It had been like having the old Sarah back, right up until the time to leave approached, and then Sarah had seemed to lose all interest in anything except getting to the theater. Nan was put out all over again.

When Suki had gone to bed, Nan sat in the half-darkened sitting room with a book unread in her hands, frowning over the situation.

Am I jealous? There was no doubt that she was *envious,* but that was a very different matter. Who wouldn't be, given the attention and treats the opera singer had lavished on Sarah, but not on Nan.

But there was more to it than just that. For their entire lives as friends, no one had treated them as anything other than equals. Not Memsa'b and Sahib, not their servants and associates, not Lord Alderscroft, not even John and Mary Watson and Holmes.

But the moment she had set foot in Magdalena's opulent suite, she had been made to feel very much Sarah's inferior. And she had absolutely no doubt that was deliberate on Magdalena's part.

Is the woman trying to drive a wedge between us?

It was a startling thought. And the more Nan thought about it, the more certain she became that it was true. Magdalena didn't need Nan, and if she knew what Nan's abilities were, she probably didn't want Nan anywhere near, where she might pick up some unguarded thoughts, or learn something from a carelessly discarded possession. But she certainly needed Sarah, especially if she was going to continue to attract the attentions of spirits. . . .

. . . or have someone sending spirits after her.

Not that there was any evidence of that. And not that Nan knew any way to do so. Still. There were, in both occult journals and folk tales, stories of the necromancers, people who could summon and command ghosts to do their will. Such an ability was of little practical use, unless you could summon precisely the spirit who knew where he'd hidden a treasure, or your would-be victim actually had the ability to *see* ghosts. That was the problem; most people didn't. For the vast majority of the population, being set upon by ghosts would be far less troubling than an irritating fly. *Some* ghosts had the power to harm the living, but they were quite few, and in all their years together, Nan and Sarah had not encountered more than a handful.

No, if Sarah was right, and she almost always was, the revenants besieging Magdalena were the common sort of ghosts. Frightening in their uncanny selves if you allowed yourself to be frightened by them, and in their persistence, but otherwise harmless.

No, it was far more likely that for some reason unknown to Sarah, Magdalena radiated something unknown that acted to attract whatever spirits were about. And it might be just as simple as the same thing that attracted spirits to Sarah; the indefinable *something* that told them, once they came into her presence, that she could see them. Except in Magdalena it was evidently much enhanced, for her to have attracted them from all over the hotel and its grounds.

It's too bad she doesn't have Sarah's unselfish nature, that seeks to help these spirits rather than just cower under the covers and scream at the sight of them, Nan thought sourly.

The question of *why hadn't this happened before* might just possibly have an obvious answer. There was one person in Magdalena's life who had been ever-present before, and now was an absolute absence: her sister Johanna. It was not uncommon for siblings to either share the *same* occult gifts or possess the polar opposite gifts. And that might hold the secret of why Magdalena seemed indifferent, even slightly antagonistic, to her sister, while at the same time keeping her present. Unconsciously, Magdalena was aware that her sister was repelling the spirits that she attracted. Yet at the same time, their opposing natures clashed.

That still didn't solve the problem of Magdalena trying to appropriate Sarah and turn her into a kind of . . . psychic sycophant.

But I can do a few things. I can make sure I don't display any jealousy, because Sarah will almost certainly react poorly if I do. And I can see what I can do about prying Sarah out of that cat's claws.

And perhaps I can be even more active than that. If a magician can shield against thoughts . . . perhaps John or Mary Watson can shield Sarah from this insidious influence.

Like the Tower, Hampton Court Palace had its Warders, who were pleased to conduct visitors over the public parts of the buildings. Most of the Palace was *not* public; for the last hundred-odd years, the Palace had become the home to the "grace-and-favour" residents, pensioners of the Crown who were granted rent-free apartments here due to great service to Monarch and Country. Victoria had opened the Palace to be toured by the general public as the Tower was in the first year of her reign, and the part that Nan and Suki had come to see—the Tudor Palace—had undergone extensive restoration. So they got to roam to their hearts' content the Great Hall, the Great Gatehouse, the Kitchens—Suki could have spent hours in there, poking about, asking how people made Henry VIII's gargantuan meals—Wolsey's Closet, and the Royal Chapel. The corridor outside the Privy Chapel was the one said to be haunted by the ghost of Catherine Howard, who had run from her own rooms, shrieking with grief and terror, to try to speak to Henry at his prayers in the chapel when she knew her adultery had been discovered. Neither Nan nor Suki saw, heard, or felt anything, however, although a lady who had been there earlier was said to have fainted.

They had a glorious time in the Maze . . . cheekily, Nan had brought ham sandwiches and bottles of lemonade with her in her big handbag, and they had themselves a nice little picnic in one of the secluded corners of the Maze. They gazed with admiration at the Great Vine, said to be the biggest grapevine in the world, and certainly the biggest in England. And then, walking around to the south of the Palace—neither of them were very much interested in the Stuart or Baroque parts—they discovered a virtual wilderness.

"What on earth—" Nan said, turning to the guidebook, for their Warder-guide had long since deserted them at the mouth of the Maze. "It says here, this is the old Privy Garden, which has been left to go to the wild."

Suki looked up at her with a face full of hope. "C'n we go in?"

So far this had been the best day, ever, so far as Suki was concerned. She had had her first train ride. She'd roamed over a place she had only *read* about, and now things that had only been chapters in a history book were real to her. She'd gotten to play in the Great Maze—never before had she been in a place where everything around her was shut out by walls of greenery. Their little picnic had felt as private as if they were the only people for miles around.

But this was the closest thing to real wilderness that Suki had ever seen, and she was clearly eager to plunge into it like a young rabbit.

"Of course we can," Nan said with a grin. "Go on! I'll catch up with you. And don't worry about your clothing. Fun comes first."

Suki dashed off down a narrow path. Nan followed her more slowly. She knew that she could trust Suki not to do something potentially bad—like picking flowers. Even if this garden was completely gone to the wild, it still would be a terrible *faux pas* to pick flowers here. As for her, she strolled along the path Suki had taken, enjoying the clean, fresh air of the countryside and the sensation of being somewhere wild again.

A sudden swirl of wind twisted her skirts around her ankles as it spun leaves around her. With a good-natured curse, she pulled her skirts loose and shook them out, then reached up and pulled leaves out of her hair. *Oak. Ash . . . and Thorn?*

"'What hempen homespuns have we swaggering here, so near the cradle of the fairy queen?'" quoted a young male voice full of mirth.

"Robin Goodfellow, we are *not* 'hempen homespuns,'" Nan retorted, spinning, to find Puck standing behind her, hands on hips, chuckling.

Today Puck wore the semblance of a tall young man in the sort of outfit most of the gardeners here at Hampton Court Palace wore: a pair of sturdy trousers tucked into Wellington boots, a weskit with a watch-chain strung across the front, a shirt with no tie and the sleeves rolled up, and a soft cap. To complete the disguise he had a bamboo rake in one hand—although, being Puck, he could just as well have had a spade. Cold Iron troubled him not at all, being the Oldest Old One in England.

"True, true. I've missed you, Nan Killian, that I have. Where's your feathered fiend?" Nan crossed the distance between them and hugged him; he returned the hug with equal warmth.

"We left him at home. He didn't feel like being chased off by well-intentioned guides and gardeners and waitresses. Don't feel too sorry for him, it isn't as if he can't fly here on his own any time he chooses." Nan stepped back and moved over to the side so they could walk the path together.

"Eh, welladay, and that's true too. Who's the wee, fearless mite you have with you?" Puck glanced at her sideways. "None of your get—"

"Nor of my blood," Nan confirmed. "Suki shares my powers;

we rescued her from a fake medium who was using her to 'read' the clients. Rather than allowing her to go starve and go mad in an orphanage, or worse in a workhouse, we took her on ourselves."

"Brave lasses." Puck shook his head. "You must have had a time with her."

"Less than you'd think." Nan spent the next fifteen minutes or so catching Robin up. He laughed several times and teased her often, until she got to the part about assisting John and Mary Watson, when he nodded thoughtfully. And then, when she described how they had entrapped the Shadow Beast and turned it over to the Sea Elementals to dispose of, his eyes widened, then at the end, he clapped and did a little skip.

"Oh well done, *very* well done! It's time and more than time for that thing to have been done away with." He shook his head. "Your guess at how long it has been a terror and a torment is a good one. I am glad to see this England rid of it."

"Why couldn't *you* have got rid of it?" Nan wanted to know.

He laid a finger alongside his nose. "Rules, lass. Rules. There's things I can do and things I cannot, not without starting a war that would have no winners, and leave the poor Earth and the Sons and Daughters of Adam and Eve all torn and bleeding. And whilst it is true as true that in these latter days, I've less to worry about on that head, the Shadow Beast was confined within the bosom of Londinium, and there, it is hard even for me to go."

"But once we mortals had trapped and confined the thing, it was perfectly—well—*legal* for us to turn it over to Elementals to hide away?" she hazarded.

He nodded, solemnly. "I do not often trust Lyr to treat mortals fairly, but in this case, he will not want *that* escaping under any circumstances, for it is an enemy to all that lives. As much to us as you, if not more so. Full many an Elemental has fallen to it in centuries past. So, then, tell me what it is that you and Sarah are about now? And why is it the fair maid is not here?"

Nan sighed, feeling her mood sour. "*That* is a very short story."

She told him how Magdalena von Dietersdorf had called, looking for their help with her problem, how Sarah had been treated and *she* had been snubbed, and now how Sarah was spending every waking moment, almost, dancing to the tune

Magdalena sang and being treated like a little diva herself.

"Oh, my, dear Nan. I do detect jealousy there," Puck said shrewdly.

"No!" she denied sharply, then, shamefaced, admitted, "Yes. I can't help it. We practically grew up together, we've saved each other's *lives,* and now it's as if I'm some casual acquaintance who doesn't matter, and I don't like it, not one bit. I don't like how she's abandoned Suki, either. It's not fair."

"No, it's not," Puck agreed. "But if you are that firm in each other's affections, and this is no unnatural influence the singer has on her, then once all the glitter and gay times wear off, or once the lady decides she no longer needs to treat the lass like a princess and reverts to treating her like a servant, then all will be as it was. *If* you can keep your own temper in check, and jealous words behind your teeth. But you mustn't say things you'll regret, or utter words in heat that still sting in coolness."

"I know," Nan sighed sadly. "And it's a *damned* hard time I've had keeping those words to myself. But—what did you mean, *no unnatural influence?* What are you trying to say?"

She gave Puck a sharp look. He quirked a corner of his mouth up in something that was not a smile. "I am the Oldest Old Thing in England, and there are many sights I have seen. And sometimes, when a friend forgets all her old friends and goes a-scamper after a new *friend,* it isn't her own thoughts she's thinking, but ones that got put there. I'm not saying that's true now," he added, putting up a cautioning hand, "but I'm not saying it *isn't.*"

"Is there any way I could tell?" Nan asked sharply.

"You'd have to be there when the influence is put on her. You couldn't tell it from scrying her thoughts yourself, though if the influence were magical, there might be a trace of it yon Watsons could read." He shrugged. "That's the only advice I can give."

"It's more than I had before," Nan pointed out. She might have said more, except that Suki came tearing around a clump of trees and stopped dead on the path before them.

She had clearly been having a glorious time, for she had lost her cap, her hair was full of grass stems and leaves, and there was a grass stain on her pinafore. She stared at Puck with her eyes gone all big and round, and it was pretty obvious to Nan that she "saw" Puck for what he was, or at least, saw enough to know he wasn't just a Royal Gardener.

"Oh!" she breathed. "Who are you?" Then before Nan or Puck could say anything, she clasped her hands tightly just below her chin, and squealed, "You're *him*! You're The Puck! You're Robin Goodfellow!"

Puck snatched off his cap and bowed deeply. "I am all those things, Suki, Daughter of Eve. And I am also Nan's friend."

"Oh!" replied Suki, who then seemed to have been struck speechless.

"Now, since this Royal Garden has been given back to nature and to *me*, would you like to see what grows in it besides plants and trees and birds?" His eyes twinkled. "I could use another such as you, to come and go and look and know. What say you?"

"Oh! Yes! Please!" she breathed.

What followed was definitely the best day of Suki's life.

She was almost—*almost*—too tired when it was over to eat the sumptuous tea that Nan bought for them at a tea shop outside the Palace grounds. She fell asleep, cuddled into Nan's side, as they waited for the train back to London to arrive. Nan actually had to pick her up and carry her to the train, where she continued to sleep. She revived enough to walk under her own power to the cabstand, and she stayed awake long enough to trudge up the stairs to the flat. But all she could manage was to give an astonished Sarah a kiss and be helped out of her clothing and into her nightgown. Her head had barely touched the pillow when she was asleep again.

"You *wore her out!*" Sarah said in shock, when Nan came back out into the sitting room. "You actually *wore her out!*"

"Oh, it wasn't my doing," Nan replied. "It was romping with fauns and sylphs and every other creature Puck could coax out of hiding. The Privy Garden's been left to go wild, and Elementals are as thick as pigeons in Hyde Park there."

"You saw *Puck*?" Now Sarah's voice held a tone of dismay. "Oh why didn't I go with you?"

Nan, mindful of Puck's advice, bit her tongue. "Now that we know he can appear there, we can go another time. Suki will be wild to see him again, and she's been given leave to *come and go and look and know,* just as we were."

"I would have liked to see him again now, though," Sarah lamented. Nan could not help but think the sharp-edged little thought that *if you weren't trailing around after that blasted singer, you could have!* But she controlled her voice and expression, and said, "Another time. And meanwhile, he gives us a *well done* for helping John and Mary, and another for turning that *thing* over to the Water Elementals and Lyr."

Sarah heaved a sigh full of both relief and regret. "That's a comfort. I want to hear all about it when I get back." She got up, and picked up her shawl and handbag, preparing to go out—as usual.

"You're usually half-asleep by the time you get home," Nan reminded her.

"I'll drink enough coffee at breakfast to stay awake to hear about it," Sarah replied, heading out the door. "Oh, I *wish* I could have been there!"

The door closed behind her.

"So do I," Nan said, softly, to the closed door. "So do I."

9

For once, Sarah had been the silent one as Suki and Nan had their (much plainer) breakfast. Suki was full of all the wonderful things Puck had showed her, and who and what he'd introduced her to, and what games they'd had. Besides showing her to Elementals, and them to her, he'd also coaxed out many of the wild creatures inhabiting the overgrown garden, which was over three acres in size. Rabbits and hares, funny little hedgehogs and red squirrels, a pair of foxes with a litter of kits, a badger, and even a deer came out of hiding at Puck's behest, and introduced themselves to the enchanted child.

Since Suki, child of the London slums as she was, had never seen any of these creatures except in picture books, she was still head over heels about the experience.

"But I'm 'fraid I ruint my dress," Suki finished, glancing at Sarah sidelong. "There's big stains on't naow. . . ."

"Stains don't matter," Nan said firmly, before Sarah could respond. "Not in the least. What's a gown compared to meeting *him*? Besides, we can save that gown for the next time we go to the country to romp. It's a good thing to have a gown that's already ruined, just so you don't have to worry about your clothes."

Suki broke out in a sunny smile.

"Exactly," Sarah said. "That's why Nan and I have old things we don't care about, so we can do whatever we need to without fussing over a dress." She might have said more, but she interrupted

163

herself with a huge yawn. "And—"

"And now the coffee is wearing off, and you will fall asleep with your nose in the butter," Nan said firmly, getting the tray and gathering up the dishes to put on it. "Go to bed."

Sarah had gone to bed, still lamenting that she had not gone on the excursion, as Nan put the breakfast tray on the stand outside their flat door for Mrs. Horace.

There was no sign of Mrs. Horace, who usually came to tidy up about now, but then she was probably finishing her own breakfast. Nan and Suki got out her schoolwork, feeling much more inclined to tackle it after such a wonderful holiday. Outside, the sun was shining, the windows were open to a lovely breeze, and they were both looking forward to more Tudor history, having *seen* where a lot of it took place.

But they were interrupted by a knock at the door. Since Mrs. Horace generally just tapped and came right in, this had to be someone else. Nan and Suki exchanged a puzzled glance. "I dunno," Suki said, with a shrug. "Sarah didn' say naught about 'spectin' a parcel or such."

Then Nan got up to answer it, as a second knock came. It was John Watson, looking just a bit worried. He snatched his hat off as soon as she opened the door, gentleman that he was.

"Oh good, you are home," he said, looking relieved. "I tried yesterday, but no one answered when I knocked. I was afraid you might have been called out of town."

"Suki and I went to Hampton Court Palace, and Sarah could sleep through the house tumbling down around her," Nan told him, and gestured to him to come inside. He did so, but did not take a seat.

He turned to face her as she closed the door. She was about to tell him that Sarah was still dancing attendance on Magdalena, so if he needed both of them, he was rather out of luck. "Sarah—"

"Sarah is not who I need," he replied, interrupting her. "Lord A and I have something that could be rather urgent that I need *your* Talents for. Sarah's would be superfluous; useless, really. The thing is, this will require a journey of several days. As few as four, as many as a week." He cast a glance at Suki. "I'm not certain how you would want to handle your charge."

"That's a problem," Nan replied, frowning a little. "I can't exactly leave her in the charge of a bird. Or that is, I *could*, because Grey is quite good enough to keep an eye on things, but Grey has the instincts of a parrot, and must sleep when the sun goes down, which is precisely when Sarah is gone. While we've left Suki at night before, it has always been in the charge of Mrs. Horace, and I don't want to impose on her good will, even with extra pay, too often."

I'm glad Suki agreed to go to school with Memsa'b. Things will be easier to manage then. Of course, once she's in her teens I shan't have to worry about leaving her here alone, she'll be fine.

John frowned, but his expression was of someone who was frowning in thought, not disapproval. Finally he seemed to make up his mind about something. "Would Sarah object if we took Suki with us?"

At this, Suki tried to be on her very *best* behavior and not jump up out of her seat to run to Nan and beg. That much was evident by how she dropped her eyes and clutched her book to her chest. But Nan didn't have to see her jumping up and down to know that she wanted to go, badly.

"Given that Sarah has already taken on a commitment of two-thirds of the day, I don't see where she has any right to object," Nan replied, a bit more sharply than she intended. "The question is whether *you* object."

"It will complicate the journey, but I don't see it as insurmountable. Could you and Suki pack for a journey of three or four days and come with me? We can consult with Mary, then leave from Baker Street." John seemed extremely anxious to be gone, which told Nan that in his eyes, this was a serious situation. "I believe you said once that Suki's Talents are not unlike yours? She might be able to learn a great deal by watching you."

That's a good point.

"Let me see if Sarah has fallen asleep yet," she temporized. Without waiting for John's reply, she went to Sarah's door, tapped on it, and poked her head inside.

It was quite dark, because, of course, Sarah had closed all the curtains. "Mmmph?" Sarah said. She wasn't much more than a shape in the bed, but the lump on the pillow rose up a little, so it appeared she was awake enough to do that much.

"John Watson needs me for several days. He suggested I bring Suki so you aren't troubled with her," Nan replied, stating it as if it was a *fait accompli*, knowing that Sarah would be too sleepy to think of reasons to object. "I'll tell Mrs. Horace, and she'll bring up Grey's food as usual, and your tea and supper if you want it. Grey should be fine here alone at night, and I'll take Neville with us."

"Ah—all right?" Sarah replied, sounding bewildered. Nan did not wait for any other answer. She closed the door and went to the birds' room.

"Neville, you and I and Suki are going on a trip. Put anything you want in your carrier," she said, as the two birds looked up from a horseshoe-nail puzzle-toy they were trying to work out between them. "Grey, you will need to keep an eye on Sarah and on the flat while I am gone. I will have Mrs. Horace bring you your meals as usual."

Grey spread her wings and bobbed her head as Neville strode over to their box of toys and began contemplating the contents. "If something seems . . . odd . . . with Sarah, I count on you to tell me when I return, all right?"

"Yessssss," Grey agreed, and cocked her head, which suggested to Nan that Grey had already noticed that *something* was up, but had not yet worked out what it was.

Satisfied, Nan went to Suki's room and helped her pack two portmanteaus, one with toiletries and clothing for an outing in the country, and one with books and toys. Suki was so tiny that two weeks' worth of clothing fit in the portmanteau, with room to spare. Then she went to her own room and packed up her own things. Nothing that might outrage the sensibilities of people living in the country, of course, and mostly all plain and dark, with a pair of sensible boots, in case she found herself tramping in the woods or across fields.

It didn't take long, as she was used to packing and traveling light; by the time she was finished and went back to the birds' room, Neville was sitting on top of his carrier as a sign he was satisfied with his selections.

He hopped inside, and Nan fastened the opening, then went

back out into the sitting room with the carrier and Neville inside. Suki had already laboriously brought the portmanteaus into the room, and John Watson had taken charge of them; just as well, since they were far too heavy for Suki to carry for any distance.

"I am glad to see you are swift packers," John said with a slight smile. "I shall procure a cab, and we will be on our way." He headed down the stairs.

Nan paused just long enough to fasten Suki's bonnet over her curly hair and drape a shawl over her, then put on her own bonnet and shawl before following him. She stopped long enough at Mrs. Horace's door to apprise her of the situation and get her assent to make sure Grey's food and water were taken care of, then she and Suki left to wait at the curbside where John had left the bags while he obtained a cab.

It took him some little time, since the street was not terribly busy at this time of the morning. Suki looked hopefully up at Nan. "We goin' on a train?" she asked, hopefully.

"Almost certainly, I think," Nan told her, and her little face lit up. "I also believe we may be in the real countryside." The cab came at that point, and they all squeezed inside it. Fortunately, as usual, Suki took up very little room. She fitted between Nan and John and spent the trip to Baker Street grinning up at both of them.

The train carriage rocked gently, as it was not going particularly fast. Faster than a horse coach, but this was a local, not an express. Suki knelt on the cushions of the seat with her hands and nose pressed against the train window. Mary Watson smiled every time she looked up from her book and saw her. When John had arrived at Baker Street with Suki and Nan in tow, he found Mary had already packed their own cases and was ready for him. Presented with Suki, she not only made no objections whatsoever, she immediately hit upon the logical answer to why they were all traveling together—that Suki was their daughter and Nan was her nurse. All the details that needed to be roughed in were easily completed in the cab to Victoria Station.

Thanks to the fact that Lord Alderscroft was funding this little expedition, they had their own compartment in the train from London to Sevenoaks, a village on the Kent Downs. Their journey would have been faster if there had been an express, but since the only train available was a local, which stopped at every station along the way, it would probably take the better part of the day.

Suki *clearly* did not mind this at all.

Since they had their own compartment, Neville could remain free, also. Nan had taken the precaution of purchasing a newspaper so he could relieve himself like a civilized creature. There would be a luncheon trolley, rather than a dining car, on this train, and he had expressed that he was willing to partake of chicken and cheese for his luncheon, so that was sorted. There would certainly be one or both in the sandwiches on offer.

"Now," Nan said, when Suki and Neville were accommodated at the windows, Suki kneeling on one seat, and Neville on the perch that served as the handle to his carrier on another. "Just what is it that is so urgent?"

"Lord Alderscroft has gotten information that suggests there might be a practitioner of blood magic at Sevenoaks in Kent," said John Watson, soberly, clasping his hands on the newspaper in his lap. "More often than not, those who take up blood magic are Earth Magicians, so Mary and I are not going to be of much help in finding him."

"And just how am *I* supposed to be of help?" Nan asked, looking at both of them quizzically. "I am not a magician at all."

"Two things; your ability at—what was it Lord Alderscroft called it?" John looked over at Mary.

"Psychometry. The ability to read the history of an object by handling it," Mary supplied.

"Exactly. That, and telepathy. The young mage who conveyed this information was walking the Downs on holiday and came across what he describes as *a heathen altar*. Now, there are a great many altar stones and standing stones and megaliths in the Downs, and he thought nothing of it, until he got nearer and sensed the unmistakable signs that it had been used for a sacrificial table within the last several months. He thought it urgent enough to cut short his holiday and come straight to London to report it to Lord Alderscroft." John glanced over at Suki, but she didn't seem to have noticed what he was saying; she was chattering away to Neville, who was responding in *quorks* and occasional words. Neither seemed inclined to resort to the toys that had been packed for the purpose of entertaining bored children and birds. Both seemed enraptured by the changing landscape going past the windows.

"Why is that so urgent?" Nan asked, curious now. *It isn't as if there wasn't plenty of blood sacrifice in Africa carried out by perfectly good and decent shamans.* Sarah, of course, was used to such things, having spent the first ten or so years of her life among the natives. When she and Nan had gone to visit Sarah's parents at their hospital, Nan had very quickly come to accept such things as ritual dances, body scarification, and blood sacrifice as a matter of course.

"Because we want to head this off before the mage in question graduates from animals to humans, of course," Mary said patiently. "Blood magic is generally associated either with mages who have gone to the bad, or with people who are not mages at all, and are raising power with death because they have no natural way of tapping into it as Elemental Mages do."

"Oh," Nan replied, thinking that this was a bit of an ... assumption. Then again, England had been civilized for a very long time, so perhaps John and Mary were right, and she was the one making assumptions.

"At any rate, our plan is to settle in at the Railway and Bicycle Hotel in Sevenoaks and investigate from there," John told her. "I hope Suki is up to some long walks; I do have directions to the altar stone, but they are not exact."

"Suki is quite sturdy, I do assure you," Nan promised. "She can probably out-walk all of us together."

But that put her in mind of something *else* they might meet out in the countryside ... or indeed, the wilderness or part-wilderness, as the Downs seemed to be. *Hmm. Probably time I should mention this. ...*

"You do know that Sarah and I have gotten the blessing of Robin Goodfellow, right? And that he has a habit of showing up to see what we are doing when we are out of the city." She tilted her head to the side. "I should also mention he seems to have taken a liking to Suki as well."

That made both of them stare at her, dumbfounded. "Ah, no. Lord Alderscroft didn't mention that," John said, after a long silence. "That could come in handy, if he's inclined to help us out."

"No promises," Nan warned. "But the possibility is there. So, we're to take some long, healthy country walks until we find this altar stone, and I am to 'read' it and see what I can learn?"

"That's the essence. I hope you'll be able to see who's using it. Then we'll try and match the face to someone who lives in the village. Alderscroft has no record of any mages at all there—which isn't at all unusual." John shrugged. "He knows everyone who's titled, of course, but there are plenty of mages out there without a drop of noble blood in their entire pedigree, and they don't bring themselves to the attention of the White Lodge as long as they've got their own local mentors."

"If they don't have their own local mentors to train them—if they *do* come to the attention of the White Lodge, it's generally when something has gone wrong," Mary observed.

"Like now," John added.

Nan was still not so sure. "Well, those mentors of their own—might they not be like Beatrice? Hereditary witches and that sort of thing? Wouldn't they have all sorts of family traditions and so forth?" She was *trying,* as diplomatically as possible, to get the Watsons to see that there might be other ways of doing things than they were used to, ways that were just as valid as their own paths. Unfortunately, they didn't seem to be getting the hint.

"They generally are. And as a consequence, they can have all sorts of muddled ideas," John told her dismissively. "They've got no real understanding of what they're doing. Witches like Beatrice, who *do* know what they are doing, are the exception rather than the rule."

Considering that I know a Water Master who's been taught by an Elemental—one of the Selch that you entrusted the amulet of the Shadow Beast to—I think perhaps I have a better idea of what someone like that can do than you do.

But she didn't say that aloud, and really, it didn't lessen her respect for the Watsons at all. This just had opened her eyes to a weakness in their thinking. And this was probably one of the reasons why Lord A had wanted her working with them in the first place. *Though I would think, having been in Afghanistan, John might be a little more broad-minded . . . but then again, probably the native magicians—the real magicians that is—were all on the side of the enemy. That does tend to color your feelings about them.*

About that time, the luncheon trolley came along, and they had to turn their conversation to much more ordinary things—such as what sandwiches were available, who wanted lemonade, and who wanted Eccles cakes. Then they were occupied with eating, and when the eating was done, Suki was full of questions about the countryside they were going through, the stations they were stopping at, and the people who were waiting at the stations. Enough of these stations were still serving little villages, in which people still dressed in the manner of the countryside as their grandfathers and grandmothers had, that Suki was intensely curious about what their garments were and why they wore them. The train to Hampton Court Palace had brought no such questions, because it had gone through genteel or middle-class suburbs populated with people who dressed just like those in London. Here she was seeing farmers in their working smocks, country women with cloth bonnets or little cloth caps, blacksmiths in leather aprons. And she was seeing enormous shire horses, much bigger than the horses still drawing carts and carriages in London. "El-eph-an-tine," she breathed, sounding out the word carefully.

She hadn't quite got all her questions answered when the train pulled into Sevenoaks, and it was time for Neville to go back in his carrier and all of them to gather up their baggage and disembark.

The Railway and Bicycle Hotel was a real hotel built of cream-colored stone and red brick; the biggest lodging place in Sevenoaks, although it was small by London standards, and nothing like the capital's grand hotels. It was located very near the railway station, which certainly made things easier for all of them. It had two floors of guest rooms over the pub; their rooms were on the second floor. Nan and Suki were established in one room, and the Watsons next door in another. Suki was mightily curious about the lack of a bathroom, but there was an advantage to having been a London street Arab; she was quite well acquainted with, and not offended by, the fact that she was going to have to use a privy in the stable yard.

Nan let Neville out the window between their beds to scout, settled their belongings in the dresser at the foot of her bed, and established a perch for Neville on her iron bedstead by lashing the tin cups from the carrier to the footposts and spreading newspaper beneath. The maid would probably be astonished, but Lord A was supplying enough money that the maid's astonishment would be tempered, if not suppressed completely, by a shilling or two.

Some chicken left over from luncheon and some digestive biscuits broken up would do for Neville's supper, and there was fresh water in the pitcher for the other cup. And that was assuming he didn't manage to catch himself some mice while he was out. Nan had long ago convinced him to suppress his instincts and leave baby birds and wild bird eggs alone, but she had given him *carte blanche* to catch and eat mice.

Suki immediately set to exploring every bit of the little room, even to the underside of the bed, and was voluble in her astonishment at finding that it had ropes supporting the mattress rather than bedsprings as they had in London.

It's like traveling with a monkey, Nan thought with amusement.

The room itself was just big enough for the two narrow beds, with a scoured wooden floor with a rag rug between them, a dresser, a low table with a bowl and pitcher of water for washing up and a tiny mirror over it, a small table with a candlestick on it between the beds under the window, flowered curtains on the single window that overlooked the main street of Sevenoaks, a metal matchbox fastened above the head of each bed so that one could find matches in the dark, and a framed picture of the Queen on the wall, which was covered in a rather plain wallpaper of yellow and ochre stripes. She suspected that, as the married couple, John and Mary had gotten a much better bedchamber.

Still, this wasn't bad. And the air coming in the open window was absolutely delicious. Even Suki finally noticed it and went over to the window to lean out, breathing in huge gulps of it.

"Wot's thet loverly smell?" she asked, finally.

"Flowers of some kind. I'm not good enough at plants to tell you what they are by scent," Nan admitted. "Roses, probably, though. Everyone in the country seems to grow roses. Are you hungry yet?"

"Perishin'!" Suki said decidedly.

"Then let's go find John and Mary, and we'll all go down to dinner," she held out her hand for Suki's, who scampered away from the window and took it.

"Why've we gotter go *down* fer dinner?" she asked, as they left their room and tapped on the next door. "Missus 'Orace gives us meals i' our rooms."

"Because we'll be eating with everyone else here in this hotel, and probably some local people, and travelers that might be staying elsewhere, in that big room downstairs," Nan explained. "Downstairs is a pub. Like a tavern or a pub in London."

"Niver been in no tavern," Suki observed, just as John opened the door to a room which, as Nan had suspected, was much nicer than the one she shared with Suki. It was at least twice the size, and wallpapered in a much more fashionable pink, cream and green stripes with a pattern of cabbage roses between the stripes. It had at least three braided rugs, a wardrobe, two dressers, a toilet table with a magnificent china bowl and matching pitcher, a huge mirror over the bowl rather than the miserly little book-sized one in their room, an absolutely enormous four-poster bed that looked at least a century old, with a beautiful quilt and plump pillows atop it and bed-curtains around it, three chairs, and a couch. From the thickness of the mattress, Nan also suspected it was a featherbed atop a horsehair mattress, rather than the tufted wool mattresses on the beds in her room. On the walls were more framed prints, all of the Royal Family.

"Cor!" said Suki, gazing with big eyes at the lofty featherbed.

"Go jump on it," Mary said with a twinkle in her eye. Nothing loath, Suki raced across the room and flung herself on the bed, disappearing in an instant.

"Cor! 'Slike a cloud!" came her muffled voice from somewhere in the center.

There were also three chairs—they didn't match in style, but someone, probably whoever did the leatherwork on carriages and furniture hereabouts, had carefully upholstered them in a dusty-rose canvas that matched the sofa and wallpaper. "Are we too early for dinner?" Nan wondered. Suki wasn't the only one who was hungry.

"I don't think so. People keep country hours here," Mary pointed out. "We can eat and have a walk around the village and get our bearings before bed."

The pub appeared to be quite popular; the beer was excellent, the fare was limited, but the serving girl promised them that the main offer changed every night. Tonight was stewed rabbit, and Nan knew enough of country life not to enquire too closely about the origin of the rabbits.

Suki was uncharacteristically quiet and watched everything around her with big eyes. She was not allowed beer, nor, despite begging, the scrumpy that Nan ordered, but the serving girl did bring her a big tankard of unfermented apple juice. John finished first, had a word with both the landlord and the girl who would be their chambermaid about Neville, and came back.

"The girl was a little apprehensive about a raven, but when I pressed a couple of shillings into her hand and told her that if he was in the room, all she had to say was 'Go in the box, Neville' and he'd go in the carrier, she seemed more at ease. The landlord is going to get the cook to save him chicken offal and meat scraps." John smiled at Nan, and she grinned back.

"I couldn't have arranged better myself. And really, Neville is likely to be out from sunup to sundown, so she probably won't encounter him." She looked down at Suki, who was valiantly trying to eat the very last scrapings of her apple tart and cream and blinking sleepily. "Do you want to walk with us, Suki, or go to bed and read?"

"Read, please," Suki said with an enormous yawn.

"Then you may be excused. Leave the window open for Neville, please," said Mary. She was doing a very good job of pretending to be Suki's mother, at least in Nan's estimation.

Suki climbed off the bench where they were sitting and trotted over to the stairs and up out of sight. "I don't think she's going to read for very long," Nan observed. "We had a long, long day yesterday, and this was another."

"I'd be very surprised if she read more than a page," John said dryly. "Let's go take a stroll and get our bearings."

The village turned out to be surprisingly large; really it qualified as a market town, because it had two markets a week. That was why they had several flourishing hotels; the Royal Oak, the Railway and Bicycle, and the Sennoke—which John said he thought was probably local dialect for Sevenoaks. The walk to the edge of town was quiet and pleasant. It took a bit of walking before John found the spot referenced on his crude little map, drawn from memory by the young mage who had reported the altar in the first place—the spot where the walking path he'd taken began just off one of the main streets.

By this time, it was dusk. The three of them strolled back, with Neville landing on Nan's shoulder when they were about halfway back to the hotel.

"*Mice*," said Neville, with satisfaction.

"I know," Nan replied. "I can smell them on your breath."

Neville gave an indignant *quork*.

He lifted off just as they reached the hotel, and with a few heavy flaps of his wings, reached the open window and ducked inside.

Nan bade Mary and John goodnight; they arranged that whoever woke first should wake the others, and she opened the door of the little room to find Suki asleep with her arms wrapped around her book and Neville sitting with one foot up on the foot of her bed.

"Comfortable? Or should I pad it with a bandage or a towel?" she asked him.

"*Good*," said Neville, and, relieved of his duty to play sentry over Suki, tucked his head under his wing. Nan took the book away from Suki and put it down on the little table between the beds. She changed quickly into her nightdress, blew out the candle, and got into bed. She didn't expect to fall asleep soon, both because of the strange bed and the strange country sounds coming in the window, but no sooner had she put her head to the pillow than she felt herself drowsing.

Must . . . have been . . . the scrumpy, she thought. And the next thing she knew it was morning, and Mary Watson was tapping on the bedroom door.

* * *

Nan was very glad she had packed sturdy boots for herself and
Suki; these country paths, as she knew from her time in Cornwall,
were no joke to be hiking over in city shoes. Suki was doing a
fine job of keeping up, and Neville performed yeoman's duty as
an aerial scout. Although it was likely thought by people outside
the city that Londoners took cabs everywhere, the fact was most
people in London did a great deal of walking, and the four of
them were no exception.

Because this was a market town and right on the railway,
there were a lot of strangers coming and going. They attracted
no attention at all. And a lack of attention was exactly what they
wanted. People probably assumed they were going to visit the
famous "country house" of Knole, one of the largest houses in the
country; the fact that John was carrying a picnic basket packed for
them by the staff at the hotel reinforced that. And it was possible
that the altar they were seeking lay within the heavily wooded
parklands belonging to the house.

It didn't take them very long to find the path marked on the
rough map that Lord Alderscroft had sent John. At first, they
walked mostly through meadows dotted with sheep and a few
cattle, with Neville soaring overhead, occasionally uttering a
quork to urge them to keep up. The path took a turn between two
planted fields, then plunged into a wooded valley. That was where
Neville joined them, changing his flight style from gliding above
them to short flights along the path, keeping just ahead of them
and serving as a sort of scout.

Suki was enraptured. She had adored the overgrown garden
at Hampton Court Palace, but this was her first real experience
of woodlands.

The trees were enormous. Not that Nan was any stranger to
enormous trees, but not growing so closely together as these. There
was a deep sense of *age* under the cool of their thick branches.
Would Puck appear? Nan thought probably not; he didn't know
John and Mary, and he was likely to be cautious around them.
But in addition to hearing and getting glimpses of wildlife under
these trees, she was hearing and getting glimpses of the *other* life
in this protected place.

Here, a rustle and a glimpse of a tiny thing scuttling away from the path, a creature that seemed as much made of twigs and leaves as flesh and blood.

If Earth Elementals have flesh and blood . . .

There, a brief flash of eyes and hair, which faded into a tree trunk. The drumming of tiny hooves—a lamb? A kid? Or a faun? A momentary flurry of faint color overhead—that was surely a sylph.

Suki led, romping along the path, stopping to crouch and look at something in the grass or turning and running backward to make sure they were keeping up. John walked a little ahead of Mary and Nan; Mary kept glancing over at Nan, with a quizzical look on her face.

"Can you see them?" she asked, finally. "The Elementals, I mean?"

Nan nodded. "Fauns, dryads, some little gnome-y things, things that fairy-tale books Suki reads call 'elves,' although I don't believe they are using the word correctly. Sylphs, I think. I wouldn't expect to see Fire Elementals out here, nor Water, unless we happen across a pond or a brook."

Mary glanced at Suki, who was bent over and talking to something in the grass. "And now she can see them, too. It must be some sort of spell."

"Probably. Although if what Lord Alderscroft has told us about the Great Elementals is true, he could simply have *willed* the ability to us. Puck also gave Sarah a charm that protects her against harmful ghosts, although at the time he said that even harmful ones don't have much power, and warned her not to depend on it against anything that wasn't a ghost." Nan half-smiled. "That's why we didn't use it on the Shadow Beast. That, and we wanted the Shadow Beast to think we were helpless so we could be proper bait."

They had been walking along a line of twisted, gnarled, very old trees for some time now. The fact that they were at least twenty-five feet high testified to their age. A line that was as perfectly straight as if someone had planted the trees deliberately. Trees that . . . now that she came to think of it . . . looked all alike.

She looked over at Mary. "What are these trees?" she asked, waving her hand at the row.

"Hawthorn," Mary said. "Why?"

Hawthorn! She looked at them again. But they were so tall! The hawthorns she had seen in Cornwall hadn't been nearly this tall; most, in fact, had been hedges. It was the size that had fooled her; this was a line of the "thorns" of "oak, ash, and thorn," the trees of Puck's magic, and—yes, sure enough, on the other side of the path were equally ancient oaks and ashes. Those weren't planted in a straight line, and they were mixed with limes, beeches and yews, but they were certainly there. This meant something. She didn't know, what, yet, but it surely meant *something*.

The stretch of woodland through which they were walking ended abruptly up ahead; Nan could see sunlight beating down on meadow grass up there. Suddenly, she didn't want this to end. It was so very peaceful, walking beneath these forest giants, birds everywhere, in the close, still, cool air beneath their canopy. This was a fairy-tale forest, and every breath she took in it was scented with magic.

The path broke out from under the trees into an irregular patch of meadow; their appearance startled a herd of deer, who all looked up at them in alarm and dashed away. The path went on through the meadow and into another patch of younger woodland, but Nan looked uphill and saw that the top of the hill was crowned with oaks just as ancient, if not more ancient, than the patch of forest they had just left. And she knew, although she did not know how she knew, that their goal was there.

"Up there," she said, pointing. Neville flew to her shoulder and regarded the oaks, then nodded once. Then he flew off and vanished into the trees, and from somewhere ahead they heard him calling.

Suki edged closer to her and took her hand. John nodded, and took Mary's, indicating to her that she should take the lead.

Neville continued to call at intervals, modulating his voice to his normal *quorks* as they drew closer to him. There was a dense thicket of younger hawthorn—a hedge almost—around the base of the oaks, and she couldn't see any way to get in. But she followed the sound of Neville's voice and, just when she least expected it, she all but stumbled into the gap in the hedge that let them all inside.

And there was another, moss-grown path, leading off to the

right, curving gently between two walls of thick growth. She looked back at John.

"This fits the description Lord Alderscroft relayed to me," he replied, and gestured that she should continue to lead.

The path was barely wide enough for a single person, so Nan put Suki behind her, between herself and Mary Watson, with John Watson bringing up the rear.

The path seemed to go on, and on—for far longer than it *should* have, since they never started downhill again, only up. It was John Watson who finally said, "I think we are going in a circle."

"Easy enough to tell," Mary replied, and pulled off the pretty ribbon she wore at her throat instead of a necklace. They all stopped while she tied it to a twig, then they went on, leaving the bright bit of color hanging limply in the still air.

Nan counted off the paces as they walked. When she got to a hundred, she heard Mary call out. "I see the ribbon! Look through the hedge to the right."

At first Nan couldn't imagine what Mary thought she saw, but then she moved her head, and got the flash of bright blue on the *other* side of three feet of trees and underbrush.

"Not a circle then, a spiral," John grumbled. "I wish Lord Alderscroft's informant had given us that little detail."

"The boy probably had more hair than wit," Mary muttered. "Wandering about the Downs composing odes to ferns, no doubt."

Nan smothered a laugh, and said over her shoulder, "Air Magician?"

"Head full of air, more like," John retorted. "Yes, I believe he was Air."

Mary laughed aloud. "Sadly, my love, Air Magicians cannot all be as level-headed as I. Well, the stone we are looking for must be at the heart of this spiral, and it is a good way to conceal such a thing. Press on, Nan."

Try as she might, Nan could not sense anything sinister *at all* about this place. On the contrary, it seemed solemn, as if she was walking down an aisle in a little green church.

She glanced back at Suki, who had been remarkably quiet since they entered this grove, and saw in the child's face some of the same solemnity that she felt. There was nothing of the smoldering repression Suki sometimes showed when she was being "quieted" against her will. It appeared more as if she felt she was in the presence of something that required silence and attentiveness.

And then, without warning, the path ended in a clearing.

It was about twenty feet across and open to the sky, full of flattened grass, as if deer came in here to lie down on a regular basis. In the center was a great stone slab, propped up on four rough-cut stone legs. The rest of the clearing was nothing but grass and flowers, hundreds, thousands, of clover flowers. The still air was full of their faint scent. Nan quickly moved out of the way so the others could enter.

John cleared his throat self-consciously. "Well . . . this seems to be it. Nan?"

"Wot 'bout me?" Suki asked.

Nan considered that for a moment. Suki was absolutely no stranger to violent death. Like Nan, she had probably seen more murders in her first nine years of life than anyone other than a soldier ever would even be able to *imagine* in an entire lifetime. And Suki might well see something that she would not; no two psychometrists ever got the same visions from the same object.

"Surely not—" Mary objected, but Nan waved her off.

"Let me see if it's dangerous first. If not, then you may help me, Suki." Suki's face was still solemn, and Nan added, "Don't be disappointed if you don't see anything either. You're still just learning how to use the Talent."

"Oil roight," Suki agreed, and hung back as Nan approached the stone table, knelt down in the soft grass next to it, and gingerly placed her hand—

Blood. Blood poured over her hand, soaking her sleeve, blood streamed over the stone and—

She took her hand away, blinking. Because, yes, the image had been horrific . . . and yet . . . completely lacking in any emotional impact. No horror. No terror.

"What did you see?" John asked anxiously.

"That this place has been used as a place of sacrifice, and very recently, too," she said. "Let me try again."

She placed her hand on the stone again, this time prepared for the image of blood pouring over the stone and onto her hand.

The blood poured over the stone, down grooves cut into it for the purpose, over her hand and into a bowl placed to receive it. There was an animal on the stone; it blurred before her eyes, but she concentrated, and then she could see it. It was a fallow deer, a stag, with huge, heavy antlers, its eyes were closed, and its throat had been cut. It was dark. The only light came from four torches thrust into the earth around the stone table.

There was a man . . . a shadow against the starry sky. She struggled to see him. Slowly, he came into focus. Blond, square-jawed, in his midtwenties, she thought. He wore a pair of stag antlers on his head, and in his right hand, he held a bloody flint knife. He had painted his face and chest with the blood.

And now she felt emotion, from that ancient warrior she once had been. Rage. Rage rose up in a flood over her, overwhelming everything else. Red, hot, raving anger so great she could scarcely contain it. She reached for her bronze sword—

And broke contact with the stone. The vision vanished, and so did her anger.

"Suki, come here," she said carefully. Unlike her, Suki did not seem to have the spirit of a long-dead Celtic she-warrior in her. Suki might be able to see more than she could. Mary made a strangled sound, but John hushed her.

Suki knelt beside her in the grass, carefully not touching the altar, not yet. "Suki, a man came here and killed a deer on this stone. There will be a lot of blood. Do you think that will frighten you?" Nan said, knowing already what the answer would be.

Suki's little face twisted with scorn. "Oi bain't skerrit," she said, dismissively. "Oi weren't skerrit when Bob Malsey tookit 'is shiv an' cut up Black Reggie so'is guts run out in street. Oi ain't gonna be skerrit fer a liddle blood wot ain't really there."

Mary made another little strangled sound. *Poor Mary. She looks at Suki and thinks 'delicate little flower' when Suki is about as delicate as a ferret.* "All right then, Suki, go ahead and touch the stone and see what you can see. If you don't like it, just pull your hand away. I'll be right here."

She took Suki's left hand in hers so Suki could reach out to touch the stone with her right. The child's eyes glazed over, but she gave no sign of being afraid. Nor did she give any indication that she felt the same incandescent rage that Nan had. Rather, she had a look of profound concentration, as if she was committing everything she saw to memory.

Finally, and with no sign of any distress, the child's hand dropped from the stone, and she sat there, blinking slowly, as she came back to herself. Then she looked up at Nan. "Oi sawr 'im. Sawr 'im good. Oi'll know 'im."

Now Nan looked back at Mary and John. "So did I. I am fairly certain I'll know him if I see him. I think we're done here."

10

"I cannot believe the two of you have any appetite at all after . . ." Mary shuddered, and looked askance at Nan and Suki, who were happily devouring buttered bread, cheese, and pickled onions. At the worst of times Nan was just as fond of cheese as Neville was, and all that walking had made her ready to devour the first thing put in front of her. There were also boiled eggs, apple tarts, and, in deference to Mary, some cucumber sandwiches—which were very nice, but not much good at satisfying a healthy appetite.

Neville was watching them all very carefully and begging for the peeled shells when they ate their eggs. She couldn't imagine how that could be tasty—but then, she wasn't a raven. He had his own two eggs, and a little bread and cheese. For drink, they had water from a sweet, clear brook that Mary's Elementals had assured them was pure.

Nan had her mouth full, so she couldn't answer. Suki just shrugged. "Weren't skerry," she said. "Wuz just a li'l blood."

Well, Suki might have been utterly unmoved by the experience, but Nan was *still* suppressing the rage of her former self at the thought of that *sagsannach feis* that had *dared* lay his filthy hands on. . . .

She cooled the temper of her former self with a long drink of water. John was speaking. "I don't think that hill was on Knole House land. I think it was a private farm."

"Well, that only makes sense," Mary agreed. "If it were on the

Sackville property, sooner or later a gamekeeper would find that altar stone. The only way it could be kept hidden all this time is if it was on someone's farm."

"Then whoever is using it probably has legitimate access to the land, and that means he's a farmer or a farmhand. There is a strong likelihood he will come to the market tomorrow. So, I propose two things. *I* will make an inquiry as to whose property that hill is on. *You*, Nan, Suki, and Mary, go spread yourselves about the market, and Nan and Suki, see if you can spot him there."

"It'll be best if we split up," Nan observed, "If you don't mind having Suki with you, Mary."

"Not at all," said Mary. "But Suki, you *will* have to behave as if you are my own little girl. That means obeying what I tell you to do without question or objection."

"Yus, mum," Suki replied obediently, winning a smile from Mary.

The walk back took longer than the walk out; for one thing, they were a good bit more tired, and for another, the adults were all thinking very hard about what they were going to do when they found the man they were looking for. Suki wore out completely when they were about halfway back. She didn't whine or cry, but she did look up piteously and ask if they could please sit down for a while. Rather than that, John gallantly took her up on his back, in spite of his bad knee.

"The next time we go hunting for something in the country, I propose that we hire some horses," said Mary, who was starting to look limp and overheated herself.

"Would you like that, Suki? If we found a nice little pony or a clever little donkey for you?" John asked.

Suki's head came up off John's shoulder, and her eyes went big and round. "Coo!" she said. "Somethin' loik!"

About the time they reached the first houses, Suki revived a little more. "Thankee, Mister Watson. I kin walk naow."

"Are you sure, Suki?" John asked in a voice so kindly that Nan smiled. It seemed he and Mary were both completely charmed by the little rascal.

"Sure's sure, Mister Watson. Don' wanter 'urt yer leg." She waited while they all stopped, and John knelt stiffly so she could slide off his back. She brushed down her frock to make sure it was neat, and smiled up at him.

When they reached the hotel, they were all tired, and showing it. Neville flew straight to their open window and disappeared inside their room. And since it was just about suppertime, and since they had long since walked off lunch, John handed the now-much-lighter picnic basket to the serving girl and said, "I believe we'll just have supper right now."

Only the fact that she was starving again kept Nan awake through dinner. Suki fell asleep with her head on her arms, and Nan picked her up without her waking to go up to their room. She herself barely managed a washup and a quick check to make sure Neville had had food and still had clean water before she, too, was asleep.

After a fruitless search of the market, they met back at the hotel pub for lunch. They all sat in a row on the bench at their table, since the pub was quite crowded, with a group of four strangers on the other side of the table from them. Nan was nearest the wall, Mary next to her, Suki between Mary and John. Suki was clutching the most magnificent carved wooden horse Nan had ever seen, a beautifully made and painted toy with a mane and tail of real horsehair. Her eyes were shining so much they looked like twin stars. Since Suki knew better than to *ask* for such a thing, Mary Watson must have seen her gazing with longing at it and bought it for her.

Suki has quite enraptured Mary, Nan thought with amusement. She looked up at Mary and happened to look just past her—and froze.

There at the bar, just accepting his pint, was the man from her vision at the altar. There was no mistake; the square face, prominent cheekbones, straw-colored hair, serious expression—she'd have known him in a thousand.

Suki, she thought, projecting the word into the girl's head. They had been practicing Suki's telepathy for a year now on a regular basis, along with her school lessons. She was very good at reception; projection was still limited to no more than a few words.

? It was more of a feeling than a thought, but Nan knew Suki had "heard" her. Good. All the excitement lately of going places hadn't interfered with what she'd learned so far.

Look past John Watson to the bar. Is that the man we are looking for?

Suki cleverly held up her horse for John's examination so she had an excuse to look up. *Yus!* came the reply.

Nan tapped Mary on the wrist and bent to whisper in her ear—or, speak quietly, since a whisper would never have been heard in the din. "Suki and I are both sure. The blond man in the middle of the bar with the pint of bitter is the one we saw sacrificing the deer."

Mary cast a startled look at her, then got John's attention with a little tap and bent to murmur in *his* ear. He nodded, as if what she had said was nothing more than a casual comment, and turned his attention back to his luncheon. Or so it appeared, anyway— but a few moments later, a tiny sylph with yellow butterfly wings zoomed in the open door and hovered over the blond man like an attendant spirit. When he had finished his pint and paid, she followed him out the door.

John seemed in no hurry to finish *his* lunch, so although Nan was itchy with the need to jump up and *do* something, she followed his example. After all, John had learned the craft of being a detective at the right hand of Sherlock Holmes, and who was she to tell him how to follow a suspected person?

"I think we should all go up to my room and discuss what we are to do this afternoon," he said aloud, when he had finished the last of his lunch at a leisurely pace. Having made his statement, he climbed off the bench and—in a gentlemanly fashion—began to make his way through the crowd in the pub to the staircase. Being female, Nan and Mary had less trouble getting through; the men usually pulled at their caps and backed out of the way with a muttered " 'Scuze me, ma'am," which most of them pronounced, in the country fashion, as "mum." With Suki sandwiched between them, they got to the stairs and trotted up, following John.

In the privacy of the more spacious room, they all gathered together, John and Mary on the sofa, Nan on one of the chairs, and Suki on the floor, playing with her new horse. "Mary put a sylph on him, one that is comfortable being in town," John said. "She'll follow him all day, then come back to me once he's gone home. I'm going to go back out in a few more minutes and find him in the market. I might be able to find out his name and possibly where he lives just by eavesdropping. If I can't, I might be able to get it by talking to him directly, especially if he's selling something rather than buying—it's easier to have the excuse to talk to a random stallholder than it is to get the elbow of someone walking about the market."

Mary nodded. "It's a pity we can't help you, but—well, too many cooks, as my old nanny used to say."

"Oh, I know!" Nan said, brightening. "I can send Neville off to be eyes as well. That way if your sylph gets bored and wanders off, *he'll* follow the fellow back to his farm."

"Excellent! All right, I am off," John said. He and Nan left the room together, he to go on his quest, Nan to go to her room and talk to Neville.

It took no time at all to impress the man's image in Neville's mind and explain what she wanted. With a grunt and a nod, he finished the last of the meat scraps that the chambermaid had left in his cup and hopped to the windowsill, then shoved off. He would certainly be able to make out Watson from above by his town clothing and hat, and eventually Watson would be in the vicinity of their target, if not actually talking to him, and Neville would be able to pick the fellow out of the crowd that way.

And then we'll corner him in his hole and— She felt that sudden rage rising in her again, the fierce anger of the warrior, and hastily shoved it down. And in doing so, she was terribly torn. On the one hand, she couldn't reconcile the fact that she had sensed absolutely nothing of evil at that altar site with the fact that it had clearly been used as a place of sacrifice. On the other hand, every time that warrior-she-had-been had manifested, she had been in grave danger, and the knowledge that incarnation possessed had been of immense importance. And to complicate matters, that grove they had found had been a place of profound *peace*—peaceful enough that deer, who were usually sensitive to magical or psychical atmospheres, used it as a safe-haven and a bedding place. It was as contradictory as the information they'd given Sherlock Holmes about Magdalena.

I'd give a very great deal for things to be nicely simple and black and white! she thought with irritation, as she returned to John and Mary's room to find Mary sitting on the couch with a book in her hands and Suki still playing on the floor with her horse.

"Well," she said aloud. "Since John has gone out to be the investigator, what are *we* to do with our time?"

"There are lessons," Mary pointed out. Suki looked up from her horse and her eyes brightened; then she looked a little apprehensive. "Mebbe not 'rithmatic?" she said, hopefully.

"I think we can skip arithmetic for a little," Nan said. "This is too distracting a place for the concentration arithmetic needs. However . . ." She transfixed Suki with a glance that brooked no argument. "We have neglected telepathic lessons in favor of history of late, and it is time we made up for that."

Suki heaved an exaggerated sigh. "Oi'll get me book," she said, and left with her horse, returning a few moments later sans horse and with a book. She opened it at a random page.

"Suki is very good receptively, but is still having trouble sending," Nan explained to Mary, who was looking on with interest. "Suki, if you can sit with Mrs. Watson, she can see what you are supposed to be sending me."

Suki hopped up on the couch with Mary and opened her book again. Frowning with concentration, she attempted to send Nan the first sentence on the page. Nan had chosen a book Suki would not likely be interested in, a botany book called *Culpepper's Complete Herbal*, that had both pictures and text. In order to properly strengthen her telepathic abilities, Suki had to learn how to send things that she might not herself understand or care about. The less she was invested emotionally in something, the harder it would be for her to send clearly.

Flea-wort, Nan heard finally, and recited the words aloud as Suki sent them. *Descript . . .* There was a sense of puzzlement, as if the word didn't look right to Suki.

But Mary said, as Nan sounded it aloud, "That's right, Suki, it's something called an abbreviation, a way to shorten a word."

The words came slowly. *Ordinary . . . flea-wort . . . rises . . . on a stalk . . .* The exercise was hard for Suki, and tedious for Nan, but it was the only way she knew of for Suki to strengthen herself. It was how Memsa'b had worked with her and Sarah, and how she continued to work with other young telepaths at the school.

"All right, Suki," she said, when Suki had sweated—literally— through half a page. "We'll do the cards now."

Suki closed the book with a relieved *snap,* and Nan took a pack of ordinary playing cards out of her handbag. She shuffled them thoroughly, then went through them, one by one, while Suki recited what they were. Suki had made about five mistakes in sending the words from the herbal, but made none in receiving the cards. Then Nan shuffled again, and handed them to Suki, who now sent the images to Nan. She was much better at images than words; flawless, in fact. They probably didn't even need to run the cards anymore, but Nan liked it as an exercise and a way to tell if Suki was tired or losing her ability to concentrate for some other reason.

Suki really *was* tired after that, so Nan assigned her a reading lesson; read a story with new words in it aloud, look them up in the dictionary, then use them in an appropriate sentence that had *not* been in the story. Like "elephantine."

From time to time, Nan checked with Neville. Thanks to John Watson, Neville found their quarry fairly easily and perched himself out of the way on the eaves of a nearby building, where he would be inconspicuous but able to see the man clearly.

John, however, was not having much luck; the man was here to buy, it seemed, and not to sell, and that made him difficult to approach. Through Neville's eyes, Nan saw him trailing the man all over the market, and she could only hope he was able to overhear something, or have some pretext to ask people who he had bought from who he was.

Finally the man moved out of the market. Neville pushed off, and followed him to the yard of the "Farmer" pub and hotel. Under Neville's watchful eye, he harnessed a cart horse to a farm wagon, went back to the market with them, and proceeded to load his purchases into the wagon. Then, as John watched from a corner of the market, he drove off, with Neville in leisurely pursuit.

Nan left Neville to his task; she could do nothing to aid it, and it would be just as well not to distract him.

"Neville's gone chasing our man," Nan reported, and Mary and Suki looked up from the book Suki was cheerfully laboring through.

"What about John?" Mary asked.

"You can ask him yourself in a minute, he should be coming up here as soon as he works his way through the market," Nan replied, and stood up to stretch. "I hope it turns out that the farmstead isn't as far away as that grove was, or we're in for another long walk tomorrow."

At that moment, there was a tap on the door, and John Watson opened it. "Frustrating," he said, closing it behind himself. "Very frustrating. Evidently he was here to buy supplies for the farm, and I could not make an excuse to speak to him. I did find out that his name is Cedric Edmondson, and he and his family have owned Sennoke Farm 'forever,' at least according to the lady who sold him a coil of rope. I also discovered that his reputation hereabouts is very good, so we should tread carefully here."

Mary handed the book to Suki and regarded her husband with thoughtful eyes. "Perhaps we should return to London and merely report this to Lord Alderscroft."

But John shook his head. "Lord Alderscroft left this in our hands. I think we will have to confront him and find out how far he has gone. No matter how much blood magic he has performed, since he hasn't yet descended to sacrificing humans, he will be no match for two Elemental Masters. And then—" He glanced at Nan. "—there is the little matter of Miss Killian's . . . other aspect."

"My other aspect, as you call it, was utterly furious at the sight of him," Nan confessed. "I fear that if he should act at all aggressively I will not be able to hold that part of me back."

"All the more reason to confront him, then," John said with confidence. "By daylight would be best; black magic of all sorts is weaker in the day. We'll wait for Neville and the sylph to return and see what they can tell us."

When the sylph returned, it was merely to give John the directions to Sennoke Farm. When *Neville* returned, however, it was with more detail. Neville had flown over the place with an eye to memorizing where each and every building was and all of the people on the farm. He had returned with every bit of information that a human scout might have.

With Suki looking on attentively, Nan sank into a half-trance, communing closely with Neville, and slowly sketched out the raven's-eye view of the farm from above. The buildings whose purposes were obvious she labeled—*house, barn, cowshed*—and those whose purposes were not, she left alone. "Neville can count up to eight, but there were more people than that there, so he counted them up by type," she said, as she "listened" attentively to what Neville had to tell her. "Four Big Skirts—that would be grown women, probably the wife, and servants or female farm folk, I suppose. Eight Big Trousers, including this Cedric. Two Little Skirts—little girls. Two Medium Skirts—girls in their teens, I think. One Little Trousers, and five Medium Trousers."

"That is a big farm," John observed. "Our best chance might be to approach him when he is alone in the fields. Otherwise there's no telling how much help he might be able to draw from the others."

"*Me go,*" croaked Neville.

"That would be the best idea, Neville," John agreed. "And you can tell us when he is alone, and where."

"A good, sound night's sleep, then," Mary declared. "A good meal before it, and John, you and I will make our preparations." She hesitated. "I don't like the idea of leaving Suki here alone, but—"

"Oi ain't stayin'!" Suki declared, crossing her arms over her chest, and glaring. "Yer cain't make me!"

Nan sighed. She knew Suki in this mood. "She's right," Nan said, to forestall any attempt at argument from John and Mary. "We can't make her stay, and if something terrible does happen, she needs to *know,* and we need to be able to send her for help."

"What kind of—" John stopped, as he realized what Nan meant. "Do you think he'd come for her?"

"More readily than for an adult," Nan replied. "Robin considers adults to be capable of defending themselves. Children, however . . . that's another story." She turned to Suki. "I'm going to give you my charm for summoning Puck; you must promise me that if things go badly, you will run very far and very fast, and when you get somewhere you think is safe, call him." She would have liked to add, "and take Neville with you," but the likelihood of Neville deserting her in a crisis was next to nothing.

Suki nodded solemnly, her curls bobbing. "Oil roight," she promised.

Nan could only hope it would not come to that.

The silence in the flat was . . . unnerving. When she got back to the flat in the morning, there were no cheerful greetings from Nan and Suki, no raucous *quork* from Neville, just Grey's happy whistle and "Welcome home, Sarah!" She made sure that Mrs. Horace had brought up Grey's breakfast, spent a half an hour cuddling her, then went to bed wishing for the chatter she had sometimes found annoying.

It was the silence that actually woke Sarah in the afternoon. Usually she slumbered, lulled by the murmur of voices in the next room as Suki and Nan did lessons. Today the only sounds were those of the street outside. It made her unsettled, and instead of lying in bed, waking up slowly, she got out of bed immediately.

She wandered the flat in her dressing gown for a bit, picking at the food that Mrs. Horace had left, feeling a bit disoriented to find herself in almost sole possession of the space. She kept expecting to hear Nan and Suki coming up the stairs, but there wasn't a single sound in the hallway, only, faint and far, Mrs. Horace singing over her work. Finally, though, she settled with Grey and a book, and the silence stopped being so unsettling. In fact, as she got herself dressed in a more leisurely fashion than usual, she began to enjoy it. It was rather *nice* not to have to listen to chatter about lessons, or answer Suki's infinite questions while she got ready for the opera. Grey expressed herself in very few words, preferring simple companionship and now and again a scratch or a cuddle. Things felt unhurried, and as a result, she left the flat in Grey's sleepy charge with a faint smile on her face, instead of feeling as if she had to rush out of the house on the instant.

She loitered in front of the house, watching the few people on the street in the evening light. A small skein of starlings flew overhead, chattering, and she reveled in the knowledge that for once, she was not beholden to anyone to set the time of her leaving and coming back. Freddy Smart turned up for her, right on time, and handed her into the cab with a little bow that made her giggle. She settled against the cushions of the hansom with a sense of relaxation for the very first time since she had begun this particular adventure.

He dropped her at the opera house early for the performance, since Magdalena liked to see her in her dressing room before the curtain rose. The front of the opera house was shut up and silent, all the lights extinguished, the doors locked. She went around to the stage entrance, where the doorman let her in without a murmur, and proceeded down the plain, even spartan backstage hall to the dressing room reserved for the Prima Donna.

"Ah, you are here!" Magdalena cried, as Alicia let her in. *"Ausgezeichtnet!"* It was one of her rare lapses into German, but apparently there was no equivalent word in English. "Sit, sit, and have some grapes, have some wine!"

The first thing that struck *all* the senses were the flowers; vases and vases of them, wreaths hung up on pegs on the wall or even a corner of the folding screen, fragrant, colorful—dying, wilting in the heat. There were always flowers waiting for Magdalena before the performance, and after, it seemed as if the entire contents of Covent Garden had been loaded into the room until they spilled out into the hall. There was a folding screen across one corner where Magdalena changed; there were costumes hung up on the walls, a chair and a couch much stained with makeup from countless previous occupants were jammed against the wall, with their worn upholstery concealed by opulent silk shawls thrown over both. The rest of the room was taken up by the dressing table, dressing stool, and huge mirror with another full-length mirror standing on the wall opposite, so Magdalena could survey herself before and behind. Lights were all around the mirror over the dressing table: the cause of the heat. The dressing table in other divas' rooms might be strewn with a chaos of makeup and hairpieces, notes from the producer, notes from lovers, notes from admirers, jewelry both paste and real, half-eaten boxes of bonbons. Not Magdalena's. Everything was precise and in its place. Stage jewels were in boxes covered with the same fabric as the costume they went with. *Real* jewels were in velvet jewelry boxes that were kept in a small strongbox under Alicia's care. The real jewelry went in there when Magdalena took off her jewelry to exchange it for the stage jewels and came back out again at the end of the performance, when Magdalena took off the stage jewels. That strongbox always returned under Alicia's guard to the hotel when the performance was over. Frequently, more velvet boxes went into the strongbox for their return than there had been before the performance. Notes from the producer, conductor, and the director went on the mirror to be studied. Personal notes went into a floral pasteboard box, secured with ribbons. Sarah suspected there was a color code to the ribbons, but Magdalena had never revealed it.

There was always fruit on the small table between the chair and the couch. There were always boxes of bonbons beside the couch, which Magdalena never indulged in, and which she gave away to the chorus the day after she had been gifted them. There was always wine next to the dressing table in a footed bucket, which she *did* indulge in, but not to excess, that Sarah could tell.

The chair and the couch were reserved for visitors while Magdalena was dressing; Sarah was the only visitor allowed before the performance. After the performance, once Magdalena had doffed the final costume and taken off her stage makeup, the chair and the couch went to admirers. Magdalena would hold court for some indeterminate time while Alicia and Sarah went to the hotel in Freddy Smart's hansom. If Magdalena planned to spend some time with an admirer, she sent a note, and Alicia and Sarah would share the feast meant for the diva and Sarah, giggling and gossiping in a way Sarah had never experienced before, because Memsa'b never seemed to gossip, and Nan didn't know how.

Sarah took her seat in the chair, curling her legs under it to as to take up as little room as possible. Magdalena's costumes for this opera were absolutely *enormous;* she was playing Violetta in *La Traviata*, and the dresses were all those huge wedding-cake-like creations of decades ago, big bell-shaped skirts held out with hoops. It was a mercy that the hoops collapsed and could be stacked against the wall, or there would never have been room for anything in here but the costumes.

Sarah ate grapes slowly and watched as Magdalena transformed herself from a healthy and hearty German woman who did not look to have had a sick day in her life to the fragile, consumptive, Violetta. It was, frankly, startling, and when Magdalena donned Violetta's black wig, which underscored her pallor by contrast, she didn't seem to be the same person at all.

Then Magdalena rose from her stool to begin donning the ball gown of the first act, and that was Sarah's signal to leave. As she edged past Alicia, who was shaking the hoops into shape, Magdalena, as always, gave her an arch wink. "Guard me from spirits, faithful one!" she said gaily, and bent so that Alicia could slip the hoops over her head.

Now Sarah made her way down into the theater—not yet open for patrons, except for those few, very special ones like herself. Behind the lowered curtain workmen were everywhere, and she took care not to get in their way. The stage smelled of dust, sawdust, and paint. She went past the curtain and paused on the stage front, as she always did, looking up into the dim half-light in front of the closed curtains—looking for spirits. She hadn't seen any yet, but Magdalena insisted that she be on the alert anyway, and the stagehands all swore the theater was haunted by the spirits of performers long dead and their own fellows who had died in accidents. When she was satisfied there were no lurking ghosts this time, she made her way down the stage steps, into the halls, and then up to the left-hand box nearest the stage, reserved, now, for her and only her. Alicia had told her that some of Magdalena's admirers were angry that they could not make use of it, but she was adamant. Only Sarah could sit there, so that if she needed to protect Magdalena from ghosts, she would not have to do so with distractions.

There was a bottle of chilled mineral water waiting there for her, in ice, as champagne would have been for someone else. And more grapes. As always, Sarah sat in a cushioned chair toward the rear of the box and drew the curtains on the side nearest the audience half-closed. She could see Magdalena perfectly, and Magdalena could see her, but it was unlikely that anyone else would know who was the tenant of that box seat.

She waited as the orchestra filed in, as noises from behind the curtain announced the final setting up of the first-act props and scenery, and as, at long last, the rest of the audience was allowed in. She waited as the limelights were lit, as the gaslights in the house were turned up, as the audience, gossiping, laughing, made their way into their seats and got themselves comfortable. It was going to be another full house. Only the Royal Box would be empty, for the Queen, even after decades, *still* thought *La Traviata* was immoral and still would not come to see it, nor allow any of her children to. The only way any of the Royal Family would be able to see this opera would be if they came without the Queen knowing, incognito.

Which was, of course, quite possible, especially for her heir, Prince Edward, who never let a little thing like "immorality" stop him when it came to pleasure. He went plenty of other places "incognito" (although he never tried all that hard to hide who he was, and he was *very* distinctive), so why not the opera?

And then the orchestra ceased its tuning, the lights came down again, the audience settled. And the overture poured, lush, faintly erotic, into the hall.

The curtain rose on a party in a fashionable apartment in Paris—probably not unlike ones Magdalena attended on a regular basis. Except that, of course, at this party most of the women present were courtesans, and the men were their keepers, for Magdalena was singing the part of Violetta, the Lady of the Camellias, the most beautiful courtesan in Paris.

Sarah did not give herself over to the music—not completely. Instead, she kept her occult senses active, waiting for the brush of chill, the hint of the otherworldly, the catch in the throat that meant something un-alive had entered the hall. But there was nothing, and Magdalena took the stage like a conquering hero, her voice soaring out over the others with a power that was positively uncanny.

It even caught Sarah, vigilant though she was, and she understood, as she came to understand over and over, every night, why so many were in love with this woman.

Sarah waited in Freddy's cab at the stage door for Alicia to come out. She always slipped out as the applause began and took the entrance into the backstage to slip out the stage door. More than one gentleman had tried to engage the cab and been sent away disappointed and grumbling that the hansom was already occupied; Sarah looked respectable enough and met them with a fierce enough glare that none of them tried anything other than a weakly bullying effort to get her to give it up. There was, as usual, a crowd around the stage door—admirers of small consequence, not important enough to be allowed inside, most of them students and the like. Some of them were impudent enough to peer into the cab to see if Sarah was anyone important; she ignored them or gave them her best basilisk glare. Finally, Alicia emerged, head held high and chin thrust out aggressively, making her way, with energetic thrusts of her elbows and kicks to shins whenever necessary, until she reached the safety of the cab. Once she was inside, Sarah knocked on the roof, and Freddy and Crumpet took off smartly.

"Students!" Alicia said, making the word into a curse.

Sarah laughed. "They're hoping to pick up pretty ballet girls."

Alicia snorted. "The pretty ballet girls wouldn't give them the time of day. Why settle for a beer and a cheese sandwich when you can get champagne and pheasant and maybe a gold bracelet?"

"From a wheezy old man, who might be fat, and will almost certainly be bald and want to put his hands all over you at the least!" Sarah pointed out. "I think I would take the beer and sandwich."

"Most wouldn't," Alicia replied. "*I* wouldn't. You and I can go on until we are old harridans, but *they* are mayflies. Dancing for pennies, and ten years, fifteen at best, they replace you with someone younger? Then, if you're lucky, you go into the costume department, or teaching little girls, and if you aren't, you hope you can find honest work at a laundry. You've got to make your hay whilst the sun shines, as my old mother says. Take that little black-eyed minx, May Fancher. *There's* a girl who knows how to butter her bread! A ruby ring she got last night!"

Sarah settled back for a nice bit of gossip about the ballet girls, who were highly sought-after by certain men, those who would not or could not support a mistress but could derive much of the same benefits of having one (without any of the inconvenient attachments) by dint of sumptuous suppers and a few gifts. As Alicia had noted, the girls of the ballet corps came and went, most were poor, and the men took full advantage of that.

This was a world Sarah had never even dreamed existed until Magdalena introduced her to it. There was the spectacle of the opera itself, and then there was the theater going on behind the scenes, which could be even more histrionic than what was presented on stage.

The cab pulled up to the hotel, and the two of them got out; for these rides Alicia—or rather, Magdalena—paid. They crossed the vast expanse of the lobby, getting friendly nods from the concierge and the desk clerk, and took the elevator up to Magdalena's room.

Their arrival was the signal for the concierge to notify the kitchen to prepare whatever Magdalena had selected for her supper before she left for the theater. While they were lighting candles, making sure the rooms were as Magdalena liked them, spritzing rose cologne about to scent the air, and making sure that if Magdalena happened to bring an admirer with her, all would be as it should be, the kitchen was hard at work. Magdalena was by no means the only guest of this hotel who wanted midnight suppers, especially not in the more luxurious rooms and suites.

Sarah reflected, as she plumped a sofa pillow, that for an artist, Magdalena was astonishingly regular in her habits. She would entertain her admirers in her dressing room for an hour; no more, seldom less. Then one of them would be allowed to take her to the hotel in his carriage. About the time she left the theater, the supper arrived at the room, and the waiter who had brought it would arrange everything, including two place settings, with two extra place settings left on the sideboard. If Magdalena sent a note, Alicia and Sarah would eat together. If she came back alone, Magdalena and Sarah would eat first and Alicia would enjoy her share after Magdalena had been put to bed—before Sarah's addition to Magdalena's entourage, Alicia had eaten before her mistress arrived, but Alicia swore she didn't mind waiting. Possibly, she didn't; there was certainly enough fruit to stave off hunger in Magdalena's dressing room, and plenty of time while her mistress was on stage for Alicia to make a sort of meal out of it.

And if Magdalena arrived with a man, Sarah and Alicia would withdraw into the other end of the room and stay behind a screen, then eat after they had dined and vanished into her bedroom.

The first time this had happened, Sarah thought she was going to perish of embarrassment, but she was used to it now. She and Alicia would play cards until the murmuring and laughter stopped and the bedroom door closed . . .

And then they would ignore whatever sounds came out of that bedroom. Or try to. Sarah still had trouble doing that.

"Doesn't that make you . . ." Sarah had asked the maid once, blushing. Alicia had just shrugged.

"If you are in service, you get used to being thought part of the furnishings very quickly," she had said philosophically. "Besides, I'm not going to wait until this lovely quail gets stone cold just to avoid listening to the bedspring chorus."

The supper came up, and the dining table and sideboard were arranged. At almost the same time, a driver and three attendants arrived from the theater with the masses of flowers from Magdalena's dressing room, which she and Alicia placed around the sitting room and dining room like trophies. When Magdalena and Alicia left to go to the theater, maids would come in and take them all away, to be replaced by the new tributes that night.

And since no note arrived with the flowers, that meant that Magdalena, or Magdalena and an admirer, would be coming shortly.

Tonight, however, Magdalena arrived alone.

She flung her magnificent sable cloak over a chair and greeted Sarah by kissing her cheek. That sable cloak had become a signature garment of hers, like Lillie Langtry's famous little black dress. "*Six* curtain calls!" she said with satisfaction. She glided into her chair and snapped her fingers in the air. "*That,* for that nasty little man in the paper who said I could not possibly equal Patti! The great Patti only got *four* when she sang Violetta in London!"

Clearly, Magdalena was in an excellent mood, and Sarah relaxed. She had only seen Magdalena in a bad mood once—but that once had been quite enough, and she was always just a little on edge when Magdalena returned until she knew what mood her patroness would be in.

Alicia served them both supper, and Magdalena kept up a nonstop stream of what could only be described as a monologue throughout the entire meal. Sarah didn't mind. Mostly she tuned it out, because it was about Magdalena's performance, or her admirers, or what they had told her, all mixed up in no particular order. Evidently tonight she'd had a new one; quite a good "catch," it appeared, a "Marquess," whatever that was. Some sort of nobleman who had come into London, on a whim obtained tickets for a box tonight, and Magdalena had enchanted him. Of course. Most women admired her, but men from six to sixty were utterly captivated by her.

It appeared that this gentleman, one George William Thomas Brudenell-Bruce, was the 4th Marquess of Ailesbury. "Call me Willie," the gentleman had allegedly told Magdalena. According to what Sarah gleaned from Magdalena, "Willie" had vast estates and profligate habits, exactly the sort of gentleman admirer that Magdalena liked best. She was just as happy to receive their admiration in the form of gowns or sumptuous furnishings or offers to pay her bills or lavish jewels as the little ballet girls were happy to get thin gold bracelets and necklaces and boxes of chocolates.

So Magdalena was in fine spirits tonight, so much so that halfway through the meal, and a little tipsy, she invited Alicia to set a third plate and join them, which Alicia was quite ready to do. By the time Alicia helped her mistress to bed, Magdalena was toasting her own triumph with a last glass of wine and singing bits of "Sempre Libera," her first-act aria. Even tipsy, her voice was glorious.

Alicia emerged again smiling. "I don't know how she does it," the maid remarked. "You or I would want to die in the morning, but she'll awaken fresh as anything and now that she can sleep at night, she'll eat her breakfast like a prizefighter." She gestured at the empty room. "I leave you to your ghastlies." Alicia had become remarkably nonchalant about the haunts, which Sarah regarded as a distinct improvement over her initial terror.

Sarah went about the room putting out lights until there were only two, and the dying fire in the fireplace. Then she composed herself on the sofa, and waited. She didn't bother keeping Puck's charm in her hand now, the spirits that were left were utterly harmless—if infuriatingly stubborn. The rooms went to silence, with only the occasional pop of an ember in the fireplace and the smell of dying roses, carnations, lilies, and, of course, camellias, in the air.

Attracted, as always, to the presence of an active medium, the last four spirits left to dismiss appeared, one by one, fading into existence between Sarah and the fireplace. These last four had been . . . remarkably mulish. So far, Sarah had not even been able to get them to communicate with her, much less move on.

Three of the four were mere thin wraiths, so attenuated by age and loss of power that they were difficult to make out, and it was only by virtue of experience that Sarah knew one was female and two were male. Like shapes of fog, they barely had a distinction between head and body. They didn't seem to have a purpose; they didn't seem impelled by anything. They had merely appeared, night after night, and . . . hovered. That would be uncanny enough, of course, for someone like Magdalena—possibly even more frightening than a spirit that actually *did* something, because having a vague shape with hollow, dark pits instead of eyes hanging at the foot of your bed and staring at you was not something most people handled well. But for Sarah . . . they were a distinct problem. She had tried invoking the door to their ultimate destinations—most spirits either went straight to it or fought to get away from it. There had been no reaction whatsoever. It was as if they weren't even aware of it. How could she dismiss them if she couldn't even get them to react to the door?

The fourth spirit she was ignoring for now, because it was not like any ghost she had ever seen before. It was bright, brighter and stronger than the others by far, but the details about it were vague, as if the spirit itself was keeping her from seeing what it was. It was definitely female, and that was all she knew about it. It wouldn't speak to her, and like the other three, it was neither attracted to nor repelled by the door. The only difference between it and the others was that Sarah got a very strong sense of purpose and a sense of betrayal and anger from it, though not directed at her.

But since it was so strong, she was leaving it for last. *If I can work out a way to get the others through the door, I should be able to use that on the last one.*

And so, for the rest of the night, she concentrated on the lone female of the three she was calling the Lost Wraiths. She tried coaxing it, tried persuasion, tried bribery, tried commanding it . . .

all to no avail whatsoever. By the time morning arrived, and the four spirits faded away in the predawn light, she was exhausted and no further along than she had been when she started.

After a breakfast she was almost too tired to appreciate, she bid farewell to Alicia and wound her weary way back to the flat, where Grey greeted her with a whistle and kissing sounds. *I cannot think what I am missing,* she thought as she greeted her friend, made sure that Mrs. Horace had given the parrot a good breakfast of peas and carrots and a little scrambled egg and bits of toast, then pulled off her dress and practically fell into bed. *I hope Nan is having better luck than I.*

11

There was something to be said for being in a hotel in a market town. No one blinked an eye when Nan, Suki, John and Mary rose at the first cockcrow and came downstairs looking for breakfast. In fact, they found four hearty souls who had arisen even earlier and were now steadily shoveling food in their mouths, drinking poisonously black tea, and looking disinclined to think about anything else, much less talk to anyone.

Under other circumstances, the silence might have been unnerving. This morning, it was precisely what they wanted.

Nan had come armed; under her skirt and over her petticoat she had strapped a belt with the Gurkha *kukri* knife that Agansing had given her when he had judged her skilled enough to have earned one. She could reach it, easily, through a false pocket in the seam of her skirt. She had armed Suki as well, with a four-inch blade that was sharp enough to cut the wind. It was hidden under Suki's pinafore; Suki knew how to use it, too.

"Now remember," Nan had told her, taking her little chin in her hand and making sure Suki was looking right in her eyes, "I gave you Puck's charm. It's in your pinafore pocket. You are not to use this knife *except* to get away. If something goes badly, I want you to run, then call for Puck as soon as you are safe. Only use the knife if someone gets between you and escape."

Suki had nodded and promised solemnly. Sometimes it made

a lot of sense to treat her as a very small adult, and this was one of those times.

They left the hotel and headed in the direction of Knole again—although this time, instead of taking the walking path, they were going to go a little further and take the road that branched off to the right immediately after the path. That road should take them to Sennoke Farm. By the time they got there, Cedric should be in the fields. Neville would locate him for them, and if he was alone, they were going to confront him. Nan was supposed to try reading his thoughts first, then John would approach.

That was . . . just about as much plan as they had.

And in case something happened to *all* of them, John had left a letter in his room, already stamped, to be mailed to Lord Alderscroft if they didn't return.

The Celtic warrior inside Nan was getting a little difficult to keep down. There was something about Cedric that had absolutely enraged the Nan-that-was, and she didn't think the blood magic had anything to do with it. It was more like a purely personal animosity. It didn't seem possible they had known each other in that past life—but it felt almost as if they *had*.

They walked in absolute silence, even Suki, all of them sobered by the undeniable fact that they were walking into a situation over which they had little to no control, on someone else's ground. And if they had not had not one, but *two* Elemental Masters with them, Nan would never have gone along with this.

Overhead, the trees were full of birds, and there was a lark soaring invisibly above them, its singing drifting down to them as it exulted in the morning. The air was cool and a little damp and smelled of green things. Nan wished profoundly that they were walking off to another picnic and a chance to enjoy the Downs, instead of heading for what could be a nasty confrontation.

The road they turned off on was not so much a "road" as a lane; it was plain dirt, pounded hard as brick with the passage of the years, with tall hedges growing on top of the banks on either side of it. That actually was good; it meant no one would see them coming. Neville stayed within sight overhead, but was cross-quartering the area to the right of the lane as they went, searching for Cedric Edmondson.

Then, at last, he folded his wings and plummeted toward them; Nan held up her arm, and he landed hard on it. He rested the tip of his bill on her forehead and shared his thoughts with her. A moment later, she knew all that he knew.

"Edmondson is just on the other side of this hedge, cutting a ditch. He's all alone, and there is no one within sight or earshot of him. There's no better time than now to deal with him," Nan said, tension rising in her and knotting her shoulders. "Neville says there's a stile a few feet along."

"All right then," John replied, sounding grim. He straightened his shoulders and looked at his wife, who nodded slightly. "Nan, is there anything you need to do to ready yourself?"

Nan considered that, then decided it was better to get her *kukri* out now and not risk its getting tangled up in her skirt. Carefully, she put her hand into her pocket, clasped the hilt, and just as carefully unsheathed it. Already she felt better having it in her hands.

John was clearly taken aback as he looked at the lethal, curved knife with recognition in his eyes. "Is that—"

"Yes," she replied. "Memsa'b's Gurkha associate Agansing taught me how to use it a very long time ago. I was only a few years older than Suki; Suki will certainly begin lessons with him when she starts attending the Harton School in the autumn."

Suki gave a little hop of happiness at this revelation. Nan patted her shoulder.

"The Hartons impress me more with every new revelation," John replied. "Mary, are you ready?"

"Oh yes," his wife said, her eyes gone very dark and fierce. "My allies are waiting. I thought you might be at a disadvantage, but if he's cutting a ditch—"

"There will certainly be water, and I don't need much to make a weapon," he finished for her. "All right then. Let's find that stile."

They strode onward. The stile was just around a bend in the lane; a set of narrow, steep, pyramidal wooden stairs not unlike a stepladder, going up the side of the hedge facing the road and down into the field on the other. John went first, followed by Mary, then Suki, with Nan bringing up the rear.

As Nan's head topped the hedge she saw the farmland spread

out before her, low, rolling hills covered in irregularly shaped fields divided by yet more hedges and hedgerows. To the right, three fields away, she spotted a lone man working along the hedgerow. Though his face could not be made out at this distance, she was sure it was Cedric.

With one hand on the splintery top step, she concentrated with all her might on picking up something, anything, from his thoughts. At this distance, alone as he was, she *should* have been able to sense at least some of his thoughts—but there was nothing. Just a kind of blank . . . a sort of shadow in her mind where he *should* have been, but was not.

John looked up at her, anxiously, as Mary kept an eye on the distant figure, who did not seem to notice them.

"Anything?" he asked, intuiting what she was doing.

"Nothing," she said with a shake of the head. "That either means he's one of the rare folk whose thoughts I can't sense, or he's got a block from something." It briefly occurred to her that the problem might be with *her*—

But that had never happened before. Why should it now?

John's expression darkened. He didn't like the implications of that any more than she did. "All right then. We have no choice but to confront him." He looked down at Suki. "Child, you are our only hope if things go terribly wrong. Now tell me what you're going to do."

Suki straightened her back, looking very proud to be so trusted. "Oi stays well back. An' if yew an' Missus Watson an' Miss Nan starts t'lose, Oi runs. Oi gets over the hedge an' runs till Oi fink there ain't nobody chasin', an Oi calls Puck."

John nodded decisively. "Exactly right. Mary? Nan?" He looked from one to the other, as if to say *if you have any doubts, this is the last chance to voice them*.

They both nodded. And at his signal, they all headed to where Cedric, all unaware, was digging his ditch. They walked the paths beside the fields, rather than through them; no matter what else was going on, they were mindful of the fact that it was acutely bad form to trample a growing field.

That is, that is what they intended to do. But as they got within about thirty feet of him, he looked up straight at them, and his face—and everything about him—abruptly changed.

Or at least, it seemed that way to Nan, who no longer saw a farmer, attired in his trousers and boots, with his smock over it all, patiently cutting a ditch with nothing more in his hands than a spade.

Once again, she saw the figure from her vision, crowned with stag horns, with symbols painted in blood on his bare chest, his face deliberately streaked in patterns with the same blood. And the Celtic warrior in her rose up and overwhelmed her.

Her vision literally misted red with rage. Screaming a war cry her civilized self didn't understand, she charged him, hand holding the *kukri* raised high. Or was it a bronze-hilted sword? She couldn't tell, all she felt was white-hot anger, and all she could see was her enemy, her hated and despised *enemy*, that she *must* slay or die herself. For if she did not, he would lay waste to everything she cared about.

At the last possible minute, he grasped the handle of the shovel in both hands and raised it above his head, catching and holding the *kukri* on it as she slashed it down on him in the move that was known to Gurkha warriors to cut their enemies' torsos in half. They struggled together, as Neville screamed and beat at Cedric with his wings and slashed at him with his beak, their faces close enough together to have kissed—but they were snarling, both of them with an absolutely feral rage. And there was nothing in Nan *but* rage and the driving need to *kill* this man, until suddenly—

"*STOP!*"

The word rang in Nan's head and drove the rage completely out, leaving her suddenly empty and stunned. She found herself looking into the face of Cedric, who looked equally stunned— and no longer painted in bloody symbols. Just a farmer, red with exertion, his face streaked with his *own* blood from the slashes Neville had put on his left ear and the side of his head.

Between them was Suki, with one hand on each of them as if she could hold them apart with her own tiny little body.

"Nan! Yew haveter *stop,* 'cause 'e ain't doin' whatcher think!" Suki said firmly. "*Look!*"

Somehow Suki had been able to read Cedric's thoughts, clearly, and now she poured them into Nan's head, so much and so fast that Nan staggered back a single pace, and then another, and finally dropped the *kukri* to the ground and stared at the man she had attacked in stunned horror.

". . . and I am the latest in the line of priests of Tyr that goes back to when my people came across the water, and fought . . . yours, I suppose," Cedric said, looking deep into Nan's eyes. He shook his head heavily. "Which will likely be where your anger comes from. 'Tisn't blood magic that I am doing, not in the way you take the meaning of it. The—life-force, I reckon ye'd say, of my sacrifices goes to the land, as it allus has been an' allus will be. 'Tis Land Magic. I take none of the magic for meself, nor my own family."

They were sitting in the shade of one of the bigger trees growing up out of the hedgerow, on the edge of a field of, of all things, lavender. Cedric had his hand up to the side of his head, putting pressure on the wounds Neville had inflicted on him. "But the altar—" said John. "The vision Nan had—"

" 'Twas a true one. But that there stag was an old friend of mine. I slay no beast that is not willin'; most of them come to me when they are old and sick and longin' for peace, and they lay down their blood in the service of the land." Cedric smiled crookedly. " 'Twas not always so," he acknowledged. "My grandfather's grandfather's grandfather sacrificed the young and prime, not the old and weary. But the deeper our ties grew to the land and the beasts here, the less we wished to choose the young and strong, in the full prime o' life. The blood of the old feeds the land as well as theirs, and 'tis kinder to send them to an easy rest."

"But why did—" John chewed the ends of his moustache. "This does not match with what Nan saw."

"Because Miss Nan and I met and fought in another time, I think," Cedric replied. "And she saw not what was before her, but her ancient enemy. And I will confess, in that dark time we did slay men on that altar, and many of them."

Neville flew down out of the tree and landed at Cedric's feet, striding ponderously up to him. The raven looked up into Cedric's face, then looked down at the ground. "*Sorry,*" he croaked miserably.

Cedric reached out and scratched the nape of Neville's neck, in the vulnerable spot Neville had offered him. "You were defending your mistress. Tain't no dishonor in that."

Considering that Cedric's ear and the left side of his face had been brutally savaged, that was gracious indeed. Nan winced. John had put a rough bandage on him made of all of their handkerchiefs together, but there was no doubt it needed better tending than that.

"You must let me do something about those wounds," John Watson insisted. "I am a doctor, you know."

Cedric got up, heavily. "We will tell my wife that I fell when the earth gave way beneath me, and the hedge slashed my face, and you came to my rescue," he said. "I do not want her worried. She knows what I am—she is my fellow priest—but there is no reason for her to be clucking an' fussing o'er this misunderstanding."

Nan gulped and got clumsily to her own feet. "I don't have enough words to say how sorry I am," she said, for what must have been the hundredth time.

"But I was fair as much to blame as you," he replied. "Even as you rushed me, I saw in *you* my ancient enemy. Had I anythin' in my hand but a shovel, had I one of my hounds with me as you have your bird, it might be I who was apologizing for wounding you." He offered his hand to John Watson, who took it and was pulled to his feet. John helped Mary stand. Suki hopped down off the branch she'd been sitting on.

"We'll go up to the cottage," Cedric said, pointing at the distant cottage with its oast house behind it. "There should be everything you need there."

"I can't believe you're not screaming in pain," Nan replied, still blushing with shame, as Neville flew on ahead of them.

Finally Cedric laughed. "I be a farmer," he pointed out. "I been worse injured than this all the time. This is one of the few times there has been a doctor to see to it; usually it is my wife."

"You have a brave wife," Mary put in, and shuddered. "I can't bear it when John does surgery."

"She is out of as many generations of healing priest as I am land priest." Cedric continued to tell them of his background and his wife's quite as easily as if blood had not been soaking through the bandages on his face and ear. Listening to his voice, you would never have known the pain he must have been in. *I can't imagine how he's bearing it—*

"I feel nothing," Cedric said abruptly to Nan, as if *he* had been listening to her thoughts, instead of the other way around. " 'Tis the gift of the land. When I am in need, it gives, and now, it takes the pain."

Nan glanced at John, who shrugged. "If he says so, Nan, it's probably true. This is older magic than anything I am familiar with. It's definitely Earth, and I suspect Cedric qualifies as an Earth Master, but what he does—it's ancient, and I don't think any of the White Lodge would understand it."

"Oh, how we could have used your help with the Shadow Beast!" exclaimed Mary, which then led to the story of the Shadow Beast and how they had rid the house at 10 Berkeley Square of it. They were moving slowly to spare Cedric, so there was plenty of time to tell all of it. Several times Cedric made muffled exclamations, but he did not interrupt them, and when they were done, he was silent for a long time.

"I know this Beast. 'Tis is an old thing, a kind of dark servant my people brought with us, and thought to use against yours," he said, finally. "There were many such; some were slain—yes, they can be slain, but 'tisn't easy, and it calls for that the slayer also be willing to die. Some were sent back to where they came from; they were as like to turn against the one that planned to use them as to attack the enemy. This, I do not know how to do. And some were lost. I be thinkin' your'n was one of the ones lost." He pondered a little more as they finally reached the farmyard of the "cottage," which was a substantial black-timbered Tudor building that probably had at least twenty rooms in it. The farmyard was full of hens scratching in the dust. A dog laying in the door to the barn looked up and laid his head back down again when he saw who it was. "I will look among the things passed down to me and see if there is something in them. If you find another such, mayhap I will be of help." He turned his head to give Nan a glance. "But if the you-that-was blamed the me-that-was for the Shadow Beast, that there is reason enough for you to come at me like a wolf protectin' her cubs."

Before he could say more, a blond, buxom woman in a brown

skirt, linen blouse, and very white apron came out of the cottage and, seeing his head bandaged, ran toward them, scolding anxiously. Cedric put her off easily with the lie he had made up. "And enough clucking, Agatha, my pretty brown hen. This man is a doctor, he helped me in the field, and he will mend me so you will not sigh and say I have lost my beauty. Let us go inside, and give him what he needs so he can patch me."

Now the woman shooed them all before her, getting them settled around the great plank table in her spacious and spotless kitchen. John asked for needle and thread, whiskey, clean cloths and boiling water. The boiling water was already on the stove; she ran and fetched the rest, and at John's direction, boiled the needle and thread and the cloths, laying them to dry on a clean towel.

Nan didn't really want to watch either; while John worked, she paid more attention to the kitchen, with its black beams and whitewashed plaster walls, the huge fireplace quite literally big enough to roast an ox, the wooden sink with its very own pump, the spotless counters, and the big iron stove that had been installed in the fireplace. Evidently Cedric was a prosperous man.

Cedric's ear was half off, but John said he was certain it would heal cleanly once it was stitched up. Half the whiskey went into Cedric, and the rest went to clean the wounds before John stitched them up. When John had done everything he could, he bandaged Cedric with the boiled cloths and called it done.

"Bread mold," said Agatha. "We should bandage him with bread mold."

"I've no objection, so long as the cloth you bandage him with is boiled well," John replied, and shrugged. "Cedric says that you are a healing priest, so—bread mold it is."

Agatha sighed and beamed at him. "Then you're the sensibilest doctor I e'er come acrost," she said, her accent much thicker than Cedric's. She patted her husband's head—the side that Neville had *not* savaged—with sympathy. "Don't let him tell you the land's taking all his pain. I've a wee bit of laudanum put by for times like this. I just thank the good gods that he's never chopped off a hand or put a tine through a foot, and may he never do. Farmin' is more dangerous work than most townsfolk e're guess."

"Amen to that," Mary replied heartily, and with the deep

sympathy of one woman whose husband regularly runs into danger to another.

"I'll go and get the laudanum," Agatha said, gathering up the bloody handkerchiefs and the rest of the mess and carrying it off, leaving them alone with Cedric.

"So," Cedric said at last. "About this 'White Lodge' of your'n. Happens I should hear more of it, I'm thinking."

"Then you'll all be havin' dinner with us, *I'm* thinkin'," said Agatha firmly, poking her head back into the kitchen.

On a farm, Nan learned, the two biggest meals of the day were breakfast and "dinner"—which she would have called luncheon. Agatha and her cook and one of the "girls" produced two kinds of pie, heaps of bread and butter, slabs of cheese, several different kinds of pickle, a saddle of mutton, roast potatoes and new peas, roast onions and turnips, three kinds of jam, honey, and pots of tea. Everyone gathered for it in the big kitchen; with four guests at the table, four of the younger farmhands were given loaded plates and told to "take themselves outside."

And everyone at this farm, it seemed, knew what Cedric and Agatha were, for the Land Magic was discussed over the table with everyone listening, although none of the farmworkers actually *said* anything. It was pretty clear that although Cedric didn't have the title of "Squire," he was the squire hereabouts in all but name. Not only did he own Sennoke Farm, he owned two more that were worked by two of his brothers, a third brother was a carpenter, and a fourth brother was the blacksmith down in Sevenoaks.

The farmhands might not have contributed to the conversation out of deference to Cedric, but from the way they were shoveling food into their mouths, it might just have been because eating was of far more interest to them than talking. They finished much sooner than the guests; Cedric intercepted one of them as he left, a grizzled, muscular fellow, and set him to finishing the ditch that Cedric had started.

"How is it even possible that your family managed to keep this farm when the Normans came?" Mary finally asked, as the last plate was cleared away.

" 'Tis a short enough tale," Cedric replied, indicating with gestures that they should all move to the "parlor," where he stretched out his body on a sofa with a little groan. "The Edmondson of the day saw what was goin' to happen, and lay in wait for the Knight who'd been granted the hall where Knole is now. Caught him out alone, huntin', and used the Land Magic to surround him with stags and boars. And he said to the feller that there were two ways this could go; he, Edmondson, could keep his freehold and farm in peace, and grant a third of the surplus to the hall. Or the stags and boars could kill the knight. 'An' it don't matter a whit to me that yon Willie of Normandy will send another,' he told the knight. 'Because I'll just wait and catch him and make him the same offer, and on and on till Willie sends a lord with sense.' Happens the first one had sense." Cedric chuckled, and winced. Agatha bustled over to him with a brown bottle and made him take a teaspoon of what was in it. Agatha had made it very clear that she intended to stick right with her man, and Cedric had just rolled his eyes when she wasn't looking and made the best of it. "So it went, with every Edmondson confirmed in the freehold, until Great Harry came in and the Edmondson of that time looked ahead himself, as the other had done, saw trouble coming, and got a proper deed all sealed and signed afore Great Harry even thought of breakin' up the monasteries and takin' away the estates t'give t'others."

"That was a good—" John stopped, and stared at Cedric. "Did you say what I think you said?"

Cedric chuckled. "That the Edmondson of Great Harry's day scried a bit? Aye."

"But . . . but . . ." John spluttered. Cedric held up a hand.

"I do a bit too. Sometimes I scries, sometimes I just knows what's comin'. 'Tisn't certain. Further ahead ye look, less certain 'tis. Further afield ye look, less certain 'tis. Ye can change things, a bit, avoid trouble sometimes. Bigger the change coming, more certain 'tis." He shrugged. "But 'tis good for tellin' best days for hayin' and hoppin'."

John could only shake his head.

There were no more such enormous revelations, though Nan was fascinated and horrified at the same time by the idea that you could peer into the future at all. On the one hand, it would be grand not to ever have any unpleasant surprises. On the other . . . you'd know bad things were coming, and you'd have plenty of time to fret about them.

I think I would rather not know.

After a while, Nan just settled back in her comfortable chair, and examined the parlor without really listening to the conversation, which had gotten on to how . . . and in some cases, "if" . . . Cedric's Land Magic differed from Earth Magic. Mary and John were taking copious notes.

Cedric was much more educated than Nan would ever have guessed. Although he hadn't gotten a formal education beyond his teens, he was a great reader; the local vicar had taught him Latin and Greek, and his library of books here in the parlor was quite impressive.

Somewhat to Nan's surprise, along with the tea table and chairs, the sofa and armchairs, there was a piano. Cedric must be *very* prosperous to have that—but it probably meant that more than one person in his household played it, which would make winter evenings ever so much more entertaining for everyone on the farm.

The parlor was not ornamented with as much bric-a-brac as most parlors seemed to be, which was something of a relief so far as Nan was concerned. Anything that was in here appeared to have been chosen to serve a purpose. It was nice not to have to worry about knocking something over every time you moved. She wondered if Agatha was the one behind this relatively simple decor, or if she lamented not having stuffed birds, wax flowers, china statues, vases, and other fashionable impedimenta crowding her parlor.

The parlor did, however, have another patent stove in the enormous fireplace . . . and two inglenooks. Nan had read about inglenooks, but until now she had never seen one. She reflected that they must be the coziest places in the whole house, except perhaps in the kitchen, when winter winds roared.

Eventually, about teatime, John and Mary ran out of things to ask, and it was obvious that Cedric's wounds were paining him again.

"You are going to bed, my man," Agatha said firmly. "Sooner to bed, sooner to mend, I say."

Cedric chuckled. "Aye, little hen," he replied, obediently. "Just a few more things. If ye'd be so kind, I'll be havin' the address of yon Lord Alderscroft. Happen I think a letter from me would not come amiss."

"That's easy enough," said John, who began to write it out on a blank leaf in his notebook.

"Also, nearest Earth Master," Cedric prompted. "Seems he and I should be havin' a bit of a talk, so there's no more misunderstandin's."

John consulted his pocket address book and added the same.

"An' one last thing." Cedric turned to Nan, somewhat to her surprise. "Ye've got the blessin' of the Old Ones on you, miss. That don't come often. I've got a bit of a feelin' that there's a patch of rough ahead of you. You remember, you cleave to them as shares that blessin' with you, come sun, come storm. Do that, and all will come right."

Nan blinked at him in some surprise. "Can you tell me more than that?" she asked carefully.

He shook his head. "'Tisn't a Sight, it's just a sense. There's summat workin' against you. Don't let it, that's all. That temper of your'n led you wrong with me, and it can lead you wrong again, if ye let it."

"Then, thank you," she replied, feeling embarrassed all over again, and grateful at the same time. She wanted to say more, but Agatha put her foot down and sent him up the narrow stairs to bed.

So, after taking their leave from Agatha and collecting Suki from the farmyard, where she was playing with a litter of kittens, they departed from Sennoke.

Thankfully, Suki did not ask for a kitten.

They walked back to Sevenoaks in weary silence; at least, Nan assumed John and Mary felt at least as weary as she did. It had been a long day, with a great many emotional ups and downs. But it was a pleasant walk, and Neville certainly enjoyed it. The lark of this morning had found a friend to duel with, musically speaking, and there were other birds calling from every bush and tree.

But the sight of town was welcome, and the sight of the hotel even more so.

Presumably, John collected and destroyed his letter once they got back to the hotel. Nan went straight to the room and changed her clothing, coaxing Suki into doing the same, since she was covered with dust from the lane, before tapping on John and Mary's door. Right at the moment, the one thing she wanted more than anything was a bath, and she hadn't the least idea of how to go about getting one.

"Ah good," said John, when he opened it. "Mary and I were just discussing our plans. We have a choice. We can catch the last train to London and go straight home, or we can spend the night here and leave first thing in the morning."

Home . . . and a hot bath! That had been one of the chief attractions of the flat when she and Sarah had taken it: it had an absolutely modern bathroom, and they were able to have a good hot bath whenever they wished. "To be honest, I would be very happy if we went straight home," Nan said, and glanced at Suki, who was already half-asleep on the big featherbed. "On the other hand, we'd be carrying Suki back like so much luggage."

"I don't at all mind that," John chuckled. "She doesn't weigh anything to speak of. Truth to tell I would very much like to get back to Baker Street and find out what Sherlock has been up to in our absence. Can you be packed and ready to go in, say, half an hour?"

Suddenly Nan longed for that bath and her own room and her own bed with an intensity that positively hurt. "Less," she said. "I'll leave Suki here and take care of it all myself."

Neville had come in the window and was devouring the food in his cup as she came in. "We're going home tonight," she told him, and smiled as he raised his wings and whistled for joy. "Hurry up and eat, then go into your carrier. I intend to be packed up in no time."

"Faster!" Neville declared.

Within the hour, they were in another first-class compartment, on the way home. Suki was fast asleep with her head in Nan's lap—not even the prospect of another train trip could keep her awake. Neville showed no particular interest in coming out of the carrier either, although Nan left the door open for him. Then again, he had probably done more flying in the last few days than he had in the previous month, and he was probably just as tired as Nan was.

Or John and Mary Watson—a glance at them showed they were both starting to droop a little. Nan was just glad that, although it wasn't an express, they would not have to change trains. It would be a straight run back to the station and a single cab home. It would be dark by the time they got to the flat, and Sarah would likely be gone, but in the morning Nan could tell her everything.

John had gotten a paper, and Mary and Nan had books, so the trip back was conducted in companionable and comfortable silence. Suki got enough of a nap that when the train pulled in to their destination, she was almost her normal, lively self and did not need to be carried as Nan had feared she might.

John got two cabs; one for Nan and Suki, and one for himself and Mary. "I'll call on you tomorrow afternoon," he told Nan as he handed her into hers. "After I speak with Lord Alderscroft in the morning. I think he'll mark this down as a job well done."

Even though I almost wrecked things, Nan thought ruefully. But there was no point in browbeating herself; it had all come out all right, and they'd learned a very great deal. On the whole, a success.

The cab rolled away, and a half an hour later pulled up at the house. Suki ran ahead and pulled the door open; Nan followed and called out "Mrs. Horace, we're back!" as soon as she got across the threshold.

Mrs. Horace popped out of her own door and threw her arms around Suki, then gave Nan a more restrained embrace. "It's been too quiet in this house with you gone!" she declared. "I'll bring up some tea and biscuits, you're probably perishing, and Neville's dinner as well. I won't be a minute!"

Nan could have done without the tea and biscuits, but a hoarse voice from inside the carrier demanded, "Want dinner!" so she shrugged internally and followed Suki up to their own door.

Where they were greeted by the exuberant cry of "Nan! Want Nan!" a feathered bullet shot out of the bird room and landed against her collarbone, and Nan found herself with a Grey parrot on her shoulder, being showered with beaky kisses.

And as she kissed Grey back and put her down on the back

of the chair, Mrs. Horace appeared with food for both birds and people, and she settled into a chair that suited *her* and no one else with a good cup of tea and a plate of shortbread, it occurred to her that . . . this was home. And she was very, very glad to be back in it.

After Suki's bath (as short as the rascal could get away with) and hers, she wrapped up in a dressing gown and peeked into her own room to see that Neville had already settled onto his perch on her bed and was asleep, then into Suki's to make sure *she* was asleep, too. She was, sprawled all over the bed like a starfish.

"So," Nan said, turning to the sitting room and leveling a look at Grey, who was waiting on the back of the sofa, shifting her weight from foot to foot. "You are *not* happy."

She padded barefoot into the sitting room and curled up on the sofa, facing Grey.

"No," Grey said. "Sarah different."

"You have a talent for understatement," Nan muttered. "It's that woman, isn't it? Magdalena."

Grey gave an impression of someone in the throes of indecision. "Yes," she said. "No. Maybe."

Nan gritted her teeth, then forced herself to relax. "Sarah is being spoilt as she has never been spoilt in her life. That might be all this is. But if it *is* something that woman is doing to her, we have to figure it out, and *how* she is doing it, before we can undo it. In the meantime . . ."

She remembered what Cedric had said to her, and gritted her teeth again. *I have many good characteristics, but patience is not one of them,* she admitted to herself. "We need a lot more information, and we'll need to be patient to get it." A thought occurred to her. "I don't suppose she could have made a mistake and gotten possessed by one of those ghosts, could she?"

Grey shook her head emphatically. "I would know," she said.

"Pity. That would be the easiest thing to undo. Well, come to my room and sleep with me and Neville. There's plenty of room on the foot of my bed and there's no reason you need to be all alone at night." She held out her hand to Grey, who stepped up on it, then leaned forward and made grateful kissing noises.

Nan smiled, brought the little head to her lips, and kissed the soft feathers. "The man we went to get turned out to be a good man. He said we need to remember that Sarah is our friend, under everything else, and not let her break that friendship."

Grey heaved a theatrical sigh. "All right," she replied. "Bed now?"

Nan yawned, caught herself, and laughed. "Yes indeed. Bed."

12

Nan was having a difficult time keeping to her resolution *not* to lose patience with Sarah. In the few short days Nan and Suki had been gone, Magdalena seemed to have cemented her hold over Sarah to the point where it was alarming.

Nan and Suki had risen at their usual time, Mrs. Horace had brought up breakfast, and a few moments after that, Sarah had come back from her nightly stint at Magdalena's suite. She had been surprised to see the two of them sitting there and eating breakfast and greeted them cheerfully enough, but . . . to Nan's mind, her greeting had not been nearly as enthusiastic as Nan would have expected after several days' absence.

Nevertheless, she sat down at the table with them, got Grey on her hand, and cuddled the parrot against her chest while they all talked, which was a better sign than that greeting and much more like Sarah's normal behavior. Suki launched into an enthusiastic recitation of her first train ride, and then another about what *the real country* was like and how she wanted to live there some day, but only if she could come back to the city when she wished. Sarah laughed and encouraged her to talk. When Suki ran dry and went back to her breakfast, Sarah turned her attention to Nan.

"So, this blood magician, obviously you came out of the confrontation unscathed, but what happened?" Sarah asked.

"*We* came out of it unscathed. The poor man himself got savaged by Neville," Nan replied ruefully.

Sarah looked puzzled. "Why do you say 'poor man'? I thought he was supposed to be some sort of . . . well, what we think of as an evil wizard!"

"He turned out to be nothing of the sort," Nan told her, and gave her a brief summation of the "confrontation." And that was when things went . . . oddly.

Normally Sarah would have been full of questions, wanting to know all the details, particularly about that Celtic warrior-woman aspect Nan sometimes took on—because when that happened it was generally without warning, and Nan had never yet been able to deliberately invoke it. But this time, as soon as Nan had finished the briefest of explanations and taken time for a few bites of toast and bacon, Sarah launched into the litany of her own past days.

Or . . . to be precise, she got on the topic of Magdalena and could not seem to get off of it. Nan was particularly startled when Sarah casually described Magdalena coming home with one of her lovers, Sarah sitting down to have supper with them both, and Magdalena carrying the man off to her bed. What was startling was Sarah describing all this with *no* sign of embarrassment.

"Isn't she supposed to be the fiancé of that German?" Nan interrupted. "I thought when people got engaged, they were supposed to be . . . well . . . faithful." She looked at Sarah doubtfully. This simply did not sound like Sarah, at all.

Sarah frowned a little. "Well, she explained all that. And really, that's just middle-class morals. Really enlightened people understand." There was a great deal more in the same vein, no *real* explanation as far as Nan was concerned, although she got the distinct feeling that the "explanation" really was "what Helmut doesn't know about doesn't matter." And since Helmut had gone back to Germany, he wasn't likely to learn, either, so long as Magdalena kept it all out of the papers. But again, that off-handed "that's just middle-class morals" did *not* sound like Sarah. Before Magdalena, she would have been embarrassed to have someone flaunting a lover in front of her, and she *certainly* would have had some tart things to say about people who were engaged going to bed with whomever they pleased.

And as for "what Helmut doesn't know doesn't matter—"

That . . . seemed extremely unfair to poor Helmut. His first fiancé vanished with a Canadian, and his second was collecting and going to bed with a string of wealthy admirers? Helmut was definitely getting a very poor set of bargains here. Perhaps he was a dull, stodgy little German businessman, but if Magdalena didn't *want* him, why had she gone and gotten engaged to him in the first place?

"What if one of these gentlemen decides he wants to marry her?" Nan asked, interrupting a description of the jewelry the latest lover, a Marquess no less, named "Willie," had presented to Magdalena last night.

Sarah stopped in midsentence, her mouth a little open, looking slightly annoyed. "That's really none of my business, nor of yours, Nan," she said, brusquely.

"Well, how are you progressing with the ghosts?" Nan asked, before she could get back on the subject of Magdalena. *Grey's right. There's something wrong with her. She certainly wouldn't have been so offhanded three weeks ago about this woman hopping into bed with a random assortment of men for the sake of their presents. And on top of that, Sarah never cared about jewelry or gowns at all, and now that's all she can talk about when she's not talking about Magdalena directly.*

Now Sarah looked like the old Sarah—a bit flustered, and unhappy, and definitely uncomfortable. "There are four I can't seem to get rid of, and I cannot make out why. Three of them are the merest wraiths, just—sketches of spirits. They've lost most of their substance, so I think they must be terribly old, hundreds of years, perhaps. Those kind are usually the easiest to move on; they get one look at the door, and they can't wait to get through it. But these three *won't move.* And I can't determine any reason for their reluctance. If there's something holding them to the earth, they haven't told it to me, or given me any hint of it. It's exceedingly frustrating!"

"I can scarcely imagine," Nan said, with all the sympathy she could muster. "What about the fourth?"

"The fourth is the very opposite. She's strong, full of emotion and determination. *She* won't go through the door or tell me what she wants, either, but I get the impression from the first three that they aren't talking to me because they *can't,* while the fourth spirit isn't talking to me because she *won't*. If that makes sense."

Now this sounds more like Sarah.

"It makes perfect sense," Nan replied, and dipped her toast in the runny yellow of her egg and ate it thoughtfully. "What if the fourth one is the one holding the other three back? Can some ghosts command others?"

Sarah blinked, as if that hadn't even occurred to her. "If that's true, that would explain why they won't move on . . . but the fourth one completely ignores everything I do!"

"Well," said Nan, after a moment, "You're being paid to keep the ghosts away from Magdalena at night, and you're doing that." She shrugged. "There doesn't seem any harm to me if they won't go away. Just keep collecting her money until her season is over. She'll go back to Germany and won't be your problem anymore."

Sarah looked alarmed at that last, as if it had not occurred to her that Magdalena would *leave*. "Oh, surely she won't do that—" Sarah replied uncertainly.

Nan wanted to shake her for being so—bloody infatuated! Did she think Magdalena would be in London forever?

"She has a fiancé she is going to have to marry eventually," Nan pointed out, trying very hard not to sound waspish. "She'll have to go back to Germany to do that. Certainly he is going to insist she live at least part of the time with him; if she doesn't, it's going to look scandalous."

"Yes but her career on the British stage—" Sarah stammered, now looking quite alarmed.

"And her career on the German stage," Nan reminded her. "And the French stage, and the Italian stage. She's going to have to sing at the Vienna Opera, probably Berlin, likely Rome, the Paris Opera, and La Scala in Milan at the very least if she's going to have the sort of reputation Patti does. My impression was that was *exactly* what she was aiming for."

"Yes, but—she hasn't said anything about leaving!" Sarah actually looked as if she was about to panic, which alarmed Nan considerably, although she took pains not to show it. Clearly, reminding Sarah that Magdalena would absolutely *have* to return to the Continent to further her career was not a good idea at this point. Three weeks ago, Sarah had only been interested in helping those spirits pass on. Three weeks ago, she had been pleased with the money Magdalena was paying her and admitted to being impressed with how Magdalena lived, but otherwise had no sort of attachment to the prima donna. Now she looked as if the mere prospect of being separated from Magdalena was going to put her into a faint.

Nan decided to say nothing more and just concentrate on her breakfast while Sarah engaged in a silent, internal struggle. Finally, as if she was talking to herself, calming herself down, she said again, with more certainty, "Magdalena hasn't said anything about leaving. And at any rate, it's almost summer, and she'll certainly be asked to come to Willie's manor for a long visit. I gather it's a rather grand house, and the company is going to be quite spectacular." The last was said wistfully, as if Sarah longed to be invited herself. Once again, Nan was taken aback, because this was nothing like "her" Sarah. Sarah enjoyed luxury, as who wouldn't, but when she had spoken of "good company" that she would enjoy in the past it was more in reference to a circle of friends like those of the Hartons—writers, artists, intellectuals, and occultists. Not a lot of jewel-bedecked aristocrats who changed their clothes six times a day and wouldn't know how to change trains without their armies of servants to guide them from one place to another.

"If she goes there for the summer, then the ghosts won't trouble her anymore," Nan said. "They are rooted to the hotel, correct?"

"I think so," Sarah agreed.

"Then once she's away from the hotel, she should be all right. But, if Willie—or anyone else—sets her up in her own establishment, make sure to impress on her it should be an absolutely modern, brand new flat, that *no one* has ever lived in before." Nan just left things at that, though personally, she thought it extremely unlikely that any such thing would happen. Setting Magdalena up in her own flat would be tantamount to announcing the liaison in public; Helmut would *certainly* want to know where the money was coming from for such a thing. Besides, why go to the bother, when at the hotel she had all the benefits of a luxurious flat without having to go to the trouble of hiring her own servants to staff it?

This attachment to Magdalena wasn't *sexual* at all; that had been Nan's first fear. But if it had been sexual, given her gifts, she would *know* if that was something Sarah was feeling. Nan knew of friends of Memsa'b's that were "special friends," and she was anything but a prude, so when that had occurred as a possibility, she had dismissed it for lack of evidence. It wasn't a romantic infatuation, either. It was more like . . .

Like hero-worship. No, like blind, unthinking adoration that allows no room for any critical thinking. Adoration to the point that whatever Magdalena does is perfectly right and good, as long as Magdalena is happy. And this made *no* sense. "Pashes" like that, especially for actresses, singers, or dancers, were normal in teenaged girls, but Sarah was far past that age now.

Nan felt herself consumed by frustration, anger, and, yes, jealousy. What had Magdalena done to deserve that kind of worship? So, she could sing! So what! That was just a mere accident of birth! And now she had *stolen* Sarah, was taking her away from Nan, and—

—and with an effort that was so physical it made her chest and stomach hurt, Nan throttled all that down. Because saying anything along those lines right now would be absolutely fatal. And hadn't she been warned?

Absolutely, I was.

Sarah yawned hugely. "It was a long night. I need sleep."

"I'm sorry I kept you up, then," Nan told her, making her voice sound sympathetic, even though she had to struggle to keep sarcastic tones out of it.

Sarah smiled sweetly. "I'm glad you're back. It means Grey won't be alone during the day."

"Get some rest," Nan replied. "We'll keep the flat as quiet as a church."

But as soon as she was sure Sarah was asleep, she got her hat and shawl and the two bird carriers and fetched Grey and Neville from their room. "In your boxes you two," she said, as they looked at her questioningly.

"Wot?" Suki asked, "You goin' someplace?"

"*We* are going someplace," Nan said firmly. "We're going to talk to the Watsons. And to Sherlock Holmes. He will probably find what Sarah had to say—interesting."

"Sarah ain't roight," Suki said, frowning, and looking at Sarah's closed door.

"No, Sarah *isn't* right. And we're going to get to the bottom of this mystery," Nan replied, firmly.

Suki ran for her shawl and cap and helped fasten Grey up into her carrier while Nan took care of Neville. And in moments, they were closing the door silently behind them.

Well, I didn't lie. The flat will *be as quiet as a church.*

They had reached 221 Baker Street very quickly, and Holmes had settled them in his sitting room just as the clock struck eight in the morning.

"Fascinating," said Holmes. He had a pen in his right hand; now he tapped it against his left. She and Suki had found places to sit in Holmes' perpetually cluttered sitting room; the birds were in their carriers at Nan's feet. "What you have been telling me tallies with some other investigations of my own. Magdalena has cut something of a swath through our gentlemen of means. The *demi-monde* is extremely wroth with her, the more so since the lovers she has discarded for those with more means have neither lost their infatuation nor blame her in any way. Instead, they seem content to hang about and continue to send her presents without getting anything in return."

"Is that—normal?" Nan asked, doubtfully. This wasn't an area she had *any* experience in. The rich were certainly . . . different. Back in the slums where she'd been born, taking a new lover would likely mean a knife fight. And in the Hartons' circle of friends, "middle class morality" notwithstanding, such a thing simply was out of the question, and would probably have caused social rifts as people took one side or another.

"On the contrary, unless one discards a wealthy man for someone with whom he could not possibly compete—the Prince, for instance—being cast off is usually the cause for a histrionic scene at the least and a lawsuit at the worst. Magdalena seems to lead a peculiarly charmed life in that regard." Holmes pursed his lips. "Unnaturally so, I would say."

This was insanity. Was *everyone* in her circle of influence enthralled by her to the point of sheer adoration, as Sarah was? "How is she *doing* this?" Nan asked, desperately.

Holmes raised an eyebrow at her. "Pray, do not ask *me*, Miss Killian. The emotional and amorous weapons such a woman has at her disposal are a complete mystery to me. It might just as well be the action of some of John's supposed *magic*. The how does not matter in the long run. What we want is the *why*, and the *what*. Why is she doing this, and what, exactly, are her intentions?"

"Marriage?" Nan hazarded.

"In most cases I would agree with you, but I do not think Magdalena would be satisfied with life as a married woman, not even to one of the highest rank in this country." He nodded, as if he was completely certain of that.

"Woi?" asked Suki. Holmes glanced down at the child, startled, as if he had forgotten she was there.

"You can say anything around Suki, Mr. Holmes," Nan reminded him. "I doubt there's much that would shock her, given where she spent her early years."

"I sore a leddy wi' three fellers oncet," Suki said meditatively. "I snucket inter th' 'all an' sore. There was a buncha fellers. They was payin' a whole shillin' to watcher—"

"Suki—that's one of the things we don't talk about," Nan warned, and looked back at Holmes. "I'm as curious as Suki. Why wouldn't Magdalena be content with being a Lady, or a Duchess, or a Baroness?"

"Because, the gentlemen who are young do not have fortunes, and the gentlemen who have fortunes are not young," Holmes replied, with a half smile. "Yes, there are any number of titled young men looking for wives on this island; one and all they are under family orders to look for rich American wives to prop up estates that are aging and *need* a fortune to be put in repair. And there are a few addled old men of fortune looking for wives who will happily marry a chorus girl, or an actress, or an opera singer, or even their housekeepers—but they would require their wives to be faithful and chaste, or at least, utterly circumspect. And they would also require their wives to give up their professions. Whatever negative things I can say about Magdalena, she is as in love with performing as she is with luxury. She thrives on audience attention. I cannot see Magdalena sacrificing her operatic career to gain a life of wealth and privilege married to an old man."

"Neither can I," Nan admitted.

"So that leaves us looking for motive, for a purpose. What is it that Magdalena wants?" Holmes asked.

"Anything that someone else has," Nan blurted bitterly, thinking of Helmut . . . and of Sarah.

Holmes blinked. "My dear Miss Killian. You might be on to something there. She's not unlike the mythical dragon, heaping up stolen treasures in her cave. A fiancé here, a sable cloak there, a pearl necklace, a Marquess . . . and to what lengths would she go to *get* them, I wonder?"

"I don't know?" Nan ventured.

"Nor do I. But I intend to find out." Holmes flashed Nan a smile. "Go on up to the Watsons; they should be ready to see visitors now. See what they have to say about all this. For all I know, they have some means to snap your young friend out of her *spell*."

Nan nodded and picked up the bird carriers. From the right-hand one came Grey's plaintive voice.

"Fix Sarah—fix Sarah!"

For the first time ever, Nan saw Holmes emotionally moved. He bent until his face was even with the screened side of the carrier. "We shall, Miss Grey," he said, in a tone of voice so kind that Nan nearly cried. "I promise you. We shall."

"I think Holmes is on to something," said Mary Watson, after Nan had told the pair the entire story. "What if Magdalena is using some sort of charm or talisman? It would account for her extraordinary ability to make people adore her, *and* for her ability to keep them adoring her after she's discarded them."

"Is there such a thing?" Nan wondered.

"I've never seen one, but there are certainly stories of such things, and I see no reason to disbelieve them," John replied. "After all, you and Sarah each have talismans from Puck, and you know those work."

"That's true," Nan mused, then her thoughts darkened. "But if that's true, it must be a terribly strong thing to work as well as it does. How can we ever free Sarah from it?"

"I don't know—but Cedric predicted this, and he was right. You mustn't give up on her, and you mustn't try to break it yourself by putting her into a position where she is forced to choose between you and Magdalena. That will certainly be fatal to your friendship." Mary pursed her lips and looked at John. "I think only one of two things will work. Either Magdalena will decide she no longer needs Sarah and discards her, or Sarah herself will come to realize that she is being manipulated. In either case, I think Sarah will probably come to herself again once she's kept away from Magdalena."

"Or we break the damn spell or destroy the charm," John replied impatiently. "I think direct action is needed here, my love!"

"Direct action would be faster," Nan said, letting Grey out of her case and putting her on the back of a chair.

"Fix Sarah!" Grey insisted. Neville nodded emphatically from Nan's shoulder.

"Patience, little friend," Mary soothed. "We should ask Beatrice Leek about this; magic intended to manipulate emotions tends to be the sort of thing witches are asked to do. We should also take this directly to Lord Alderscroft; I have no doubt he is aware of Magdalena's conquests, but he might not be aware of this aspect of it, and that will cast her influence in a whole new light."

"I've never heard of this sort of thing being a part of Elemental Magic," John brooded, tapping his fingers on the armrest of the sofa. "Could it be the result of a psychic power?" He looked up at Nan.

"That . . . didn't occur to me," she admitted. "I believe the ability to feel the emotions of others is referred to as *empathy*. I suppose, just as there is *projective telepathy,* where one can put thoughts into someone else's head, there could be *projective empathy*. But . . ."

She was lost in thought for a moment, and Mary was the one who jarred her out of it. "But what, Nan?"

"But telepathy only works on one person at a time, so I suppose empathy does, too. I would have to ask Memsa'b."

"Well then, I think we have our tasks," John said briskly. "I will go have a talk with Lord Alderscroft. Mary, you find Beatrice and see what she has to say. Nan, it will be up to you to speak to your mentor."

Nan nodded. It occurred to her that there was another reason to want to speak to Memsa'b. And if all parties agreed, the result would certainly be a test of how strong Magdalena's hold was on Sarah.

They managed to reach what had once been one of Lord Alderscroft's "country" homes (although now it was just at the edge of the suburbs of London) just before noon. Memsa'b had insisted they all have luncheon as soon as they arrived. Now the birds sat on their old perches in Memsa'b's study; Suki and Nan were in two old, comfortable chairs. Neville was within reach of Nan, and Memsa'b reached out periodically to pet Grey comfortingly.

They were at the Harton School, a school for the children of expatriate British parents, some of whom happened to have psychic abilities. Schools serving expatriate parents were dotted all over Britain—but this was one of the few where the interests of the children were put ahead of the chance to make money. Here, the littlest ones were cared for by native *ayahs* of the same sort that had cared for them where they'd been born. The servants were a mix of the peoples of India, the same sort of servants the students had been tended by at "home." And instead of the sort of unsatisfying, unhealthy foods they would have been fed in one of those money-making schools, they got the same curries and other dishes they were used to.

When Nan and Sarah had joined the school, it had been in a rather bad neighborhood in London. Shortly after Nan and Sarah had saved Lord Alderscroft from a near-fatal situation, he had turned over this country manor to the Hartons, and that was where the school had been ever since.

Memsa'b's study had been the drawing room; as such it was attractive and airy, with tall windows that looked out on the formal garden. The furnishings were all of an older style than was fashionable; Lord Alderscroft had seen no reason to replace them when he had inherited, and the Hartons preferred to leave things as they had been. It was just as well; plain, sturdy furnishings with plain or leather upholstery held up better with children about. All the truly irreplaceable or fragile objects had gone into storage.

Memsa'b—Isabelle Harton—was still a very striking woman, although no one would ever have called her "pretty." There was something about her that signaled a great deal of experience acquired without bitterness. Like Nan, she wore a suit in the "Rational Dress" style, although hers was navy blue rather than brown. She listened patiently, without interrupting, pausing now and again to caress Grey when the parrot seemed agitated. "This is very distressing," Memsa'b said when Nan finished her story. Her brows were furrowed, and her face had a look of unhappiness and puzzlement about it. "If I were not absolutely certain it would only make matters worse, I would come back to London with you and box Sarah's ears myself until I brought her to her senses."

"It's been a temptation," Nan admitted. "If that fellow in Sevenoaks hadn't warned me, I probably would have done so already. Does this sound like anything you've seen or heard of before?"

"Yes, but there was only one victim at a time, not entire swaths of them," Memsa'b replied. "And when the wretched wench lost interest in a victim, she lost power over him, too. Her discards certainly were *not* inclined to continue admiring her from afar and send her presents!"

"What did they do?" Nan asked, rather certain she was not going to like the answer, but thinking she needed to know anyway. "When they were discarded, that is."

"It depended entirely on the personality of each man—the victims were all men," Memsa'b replied. "One flung himself in the river and drowned in despair. Several joined the Army, declaring that their lives were over so they might as well lay them down in the service of their country. But one was not taking the situation quietly, and sued her for breach of promise. She thought it was all very amusing until the judge and jury handed down a guilty verdict and she was stripped of all her ill-gotten gains."

"What did she do then?" asked Nan.

Memsa'b sighed. "Found herself another victim, a wealthy old man, and married him. That was when we psychics took the law into our own hands and . . . dealt with her. When we were done, she could no longer play her tricks on anyone, and when he was no longer completely besotted, her spouse became suspicious and jealous and made sure she was never alone, night or day. He controlled every penny, accounting for the last farthing she spent, put the control of the household expenses in the hands of his housekeeper, and allowed her to establish credit with no merchants." Memsa'b's lips thinned in what was not exactly a smile. "And when she went anywhere, there was always a special secretary accompanying her. If she *tried* to gull an unsuspecting dressmaker or shopkeeper into extending her credit, the secretary would step forward and inform the intended victim that 'milady's husband will not honor any debts his wife contracts.' To put the icing on the cake, he was a great deal more vigorous than she had bargained for. He lived to be almost a hundred, so by the time he finally died, she was in her sixties, and very little joy did she get out of her inheritance. But that has no bearing on what's happening to Sarah."

"No, it doesn't sound like it." Nan sighed. "Memsa'b, Suki, there is something I want to propose to you, which is why we came all the way out here. I'm very much afraid, the way Sarah has been acting of late, that she's not . . . safe . . . around Suki."

"*Wot?*" Suki exclaimed, whipping her head around to stare at Nan incredulously. "Wotcher mean? Sarah ain't gonna hurt me! An' I c'n take care o' meself!"

"I mean, if Magdalena decided she wanted Sarah to spend nights *and* days in the hotel with her, in her current state of mind, Sarah is perfectly capable of abandoning you without any warning," Nan replied. "And if I happened to be gone—if, for instance, something came up that required me to be away—you would be all alone. And I know that you are brave, and you know how to take care of yourself, but terrible things like fires happen that you would have no control over."

Suki opened her mouth as if to object—then a strange look came over her face. "An'—if the roight bitch took th' notion Oi was gettin' i' th' way—" She shook her head. "Aye."

"Suki if Sarah was in her right mind, there is *nothing* she would let get between you," Nan said urgently. "You know that.

I know that. There is no question of it."

Suki nodded, slowly. "So. Wot then?"

"We talked about you starting at the Harton School. I'd like you to start early. Now, in fact." Nan held her breath, hoping she wasn't going to get rebellion.

"I'd be pleased to have you, Suki," Memsa'b said quickly. "You could give some of my little boys a swift, sharp lesson in how girls are not inferior creatures. It's a lesson they dearly need to learn. Most of my girls here have been brought up with the notion that if they are tormented, they must run to an *ayah*, rather than fight back."

A hint of a smile crossed Suki's solemn face. "Oi could, that," she admitted.

"I can have most of your things sent by carrier," Nan told her. "But we'll want to leave enough at the flat so that you have things to wear and play with and read when you come visit us on holidays."

The flash of grateful relief that crossed Suki's face told Nan that Suki had been afraid Nan was going to renege on all her promises—including the ones that she was to spend holidays with her foster "mothers."

"And Suki—the property belonging to this house is enormous," Nan went on. "There are some completely wild places, like that forest we walked through on the Downs. You will *certainly* see Puck there, and he will certainly come to see you."

"Cor! Rilly?" Suki's face, which had taken on a bit of a pinched look, brightened again.

"When Nan and I were your age, he came to visit us regularly here in the country," Nan assured her. "And you will finally learn to ride and drive as you wished. Lord Alderscroft has supplied ponies for the students here, and even a pair of white donkeys, and—well, you'll see. There's a menagerie of animals here; there are cats in the barn and dairy, the gamekeeper's dogs, and cows and doves."

Well, that was the touch that turned this from "exile" to "promised land," so far as Suki was concerned. After a barrage of questions, Memsa'b finally rang for one of the Hindu servants, who took Suki away to pick out a room and some of the outgrown clothing of other girls to tide her over until her own things arrived.

They walked out, hand in hand, Suki already chattering to her as if she was an old friend.

Memsa'b turned to Nan. "Now what are you *really* afraid of?" she demanded.

"Frankly, that Sarah will abandon us. And I absolutely was afraid she'd do so without even a second thought for Suki. I couldn't keep leaving Suki with Mrs. Horace; it's not fair to either of them. It was bad enough when she was spending every night at the hotel, but today I understand from Sarah that Magdalena's latest conquest is going to invite her for the summer to his estate—"

Grey gave a heartbroken cry that sounded like a sob, and Memsa'b quickly gathered the bird to her chest and held her there, comforting her.

"Grey, she will certainly take *you* with her," Nan said hurriedly. "I cannot see her leaving you behind. But I am not going to sit by and let her get into that fiend's clutches without a fight. I am going to follow; I'll hire a cottage nearby, or disguise myself as a servant, or *something*. But I cannot do that if I have Suki to care for."

"No, you certainly cannot," Memsa'b said firmly. "You're quite right. This is the only solution." She hesitated, and then added, reluctantly, "And Grey, if she becomes unkind to you, you will have Nan nearby to fly to."

Grey made another little sobbing noise, and Nan thought her heart was going to break. "I am going to cure her of this if I have to kidnap her and smuggle her here and keep her in the cellar until she comes to her senses," she snapped. "*Oh!* How I want to box her ears until her head rings like a church bell!"

"Sarah?" Memsa'b asked, dryly.

"A bit. But chiefly that wretched Magdalena. I should have started keeping a watch on Sarah's mind from the beginning," Nan replied bitterly. "Then I would have realized how she was worming her way in, and I might have been able to stop her."

"I am as much to blame for this as you," Memsa'b said with equal bitterness. "I am the one who suggested Sarah to someone who must have been one of Magdalena's early converts. Lady Dorcas came to me, looking for a '*real*' medium to help Magdalena, and after hearing her story, I suggested Sarah. I wish I had said someone, *anyone* else!"

"And if that person actually had been a medium, he or she would be in the same straits as Sarah is now, or even worse," Nan pointed out, quickly, trying to extinguish the guilt painting her mentor's features. "And *that* person would have been without any friends able or willing to help!"

Some of the guilt lifted. "That . . . is true enough," Memsa'b agreed. "And . . . yes, it is also true enough that if things come to that pass, Karamjit and Agansing are more than skilled enough to ambush Sarah someplace and carry her off here."

"Then the first thing you must do is make several plans along those lines," Nan told her. "There will be no difficulty in abducting her if she continues to sleep at home, because I will certainly aid and abet a kidnapping, but you must make contingent plans if she begins staying at the hotel—and tentative ones for if she does, indeed, go to this country house. Wherever it is—"

"I can find that out easily enough," Memsa'b told her. "What did you say this new conquest is called? 'Willie'? And he's a Marquess? Those are not all that thick on the ground, particularly not those of middling age. I can easily find someone with that nickname among his fellows and those profligate habits. Once I know that, I'll know what and where this 'country house' is."

Nan sighed with relief. That was one enormous worry off her shoulders. She had been afraid that Sarah would simply announce she was going with Magdalena, pack a bag, and vanish, *without* telling Nan where she was going.

Memsa'b held the parrot up to her lips and kissed her. "We'll make her better, Grey. Whether she likes it or not."

13

Nan managed to make it back to the flat just before tea, informed Mrs. Horace of the change in circumstances, and helped her bring the tea for two up herself. If nothing else had persuaded Nan that she had taken the correct course of action, it was Sarah's reaction when she woke up. It took her over an hour before she finally frowned slightly and asked, "Where's Suki? Is she studying in her room?"

"I took her to Memsa'b this morning and enrolled her in the school," Nan said, with a carefully calculated air of nonchalance. "We discussed this before, and we all agreed, and with you gone every night, and *me* helping the Watsons, it seemed prudent to take her there today. We cannot keep imposing on Mrs. Horace's good will."

"Oh, all right," Sarah said, vaguely, and went back to reading the newspaper.

A Sarah in her right mind would have been shouting at me, Nan thought, throttling down her anger. *A Sarah in her right mind would be demanding how I had gotten the notion into my head that I could make decisions without discussing them with her. This Sarah . . . isn't my Sarah.*

But she said nothing; she just went to the task of making up the labels for the boxes in which she was going to pack Suki's things. A carrier would be coming for them tomorrow. She tried not to think about what would happen if . . . they *couldn't* find a means to break Sarah free of this terrible woman.

I still haven't heard from the Watsons, she reminded herself. *Perhaps they will have good news.*

A quarter hour later, Sarah went back to her room and emerged dressed for the evening. "That was a good idea, Nan," she said, with an absent-minded caress of Grey's head. "I've been worried about you needing to go out some night and having to leave Suki alone. This solves everything."

"Yes, I'm sure it does," Nan replied, heartsick. "I hope you finally convince those last spirits to leave tonight."

"Even if I can't, as you pointed out, I'm doing what I promised Magdalena, I'm keeping them away from her. That's all that matters." Sarah beamed. Nan tried not to gag.

"So you say. Good luck," said Nan, wishing Sarah would finally hear how false those words were ringing and come to her senses.

But Sarah took them at face value, and gave a gay little wave as she turned to leave. And it took every ounce of Nan's self-control to keep from erupting in a fury and giving her friend a harsh piece of her mind.

She worked out that fury by packing up Suki's things—all the warm-weather clothing, most of the cold-weather clothing, and most of the toys. She left the puppet theater—there was one at the school—but sent the new wooden horse and Suki's favorite dolls. When everything was boxed up and the labels pasted on, she took the boxes downstairs and left them in the care of Mrs. Horace, along with the money for the carrier.

"Well, I'll miss the little mite," Mrs. Horace said, looking troubled. "But I will confess I've been worrying, too. What with Miss Sarah being out all night, and you liable to being called out by day *or* night, you can't leave her alone, it's not right. She's a good little thing, but children will be children, and the temptation to get into mischief or something she shouldn't—well!"

"That was what Sarah and I thought," Nan replied, sick at having to lie. "And we wrote the head of our old school, who wrote back yesterday and said there was a vacancy. Suki will be very happy there."

"And she's getting to be with children her own age, which is right and proper. And she'll lose that *dreadful* accent." At any other time, Nan might have smiled at this tiny example of Mrs. Horace's snobbery, but not today.

Instead, she ran back up the stairs, the birds went into their carriers *again*, and she headed out to find a cab and go to the Watsons.

Evidently they had been watching for her, for no sooner had she opened the door to 221 Baker Street than the door on the second floor landing popped open and Mary Watson waved to her to come up.

"We told Mrs. Hudson there will be three for supper," Mary said as she arrived. "And I've set up spots for the birds; I rather thought you might bring them. Where's Suki?"

As Nan explained the provisions she had made for Suki and Sarah's reaction—or rather lack of it—she let the birds out. Mary Watson had found a pair of old-fashioned wooden smoking stands somewhere—not matching, but equally sturdy—and she and John had replaced the ashtrays and humidors with cups for food and water. Both stands had rails that would do very well for perches, and there was already food and water waiting, and newspapers beneath them.

"I wish we had better news to report," Mary said, as John came in from another room, shrugging on his jacket. "Beatrice was unfortunately unhelpful. She agrees that this sounds very like a witch's love spell, but maintains that such things have to be cast separately, on each person one wishes to enchant. She also maintains that it is absolutely impossible for the passion inflamed by such a spell to be 'cooled' in order for the witch to take a new lover. 'It has to be broken,' she told me, 'Or else the original lover will kill himself, his rival, or his mistress in his rage. Love spells are nothing to trifle with.' And she never heard of a love spell that evokes the—let's call it *adoration,* in the old sense of worship, that we've seen in Sarah."

"And others," said John, settling down at the laden table next to Mary, while Nan made sure the birds were comfortable and sat down opposite the two of them. "I have that from Alderscroft. He wasn't alarmed before, but he damned well is now."

"Why wasn't he alarmed before?" Nan wanted to know.

"Because the men this woman has gotten under her thumb are not particularly important so far as the government is concerned,"

John replied, putting a lamb chop each on Mary's and Nan's plates, then serving himself, as Mary served mashed potatoes and new peas. "Remember, as the unofficial Minster of Magic to the Crown, his chief concerns will be things that threaten the Government and the Crown. Alderscroft frankly doesn't care how many merchants or peers bankrupt themselves over a dancer or an actress, so long as they *don't* have access to state secrets or do anything other than park their ample derrieres in a Seat in Parliament and vote with their cronies. But now that we've pointed out to him *how many* victims she's ensnared, he's taking notice. Just because she hasn't gone for bigger fish yet, it doesn't follow that she won't. And she's actually amassed enough followers that she *could* turn a close vote, if she chose to. So that has alarmed him, and he was sending for Mycroft as we left."

Nan furrowed her brows with thought, because involving herself in government plots seemed very uncharacteristic of Magdalena. "Everything she's done has been purely selfish until now, why would she risk exposing herself to change that?"

"Because, as Alderscroft pointed out to me, *she* might not have the wit or the inclination to meddle in politics, but any foreign agent who has noticed what she has been doing will become very interested indeed. And she is shallow enough that an offer of a great deal of money is very likely to be enough to convince her to exert the trifling amount of 'work' it would take to get her followers to vote as she wants them to." John Watson shrugged. "We couldn't even prosecute her as long as she leaves no trail of written evidence. She's a foreign national, so the Seditions Act wouldn't apply even if we got her victims to testify, which we wouldn't, and neither would any of the provisions against espionage. Alderscroft has very good reasons to be concerned."

"For that matter," Mary continued, "She *is* German, and German nationals do tend to be just as loyal to their Kaiser as we are to the Queen. I doubt she would stir herself for that loyalty alone, but for loyalty and money, or loyalty and a promise she'll be made the prima donna of, say, the Berlin Opera Company, I am sure she could be moved to mischief. It pains me to say this, but the Queen is under the entirely false impression that her Hanoverian relatives would never do anything to harm the interests of Britain—which is an extremely foolish thing to believe when you are faced with Kaiser Wilhelm and Otto von Bismarck."

Nan blinked. "I willingly take your word for this," she said. "I don't know half of what is going on *in* Britain, politically speaking, much less outside her borders."

"And none of it matters, except in that it gives *us* more help from Lord Alderscroft and, more importantly, Her Majesty's government," John replied. "Should we need it, that is."

Nan was not at all ready to relax. There was no telling *what* all these governmental fellows were likely to be *willing* to do—or if what they wished to do would help Sarah or make things worse. She would rather count on people she knew.

"Well, what I'm most worried about is if Magdalena goes off to this 'Willie' fellow's country house and takes Sarah with her," Nan confessed. "I don't even know who 'Willie' is—Memsa'b said she'd find out—"

"Alderscroft will see to all that," John interrupted. "I assume if Sarah does go, you intend to follow?"

"Couldn't stop me if you tried," Nan replied firmly.

"Then we'll find out *who* this Marquess is, which of his properties he intends to entertain at, and work out a plan from there." John nodded, as if were all settled. "I can almost certainly get an invitation myself as long as at least one of the guests is beholden to Alderscroft. Alderscroft can get me installed as a personal physician."

"And I can go as a personal maid; whoever we are attached to will have to be informed that we are investigating something, and will not expect any actual service from me." Mary seemed absolutely confident of this, so Nan could only assume that this was something she had done before. "As for you—" She frowned. "—I think it will depend on how near we want you to be to Sarah. We could arrange for you to be attached as another lady's maid—"

"I'm good with hair," Nan offered.

"That ought to be sufficient. But I'd really prefer you to be outside the household, in case we need to get Sarah away against her wishes." Mary glanced at John.

"I agree," he said. "Alderscroft will arrange something. Some place near enough to the manor house to be of use, but not actually *in* the household." John sat back. "I think that is as much planning as we can do without knowing the exact circumstances we will be dealing with."

Grey had been peering at all of them, anxiously, during this entire conversation, her eyes going from face to face as they spoke. When John finished, she uttered what sounded like a sad sigh, her head drooping. Nan took the poor parrot up on her hand and held her against her chest. She just didn't know what else to do.

Nan spent a restless night with both Grey and Neville perching on her bed. She was just grateful that Grey's instincts were able to overpower what must have been terrible despair, for the parrot did manage to go to sleep not long after the sun went down and was very little disturbed when she came to bed with her single candle.

As for herself . . . well, she shared some of Grey's despair. They still hadn't managed to work out *how* Magdalena was controlling people, and until they did, how could they hope to break the spell, if spell it was? And Nan didn't believe in the promises or fidelity of anyone other than John and Mary, Sherlock, and Lord Alderscroft. These governmental men would promise things they never meant to give, as soon as they had no more interest in a situation. And once Magdalena's danger to Crown and Country was negated, why would they have any reason to help Nan break Magdalena's control over her friend?

It would be easiest for these government agents just to approach Magdalena directly, offer her the spot as the Company Prima Donna for the Covent Garden Opera, and money, too, as long as she promises never to meddle in politics. Given what she had seen of Magdalena, Nan had very little faith that the singer would *ever* be moved by something as unselfish as loyalty to her Kaiser and native land. The only loyalty Magdalena had was to herself.

And if that was the approach these governmental shadow-men chose, well, then they'd walk away from the situation content. Magdalena would be thrilled to promise not to do something she'd never intended to do in the first place in exchange for more golden guineas, more fame, and a secure position in one of the best opera companies in the world.

So Nan lay awake, staring at the ceiling, quiet rather than tossing and turning so as not to wake the birds. Poor Grey had enough to deal with, without losing sleep.

She was yawning over her third cup of strong coffee, and the birds were on their perches partaking of—if, in Grey's case, not precisely enjoying—their breakfasts, when Sarah came back. And from the "I'm full of *news*!" look on her face, Nan dreaded to hear what she had to say.

"It's wonderful!" Sarah burst out, casting her shawl aside, tossing her hat in the direction of a chair, and dropping down across the table from Nan. "Willie *has* invited Magdalena for the entire summer! And Magdalena says that, as the manor is old and, according to Willie, absolutely *stiff* with haunts, she can't do without me! We're to leave two days after the last performance of the season!"

"That's interesting," Nan managed. "I suppose Willie is rather pleased you'll be ridding his manor of spirits. And at no cost to him, except for the provision of meals and a bed!"

Sarah looked hurt; under any other circumstances, Nan would have apologized, but after seeing how unhappy she had made Grey, Nan would rather have eaten a live frog than apologize.

"You're just jealous that I have been invited and you have not!" Sarah snapped.

Nan held on to her temper with both hands. "If I were at all interested in hobnobbing with a lot of empty-headed idlers whose chief recreations are changing their clothing five times a day and talking about hunting, then perhaps I might be. But I'm not," she said, coolly. "Then again, you won't be hobnobbing with them, either. You'll be staying up all night to keep the ghosties away from Magdalena and sleeping all day, so you'll be spared the hollow prattle."

Sarah looked astonished for a moment, and as if she really did not know how to respond. Nan had been anything but supportive, but at the same time, she hadn't given Sarah anything to start an argument over.

Nan avoided eye contact with her friend as she assiduously ate her breakfast. Out of the corner of her eye, she noted Sarah open her mouth to say something, then close her mouth again, whatever she had intended to retort with left unsaid. Nan would have felt a little more as if she had "won" if "winning" had been her goal.

She reached for the paper and opened it, still saying nothing to Sarah directly. "Hmm. I see there are only five days left in the current season. Are you planning on leaving directly, the next day?"

"Alicia is already packing," Sarah said, faintly. "So I suppose we are."

Nan closed the paper. "That will be tiring for you; you'll have to stay up all night, then come here to get your things, and then back to the train." She didn't offer any solutions. She didn't intend to. She might not be able to stop Sarah, but she certainly wasn't going to *help* her. And perhaps this would serve to remind Sarah that things were a lot easier with genuine friends to help.

"I'll manage," Sarah replied stiffly.

"I'm sure you shall!" Nan replied.

An awkward silence ensued, after which Sarah picked up Grey and went to bed.

Without Suki here to give lessons to and without any other task, Nan set herself to studying, with determination, a couple of books that Memsa'b had sent her home with, books about psychical power used for bad or selfish ends. She had some slim hope she might find something like Magdalena's abilities in them. About the time that Grey flew out of Sarah's room to rejoin her and Neville, she had managed to push her distractions to the side and concentrate on them.

Rather than playing with Neville, who was hard at work on yet another horseshoe-nail puzzle, Grey landed next to Nan on the couch and crept into her lap like a cat. There, she settled down as if she was on a nest, and Nan stroked her gently while she read. After a moment, Neville left his puzzle and hopped up onto the couch, gently preening Grey's head feathers with his massive beak. Both of them were trying to comfort their heartsick friend. It made Nan want to cry, knowing that there was so little they could do.

Well. I showed her. I managed just fine without her.

Sarah stood, yawning, on the train platform beside Magdalena and Alicia. By packing up one case at a time and bringing them with her to Magdalena's suite to be stored with Magdalena's things until everything she would need for the summer was there, she had solved the problem of trying to transport all her luggage by herself. *And I didn't need Nan to think of it, either.*

The last night, she had skipped going to the opera and instead brought Grey in her carrier to the suite. She had left Grey sleeping while she kept those four persistent ghosts occupied. Then she and a fascinated Alicia had shared breakfast with the parrot; then Grey went back into the carrier while the porters came and collected all the luggage.

Since she was traveling in the same private compartment with Magdalena, she didn't dare let Grey out, but Grey was so quiet she might not even have been *in* the carrier at all. Magdalena showed no interest whatsoever in the leather carrier; Sarah had a notion she just thought it was an odd piece of luggage, containing, perhaps, a hat or two, or something else equally delicate and likely to be crushed. Sarah didn't enlighten her as to Grey's presence. She didn't want Magdalena to raise an objection.

It was going to be about a three-hour train trip; Sarah kept the carrier on her lap and read. Magdalena, who was clearly bored, looked out the window while Alicia read the society papers to her. They were going into Wiltshire, a county that Sarah had, until now, only passed through. The manor they were going to be staying at all summer was called "Tottenham House," which was not a particularly impressive name. Sarah actually knew nothing whatsoever about it. She just hoped it would be large enough that there would be at least one small room for her that she did not need to share, unless she was going to share one with Alicia. Alicia had enjoyed Grey's company and been fascinated by her, and probably would not object to sharing her room with a bird— but anyone else? There was no telling. She didn't even want to contemplate what would happen if they wanted her to sleep with the servants. Willie had invited her himself, albeit at Magdalena's urging; surely that meant she was supposed to be a guest.

It was a distinct relief when they arrived at the tiny station at Burbage to see a carriage waiting for them *and* a wagon waiting for the luggage. She and Alicia trailed along behind Magdalena like a pair of geese behind a magnificent swan; she took the seat facing the front, and they took the one facing backward. Sarah was glad she didn't suffer from traveling sickness when sitting in the backward seat. As the little caravan moved away from the station, it was clear that they were going to be moving along at a very sedate rate; the horses barely picked up into an amble.

The carriage swayed along country roads for quite some time; Sarah began to wonder if they were in for *another* three-hour trip. By her watch, it was nearly an hour before the carriage made a right-hand turn and moved from the rutted country road to a smoothly graveled lane, passing through enormous gates held open by a gatekeeper. Behind the gatekeeper was his "cottage"— and to her shock, it was a three-story stone building that looked the size of Mrs. Horace's two-flat house in London!

While she was still taking that in, they rolled smoothly down the lane—or road, it was perfectly wide enough to be a road— through what looked like manicured parkland. They traveled through this parkland along an avenue between two perfectly straight lines of trees. It was driving Sarah a little mad to be sitting backward, where she couldn't see the manor. And finally, after about a mile, the carriage made a smooth left turn that became a curve, and then, the manor came into view.

And came into view.

And came into view.

When the carriage came to a halt, Magdalena was handed out by a *footman,* complete with livery, and Sarah and Alicia descended (without any such help). The carriage had arrived at the steps of the . . . "house." "Willie" was already there, having taken Magdalena's hand, and was guiding her toward the great front doors.

". . . about a hundred rooms, more or less," Willie said, with a little laugh. "Never counted 'em all, personally. You'll have the Green Suite, there's four bedrooms in it . . ."

Sarah sighed with relief.

Willie began rattling off all the members of the peerage and the wealthy and famous who were going to be at this "house party" as Sarah tried to simultaneously look at the building and try not to look as if she was gawking, because it was, quite literally, the largest single building she had ever seen in her life, excepting only

Hampton Court Palace. She could scarcely believe her eyes. How could anything this big be called a mere "house"?

Built of some pale yellow stone or brick, it had two stories and a ground floor, with a third story over the main building. Two huge, stubby, L-shaped wings stretched out on either side of the main building, embracing a circular drive, then two single-story curved sections sprang from the ends of the wings, ending in two *more* single-story buildings.

Sarah had thought Lord Alderscroft's estate was magnificent. Tottenham House's main building alone was the size of Lord A's manor.

There was a line of uniformed or liveried servants stretching to either side of the door, which was being held open by a butler. Sarah took a quick glance behind her and saw that the wagon was being swarmed by more servants, busy as ants, unloading all the baggage. She looked ahead again, and the twin lines of servants bowed or curtsied as Willie and Magdalena sailed past them.

In a front hall that left Sarah feeling dazzled, Willie took his leave of them, putting Magdalena in the keeping of a housekeeper. That worthy woman directed them to the right and into one of the wings. Eventually they were brought to the "Green Suite," which was papered in a pleasing pale green brocade, with furnishings upholstered in a darker green plush. The sitting room of the suite was nearly identical in its magnificent furnishing and size, if not in shape, to the suite at the hotel. And like the hotel, the opulent green bedroom that would be Magdalena's was to the left as they entered. It was complete with a bathroom, although it was clear that water was not piped in, and would have to be carried here by hand every time Magdalena wanted a bath. There was a separate door for that, so that pails of hot water would not have to be lugged through the bedroom.

Then again, they clearly have an army of servants to do just that sort of thing, Sarah thought in a daze.

To the right were three more modest bedrooms, papered in a simple pattern of dark green vines on a light green background, with furnishings that were older, simpler, and appeared to be suited for children. The luggage was piled up in the third bedroom, and Alicia went immediately to sort it out.

Sarah went to the further of the two bedrooms and put Grey's carrier on the bed, opening it so she could come out. The parrot walked out onto the bed and shook herself vigorously, hopping up onto the foot of the brass bedstead and peering out to the southwest at first, where she could see a formal garden, then a great deal of lawn, sparsely dotted with trees and bushes, then forest. She looked up at Sarah and looked back at the window.

"Yes, I think there are almost certainly hawks, and Neville is not here to protect you," Sarah said, in response to the unspoken wish to go out. Grey sighed. "Water," she said, and Sarah went to where the luggage had been left and pulled out the case holding the traveling perch and newspapers. When everything was set up, she filled one cup with water from the pitcher on the washstand and the other with the peas and cut carrots that had been in the traveling case.

The housekeeper emerged from Magdalena's room, having made sure that everything was to the diva's liking, and Sarah intercepted her before she left. "I have a parrot with me," she said to the housekeeper, trying to put on an air of enough authority that the woman would not challenge her right to have Grey with her, but not so much that she'd think Sarah was "aping her betters." "She's perfectly tame, and travels with me everywhere. If the chambermaid is afraid of her, all she has to say is "Go in the box," and she'll go to her carrier and not come out until the maid is gone. I will take care of any messes she makes, but I will need fresh fruit and vegetables chopped for her, about a cup full, once in the morning and once at teatime."

"May I see this bird?" the housekeeper asked, sounding a little doubtful.

"Certainly," Sarah replied. The housekeeper followed her into the second small bedroom, where Grey had just finished eating a piece of carrot. Grey looked at both of them, and bobbed her head. "Hello," she said. "My name is Grey."

"Hello, bird," the housekeeper replied with surprise. "Well, listen to it talking like a Christian and all! You're sure it'll be no trouble to the maid?"

For answer, Sarah said, "Grey, go in the box."

Grey flew to the top of the dresser where the carrier now stood, and walked into her carrier.

"Well then, this will be easier than those nasty little spaniels Lady Harrington brought with her, miss," the housekeeper said, with a little spite. "Underfoot and yapping and snarling, and if they're housebroken, *I* am a Red Indian. I'll tell the maid; you'll have Annie, she likes animals. Good day, miss."

As she left, Grey came back out and flew to her perch, which Sarah put by the window. With the most important thing taken care of, she went to collect the rest of her luggage, including some toys for Grey, which she hung from the perch. When she had finished putting her clothing away in the dresser, Alicia came in.

"They'll be ringing the gong for dinner," the maid told her. "You'll hear it all over the house. Once to warn you it's time to get ready, and twice when dinner is served. You'll be going in with Magdalena. Someone will come to show you."

"But where—"

"I'll be eating with the servants, as is proper," Alicia said, with a faint air of regret. "I'm not quite sure *where* you fit in things. I *think* you're above a governess. You'll find out when they place you at table. I'm not sure if the Marquess thinks you'll be performing séances or anything, but you ought to prepare to be asked. You might count like Magdalena, as a sort of entertaining guest."

"I hope they don't ask me," Sarah said, feeling the cold hand of dread. "Séances are . . . I don't usually do them. Spirits sometimes don't come when you call them, and when they do, if there are a lot of people, things can get unpredictable . . ."

What did I let myself in for when I agreed to this? she thought in a bit of a panic.

"Well, if they do ask you, it will probably be after we've been here a few days. Most of the guests aren't even here yet, so it will just be the Marquess and people who managed to come down from London early." She lowered her voice. "His bedroom suite is right next to this one, so it will probably be him who comes to take Magdalena down."

Ah. I hope Magdalena realizes there's more than one way in which she's going to be expected to perform. . . .

At just that moment, a maid appeared with a laden tray, standing hesitantly in the door open to the hall. After a few moments of directing and setting out, the maid left again, this time closing the door behind her, and Alicia tapped on the closed bedroom door. "Mistress," she said quietly. "There is tea."

"You may serve me in my room, I am *prostrate* with exhaustion," Magdalena replied, sounding not exhausted at all. Alicia gave Sarah a knowing nod, fixed a plate full of tiny sandwiches and cakes, and poured a cup of tea the way Magdalena liked it. When she came out of the bedroom again, she closed the door behind her with a sigh.

"Now *we* can eat," she said. "I'm famished. I'll tell you what dinner will be like while we have our tea."

INTERLUDE: *LANGSAM*

(SCHUMANN CONCERTO IN D)

The tall, spare man regarded the view out of the window of his room on the second floor of Tottenham House with a frown. Moonlight flooded the enormous lawn, and the few trees and bushes made black figures against the silvery expanse of perfectly mown grass.

It was not that he was unhappy to be here. On the contrary, it was a good thing he had been alerted to the flight of his quarry before she'd had a chance to vanish. It was an even better thing that he had managed to maneuver an invitation for himself to this "house party"—he considered himself a fit man, healthy and able-bodied, but the prospect of marching over acres of land guarded by gamekeepers and dogs every night was not one that appealed.

He, of course, had not been granted a room in the part of the "house" where the master and his most favored guests were sleeping. But his powers should be strong enough to accomplish what he needed from here. He had specified that he might need to practice at odd hours; his host had assured him this would cause no difficulty. He wondered if his host had any idea just how "odd" his "practice" hours were going to be.

There are a hundred rooms in this mausoleum. If my neighbors object, I am sure they can be moved, or I can.

He went to the bed, opened the violin case, and took out his treasured instrument and the special bow. The bow glowed with a spectral paleness in the moonlight, the bow itself luminescent, the bowstring gleaming like silk. Carefully, he put bow to the strings, and began to play.

She came immediately, bright as a candle flame in the darkness of his room. He played for her, and her alone, at this moment. Reminding her that she was here by her own choice; that she and she alone had the right to decide how this dance of life and death would end. She swayed a little, not to the music, but to some inner rhythm of her own. And as she swayed, her light strengthened as she drew in power from him, and from his own particular magic.

When he was sure that, once again, she understood, when he was sure she had accepted all of his power that she could contain, he released her. She did not leave, of course. She was waiting for more.

And then, as she waited, he summoned the others. This was an old site, and there were many restless spirits here. Before long he had given her an army. Only when she was satisfied did she vanish.

Now drained from his exertions, the violinist carefully replaced instrument and bow in the case, then closed and locked it. Only then did he turn to the darkened, farthest corner of the room.

A shadow moved in that corner. The sound of soft clapping came from the depths. "Bravo, Maestro. Bravo."

The violinist bowed his head slightly in acknowledgement. "But . . . you saw nothing?"

"I saw nothing. Then again, what I see and believe is immaterial. Or so you keep telling me." The man in the shadows rose to his feet. He appeared to be as tall, and as slender, as the violinist. "What matters to me is that you obtain results that I *can* see and believe in. So let us hope we can bring this affair to its appropriate conclusion. Until we meet again—*buenas noches*, Maestro."

"*Buenas noches,*" said the violinist—but the door had opened and closed again, and his visitor was already gone.

14

After tea, Sarah had taken a nap, knowing that without the need to rehearse or practice—and with Willie being literally a mere door away—Magdalena was very likely to stay up late. When the first gong rang before dinner, she hastily got up and put on her only evening dress, fixing her hair as well as she could, and wishing at that moment for Nan's helping hands. Somehow, Nan could always make her hair look elegant. But enough hairpins could tame nearly anything, and when Willie came to escort Magdalena to dinner, since neither of them gave her a reproving look, she trailed along behind. Willie didn't pay much attention to her, but neither did he snub her, and when the time came for the group assembled in the drawing room to "go in to dinner," he signaled unobtrusively to a gentleman at the fringe of the group to act as her escort. According to Alicia, this was not what was supposed to happen; the lady of the house was supposed to arrange escorts, and introductions to the escorts, beforehand. It appeared there was no "lady of the house," so Willie was free to arrange things as he liked. A glance at the clock on a nearby mantelpiece as she passed in to the dining room on the arm of her escort told her they were going in at a little before nine in the evening. She reflected that at least she wouldn't have to wait until midnight for her dinner while she was here.

The dining room featured a table of daunting length, but only a quarter of the possible seats had place settings in front of them. There were *chandeliers* over the table, every candle in them burning brightly. Every place had an elegant place card in the form of a little scroll curled over a rose and a sprig of fern. When her escort left her at her place, she found herself situated at the bottom of the row on the left-hand side of the table, sitting next to a tall, thin man with beautiful hands, who told her he was a violinist. "I'm afraid I don't know very much about music," she confessed. "Which seems absurd, considering that Magdalena von Dietersdorf is my patroness, I am sure . . ."

"Ah! She is a great artist, I am told," the gentleman said and, putting his hand to his chest and bowing a little, added, "I have been too busy preparing for and performing my own concerts this season to attend any of her performances, so I will trust to hearsay. We must not stand on any ceremony, then. You may call me Pablo."

"I'm Sarah, Sarah Lyon-White," she replied, and offered her hand to him to shake—trying to remember from all those etiquette lessons if that was the proper thing to do at dinner or not. Evidently it was, for he took it and bowed over it instead of shaking it, and no one gave them any strange looks.

Magdalena was the queen of the table, of course. She sat at Willie's right hand, chatting away gracefully, and attracted all eyes toward her, except, perhaps, for those of the man beside Sarah. He gave her only polite interest at best, and for the most part applied himself quietly, and elegantly, to his food. He did not ignore her, however; he asked what she did for Magdalena (she told him she was Magdalena's companion, which was not far from the truth), what sort of music she liked, what she was reading—nice, commonplace conversation that was easy to answer. The gentleman across from her was very much occupied with the young lady next to him, who had an American accent, and there was no one to her right.

It was a very long dinner; Sarah was put in mind of the history lessons Nan had been giving Suki and the royal dinners of Henry VIII with their bewildering parade of dishes. There was even a menu! Dish after dish was presented by the servants—there seemed to be one servant for every two or three guests, and after a glance at the menu card, Sarah realized that she would have to be careful and decline at least two-thirds of what she was offered.

After dinner, rather than the men settling in the dining room for coffee while the ladies took to the drawing room for the same, the guests were escorted into the music room for a concert by the gentleman who had been sitting beside Sarah—but being aware just how late her evening was going to be, Sarah slipped away to go take another nap. It was very obvious that no one was going to miss her presence. She was feeling the fact that she'd been forced to be awake for the journey here, and didn't want to fall asleep when she was supposed to be watching over Magdalena. And . . . truth to tell, although no one had *openly* snubbed her, her feelings were a bit bruised by being ignored so much. She left a request with Alicia to fetch her when Magdalena returned to go to bed, changed into her nightgown, then cuddled with Grey and a book until Grey grew sleepy. She left Grey on her night perch on the headboard, and took to her bed.

When Alicia came to fetch her, it was nearly three in the morning, and from the slightly disheveled appearance of Magdalena's gown and hair, Sarah had the notion the diva had been rewarding their host with what their host expected. Since they weren't in the hotel, and she was going to be able to go straight to sleep in the morning, Sarah stayed in her nightdress and pulled on her dressing gown for what she expected to be an uneventful vigil.

Oh, how very wrong she was.

She'd brought Puck's charm against spirits with her, and it was a good thing she had. Out of the corner of her eye, she saw movement, and reflexively turned to face it just as a transparent, balding fellow in Roundhead garb appeared out of thin air, gabbled something about witchcraft, and swung a sword at her.

Instinctively she ducked, a shriek freezing in her throat. She gazed at him in horror and some shock for a moment before she realized that, of course, Puck's charm easily kept him far enough away to be nothing more than a nuisance. Waiting for her heart to stop pounding, she watched him rage at the invisible boundary, swinging at it with his spectral sword, then beating at it with fists and swearing at her for being a vile, Popish trollop. He managed quite a colorful sort of invective without ever uttering any real profanity, but eventually even his ghostly patience ran out, and he was reduced to crossing his arms and glowering at her.

He was the first but by no means the only violent ghost. If she had not been sure of the strength of that charm it would have been a terrifying night, and as it was, it was an ordeal.

The next to appear was a woman enveloped head-to-toe in a long black veil who tried to strangle her, then came the Cavalier who was as eager to shoot her as the Roundhead was to chop her head off. When he wore himself out, there appeared the centurion in Roman armor who was as eager to take her head off with a short sword as the Roundhead was with a longer blade. The Roman was, by far, the *oldest* spirit she had ever encountered, and if he hadn't wanted to kill her, it might have been enlightening to try to get him to talk. Assuming her Latin was up to such a thing. . . .

But that wasn't an option. There was no chance of talking with spirits who were intent on violence. Nor with the two Catholic priests, who kept exploding into flames, the nun that just paced and wept, or the four children who clung to each other in the corner and stared at her as if they expected her to murder them.

Any sort of communication at all was impossible with the highwayman who actually did not *have* a head, the gentleman in an Elizabethan collar who stood off to the side, apparently muttering to himself, or the old woman who shrieked curses, then exploded into flame.

She was beginning to gather that a good many people had been burned at the stake hereabouts.

As for the man in knee breeches of the last century who would not stop leering at her and trying to fondle her—well, she wanted, badly, to have been able to open the door to the afterlife right *under* him.

And those were just the ones who pushed themselves into her attention. She got the distinct feeling that there were more who had chosen not to manifest themselves . . . yet.

In the end, she only managed to send the Roman and the Roundhead on through the door before the first thin light of day came creeping in through the windows and the rest of the spirits faded away.

It had been a long, exhausting night.

Sarah was very glad that all she had to do here at Tottenham

House when the night was over was get as far as her room, pull off her dressing gown, and fall into bed. If this had been the hotel—she didn't think she'd have gotten much farther than the elevator after the grueling night she'd just endured.

But before she went to bed . . . she was starving. Wishing she could somehow drink a breakfast, she rang for the maid—poor things, they were up at daylight regardless, or so Alicia had told her—and when the girl arrived, looking shocked that any of the "gentry" were awake at this hour, Sarah begged for something to eat. "It doesn't have to be anything special. Whatever you're eating in the kitchen. Porridge is fine, or whatever was cold from last night."

The girl returned with hot bread, butter, fruit, biscuits, and a leg of cold chicken, which seemed like a feast to Sarah. By this time Grey was awake, so she shared her fruit and one of the biscuits with the parrot, then went straight to bed.

When she woke, it was midafternoon. The rooms were very quiet, but her bedroom had been tidied a bit and Grey was eating some carrots and peas, so evidently the maid had come in and done her work and gone without waking Sarah up.

She had a headache after that grueling night, but more often than not that sort of headache could be cured with food and especially drink, so she dressed and went out looking for Alicia. She found the girl in Magdalena's room, shaking out one of Magdalena's magnificent gowns; Magdalena was nowhere in sight.

"Mistress is playing tennis," Alicia said without prompting. "You probably can too, if you like."

"I'd rather stay here and read," Sarah replied. "I'm not really here to—" She shrugged.

"Then let me have the maid fetch you something to eat," Alicia replied, and before Sarah could say anything, she had already pulled the bell. A few moments later the maid appeared.

"Miss Lyon-White requires a late luncheon," Alicia said, loftily; the chambermaid gave a quick curtsey and hurried off. "You'll probably get whatever was left over," Alicia told her with a shrug. "But you never know. The staff might already have eaten everything, so you might get something new-made and nice."

In fact, she got a nice big plate of finger sandwiches, scones, clotted cream, and sliced strawberries, which she shared with Alicia and Grey. "Is anyone going to notice that I have only the one evening gown?" she asked, nervously.

"I doubt it," Alicia replied bluntly. "You're here as Magdalena's companion. Mistress has made no secret of the fact that she's sensitive to spirits, in fact, she's rather boasted about it. They know you are here as a medium, you are here to keep her from being disturbed by them. I did a lot of listening while I was having luncheon with the house servants. You may be a guest, but the only reason you are at the dinner table is because Magdalena wants you, and you make up the matching woman to go with that Spanish violinist who was invited."

"Oh," she said, feeling rather hurt. *I've been invited to Lord Alderscroft's parties!* she thought. *And he's in the Cabinet! This Willie is just one of those peers who turns up twice a year to sit in his seat in the House of Lords and otherwise just . . . fritters his time away with actresses and dancers!* But she did her best not to *show* she was hurt. *Besides, most of these people are horribly dull. They've never done anything in their lives, or with their lives, except to spend money.*

Except perhaps that violinist. There was something about him— something that reminded her, oddly enough, of Lord Alderscroft.

I'm not here to socialize. I am here to protect Magdalena. Nevertheless, this was very like a snub, and as such, it stung.

Alicia gave her a sidelong look, as if she wanted to point out that the only real difference between her and the maid was that the maid worked by day and she worked by night. It was clear to Alicia that it was only purest accident that Sarah wasn't eating in the kitchen with the rest of the servants.

Now feeling both hurt *and* irritated, Sarah left the remains of the luncheon to Alicia to clean up, although she had generally, in the past, helped with putting things on the tray and getting the tray out to the hall for the hotel maids to deal with. She retreated to her room, her head still aching, closed the door behind her, and decided to open the window to get some fresh air in.

Then she sat down in the lone chair next to the window—one that was not particularly comfortable, and appeared to have been given a quick reupholstering job then left here as being "too good" for a servant's room but not good enough for the real guests. She rested her aching forehead on her hand and tried not to cry. None of this was what she had expected. She'd thought it would be a small group in a much smaller house, and much less formal. She'd thought she'd be treated the way Magdalena treated her, as someone valuable, even necessary. Instead she was this . . . well, not insignificant enough to ignore, but not important enough to pay any attention to.

"Want Nan," said Grey.

"Well, you won't get her!" Sarah snapped. "She's not interested in petty things like banishing ghosts." Which was unfair—Nan hadn't refused to come. It was Magdalena who had pointedly *not* invited Nan, who probably would have come if she *had* been invited, but—

Magdalena probably saw through all that veneer of civilization that Memsa'b put on her to the dirty little street urchin underneath. Magdalena probably knew as soon as she saw Nan that you couldn't put her in this kind of society without her embarrassing us.

And as soon as she thought that, she was ashamed of herself. Why should she think that about Nan? Even if Magdalena thought Nan was "common," she had never been anything other than the best of friends and partners to Sarah! And as for her lowly origins, when had Nan *ever* put a foot wrong with Lord Alderscroft and his guests?

And then she was angry with herself for being ashamed. After all, Magdalena must have seen *something* wrong with Nan— or why should she have pointedly excluded her from the very moment Sarah started protecting her from spirits?

"Want Nan!" Grey insisted. "Want Nan. Want Neville. Want Suki. Want Nan!"

Sarah glared at her. Grey glared back. It was very clear that she was going to *continue* to chant that she wanted her friends like a little repeating clockwork, whether Sarah liked it or not.

"*Will* you *shut up,* you stupid bird!" Sarah snapped, and got up and thrust her hand roughly at Grey, intending to shove her into her carrier, close her inside, and cover it with a cloth so she'd go to sleep and stop with her irritating litany of *Want Nans.*

Grey growled—something she had *never* done to Sarah

before—but Sarah ignored her, and shoved her hand at the bird again. "Up!" she barked.

And Grey looked at her face, then at her hand—and quick as a cobra, darted her head down and *bit* Sarah, hard, so hard that blood spurted from the bite as she clung on, grinding her beak on the finger.

Too shocked to shriek, Sarah instinctively shook her hand, roughly, and Grey was off like a shot through the open window. In a moment she was at the edge of the formal garden, flying hard for the trees, not looking back.

And as Sarah stood there, stunned, a black shadow dove from the roof after the flying parrot, flying swiftly in pursuit of her.

Now she shrieked, *"Grey!"* and dashed out of the room, injured hand forgotten, trying to find a door to the outside. It took far too many minutes to find one, far too many to run around to the southwest side of the building where the formal garden was—

And by then, there was no sight of her, nor of the predatory bird that had followed after her. But she ran for the distant line of the forest anyway, because if Grey had been able to get that far, that is where she would have gone. She ran as hard as she could, holding her injured hand in the other against her chest and sobbing, over and over, one word.

"Grey! Grey! Oh, Grey!"

But there was no reply.

Sarah's side was aching, along with her head, and her eyes were sore from crying, as she craned her head to peer into the trees above her, looking for a sign of that red tail, listening for a reply. "Grey!" she sobbed, hoarsely. "Grey! Please come back, Grey! I'm sorry! I'm so sorry! You were right! Magdalena is *horrid*. I never should have come here. I should have stayed with Nan and Suki, and now you're gone, and it's all my fault!"

Then her eyes dropped, and she saw it. A single red feather, lying on the grass.

And a vision flashed through her mind, of a hawk, talons outstretched, snatching Grey out of the tree where she had landed, as Grey writhed and gasped her last breath, and carrying her off,

259

leaving behind a single, red tail feather to fall to the ground.

All that was left—

"*Grey!*" she cried, and dropped to the grass, picking up the feather and sobbing over it hysterically. "Oh, this is all my fault! It's all my fault!"

"Why yes," said a dry voice, "It is. You are the one with psychical powers. You know what they can do. You *let* Magdalena get into your head, and this is where it's brought you."

Her head shot up and she stared in shock at Mary Watson, who was standing just inside the forest, arms crossed over her chest, frowning.

It didn't even occur to her to ask how Mary had gotten there, or why she had come. She had thought she could not possibly be more miserable until that moment, but grief piled upon grief as she realized Mary was right. She'd been so proud of herself, she'd been so thrilled that *she* had been singled out by Magdalena, made a pet of, flattered and spoiled, that she'd been pushing her friends away, pushing *Grey* away . . .

. . . and now . . . now it was too late.

All she could do was sob.

Mary let her weep hysterically until she ran out of breath from sobbing and began to cough. Only then did she push her way through the heavy grass and make her way to where Sarah was half-collapsed and offer a hand. "Come on," she said. "Get up. Crying won't change anything."

The sure and certain knowledge that this was true only made her cry harder, until at last Mary grabbed her by the elbow and yanked her to her feet, then gave her a little shake. "That's enough. Come with me," she said, and turned on her heel and strode along the tree line.

Sobbing and shaking, Sarah stumbled after her, cradling the precious feather in her injured hand. Every throb of pain was welcome to her, a reminder of how much she *deserved* to be hurt for being so stupid. *Now,* now that she wasn't blinded by pride, blinded by thinking she was somehow superior to Nan, she could see it. Magdalena had shamelessly manipulated her. And now everything was lost. Nan would never forgive her for what she had done to Grey. She would never forgive herself.

Her thoughts circled endlessly in the same heartbroken circle as Mary led her around the front of Tottenham House to another hard-packed gravel lane that formed the top of the circular drive at the entrance. They followed that lane to the northeast, then it curved to the northwest, passing through a shorter avenue lined with trees, until they reached a huge, square building, two stories tall, made of the same pale yellow material as the main house. It was built in the same style, with a tall arching entrance into a central courtyard and a clock tower over the entrance. Grooms leading saddled horses into it showed what it was: a stable. There must have been room for fifty horses here. Mary took her elbow and led her through the arched doorway, beneath the clock tower and into the square courtyard. Open doors onto the courtyard showed various sorts of carriages and wagons all along the rear and the stable doors to the right and left. Grooms took horses in and out through the stable doors, casting curious, but averted, glances at the two women.

Mary, however, continued to lead Sarah on to one human-sized door in the middle of the left-hand side of the block. There was a staircase immediately inside; Mary pushed Sarah at it, and Sarah climbed it, half-blinded now with tears and her swollen eyes. At the top of the stairs, Mary took her elbow again and dragged her through an open room with beds lined up on either side beneath the windows—this was where the grooms and stable hands must live, at least the lowest and youngest ones on the staff. At the end of the room was a door, which Mary opened, pushed Sarah inside, then entered herself, closing it behind her.

"I hope you're properly ashamed of yourself," said Nan, with Neville on her shoulder, cradling Grey in her lap.

Sarah burst into tears all over again.

Mary Watson pushed her down onto a narrow iron-framed bed, and Grey leapt into her lap with two awkward flaps of her wings. Nan handed her a handkerchief, then Mary handed her another, then John Watson handed her *his* when she'd turned the first two into soggy messes, and she cried until her throat was so hoarse she could scarcely speak.

Then she croaked out apology after apology: to Grey, to Nan, to Grey again, to the Watsons, to Grey, to Nan. She thought she would never be able to apologize enough, until Nan finally told her, in the kindliest voice possible, to "Shut up, you're starting to babble."

Then Mary Watson handed her a glass of water, and she realized that she had cried herself literally dry. She drank three glasses in quick succession while John Watson bandaged her bitten finger. It hurt abominably, and she welcomed the pain.

All the time she kept Grey cuddled in her lap, until at last, the parrot looked up at her and said, "I forgive you. Don't do this again."

Which only made her burst into tears again.

"I don't understand this," Sarah croaked, Grey still held against her chest with her bandaged hand; from time to time Grey rubbed her head gently against Sarah's thumb. "Why are you here? How did you get here?"

The room they were in was about the size of the sitting room in the London flat; it held two beds, a chair, a washstand, and two chests. There was a second door opposite the one they had come in; it was open, and Sarah guessed it led to another bedroom like this one; both were probably for "superior" stable staff. From the tweed coat draped over the foot of one bed and the skirt draped over the other, Sarah guessed the room was being used by John and Mary.

"*How* is simple enough," John Watson said with a shrug. "Lord Alderscroft. The Stable Master here is an Earth Magician, and shortly after you told Nan that Magdalena was going to bring you here, Alderscroft began making arrangements. Alderscroft sent us by carriage with very fast horses the same day you left; we arrived not more than an hour or two after you did; we came in by another road, straight to the stable. No one knows we're here but the stable staff, and they are under strict orders to say nothing."

"That was a hawk you saw chasing Grey when she flew away," Nan added. "What you *didn't* see was Neville showing the hawk that his friend was not to going to become her dinner."

"As for *why* we are here, it was abundantly clear to all of us that you were not yourself," said Mary. "We certainly weren't going to leave you alone with her, every day, and give her the opportunity to separate you from your friends permanently. What we couldn't figure out was how Magdalena was manipulating not only you but anyone else she cared to use. When we spoke to Alderscroft about it, he became alarmed."

"Why?" croaked Sarah, blinking her sore eyes in surprise.

"Because, although she had not done so yet, it was entirely possible she could use her power, whatever it is, to meddle in the business of Her Majesty's government in the future," replied John. "At that point, she became a risk to our national interests."

If she'd been able to do so, Sarah would have widened her eyes in alarm. "But—all she ever did was—get men to give her presents—" she said, feebly.

Nan snapped her fingers in front of Sarah's nose, and she started. "Wake up!" Nan said sharply. "She's *far* more dangerous and ruthless than you think!"

"I think," drawled Sherlock Holmes, as he opened the door and entered the tiny room, "This is where I should join the conversation." He sat down on the bed beside John Watson, who moved over for him. He leaned over and looked sternly into Sarah's eyes. "As you know, I was originally intrigued by Fraulein von Dietersdorf because of the absurd story about her missing sister." He held up a hand, forestalling any protest on Sarah's part, but she actually hadn't intended to protest. "I've never heard a more feeble story in my life. And when, after sending me frantic letters begging me to look for her, her parents and her fiancé suddenly decided to accept that story, I became very suspicious, although I was not sure *what* to be suspicious of. Nevertheless, you and Sarah had just proven to me that psychical gifts are a reality, and I wondered if something like that might be at work."

"You thought Magdalena might be—changing peoples' memories and thoughts?" Nan asked, as if all this was new to her. From the looks on John and Mary Watsons' faces, it was new to them, too.

"It seemed to me to be a possibility," Holmes replied. "So I went to Germany to speak to Johanna's friends, where I learned several very interesting facts. It was Johanna, not Magdalena, who first began an operatic career, although both girls were given singing lessons by the most able of teachers. Magdalena only became interested when Johanna succeeded in eventually singing a leading role; once Magdalena applied to the opera, she quickly shunted Johanna aside. Then Johanna stepped back and devoted herself to the more conventional roles of a girl of her class and station. Magdalena confined herself to lording over her sister with new accomplishments . . . until Johanna became engaged at about the same time that Magdalena accepted the engagement to debut at the Royal Opera. The engagement was a complete surprise to everyone except their parents, and young Helmut was considered a fine catch. Johanna's friends say Magdalena was livid."

"And what did Magdalena's friends say?" Sarah managed.

"Ah! Now *that* is fascinating indeed!" Holmes said, resting his elbows on his knees and steepling his fingers together. "Because although Magdalena left behind a plethora of friends and admirers when she traveled to London, by the time I had arrived . . . there were none who would admit to being a friend *or* an admirer. And every person I queried about her would respond in the tones of acute bitterness that only a baffled German can produce, indicating that he could not imagine what he—or she!—was thinking when he allowed her to lead him about like a monkey on a leash. I must say it was mostly males, however. Magdalena does not often exert herself to charm females. You, Sarah, are an exception to that rule."

"So it wears off!" Nan exclaimed. "The—charm, or fascination, or call it by the ancient name, *enchantment*—I mean."

"Indeed." Holmes nodded. "So, at that moment, Magdalena is going to London. Johanna has no reason to go, and indeed, one would think she would embark on a round of engagement parties and outings where she and her fiancé are displayed together. And yet, she *does* go. Why, she agreed to, we will never know. But I believe I know why Magdalena asked her." He raised an eyebrow. "I believe she intended to eliminate her. Possibly because she knew that Johanna was her only real rival, as they share the same talents. The difference between them was that the only talent Johanna *used* was the gift of song."

"Johanna was going to get her old position in her old opera company when Magdalena left!" exclaimed Mary, looking to Holmes. "Because whatever *else* Magdalena had done to get it would wear off eventually!"

Holmes smiled thinly. "And Johanna had something else that she would *never* allow Magdalena to take from her. Herr Helmut. While on Magdalena's part . . . well, you, Miss Nan, put your finger on why Magdalena would want the young man."

"When I said that Magdalena wanted anything that someone else had . . ." Nan replied, slowly.

Holmes nodded. "Perhaps Johanna thought this trip was a sort of chance for reconciliation with her sister. Perhaps she only wished to keep an eye on her, to keep her from piling up dupe after dupe. In either case she was sadly mistaken when she thought she was safe from Magdalena. I am convinced that Magdalena murdered her."

Shocked, Sarah protested—much as she now felt sick about how much Magdalena had been using her and anyone else that crossed her path, she could not believe *that*. "No body was ever found!"

"Not . . . quite . . . true," Holmes told her. "No body was found at the time Johanna supposedly went missing."

"Ah!" Watson cried. "I see where your logic is leading you! You think Johanna was murdered earlier!"

"Precisely. In fact, I believe Magdalena murdered her sister by throwing her off the boat as it approached London." Again, he held up his hand. "And you will tell me that letters came from Johanna in London, and Johanna was seen in the hotel. But I point out to you that siblings can often forge one another's handwriting, that the letters in question sounded suspiciously as if they had been copied from a guidebook, that the ladies were known to wear each other's gowns, and that the specious 'Johanna' was never seen without a veil."

Sarah felt . . . stunned. Too many shocks in too short a time.

"Now, countering this was the testimony of the hotel porter that he had helped Johanna with her luggage and sent her off in a cab to the King's Cross railway station, at an hour when Magdalena was normally asleep. Surely the maid Alicia would have noticed! But! The maid Alicia was not engaged until after Johanna had 'eloped.' I established this at once."

"So there is no alibi for the time in question," John observed. "And Magdalena has been known to exert herself when necessary. She only needed to get up very early, ring for the porter, and get as far as King's Cross and back. Porters and elevator operators are not known for noticing what a lady is wearing, only her face. Without her veil, she could feign to be returning from a festive night."

Holmes nodded. "So I went to King's Cross and looked for the most remote destination possible from there, which was Thurso, in the Highlands. Then I took the journey myself and made enquiries at the left-baggage office. And there, as I had expected, was 'Johanna's' luggage. It was without an owner's label and contained a few outmoded gowns with German seamstress labels, cheap jewelry, a picture of the Von Dietersdorf family, some toilette articles, letters, and quantities of dead flowers. Now that I knew I must look for a dead woman found much earlier than I had thought, I returned to London, and that was when I had my great piece of luck."

He paused.

Watson shook his head. "You never admit to mere luck, Sherlock."

"I shall this time. The morgue attendant told me of a young man, with a photographic hobby, who was attempting to get himself hired by Scotland Yard. To that end, he had been photographing the faces of victims that were unidentified in morgues all over London, so that even after the bodies were interred, the victims might be identified. I already knew the date at which Magdalena had arrived. I suspected she would not have murdered her sister until the ship was near to port—otherwise Johanna would have been missed. She probably threw Johanna over the side at the stern, when all the other passengers who cared to watch the arrival were clustered at the prow. I knew the ship, its course, and the currents, and I asked him for the photographs of unidentified blond women within the correct date range."

Holmes reached into his tweed jacket and emerged with two photographs. The first was the one that he had shown the girls when they first discussed the case with him, the photograph of Johanna that her parents had given him. The second—

Well, the features were bloated and softened—but it was still unmistakable as being Johanna.

Sarah gasped.

"I will not say that you have had a near miss, my dear lady,"

Holmes said. "You are exceedingly useful to Magdalena. But if you had cut yourself off from your friends and followed her into the world, on the day that you ceased to be useful to her. . . ." He let the sentence trail off. "Perhaps nothing would have happened, and you would have been left like all those others she used and discarded, wondering *how* you had come to let yourself be manipulated. But . . . perhaps not. And if she had, indeed, succumbed to the temptation to meddle in the affairs of government, she might have found a way to cast all blame on *you* if she was caught."

Sarah swallowed, and Grey reached up and took one of her uninjured fingers gently in her beak.

"At any rate, that was when I spoke with Miss Nan about Magdalena, and became . . . alarmed at the prospect of what she might do. I turned to my good friend John for an explanation of how she might be doing these things." He bowed his head at Watson, who picked up the tale.

"I went to Alderscroft, who also became alarmed. He in turn took my information about Magdalena and her summer plans— and you and your part in them—and did what Alderscroft does best. He found allies, some in unexpected places, we formulated an interim plan of action, and here we are."

Holmes laughed dryly. "Yes. About those unexpected allies—"

"*Señors, señora, and señoritas,* I trust I have arrived at the correct time for our meeting?" A new voice spoke gently from the door, and Sarah gaped as she recognized the newcomer.

It was Pablo, the famous violinist.

15

Nan, John, and Mary had been expecting this. Nan had been waiting for this moment. Holmes had not spoken to Alderscroft, as they had, but Holmes had his sources, too.

Holmes leapt to his feet. "Maestro Sarasate—" he said, with a bow. The elegantly clad violinist raised his hand.

"*Un momento*. First of all," Pablo Sarasate said, with a little bow toward Sarah, "I must apologize to you, Señorita Sarah, for I have been the cause of much work, perhaps even distress, to you."

She blinked at him. Or at least as much as her tear-swollen eyes would allow. "I don't see how that is possible," she said dubiously. "We only met last night."

"Ah, but I fear that you have been battling the fruits of *my* labors for some time," he replied.

She stared at him blankly.

He smiled and elaborated. "I am the one responsible for invoking the spirits that *you* have been sending to their rests. Or at least, to their just rewards or punishments, as the case may be."

Now Sarah gaped at him. Nan was enjoying this. She and John and Mary had had the pleasure of meeting Pablo Sarasate three days ago, so they had heard all this before. Sarah, however, was completely in the dark.

"*How?*" Sarah demanded. "That's not possible! Spirits can come of their own accord, but no one can actually *call* them!"

"Actually, *señorita*, it is possible," the violinist said apologetically.

"I am an Elemental Master. And what you have been told, that there are four sorts of Elemental Masters, is not precisely true. There are five; I am one of the fifth kind, a Spirit Master, Spirit being the fifth element." He looked around for a place to sit and settled on the windowsill, after dusting it off with his handkerchief. "We are rare, which is just as well. The gift is not . . . terribly useful." He shrugged. "It is not unlike your ability as a medium, save that I cannot open a door to the next world. All I can do is answer the call of a spirit in distress, summon spirits who remain in this world, and strengthen them. This is how I became involved with Magdalena von Dietersdorf in the first place."

Sarah tilted her head to one side, bafflement showing on her face. "I don't understand. How does that have anything to do with what I have been doing for Magdalena?"

"Because," Pablo said, with a little gesture of conciliation, "I was asked for help by the spirit of Johanna von Dietersdorf."

The look on Sarah's face was absolutely without price. Nan wished there was a camera there, so she could capture it. Even Grey gaped at the violinist. If the situation hadn't been so serious, Nan would have laughed until her sides hurt.

Then Sarah's face took on another expression, this one of a revelation. "The very strong ghost—the one who wouldn't talk to me, wouldn't listen to me, and wouldn't go through the door—"

Pablo bent his head. "Indeed," he replied.

"That explains a great deal," Sarah replied without rancor, then sighed. "So what are we to do about this?"

"Ah!" said Sarasate, with a slight smile. "That is what we are here to decide."

Sarah walked back to the manor with the violinist. She held Grey against her chest with both hands the entire way as he escorted her right to the door of Magdalena's suite and knocked for her. She found his presence incredibly soothing, and hoped that at some point she would be able to ask him questions about being a "Spirit Master."

Alicia opened the door *immediately,* and her face was suffused with relief when she saw Sarah had Grey. "Oh thank God!" the maid cried. "You found her!"

"Maestro Sarasate helped me, she came to him when she heard his practicing," Sarah replied, making up a story on the spot. "If she hadn't heard him playing and gone to him, I don't think I would ever have found her."

Pablo gave a little bow. "It was my pleasure to be of service, *señorita*," he said gallantly, with a sidelong glance and a little twinkle at her lie. "Now I must return to my practice, and you should rest after your fright." With that, he turned and walked off, presumably back to his own guest room.

"Get in here! You must be completely knackered!" the maid said. "And your poor parrot! She must be half-dead with fear!"

"I think she was, I think there was a hawk chasing her," Sarah murmured, allowing herself to be drawn into the sitting room and fussed over.

"Is she hurt, or did she bite you? There's blood all over your waist and skirt." Alicia began *tsk*ing over the stains. "That is never going to come out—"

"She bit me when she saw the hawk and flew out the window, I think she was terrified," Sarah lied, a little appalled at how many lies she was telling lately. "She came to me as good as gold when Maestro heard me calling for her and called me back."

"Did he bandage your hand? He's as good as a doctor! Here, let's go in your room and get you out of those clothes, and I'll see if there is anything to be done about the stains." Alicia chivvied her into her room, shut the window firmly, and waited while Sarah put Grey on her stand before helping her out of the skirt and waist. Sarah was a little surprised at the amount of blood on them; she hadn't realized how bad the bite had been.

"I don't think there is anything I can do to save this shirtwaist," Alicia said, holding it up critically. "But I might be able to get the blood out of the skirt, at least enough that it's not noticeable anymore. It's a good thing you like browns."

"You don't have to go to all that trouble," Sarah protested. But Alicia just smiled.

"Mistress rarely needs anything done, she's so careful about her clothes. I don't mind. Now *you* look a sight. You have a nice lie-down with cucumber slices and a cool cloth on your eyes while I see what I can do." It was very clear that Alicia was not going to accept "no" for an answer, and truth to tell, Sarah was utterly exhausted. Her eyes were still swollen, her nose felt twice its normal size, her hand throbbed, and so did her head.

I should try to think of something to add to the plan, she told herself. But her head hurt so badly, she really couldn't think at all. So she did as Alicia had advised and laid herself down on the bed, changing the cloth over her eyes whenever it got warm. At some point her head finally stopped pounding, and somehow she drifted off to sleep.

She woke to the sound of the first dinner gong with a start. Wrapping her dressing gown around herself, she took a peek into the sitting room.

Alicia was there, mending something. She looked up when she heard Sarah's footstep. "Oh, you look much better. I got most of the blood out of the skirt, but I advise you have that shirtwaist dyed if you really want to keep it. I was going to wake you, then thought I had better let you sleep. Would you like me to ring for dinner to be brought here?"

"Would you share it with me?" Sarah asked.

Alicia laughed, and they were on friendly terms once again. "I would love to, thank you. There's a ladies' maid here that used to serve Willie's mother; she's an absolute cat, *terribly* superior, and I have to sit right next to her in the Hall. I'll ring for the maid, tell them you've got a sick headache still, and you need to be fit to watch over Mistress tonight. They've got enough servants here they can make us a tray before the dishes go up for dinner."

"Where *is* Magdalena?" Sarah asked.

"She went down early; Willie asked her to play lady of the house. Almost everyone that's supposed to be here for this house party arrived this afternoon." Alicia waited for her to take in and understand what that meant.

"He isn't thinking of proposing to her, is he?" she asked.

"Well, I don't know, and it's not my place," Alicia admitted, ringing for the maid. "It might only be that now *everyone* is here and he can't do without someone to act as hostess—and he discovered last night that Mistress can do the thing proper, without embarrassing him. So she can play hostess, and the guests can think what they like. He's a Marquess *and* an Earl, *and* has pots of money, there's no reason he can't suit himself. After all, we've got half the peerage marrying these American heiresses with silver mines who don't know a soup spoon from a demitasse spoon, why shouldn't he marry a prima donna who was properly brought up?"

I need to sound the way I did when I was still worshipping the witch, Sarah realized. This was going to be harder than she'd thought. "True enough. Would you *like* it if Willie proposed?" Sarah asked, making an effort to appear curious, and not appalled. "You'd be the lady's maid to a real Ladyship then!"

"If I could get that cat dismissed, I'd love it," Alicia replied, and giggled. "No, that would be too easy. I'd have her as my under-maid. And I'd be sweet as sweet to her, because that would pour vinegar in her wounds of coming down in the world." She eyed Sarah. "You go get into your nightdress and dressing gown and lie down again. I'll get you when the dinner comes."

Sarah was not at all averse to following that advice. It was quite lovely to get into her night-things and the heavy silk dressing gown that Lord A had given her last Christmas. Coming from any *other* gentleman, such a gift could have been considered scandalous, but Lord A frequently bought her and Nan garments appropriate to roles they might need to play, if those roles were of ladies in the higher ranks of society. He'd bought Nan a silk dressing gown, too. And once again, she found herself overcome with shame that she had considered Nan somehow *inferior* to her, even if she *had* been under that witch's fascination. After all, Lord Alderscroft treated them exactly as equals. . . .

"Are you all right?" she asked Grey, who was watching her curiously, as if the parrot was reading her thoughts.

"Hungry," said Grey, and yawned. "Sleepy."

"We'll both eat and sleep, and then . . ." Then, well . . .

Then we'll have to see. Not even Pablo knows what's likely to happen tonight. He was going to *try* sending some of the worst of the ghosts back to "sleep." The rest—well, he and Sarah shared a concern: that they must be helped to move on.

He was also going to try to explain their plan to Johanna. Or rather—he was certainly going to be able to explain it to her; as a

Spirit Master, that was his forte. He could communicate perfectly with spirits. The question was what she was going to do, once she heard what they planned.

"I have no control over that, Sarah," he had said apologetically. "I do not control spirits; that would be the work of a necromancer, and such things, I will not do. So—we will see what we will see. If she does not like our plan for her sister, then . . . it may be she will do as she will do, and we will have to adapt ourselves to that."

About a half an hour after Alicia rang for the maid, she came to get Sarah again. Sarah brought Grey with her into the sitting room, where quite a repast was laid out. Certainly enough food for two, and then some; it looked as if someone had asked the servant who had served her at dinner last night to make up plates, for there was nothing there she would not have chosen for herself.

The two of them—three, if you counted Grey—sat down at the table; Grey was between them, and they took turns offering the parrot bits of things they thought she would like. It was a much more pleasant dinner than last night's, and Sarah was able to relax and chat with Alicia quite naturally as long as she didn't think too hard about Magdalena's manipulations.

When they were finished, Sarah went back to her room to doze until Magdalena returned. It turned out to be a "nap" of about five hours, as Magdalena came in at around three, just as she had the previous night. Tonight she was as pleased as a cat who had gotten into the cream, and brought a half-empty bottle of champagne and a full glass with her. Alicia raised her eyebrows when Magdalena wasn't looking; Sarah shrugged. Alicia coaxed her mistress into her room, and Sarah settled down to see what the silence of the night would bring.

The clock on the mantelpiece had struck four before the rooms quieted down. And as soon as the last chime had struck—so did the Cavalier.

With a sigh, she resigned herself to another grueling night. The only good thing about it was that the later Magdalena stayed up, the shorter the night was. And the more sleep *she* was going to be able to get after it was over.

* * *

Their quarters in the stable block were not nearly as uncomfortable as Nan had feared they might be. The Stable Master had cleared out the two rooms at the far end of the left-hand quarters over the stables; that put them over the tack room rather than over the horses. The rooms were plain and spare, but scrupulously clean, and scented with nothing more objectionable than leather and clean hay. Since the stable was set quite a distance from the manor, it was in a little bit of forest and meadow all its own. What came in the windows was a great deal of lovely, fresh air, birdsong, and, at night, the occasional bat. It was four days since the rescue of Grey. *I wouldn't mind staying here a week or more,* Nan thought. *Well, except for the food . . .* Since they weren't supposed to be here, they were having to make do with whatever could be brought over from the nearest village, and she was getting tired of bread and cheese, carrots, and pickles. She tried not to think of how Sarah was eating. She kept reminding herself that her younger self, before Memsa'b had taken her in, would have cheerfully subsisted on any of the four alone and considered just having a full belly to sleep on enough.

Holmes, the Watsons, and Pablo Sarasate had joined Nan in her room; since there was only one bed, and it had only one door, it was easier to fit chairs into it. Nan sat cross-legged on her pillow while Mary Watson sat properly at the foot. The violinist had taken the chair nearest the window and sat with his back to it, sun streaming over him. He had removed his coat but seemed entirely happy where he was, basking in the warmth like an elegant cat.

"The difficulty is," said Holmes, "I believe we need to exclude Miss Sarah from most of our plan."

He glanced at Nan, as if he expected her to object, but she nodded agreement. "You're right," she concurred. "She's free of Magdalena's influence *now,* but there is no telling how long she will continue to be free. I would like to think that now that she is aware of what Magdalena is doing, she'll keep her wits about her and her mind as her own, but . . . since we don't know *how* Magdalena does what she does, I see no way of ensuring that she can't control Sarah again."

Pablo shrugged as they all looked at him for his opinion. "I think that she is best left out of most of it. And for the same reason."

"We cast protections on her, but whether they will hold . . . I don't know," said Watson. "But at least I *think* I may know where Magdalena gets her powers from." As they all gazed at him expectantly, he said, with a little pride, "Once I knew she was making people worship her *en masse,* it came to me. I believe she has lorelei blood—and so did her sister."

Holmes laughed, his face full of incredulity. "Oh, come now, Watson! This is more of your superstitious farradiddle! The lorelei is a romantical German legend—why, the story isn't even a folk legend, it's from this very century—"

"Wait, hear me out, Holmes. Will you admit that nearly *every* nation with significant bodies of water has legends of beautiful singing women who enchant entire boatloads of men onto the rocks to their doom, or otherwise enchant them with song?" Watson waited expectantly.

"Well . . . yes," Holmes admitted. "The Greeks had the sirens. The Russians have the rusalkas, and the sirin. The Chinese—"

"Indeed," Watson replied, interrupting him. "Make the assumption that these legends have an origin in a real power— perhaps psychical in nature—perhaps merely the ability to manipulate harmonic sounds in order to render the human psyche susceptible to suggestion—"

Holmes brightened. "Of course! My own experiments on the behavior of house flies in response to musical tones—"

"Yes, yes, precisely," Watson interrupted him again. "Let us assume that because of their higher-pitched voices, the ones who inherit this power are exclusively women. And because, unlike psychical manipulation, which depends on one mind projecting thoughts directly onto the mind of one other, *sonic* manipulation depends only on the response of however many people there are listening to the music, these sirens can affect more than a single person at a time." He coughed slightly. "Then, of course, if the siren concentrates her efforts on one particular person, her results are more profound."

"By Jove, Watson . . . that is a tenable theory." Holmes nodded. "Logical, and scientifically sound. There is hope for you yet."

Nan caught Watson's wink at her when Holmes turned his head, and did her best not to snort. It was *amazing,* the contortions that

Holmes would put his own logic into in order to avoid the simple conclusion that magic was real, and worked.

"Now, to change the subject, the last obstacle to our plan has fallen," Holmes continued. "The Marquess's valet is none too fond of Magdalena, and is not anxious to see her become the lady of the manor. He has agreed to 'make sure his lordship sleeps *alone* tonight' by drugging the brandy he habitually takes before entertaining the lady in his bedroom. Sarah assures me that Magdalena's maid will not expect to see her before three in the morning at the earliest."

"Have you prepared the note, Sherlock?" asked Watson.

Holmes nodded, took a folded note out of his vest pocket, and handed it to Nan. "Maestro, can you arrange for the Marquess to be engaged in something exclusively male immediately after dinner?"

"Easily," said Sarasate, with a brisk nod of his handsome head. "I shall ask him about the British custom of billiards and cigars after dinner, and beg to have a taste of it. He is excessively fond of billiards, and the rest of his male guests are weary of musical gatherings after so many nights of them. I think it will take no effort at all to persuade them into an evening that excludes the ladies."

"And I've purloined one of the maid's uniforms," said Nan. "Magdalena has only seen me the once, and paid no attention to me. I can easily slip her the note, and she'll think it is from Willie."

"And Sarah?" asked Watson.

"I can tell her to come to the conservatory at eleven during dinner," Sarasate assured him. "We are linked in partnership at dinner, it seems, for when she is not there, I have an empty place beside me. I suppose we are equally awkward to place, socially; we are too important to send to dine with the servants, but not important enough to put anywhere except at the foot of the table. If for some reason she does not come to dinner tonight, then I can bring her a note to that effect under the guise of being concerned about her."

Watson and Holmes both nodded with satisfaction. "I have one small item I would like to add to the plan," continued Sarasate, and he reached down to his feet for something. When he stood up, he handed Holmes a violin case he must have brought with him. "I hope you know the *Danse Macabre* by Camille Saint-Saëns?"

"I am familiar with it," Holmes said with surprise. "Why do you ask?"

"Above all things, we will not want Magdalena to employ her powers on us. We know they are sonic in nature. I have taken the liberty of writing a little variation for two violins on the *Danse Macabre* and left the manuscript in the case with this spare instrument of mine. I believe that if there are two of us playing, the effect will be too confusing for Magdalena to counter."

Holmes stopped just short of opening the case, turning just a little pale. "This is surely not—"

"Not either of my Stradivarius instruments, no," Sarasate chuckled. "It is a very good violin that I take with me for the purposes of playing at picnics and other places where I would not risk my beauties."

Holmes sighed with relief and opened the case. He took out the violin, quickly tuned it, then played a few bars of the music he had found with it. Nan shivered; there was something about that piece that was . . . wild, and uncanny. She had the notion that Sarasate had put something of his Elemental Mastery into the composition.

"You play well, Señor Holmes," said Sarasate with great satisfaction.

Holmes actually flushed a little. "Praise from the master is praise indeed. I never would have had the temerity to think I could ever play *for* you, much less *with* you—"

Sarasate chuckled. "You will perform to great effect, Señor Holmes, I am certain of it."

"If I am expected to perform well, I had better go to practice," Holmes replied. "Midnight will come all too soon." He packed up the violin and, with a slight bow to all of them, took his leave.

"Where is he staying?" the violinist asked curiously. "Since he is not in the stable here with you?"

Watson shook his head. "That is one of Sherlock's little mysteries, although my suspicion is that he is camped out in a building used to store game known, appropriately enough, as the 'Game Larder.' Virtually all game is out of season now, so it would be empty. He probably has a local urchin bringing him supplies, as we have the wagon-driver who fetches items daily from the village picking up things for us."

"Well, good; he will be far enough from the manor that his practicing will not be heard, then. I gave him the easier of the two parts, obviously, but it is clear he is a competent player. And—something I would not have suspected, given his devotion to logic—a sensitive one." Sarasate nodded with satisfaction. "His playing will echo my magic almost as well as if he were one of us."

Nan looked from the Watsons to Sarasate and back. "I assume that business about Magdalena's power being some sort of sonic influence on the nerves is all gammon?"

Watson laughed. "Completely. I *do* believe that Magdalena is a member of that class of Water Elementals known as the sirens, or rather, has a siren ancestor. I can tell you that sirens, like the Selch and the Selkies, are quite real, and like them I suspect they can intermarry with humans. Or at least, interbreed. Since they are exclusively female, they probably only keep the female infants and abandon the males."

"So, if a male infant was found—it would be easy enough to introduce siren blood into a family," agreed Mary. "That makes perfect sense. The family would never know."

"Their magic is probably related to mine," observed Sarasate. "Music is an excellent conduit for my magic. Well! That is extremely satisfactory; if her magic is based in music, she should be more susceptible to mine."

"Let us hope," said Watson.

"I think we are as prepared as we can be," Mary put in. "So the wisest thing we can do is rest and be ready for midnight."

"Tonight, at eleven," Sarasate said, over the soup. Then later, over the fowl course, he added, "The conservatory." He had interspersed both these bits of information with normal dinner conversation, choosing a moment when the others were laughing at something Magdalena or one of the other sparkling conversationalists had said to give Sarah her instructions in an undertone.

Sarah was both relieved and terrified. Relieved that the others had finally come up with a plan; terrified that it wouldn't work. All sorts of things had occurred to her as the outcome of the latter. The least of the disasters would be if Magdalena simply denounced them all to her host and had them thrown out, or even thrown into the local gaol. *That* scenario was one that could be salvaged; with all the tricks they had up their sleeves, they could easily escape from a simple country gaol and get to where they could contact Lord Alderscroft, who would smooth things over. Magdalena would still be free to act, but no longer unnoticed. And without Sarah, or some other medium to protect her, the ghost of her sister might just drive her back to Germany. She would still have gotten away with murder, but at least she wouldn't be a threat to the British Government.

But the worst—well—she could *use* her powers on all of them, turning them against each other. And she could exert herself to put Sarah thoroughly under her control, like a mediumistic lapdog, serving with adoration as long as Magdalena was plagued with spirits.

As she was making dinner conversation with Pablo, she wondered what the plan actually was, and how much chance of success it had. She knew *why* she had been left out of the planning for tonight, and she absolutely agreed with the others. *It would have been far too much of a risk to tell me anything. What if Magdalena got me under her control again? I could have run to her with what I knew. Could have? More than likely would have.* But not knowing the plan—the uncertainty naturally made her imagination run wild—this was actually making her hand shake so much she was glad that the soup course was over.

As usual, she excused herself from the after-dinner activities— but just in time to hear that the men intended to have an evening of brandy, cigars, and billiards, leaving the ladies to their own devices. She had thought that Magdalena would be displeased by this, but in fact, she seemed delighted. *I wonder why?*

But this was not an evening to give in to curiosity. She headed straight for her room. Eleven was not that far off.

It was so dark in the conservatory that Nan could only see shadows. Pablo had been in the conservatory earlier that day with a compass, and had made what little preparations needed to be made; mostly deciding where they were all to stand. Now he arranged them all with the help of a dark lantern. "You, John, stand here," he whispered, removing a clay pot he had used to mark the spot. "You, Mary, here. *Señorita* Nan, here, and *Señorita* Sarah, here. *Señor* Holmes, you will be opposite me. You form the point of one triangle, I the point of another, interlocking to make a star of six points."

"Is this relevant?" Holmes whispered. Nan couldn't see his expression, but she fancied he had an eyebrow raised.

"*Si*," said Pablo. "Acoustics. Soft human bodies will resonate differently than the thin forms of plants or the iron frame of the conservatory. *You* know this; you know how an empty concert hall sounds significantly different from one that is full. We must take full advantage of the resonance between your violin and mine."

More gammon? She couldn't tell from Pablo's voice; he sounded completely in earnest.

"Ah, of course," Holmes murmured, sounding satisfied.

Well, all that matters is that he does what he needs to do. It doesn't matter that he believes or disbelieves in magic. He ought to be so busy concentrating on his part of the music that he won't devote any of his mind to disbelieving, anyway.

Not for the first time, she wondered if that had been Pablo's plan all along, to give Holmes something he had to concentrate on so that his skepticism wouldn't disrupt the delicate workings of the magic he, Mary, and John had worked up among the three of them. She knew, more or less, what it was intended to do—

"*Hush!*" Pablo whispered urgently. "*She comes!*"

Neville tensed on Nan's shoulder; she felt his talons digging into her skin through the maid's dress she had forgotten to take off.

Too late for second thoughts now.

16

"Willie?" called Magdalena, in the darkness of the conservatory. "Willie!" She made a little song of the name, and Nan shivered. "Where are you, my darling! I hope you are not trying to frighten your Magda!" She laughed, and even the laugh was a kind of song, and beneath that song was *power*. There could be no doubt that Magdalena was using her abilities to manipulate, and only the fact that they had protection from the three Elemental Masters saved them from being played like puppets.

Footsteps crunched on the graveled path, and Nan could hear the singer drawing nearer, step by step. Suddenly, there was a *thunk*, and Magdalena cursed in German under her breath. "Willie, some fool left—"

"*Now!*" roared Pablo, and the conservatory erupted with light. Magdalena stood right in the middle of all of them, gowned and coiffed impeccably in a scarlet evening dress with a tight bodice cut low across the chest, tiny puff sleeves, and a long train. She must have come straight here from the drawing room where the ladies were all gathered. She held up gloved hands to shelter her eyes from the blazing white light that surrounded her.

The light came from *them,* or rather from the magic that Pablo, John, and Mary had invoked. There now were the two interlacing triangles, inscribed in white brilliance, on the floor of the conservatory. One triangle connected the Watsons and Pablo, the other connected Holmes and the girls. Trapped in the hexagon of light in the middle was Magdalena, and as she lowered her hands, her face registered only surprise and shock.

Pablo already had his violin in playing position with a white bow poised above the strings; the moment after he shouted *"Now!"* he began the first notes of the *Danse Macabre*. Holmes followed flawlessly with the next, in answer to his opening phrase. The music rang strangely in Nan's ears, as if there was music *beneath* the music, a tune she could not hear, only feel.

Holmes had his eyes shut tight in concentration; Pablo's eyes were open, focused on Magdalena.

Now Magdalena lost her initial surprise; she crouched and hissed, her features becoming feral, like some strange creature you might expect to find in a deep jungle—not quite human, not quite reptilian. She made a dart at Pablo, but the incandescent line at her feet stopped her.

She jerked back from it, and stared at it, astonished. "What is this?" she spat. "What are you doing, Sarasate? Is this some sort of joke? Because I am not finding it funny!"

Pablo did not answer . . . but as he played on, something else out of the darkness *did*.

Nan had seen ghosts before, when Sarah had given them form—but she'd never seen one that was on fire, rippling with pale green flames. It—it seemed to be wearing a nun's habit—literally rose up out of the ground between Nan and Holmes, its mouth open in a silent scream. Then another did the same, another burning nun, this time between Sarah and John Watson. Then another, this time a burning priest, and another, an angry child, until there were six spirits ringing Magdalena, all of them with their eyes fixed on her, all of them concentrating every bit of their attention on her. A green-blue haze of light linked all of them; this was the barrier Mary Watson had told Nan to watch for, a sort of wall of magic that would keep Magdalena from leaving the circle, but would allow other spirits to enter from outside.

The hexagram might *keep her pent, but the thrice-cast circle* will *prevent her from escaping.*

But rather than being terrified, as Nan probably would have been in her place, this only seemed to infuriate the diva. She drew herself up to her full height, opened her mouth—and *sang*.

She sang a single, pure note with no tremolo, straight at one of the spirits, a fat man in Georgian knee breeches who stood directly in front of Sarasate. And suddenly, the spirit looked as if he was attempting to hold his place against a strong wind. And more than that, the barrier at his position weakened; the blue-green light dimmed, and Nan sensed from the feral light in Magdalena's eyes that this was exactly what she intended. *They* needed to hold her, and—do whatever it was that Pablo intended to do. All *she* needed to do to end their threat was to escape. If she could break out of the prison they had built to hold her, the simplest thing for her would be to run for the manor, and she would be completely safe from them forever.

Of course, no one would believe her if she told them she'd been attacked by magicians—but no one would believe *them* if they claimed the prima donna was a magician herself. If she escaped, *their* only choice of action would be to flee. They would never get a second chance at stopping her, once she was warned against them. If they stayed, they'd be caught by the servants, and of all of them, only Pablo and Sarah had invitations to be on the property. And yes, Alderscroft could come up with another plan to deal with her, but it would never accomplish more than controlling the damage she had done already.

Gritting her teeth, Nan *willed* strength into the spirit; she felt that peculiar tingling that meant the Celtic warrior within her was about to break through, and she *let* it. This was no time for half measures!

That other *she* manifested with a snarl of triumph, and Neville gave an echoing scream. In time with the music, the warrior began to chant, and whatever it was she was invoking, it strengthened not only the spirit against whom Magdalena was exerting all her power, but the rest of the circle, too. The lines on the ground blazed up whiter, and the blue-green wall of light grew brighter.

Magdalena's song became a scream, and still the wall held, although all six spirits braced themselves against her invisible force to maintain it. And now Nan felt that force, too, exactly like a powerful storm wind trying to blow her over. She reached out blindly and somehow her hand touched the handle of a spade, which became a sword the moment her fingers closed on it. She drove the blade down into the earth at her feet and hung on, still chanting.

Across from her, Sarah stood stock-still, eyes closed, hands spread out. Grey was on *her* shoulder, and at a glance from Nan, began echoing the words of Nan's chant. Then Neville did the same, until the conservatory blazed with light, and reverberated with sound, the two musicians playing, and the three voices chanting in time with the music.

This isn't getting us anywhere, Nan thought, although she did not stop her chant. *She can't get out, but we can't do anything to her—*

"Now, *mi querido!*" Pablo shouted over the music and the chanting. "Come to us now!"

A shape of golden light so bright it brought tears to Nan's eyes appeared behind Sarasate. It was human in general outline, but it was impossible to tell if it was male, female, or something between the two. It moved up beside the violinist, who continued to play, eyes fixed on Magdalena, wearing an expression of absolute concentration. It touched him briefly on the shoulder, then moved across the lines, past the spirit, to stand in front of him, between him and the diva.

Magdalena broke off her scream of power with a gasp. Her lips moved, but nothing came out.

The spirit passed through the wall of blue-green light and stood no more than a pace or two away from Magdalena. Magdalena stared at it, face expressionless with shock, pupils so contracted they were mere pinpoints. The singer had gone white to the lips, and looked as if she might faint.

"No—" she said, a mere whisper. Then, suddenly gathering herself together, she roared out in a red-hot fury, "*No!* You are *dead!* Go back to the dead, where you belong!"

Then she opened her mouth wide and . . .

What came out was . . . Nan didn't have a word for it. It wasn't music.

It was the screams of dying men, slaughtered in battle. It was the trumpets of a thousand angry stallions. It was high, thin cries of women in torment. It held the tumult of all the choirs that ever sang in honor of the gods of darkness and death and evil, shouting out the superiority of those they worshipped.

It was a whisper so soft it was nothing more than a thread of sound. It was a deafening howl that shattered not only the ears, but the mind.

It was pain. It was pleasure. It could lull you to sleep and stab you awake. It promised and betrayed in the same breath. It was impossible to withstand and impossible to yield to.

The six ghosts all straightened up, turned their faces upward, and cried out their agony to the stars. The howls somehow blended with the sound Magdalena was making, even though *nothing* in this world ever could have *blended* with a thing like that.

Nan clapped her hands over her ears and continued to chant, and somehow, in some way, she could *still* hear her chant and the music of the two violins, high and pure and holding out against that cacophonous chaos that emerged from Magdalena's rage-twisted lips.

More to the point, the sound had no effect on the other, the golden spirit. The thing stood, implacable, untouched, like a spear of golden ice.

Magdalena redoubled her efforts.

The blue-green wall flared up, so bright now it was hard to see Magdalena and her opponent through it. Nan continued to chant, hoarsely, wondering in some place deep inside herself just how long this could go on.

Dawn?

Are we going to have to fight her until dawn?

And *then* what? At dawn the ghosts would vanish, leaving Magdalena with the upper hand.

Just as she thought that, the golden spirit moved. Slowly, almost too slowly to see, she closed the distance between herself and Magdalena. Magdalena's eyes widened, and her expression took on a cast of panic. In a gesture of utter futility she tried to shove the spirit away from her, but of course, it was not a solid, material creature, and her hands passed right through it. She backed up a step. Then another. Then a third, and a fourth, and at the fifth step she found herself backed into the all-too-solid incandescent green of the barrier wall. The horrible, beautiful, indescribable *sound* she had been making cut off as she closed her mouth, ducked to the side, avoiding the spirit, and ran straight at Sarah. She was stopped by the wall of light, but she flattened herself on it, pounding on it with both fists, calling out Sarah's name in tones of absolute desperation.

Pablo and Holmes continued playing like a pair of madmen, but Nan and the birds stopped chanting.

Magdalena redoubled her cries to Sarah. And in that cessation of chanting, Sarah opened her eyes and stared at directly at her.

Magdalena slid to Sarah's feet, arms upstretched to Sarah, imploring. "Let me go, Sarah! Let me out! I am sorry I tricked you, I am sorry I tried to part you from your friends, I am sorry I used you! I promise, I will leave this country, I will go back to Germany, no one will ever hear of me again, only please, do not leave me to *her!* Do not leave me to Johanna!"

"I think," Sarah said, in a slow, thoughtful voice. "It is not I you should be asking pardon of."

At this point, the golden spirit was breathing down Magdalena's neck. The diva whirled to find it "face" to face with her. She screamed—and then it engulfed her.

There was no longer a vaguely human-shaped form of golden light within the hexagon; there was a swirling, amorphous, golden whirlwind with a struggling human at its heart, a vague darkness in human shape that was all that could be seen of Magdalena.

"Sarah!" Sarasate cried warningly, as the wall that had protected them all collapsed, and the six spirits collapsed with it, still present, but faded to mere sketches of mist. But Sarah remained upright and unafraid as the struggle continued before her.

Then she raised her hands above her head and sketched a sort of arch in the air with them, stepping back once she had finished.

Blimey! I know what that *is! But—*

A very faint haze filled the archway, and Sarah spread her arms wide, as Nan sensed energy passing between Sarah and the door she had formed, keeping it open.

And the moment that the door appeared—the golden swirl began to edge toward it.

And Magdalena began to scream from the heart of it. No words this time, no music, no power; just mindless panic.

The closer the whirlwind came to the door, the higher and more desperate Magdalena's screams became. And then, just on the threshold, the whirlwind stopped.

Nan began chanting again, and the birds joined her, but neither the chanting nor the *Dance Macabre* made any difference. The whirlwind seemed . . . stuck. Nan sensed Johanna was trying with all her might to carry herself and Magdalena through that door, but Magdalena was holding them back, right on the brink.

That was when the spirit in front of Nan, one of the burning nuns, drew itself upright and rushed at them, joining her force to Johanna's. Then the second nun joined, then the priest, until all but one, the stout man in knee breeches, was all that remained. He hesitated. He looked imploringly at Sarasate.

Sarasate slowly shook his head.

With a shrug of resignation, the spirit slowly moved across the circle and added his force to the rest.

Magdalena's shrieks rose to an ear-shattering level as the whirlwind edged its way through the door under the combined powers of all six spirits and the golden light that was Johanna.

Without warning, the door erupted in a soundless explosion of light—soundless, but by no means without force, as an unseen blow struck Nan in the chest, lifting her off her feet, throwing her backward and knocking her to the ground. The door, the lines on the ground, the wall of power, all vanished in the same moment, leaving them in darkness and silence, a darkness and silence so profound that Nan wondered for a moment in a flash of panic if she had gone blind and deaf.

"Well," came a calm, accented voice out of the darkness to her left. "That was quite the *finale*."

"Indeed," said Holmes, to her right. "I don't suppose you can put your hands on your lantern?"

"*Si,* provided it has not gone out—" A moment later, and Sarasate lifted the lantern over his head, shining the weak light over them all. "Most undignified," he continued, since all of them were sprawled in various ungainly positions. "Is everyone well?"

"I seem to be in the embrace of a rose vine," Holmes said, sounding rather put out. "I hope I have not damaged the instrument you loaned me . . ." He struck a match of his own and looked around himself. "Ah, here it is. It seems intact." The match went out. "Give me a moment to extricate myself."

"I am still blinking dazzle away from my eyes, but I am

otherwise fine," said John Watson. "Mary?"

"Attempting to get up without embarrassing everyone, including myself," Mary replied with a laugh. "I landed with my skirts clean over my head."

Neville quorked from somewhere behind Nan, then added, "Bloody 'ell!"

"Sarah? Grey?" Nan asked, fear rising up in her.

"We're here!" Grey replied.

"We are," said Sarah. "But so is someone else. Pablo, we need your lantern."

Sarasate made haste to get up and widened the aperture on the dark lantern to its fullest. He made his way to where Sarah was still crouched where she had fallen, Grey on the ground beside her.

Crumpled in a heap on the conservatory path, was Magdalena. *Oh no—don't tell me we went through all of that for nothing!* Nan thought in dismay, and unconsciously grasped the shovel with both hands as Neville landed clumsily on her shoulder.

They all gathered around, Sarasate with his bow and violin held in one hand, lantern in the other, Holmes with bow and instrument as well, John feeling the back of his head, Mary shaking bark out of her skirt, and Nan holding the shovel—though she couldn't think what she was to do with it if Magdalena used her powers against them all—

Finally the crumpled figure on the gravel stirred, and raised her face to Sarasate.

But there was something—odd—about it.

She had Magdalena's *features,* yes, but there was a softness to her, and a slightly bewildered look in her eyes. She raised one hand to her cheek and felt it, as if she could not believe there was flesh beneath her fingers. Then she looked down at herself, and up at Sarasate again.

"M-m-maestro?" she faltered.

That's—not Magdalena's voice—

There was none of the power in that voice that Nan was used to hearing, none of the sensuality, none of the calculation. It sounded like the voice of a younger woman, a much less experienced woman. And the German accent was much more pronounced.

Surely Magdalena is not that good of an actress! And yet,

she had fooled so many for so long, it was within the realm of possibility that she was feigning something.

Sarasate got down on one knee beside the woman, and peered into her eyes. "Johanna?" he gasped, incredulously.

"*Jawohl*," she replied, and laughed, shakily. "My sister stole my life. *Lieber Gott* has given it back to me, it seems, though in her person."

"Maestro, does this make sense to you?" John asked urgently, saying what the rest of them were all probably thinking. "Could this be a ruse?"

Sarasate shook his head, slowly. "It is no ruse. I would know." He looked up at all of them. "Magdalena has gone. This is Johanna. But how this came about—I do not know. It was none of *my* doing!"

Although Nan was loath to leave her alone with Johanna—because she still suspected a trick—Sarah insisted on taking the woman back to her rooms alone. After the third time Nan asked her if she wanted someone else—meaning herself—along, Sarah finally smiled and replied, "Nan, I have Grey. And I *know* that the Maestro is right. This is Johanna. We'll be fine."

With that, Nan was forced to let her have her own way and trust nothing bad would happen, even though every bit of her revolted against doing so. "I would invite you to my room," said Sarasate, watching them go, Sarah helping Johanna (if Johanna it really was) make her way slowly to the suite they shared. "But that would mean attempting to smuggle *all* of you past other guests and many servants."

"The stable it is, then," John replied. "Nan should get out of that maid's uniform anyway, or someone is likely to order her to bring them a late-night brandy."

Wordlessly, Sarasate handed John the lantern, and he led the way back to the stable.

Once there, Nan closed them all out of her room while she changed, then they gathered again in the light of much brighter lamps. Mary brought out their hamper of current provisions, and John rummaged behind the bed and emerged with bottled beer for all of them. Although Nan normally did not care for beer, at the moment, she felt strongly in need of a drink of *some* kind, and from the way the rest were behaving, so did they all. Mary passed around rough-cut chunks of bread and cheese and sausage, and they all took their usual places; Mary and Nan on the bed, the rest in chairs or on the chest at the foot of the bed.

"Assuming that it really *is* true that Johanna replaced Magdalena in Magdalena's body, Maestro," said John, as they settled into chairs and on the bed. "In God's name, *how*?"

Sarasate took a moment to examine his violin minutely before replacing it in its case—although he left the bow out. "It is nothing that I caused," he said, accepting a beer. "But it is something that is known to occur. *Usually,* the spirit that was wronged displaces one that is—weak. I have personally known the spirit of a man to displace the spirit of another who was ravaged by addiction to drink and drug, though I myself only intervened enough to suggest that the thing was possible. I have *heard* of other such cases, although that is the only one I know of, personally. But for such a strong spirit to have been replaced—" He shook his head. "It is a circumstance that, I think, is not likely to happen again in my lifetime."

For once, Holmes seemed to have lost every bit of his skepticism. "There was the—portal—that Miss Sarah created. There was Johanna herself, and all the power that all of us put behind her. And then there was the intervention of the other six spirits. I suspect it was that last which turned the trick, so to speak."

"You saw that, Holmes?" John Watson gaped at his friend. "And you actually admit to seeing it?"

Holmes frowned a little. "Do not press me, John. I am open-minded enough to accept the evidence of my own eyes. I still think your *magic* is mostly imagination, air, and shadow."

Watson knew when to leave well enough alone, evidently, for he said nothing more on the subject.

Nan put her head back against the wall behind her and ate, slowly. She was starving, but feeling so exhausted that if the others had not been there, she probably would have gone to bed hungry.

"But what is *Johanna* to do now, Maestro?" Mary asked anxiously, as an owl called from the trees surrounding the stable block, and another answered from farther away. "And you are utterly *sure* it is Johanna, and not Magdalena somehow feigning?"

Nan took another bite of bread and cheese, wanting very much to hear the answer to that question herself.

For answer, Sarasate held up the bow with which he had played the violin. "This tells me. I made it from the bone and hair of Johanna's—"

"Good Lord!" Holmes exclaimed, going white as a sheet. "That explains the mangled arm! The morgue attendant drew my attention to that; the explanation given was that her right arm had been bitten by sharks, but that didn't explain the removal of a single bone without taking off the entire arm. I don't know whether to admire you for your audaciousness, or denounce you as a necromancer!"

"It was with Johanna's permission and guidance," Sarasate replied, calmly. "It was the channel through which I strengthened her and kept her sane. When one dies—as Sarah will likely tell you, if you ask her—unless one travels to the fate which one has earned, the spirit that clings to earth grows weaker and loses more of itself and its memories the longer time passes. This is why only those spirits who have very powerful, emotional reasons to remain retain even a fraction of their former selves. Johanna came to me, asking for help to bring her sister to justice. I explained what I needed to keep her from dissolution. She gave me permission to take it."

"Bone and—good God," John Watson said, suddenly. "It was *you?* You, out there on the mud of the Thames at midnight?"

Sarasate smiled slightly. "I thought I might have been seen; I had the sense that someone was watching me, so I took care to cover my tracks on retreating. But nothing ever came of it. Was it one of the Irregulars?"

"Tommy Grimes," John said, absently, staring at Sarasate. "You terrified the boy. By the time he got around to telling me about it—he flatly refused to tell *you*, Holmes—it was weeks later, and I couldn't even find the girl in the morgues. And here I have been waiting for the emergence of either a murderer who takes trophies, or a *real* necromancer, and all the time it was you!"

"Sometimes I am required to do terrible things in the name of justice," Sarasate said, simply.

Watson shuddered. "Better you than me, old man."

Sarasate shrugged. "One becomes accustomed." He turned to Holmes and extended the white bow—which now Nan would not have touched for any amount of money, knowing it had been made of a dead girl's bone and hair. "Under most circumstances, I would destroy this . . . but I do not know if doing so would have any effect on Johanna."

"Then I think we should wait," replied John.

"I think we should wait as well," said Holmes, who took a long drink of his beer. "I think we should wait and see if in the morning *she* is still Johanna." He raised one eyebrow. "After all, it's never wise to throw away a weapon unless you are absolutely certain you will not ever need it again."

Nan expected to wake at the crack of dawn; she had scarcely been able to get to sleep, worrying about Sarah, worrying that they'd all been gammoned by Magdalena, worrying that when they all woke up in the morning they would discover Magdalena *and* Sarah gone.

But when she finally did fall asleep, every bit of her exhaustion caught up with her and kept her sleeping, and she didn't wake up until Mary Watson shook her awake. She floundered up out of darkness with a start, staring at Mary with her hair in her eyes, confused for a moment about where she was and why Mary was shaking her shoulder.

Mary let go of her as she sat up. "Get dressed. Sherlock wants us at the manor; he sent one of the hall boys down here to the stables to deliver a note to John and one to you and I. John has already gone."

Nan shook her head hard to chase the cobwebs out. "Just give me a moment. And let me see the note."

She scrambled into her clothing, silently grateful that she had thought to pack one shirtwaist and skirt that would pass cursory muster up there at the manor, and read the note while she swiftly did up her hair.

Come to the manor immediately; we are on the steps of the front entrance. Things have been moving apace this morning.

Allegedly, I arrived last night to tell "Magdalena" of the tragic death of her sister. Johanna has informed the Marquess, and now is persuading the Marquess that the affair is over in the kindest way. I believe the Maestro was right. I cannot imagine Magdalena letting the Marquess out of her clutches under any circumstances, so it seems that Johanna has triumphed and evicted her murderous sister for good.

"Is John already there?" she called, sticking the last pin in her hair.

"Yes." Mary poked her head—crowned with an extremely fashionable little boater—in the door. "You look splendid. Let's go back him up."

They hurried over to the manor and found the little group actually standing on the front steps. Willie was in boating flannels—evidently there was a boating expedition planned, and he had been interrupted by "Magdalena" coming to him. He seemed very distressed, although whether that was for "Magdalena's" sake or his own, it was impossible to tell.

Johanna—and the young woman's very *posture* was unlike Magdalena's had been—was all in mourning black, despite the fact that she had "only been told" about the discovery of Johanna's body last night. Nan blinked to see *that*. Had Magdalena literally packed an outfit for *every* occasion, including a death?

Johanna stood a little apart from the Marquess and made no attempt to touch him. "Willie, you must see, with this terrible news that *Herr* Holmes has brought me, I *must* go home. My parents are alone now—and I must be the one to tell them what has happened to my sister." She clasped her hands together and looked at him pleadingly, moving slightly out of reach when he tried to touch her arm.

"But you can come back," replied the Marquess forlornly. "Surely—"

"Ah," said Holmes, "Here are the fine wife of my colleague and little Sarah's companion. Miss Killian, Mrs. Watson!"

"Mr. Holmes," said Nan, agreeably. "Mr. Holmes brought us, since he felt that Fraulein von Dietersdorf would wish to leave immediately, and would be relieved to have Sarah taken care of for her. And you are, sir—?" She looked at the Marquess enquiringly.

"Willie," the Marquess said, miserably. He turned back to Johanna. "I—understand how you must go but—"

"Willie," Johanna interrupted. "You will soon cheer up. You will have a *splendid* summer. You have so many friends here, and I am sure you have even more you could bring to help you when I am over the Channel. But my parents have only me, now."

She reached out and took both his hands in hers—which had the (intended, Nan was sure) effect of forcing him to stay at arm's length. Finally, he sighed dolefully, and nodded.

"You're right. I'll send for Hammond. Never mind going by train, take my traveling carriage and go in comfort." He bent and kissed the backs of both her hands, since it was obvious she wasn't going to let him come any closer, and went back into the house, presumably to order his servants to get things in motion for Johanna's departure.

"Where's Sarah?" Nan asked bluntly.

"Packing," Johanna told her. "Alicia has been packing since dawn. I told Alicia last night that Mr. Holmes had intercepted me after dinner and informed me of my sister's death, to account for how we looked when we came in. And I told her that we were leaving immediately last night, then sent her to bed. Sarah *was* helping Alicia, but I sent her off to take care of her own things. Now that Willie's gone, and we are out of earshot of any servants—*Herr* Holmes, what are we going to do?"

Holmes looked at her curiously. "About what?"

"The time the body was found, and the time Johanna allegedly ran away do not . . . precisely . . . correspond. . . ." She bit her lip and looked at him worriedly.

"Ah, that." Holmes waved it away. "I take it you wish to take Johanna's body back to Germany?"

"I think it would be wise. *And* kind. I cannot imagine that my parents would accept her resting anywhere but the family plot. It would be dreadful for my parents to make the sad trip back here to fetch it, would it not?" she asked.

Holmes nodded. "It would, indeed. Well, if that is what you plan, then that solves the problem. They will never learn that the dates are . . . contradictory. I'll arrange the disinterment for you. As for the date discrepancy, you'll give the probable date of death as, oh, say, the day after she allegedly ran off with the Canadian. And since . . . *Johanna's* disappearance was never a matter for the police, there are no official records to amend, and no one will be the wiser about the discrepancy."

Johanna went a little limp with relief. "*Herr* Holmes, that is very kind of you."

He waved it away. "Think nothing of it. I will take care of all of the necessary details. Even if *I* were not owed more than enough favors to make this trivial, Mycroft has but to wave his hand and all is made smooth. I suggest you return to your suite at the Langham. I will find you there, and together we will make the rest of the arrangements for your return home."

"Fraulein Killian, would I be correct in assuming that Sarah would probably prefer to return to London with you, rather than with me?" Johanna asked.

And *that* was what finally persuaded Nan that it really was Johanna in there, and not the former occupant of the body. After everything she had just gone through, and with the possibility that Johanna's spirit, backed by Sarasate, could return to attack her at any moment, *Magdalena* would not have allowed Sarah out of her sight for a moment. There was no chance that it was Magdalena feigning to have been driven out. The diva might well have bidden farewell to Willie. She might well have left to return home to Germany. After all, she could still build a fortune and an immense career on the Continent, given her vocal and arcane talents.

But she would never, ever, have released Sarah. In fact, her need for Sarah would have been greater than ever.

"I think she probably would, but why not ask her yourself?" Nan replied.

Johanna smiled. It was a sweet smile, and nothing at all like the expression Magdalena used as a smile. "I have, and she said it was up to you. I think she is afraid that she has somehow disgraced herself in your eyes."

"Bosh," snorted Nan. "I'll go and tell her myself."

She didn't need directions, since she had explored that part of the manor in her maid disguise yesterday. *Was it only yesterday? It seems like an age.* She marched straight to Magdalena's suite and knocked on the frame of the door, since the door itself was open.

There was a pile of luggage in the middle of the sitting room, and Alicia entered carrying a hatbox just as Nan knocked.

"Yes, miss?" Alicia asked.

"I'm looking for Sarah Lyon-White," Nan told her. "I'm her friend, Nan Killian. Magdalena sent me."

"Oh, she's packing the last of her things. Over there—" Alicia inclined her head to the right, and Nan took the unspoken invitation to enter and headed for the door in that direction.

She found Sarah in the third bedroom, fastening the food and water bowls into Grey's carrier. "Well, you look ready to go with us," Nan said, startling her.

"Oh!" she replied, her hand to her throat, as Grey looked on from the dresser. "I am . . . unless you'd rather I traveled with—"

"Us, of course," Nan replied. "I just hope Holmes and Watson have figured out how we are going to manage your mountain of things. Didn't you *ever* learn how to pack lightly?"

EPILOGUE

Johanna's suite in the Langham looked strangely bare. There were no masses of flowers, no silk shawls tossed idly over the backs of chairs, no framed photographs or boxes of sweets or other trifles from admirers left lying about. Most of Johanna's luggage was already aboard the ship back to Germany. So was the sad little white casket that held the remains; Johanna had actually had the temerity to look at what was left of her old self before the new coffin was sealed, and the white metal casket sealed over that.

Johanna had elected to say her goodbyes here, in the hotel, rather than on the dock. "It will be too crowded and chaotic at the dock," she had told Nan. "Besides, I won't be able to give you my presents." She had hesitated. "I hope you will not mind that they are not precisely new. . . ."

Nan had laughed. "So long as they aren't any of Magdalena's dresses. Sarah is too short for any of them, and I am too tall."

The birds were back in the flat; neither Nan nor Sarah felt inclined to subject them to their carriers after all the time they'd had to spend in them lately. And the birds themselves had shown no interest in saying goodbye to Johanna, who was not in the "flock" that they considered "friends."

So Holmes, the Watsons, Nan, and Sarah were waiting in the sumptuous sitting room as Johanna put the finishing touches on herself and came out to say her goodbyes. Alicia was already at the steamer; she had elected to come with Johanna and remain as her personal maid in Germany. "It won't be as exciting," she'd told Nan. "But Mistress is much kinder these days. And she says there is not the stigma to being a ladies' maid there that there is here, and I just might find myself with a handsome blond gentleman of my own."

Finally the lady emerged, clad in mourning, as she had been since she "got the news," although truth to tell, she had probably been putting on the acting performance of both lifetimes, pretending that she mourned for and missed her sister. She had everyone convinced but the people in this room that discovering her sister's death—which had been ruled an "accidental drowning," thanks to Mycroft—had left her prostrate with grief.

She surveyed them all with a smile. "I must say, it seems peculiar to be in mourning for myself," she observed.

"I can see how that would be rather disconcerting," Holmes agreed. "And probably most amusing, if it were not for the real grief this will cause your parents."

"I intend to use my powers to ease their grief," Johanna declared. "And when I think they are sufficiently recovered, I shall marry my Helmut, and when he calls me Johanna I shall not correct him."

"Forgive me if I have been occupied with another case," interjected Holmes, looking morbidly curious, "But just what Banbury tale did my brother concoct for you?"

"A great many people apparently 'fall into the Thames,' he tells me, and he found an unidentified young man to stand in for the specious Canadian lover." Johanna's mouth thinned a little in something that was not quite a smile. "He concocted a tale of an accident whereby they both ended in the river on the way to the railway station—and I *know* this makes absolutely no sense to a Londoner, but we are not attempting to fool Londoners. My parents are not likely to enquire even so much as looking for newspaper stories about the accident. I have it all beautifully written out by a purported police inspector."

"Who is, in fact, Mycroft," stated Holmes.

She nodded agreement. "I think that Helmut will not care. Magdalena entranced him completely; by the time the entrancement wears off, he will be in love with *me* all over again."

"And singing?" Nan asked. "You *do* have a great gift. . . ."

"Which I shall employ at charity concerts," she said firmly. "And perhaps, recitals. It would be different if Magda had not . . . gone into so many beds. I do not want to be looking out at an audience and wonder how many of the men gazing down at me from the expensive boxes had seen me in theirs." She blushed, nearly stammering that last, then recovered. "So, before I leave for the steamer, as you know, I wished to bring you all here to give you something to remember this adventure by. Several things, actually."

She turned to John Watson. "I know that every man would like to shower his wife in jewels at some point." She picked up a jewelry case from the mantelpiece and put it into his hands. "Now you can." She smiled at him—amazingly, *Johanna* produced a little dimple that had never appeared when Magdalena had smiled. "They are some gifts of Willie's. He would not take them back, and I did not feel right about keeping them. May they bring both of you joy."

She turned to Sarah and Nan. "I have gifts for you, but *these* are for your birds." She picked up a pair of what Nan had thought were black velvet pillows from the sofa, behind her, and handed them to Nan and Sarah. But when Nan took the object in her hands it proved to be a sable muff, lined with wool plush. "I know that the grey parrot, at least, is delicate to the cold. If you must take her in her carrier in winter, have her crawl into that as into a nest and stick her head out, then put the whole into the carrier. It should keep her warm as toast. If you are still concerned, there is a pocket inside it with a smooth granite stone that you may warm on the stove to add to the heat. I think that the raven will enjoy the heat of a muff, too."

"Oh, this is wonderful, Johanna!" Sarah cried. "It's perfect—"

"But it is not all," Johanna replied, and went into the other room. She returned with her arms full of sumptuous black fur. "Here," she said, depositing a sable cloak in the laps of each of the three women. "Magda would never be seen without her cloak of sable, and her admirers gave her far too many. May they keep you warm, and remind you of my gratitude."

Already the fur was warming Nan's lap, and she could only think of how wonderful it would be in the dead of winter.

"And last of all, *Herr* Holmes, I have two things. The first—" She put an envelope in his hands. "I have pried from out of your brother your usual fee. You will find this is rather more than that, but how could I put a price on my life, which you have given back to me?" Before Holmes could say anything, she picked up a long, slender case, and handed it to him. "And this is by way of a souvenir, from myself, and from Maestro Sarasate."

Holmes tucked the envelope in his breast pocket and opened the black leather case.

There, lying like a jewel on the black velvet, was an ivory-white bow, strung with golden-yellow hair.

This was the bow that they had all last seen in Sarasate's hands.

"By Jove—" said Holmes, taken aback.

"I know you are not the squeamish sort," Johanna told him, calmly. "And we both felt it was better not to destroy it, as he ordinarily would have done with such a thing at the end of a task. So, let it be a memento of one of the cases that *Herr Doctor* Watson dares not write about. *Ja?*"

"*Jawohl,*" Holmes replied, closing the case, and casting a glance at Watson. "Because if he dares so much as *hint* that I paid heed to his superstitious twaddle, I will not be responsible for my actions."

"Really, Holmes!" Watson said, affronted. He might have gone on to say more, but all four women burst into laughter.

"Come along John," Mary said, throwing her sable cape over her arm and standing up. "You should know better by now. Let's be on our way and allow Johanna to be on hers, or she might miss her steamer. And then what would you do?"

She and John left; Holmes was the next to stand. He took Johanna's hand and bowed a little over it. "I wish you well, and a long and prosperous life," he said with feeling. "Surely no one could have earned it more than you."

"But it was gifted back to me, thanks to you," Johanna replied. "And if I ever may be of service to you, you have but to call on me." She smiled. "Even if it is to assist you with something naughty my countrymen are attempting against yours. I think that you have more than earned that sort of aid."

With the bow case tucked under his arm, Holmes left, his step brisk and his brows furrowed in thought. But not, Nan would wager, over anything having to do with Johanna. No, in his mind, he was already contemplating the next case.

"Well," said Nan, getting to her feet. "This—"

"Was strange for all of us," said Johanna. "And I am sorry it brought you two grief. Come, I am done here. Let us all go down to catch our cabs."

"Not nearly what it brought you," Nan pointed out, as they made their way down the hall to the elevator. "The one thing nobody's quite said is that you were *dead*. And if it hadn't been for your not giving up on bringing Magdalena to justice, I don't think she would have stopped at murdering just you."

Johanna looked at both of them, soberly, as they waited for the elevator to arrive. "She would not. Her memories and thoughts are fading the longer I live in this body, but I can tell you, Fraulein Killian, if she had thought for a moment that you were going to interfere with her wishes, she would not have scrupled to find a way to make you vanish, too. And if she had known that Sarah's Grey was more than just a pet—well."

The elevator turned up just at that moment, and they all stepped inside. They held silence until it had reached the ground floor, then picked up their conversation as they strolled across the lobby.

"Then it's just as well she didn't find out," Nan replied, and nodded at the doorman as he held the door open for them. "And speaking of Grey and Neville, 'tis time we got back and found out what mischief they've been into while we were gone."

"I expect to find the biscuit-case dismantled and all the ginger nuts reduced to crumbs," Sarah sighed. "Living with Magdalena spoiled Grey. She may never be content with humble digestives again."

"Then I shall have to see to it that a box of *lebkuchen* and *pfeffernusse* comes to her every Christmas," said Johanna with a twinkle in her eye.

"Oh, I know what she would have to say to *that* idea," Nan laughed.

"And what would that be?" asked Johanna, curiously.

"*Clever* bird!" Nan and Sarah answered in chorus.

They were all still laughing as they parted to catch their cabs.

ABOUT THE AUTHOR

Mercedes Lackey is a full-time writer and has published numerous novels and works of short fiction, including the bestselling *Heralds of Valdemar* series. She is also a professional lyricist and licensed wild bird rehabilitator. She lives in Oklahoma with her husband and collaborator, artist Larry Dixon, and their flock of parrots.

www.mercedeslackey.com